Body Of Evidence

Juanita B. Tischendorf

Body of Evidence

By Juanita Tischendorf

Published by J. Tischendorf Services
This is a work of fiction and any resemblance between the
characters in this book and real persons is coincidental.
nitatischen@hotmail.com

Printed in the United States of America
ISBN: 978-1-928613-72-5

ALSO BY JUANITA TISCHENDORF

Who Says I'm Small
Til Death Do Us Part?
The Madman The Marathoner
An UnFair Advantage (A Murder In Oklahoma)
The Selfie (Adolescent/Teen Girl Self Development

Acknowledgements

A good book in fiction must mimic reality. Keeping that in mind, a fiction writer needs to call on sources to keep it real. In writing this book I had wonderful help and support from Dave Addelman, an attorney in Buffalo New York and Doug Pollock, a recently retired Irondequoit Police Officer. Even with the internet, you can't get information as accurate and precise as you can from individuals who work in the field. I learned so much from them and I believe their input is what makes this book good.

July 31, 2015
Prologue

Rochester, New York

All day people stopped along the road that ran through the woods by the Great Embankment Park in Pittsford, New York. The yellow tape wound around trees that circled the area where it had occurred, but beyond the muddy ruts in the dirt road entrance there was nothing to see.

In cars and on foot they wanted to view the site that had been reported on the news, because they needed to see it in person to make it real. This not being a suburb where one became familiar with a crime scene made it even more interesting. They looked forward to the trial that they knew would come and hopefully soon so that the incident could be laid to rest and they would have all the answers to their questions.

As they gape at the area they wondered what was the truth of it all. They wondered if she had been raped or exactly what had taken place that night and those in the know looked forward to the forensic reports that could solve the mystery of why a man was murdered and a woman raped in this high-class suburb of Rochester.

Those forensic pathologists would examination the entire body of the woman. They would check her hair and fingernails, all bodily orifices, the skin and all external wounds and bruises. Nothing would be left out in discovering the evidence such as fibers entrapped in the hair on her head and pubic area. Evidence of semen or body fluids would help prove the truth of her claim.

As for the murdered victim, the gunshot entrance and exit wounds would be thoroughly examined and probed to reveal bullets or bullet fragments. They will also probe to determine the position of the shooter in relation to the victim at the time of the shooting. Trace evidence will be collected from the body surface at autopsy so that they will hopefully have hairs, fibers, small fragments of plastic, paint or glass that may have come from the murder weapon or the crime scene.

Though the location where they now stood was said to be the site of the rape, it would not be definite until the dirt or soil on the body or on the victim's clothing identified it as so. Yes, from all the crime shows on the television no one was clueless to how it worked. The forensic autopsy should determine with reasonable certainty how the victim died and estimate the time of death. However, it cannot determine where or why the victim died or if the two crimes were connected but the findings would be an integral part of the crime investigation and in many instances guide investigators in the right direction.

***

Big-city culture and small-city charm combine in Rochester, a mid-sized city in Upstate New York on the shores of Lake Ontario. Rochester has always been defined by water from its early beginnings as a small village on the Genesee River, to the construction of the Erie Canal routed through Rochester, and turning the small village into America's first boomtown.

But cities are populated with people and people are what shape the reputation of an area. There was a murder and it happen in Upstate New York. For many 'New York' is New York City and since there is no clear official boundary between Upstate New York and Downstate New York it is a reasonable assumption. In truth, Upstate New York is the portion of the state of New York lying north of New York City and includes the major cities of Buffalo, Rochester, Albany, and Syracuse. Murders happen some place, and this one and the subsequent trial took place in Rochester, New York, a city that is not the murder capital of the country, but it does have the highest rate of murders, per capita, in New York State.

Rochester has had its share of murders and high profile cases. The alphabet murders (also known as the "double initial murders") occurred in the 1970s in the Rochester, New York, area.

7

Three young girls Carmen Colon in Churchville, Michelle Maenza in Macedon, and Wanda Walkowicz in Webster were raped and strangled. The case received its name from the fact that each of the girls' first and last names started with the same letter. Furthermore, each body was found in a town that had a name starting with the same letter as the victim's name.

November 1990, Arthur John Shawcross an American serial killer, also known as the Genesee River Killer in Rochester, New York was tried by Monroe County First Assistant District Attorney Charles J. Siragusa for the 10 murders in Monroe County. Shawcross pleaded not guilty by reason of insanity, with testimony from psychiatrist Dorothy Lewis that he suffered from brain damage, multiple personality disorder and post-traumatic stress disorder, and had been sexually abused as a child

In 1993 $7.4 million was stolen from the Brink's Armored Car Depot in Rochester, New York, the fifth largest robbery in US history. Four men, Sam Millar, Rev. Patrick Moloney, former Rochester Police officer Thomas O'Connor, and Charles McCormick, all of whom had ties to the Provisional Irish Republican Army, were accused.

April 2006, a grand jury indicted three Rochester men in connection with the March 9 murder of Herschel Scriven, a young minister and church organist, in southwest Rochester and the night before the Scriven indictments, two men were shot in northeast Rochester. On Sunday morning, two others were shot in the same area of the city, and a third was fired at as he drove his car. None of those shootings were fatal, but the repetition underscores the severity of Rochester's violent-crime problem.

Part 1
In The Beginning

Chapter 1

The sound of the boat engines continue as I drive up Thomas Avenue in the suburb known as Irondequoit. It is a warm moonlit Sunday evening in August and I am arriving home from a long weekend of golf at Bristol Harbor Resort. There are great golf courses closer to home, but I needed to get away for a bit and going here gave me a chance to meet up with my friend Travis Jones. Even though Travis lives in Canandaigua he enjoys a stay at the resort and my visit gives him that opportunity. We have been golfing friends for a long time, Travis and I and like myself Travis is an avid golfer who prefers to spend full days on the course. I can understand because we also have in common the fact that we both lead a busy life. He works hard as a marketing manager and, in his spare time, enjoys golf and basking in the sun. One look at his tanned body, the permanent dent from wearing his brimmed hat and it is no secret where he does spend his off-hours. So that's Travis.

As for me, extraordinary people have realistic optimism. That describes me to a tee. It takes optimism to succeed in this world. I was born in Manhattan so I can claim attachment to both upstate and downstate. I attended UCLA law school and began my career as an attorney in 1994. The firm I joined handled the legal matters of many notable individuals and I believe wholeheartedly I was hired because I had the 'look'. "The look" had everything to do with appearance. Standing inches above six feet, with what my clients called, piercing blue eyes, I made the grade. People found me handsome and commended on me having a captivating smile and wearing only designer suits added to the image.

Lawyers do not enjoy the best of reputations. Some people hate them just by default. But behind every cliché is a kernel of truth, and each year brings no shortage of lawyer scandals. I didn't care at first, even managed to ignore the rumors until it was splashed across the media that this single law firm orchestrated an elaborate web of offshore tax havens and shell companies. The publicity unveiled ties to the Watergate scandal and a bank heist dubbed the 'Crime of the Century'. The firm became the choice for some of history's most notorious politicians, bank robbers and drug lords. I tried to ignore all these scandalous claims because the money was more than I ever dreamed of making but there came a time when money was not as important as reputation. It was at that point I left to seek a smaller city environment with hopefully less notoriety. That is how I landed back in Rochester, New York.

***

I took the scenic route home and it was almost midnight as I made my way down Seneca Point Road and on to NY 21 South. Traffic was nonexistent so I could easily occupy my mind with thoughts of the past. These days I traveled this way often and knew each turn by heart, so much so that even in the dark I could mentally visualize the beauty of this remote area, when depending on the month there would be an array of colors from the bur marigold, bluebells, buttercups, white and red clover, daisies and lilacs. In May, there would be the flowering trees, but by June they would have passed and blend in with the ash, oaks and maples. From North Bloomfield Road and then onto New Michigan Road, I am exhausted when I reach Titus Avenue in Irondequoit, minutes from my home, only I need to make a stop first over on Florenton Road to check on my mother's house. As my car turns the corner the headlights sweep over the rows of tall maple and oak trees lining the street and shine into the darkened windows, shades up and curtains open; just like my mother likes to leave them.

I love my mother. She is a beauty inside and out. From her smiling light, brown eyes full of warmth and tenderness and her gentle smile she can lighten life's bitter trials and bring calm and peace to heavy hearts and she has been a vital, respected lady all my life. Her personality is potent, even over the phone; her passionate, funny, wised-up remarks come through in capital letters, especially when she agrees with you. You imagine that she could persuade anyone of nearly anything and that she is her own person. Her shining grey hair she wears in a feminine style of fluff, even when she works in her garden in oversized plaid shirts that once belonged to the love of her life; my father who she was married to for almost 50 years before he passed. Once I asked her if she still missed him after all these years and she said, YES in capital letters, but I keep that idea, that happiness is a decision, and so I'm going to do today the things that will make me happy, I'm not going to focus on this or that. That is what she did for me on my return to Rochester and I in turn would do anything she asks.

That is why even though I am exhausted and want to go to bed and even though I know the house is locked up like Fort Knox and doesn't require watching, I nevertheless swing by. I park in the driveway and wall around the perimeter, peeking through windows as I go. Everything is quiet and undisturbed so I go back to the front and climb into my car.

All I want to do is go home now but there are obstacles in my path. Reaching Titus Avenue, I brake for a staggering man as he emerged from the direction of the I-Square and did not stop to wait for the light to change. I find it strange for anyone to be out this late, but pay little attention to him as I finally am on my way again. Minutes later I pull into the drive of my home on St. Paul Boulevard.

I drive my car up the driveway, park and then climb out and go to the back to unlock the truck and take out my golf clubs. I rest the clubs against the side of the car and look up, admiringly. The autumnal moon beams its mellow light, looking beautiful in the deep navy blue sky sprinkled with stars and planets. Here and there a few patches of white clouds float swiftly and the moon plays hide-and-seek behind them. I must have stood there for at least five minutes before finally pulling my attention back to the task at hand and reaching in the trunk to grab my weekender before closing the trunk lid. I pick up and place my golf club bag over one shoulder and the weekender over the other, press the lock button on my key chain and start walking up the driveway.

"How was golf, Richard?" someone says, emerging from the shadows next door. It was my neighbor, Marcus Peterson. Marcus had been a cop on the Irondequoit police force for as long as I could remember. He was raised in Amityville, New York, the eldest son in a family with six siblings which at an early age had him on the alert always. He had attended high school in a small town where everybody knew each other's business so he naturally came by being on the lookout for his neighbors.

"Fine, very fine, Marcus," I said, rubbing my unshaven cheek. "I golfed enough to last me for a while."

"Suppose you heard about the murder?" Marcus said, moving closer. "It made the papers and is all over the internet."

"No, Marcus," I said. "I just got in, as you can see. I haven't seen a newspaper or turned on a computer, thank God. I was with my old golfing buddy Travis who believes vacations mean being disconnected. Trust you caught the murderer?"

Marcus shrugged. "It's not our headache, Richard. It happened out of our jurisdiction on Friday night. As I heard it some bigwig blew his top and fired five bullets into a man named Noah Arietta. It happened at the Academy building in Pittsford that is owned by this Arietta person. The early reports say that the person who killed Arietta claims that he raped his wife. In any case, the state police have taken over, thank goodness."

"Hmm," I said, the legal gears beginning involuntarily to turn as I face Marcus. "Well, I'm going to call it a night." I turn and march up the drive to my front door.

Once inside my home I unshoulder my golf clubs and put them in the hallway closet. It is now somewhere around one or maybe two in the morning so I am surprised to hear my landline ringing before I can make it halfway up the stairs. I want to ignore it and continue on my way, but it could be some kind of emergency so I hurry up the remaining stairs, taking them two at a time. I turn the corner and enter my bedroom in time to pick up the phone on the nightstand. By the time I move the phone up to my ear it has ceased ringing, so I set it back on its charger.

I shrug my shoulders, grab my pj's from under the pillow and head into the bathroom. When I emerge, I am clean and anxious to just climb in the bed and get some rest. Luck is on my side.

***

Saturday morning and I overslept! For the 9 to 5 guy, this would be the morning to sleep in, but not for a lawyer in private practice. I jump out of the bed and rush to the bathroom where I put toothpaste on my toothbrush and start brushing as I leave the bathroom and go to my bedroom to gather my clothes and lay them on the bed.

I head back into the bathroom to spit and climb quickly into the shower, not even waiting for the water to warm up as I begin washing my body. There is no time to linger as I hurriedly dry myself off and rush into the bedroom to put on my clothes. Yes, it's great being my own boss I think, but it comes with responsibility too. A swift trip to the mirror to brush my hair and I am finally on my way downstairs where I pick up my briefcase, grab my keys from the hook and after a check to make sure I have everything, I head out the door.

I climb into my car and back down the driveway, carefully pulling out onto St. Paul Boulevard and head toward downtown. It is best to arrive early than late if I want a good parking space, but it is also important to do the speed limit or risk getting pulled over and waste even more time so I keep an eye on the speedometer, something that wouldn't be necessary in Manhattan in its bumper to bumper traffic jams.

True to form, getting to any area in Rochester is no more than 20 minutes when the roads are not covered with snow. I find I am indeed lucky as I pull into the East End parking garage and spot a space on the main level, near the exit for Main Street. I don't even stop for coffee as I hurry down the sidewalk to my office building where I stop to admire the sign on the frosted-glass door that reads, Richard Dandridge, Attorney & Counselor At Law, 106 East Main Street, 585 467-9191, www.RDandridge.com

Underneath these words is a thick arrow pointing toward Theresa's door, accompanied by the words, "Entrance next door." It never ceases to amaze me how few people ever followed the arrow, but instead stand there gripped by a sort of confusion that has them pounding on this entrance door.

I find the right key on my keychain and open the door entering the private entrance. The two-story brownstone building use to be the home of my grandparents who lived here for many years and now it was my law offices and when working on a case late into the night, I had bachelor quarters up on the second floor where I kept some clothes and a stocked refrigerator. Outside the building seems much as it was, except for the addition of oversized windows.

My law office does not fit the mold of those in Rochester. My mother Laurel approvingly claimed that my office looked like anything but a law office and most agree with her. It is neat and clean with wood floors, glass walls and high ceilings. There is one bright office and one workstation with an internet connection and secure wireless, a modern phone system with voice mail, copy/scan/fax and postage machines along with a T1 internet connection. The large glass walled conference room is immediately off the reception area and all business machines are available behind the high-end workstations that are outside the windowed office with a large corner office that has big bay windows offering a very bright corner space easily accommodating two professionals. It meets my criteria of lots of wood and glass, high ceilings and lots of light. Even my personal office is less formal apart from the New York supreme court reports and other law books stored on narrow shelves against an entire wall, but completely hidden by a sliding wooden barn door. Modern furniture, bright upholstery and carpets were chosen to give my clients more comfort but my friend Pete Adams, would occasionally tease me that the environment works well for testing the virtue of my female divorce clients.

In one corner of my office is a tufted back leather rocker with a matching footstool. This is situated under recessed lighting as it is my go-to reading spot. On the walls are some small color prints and photographs. Where the wood burning fireplace use to be is now a sleek electric one camouflaging the area all the way to the ceiling with glass tile supporting a mounted flat screen television and the final touch; the room is wired for sound so that music plays softly in the background.

I sat down at my desk and turned on the computer hoping to gather some information on the murder that had taken place and see what cases I needed to work on. I begin my routine. I pick up a copy of the Financial Times and scan both the headlines and the section that lists what companies are in the news. I'm looking to see if there is any news about any of the clients I'm working with now. I check my emails to see if anything has arrived in my inbox that is urgent and respond to anything I can straightaway.

I next search the internet for information on the murder. From talking with Marcus, I know it happened at the Academy building and that a Noah Arietta was the victim. That's enough to get me started as I search the internet and flip through pages of the newspaper for additional details that I mark for copying. Online I send web pages to the printer, making a copy for myself and one for Theresa, my office manager.

Theresa was a god sent. I had worked with many office managers but none compared to her. She was smart, forward thinking and knew the law. That plus her personal attributes of rich chocolate brown skin and eyes of the same shade housing a sparkling witty personality made her easy to approach also helped. Then there was her kindness and her way of looking at a person with eyes that expanded, and made them feel like she thought their words important. Standing only a few inches over five feet, her intellect and demeanor commanded respect. During our initial interview, she would impress me by saying, "The only thing that separates women of color from anyone else is opportunity."

Over the years I learned that Theresa was raised in a small town in South Carolina, in her grandparents' house and she was the youngest of five siblings. Her father was a horse trainer and her mother was a maid, factory worker, and homemaker. Her family moved to Central Falls, Rhode Island, where they lived in abject poverty and dysfunction" until they finally moved to the Rochester area. It took little time for Theresa to realize if she wanted more out of life she needed to step up so she enrolled in community college and obtained a business degree.

Breaking into my reverie, the telephone began to ring and as it was too early for Theresa to be at her desk, I answered it myself.

"Hello," I said, "This is Richard Dandridge."

"This is Paige Trapp," a woman said. "Mrs. Paige Trapp. I'm sorry to be calling you so early, but I've been trying to get you all weekend. I finally reached your office manager and she said she thought you might be in early.

"Yes, Mrs. Trapp?" I said.

"My husband, Vincent Trapp, is in the county jail here in Rochester," she went on. "He's being held for murder. He wants you to be his lawyer." Her voice broke a little and then she went on. "You've been highly recommended to us." There is a pause. "Can you take his case?"

"I don't know, Mrs. Trapp," I answered truthfully. "I'll naturally have to talk with him and consider the situation before I can decide."

"Yes, I understand," she said.

"When I go to the jail, the conversations between your husband and myself is considered confidential." I said. "The most basic principle underlying the lawyer-client relationship is that lawyer-client communications are privileged, or confidential. This means that I cannot reveal a clients' oral or written statements nor my own statements to clients to anyone, including prosecutors, employers, friends, or family members, without the clients' consent," I add because sometimes when approached by someone other than the client, that person assumes they will be kept informed of all details so I need to be sure she understands this.

"Yes, of course, Mr. Dandridge. When can you see him? He's awfully anxious to see you."

I had already looked over the cases lined up in the computer but they were mostly routine stuff that could wait. "I'll go see him around eleven today. Do you plan to be there?"

"No. I have to go to the doctor's. I don't know if you've heard the details, but I...I had quite an experience. I'm sure I can see you Tuesday, though—that is, if you can take the case."

"I'll plan to see you Tuesday, then," I said, "if I take the case."

"Thank you, Mr. Dandridge."

"You are welcome, Mrs. Trapp,"

I hung up the phone and then leaned back and watched the windows become illuminated with the morning light. Outside the window, cars were passing by more frequently now as the city began to come awake.

Chapter 2

The Monroe County District Attorney's Office, is charged with prosecuting felony and misdemeanor crimes and violations occurring in Monroe County. Since returning to Rochester I had served as Chief of the Felony DWI Bureau for a year, then as Deputy Chief of the Major Felony Bureau for two years. Later I had served as Homicide Bureau Chief. All this I did to get accepted in the legal community not as most expected, because I set my sights on the office of District Attorney. That I knew was what Randall Walker wanted and I was not stupid enough to take him on.

Randall was a powerful figure of a man, standing over 6 feet with muscular arms that challenge the seams of his starched shirt. He wore his straight, short blond hair in a sleek style of a stock broker on wall street and his choice in tailor made suits and shirts supported that image. He had money and was not above flaunting it. He also had a style of using his large hands that seemed to be out for display as he moved them constantly whenever he was in the courtroom as if they were the power of his controlling the situation. Randall was quite a football player in the day too, a star at his high school and later at his university. But his fame did not end there as he fought in the Iraq War, a prolonged armed conflict that began with the 2003 invasion of Iraq by the United States collapsing the government of Saddam Hussein. The conflict continued for most of the next decade as a rebellion emerged to oppose the occupying forces and the post-invasion Iraqi government. After the United

States officially withdrew from the country in 2011, Randall's military career ended. I tried to do my part in the war, but received a 4F classification; in other words, found unacceptable for service in the Armed Forces.

There was no doubt in my mind that Randall, with his rich personal history, deserved the position, but there was something unlikable about him and whenever we met it was not a pleasant encounter. Now as I sat there in my office looking down at the traffic, I had to admit that I enjoyed being a lawyer and having my own law firm. I had run with the big dogs and I didn't like it and I didn't like having more than the law controlling my actions.

As usual when I think about where I started, I think of my old friend Pete Adams. Here was a man who was my mentor and who I would later learn had lived a difficult life. Pete, after attending Dwight Morrow High School moved to New York City on the pretense of attending college, but instead missed too many classes and was asked to leave. That straightened him up and he landed in Syracuse, New York where he buckled down and got his law degree. He would pass the bars on his second try and from there his life went downhill.

Pete met the woman of his dreams, only to have her die of breast cancer just a year after their marriage. He had loved her dearly and her death was unexpected. After that Pete dissociated from the situation which was his way of handling the trauma because her death had a huge impact on him. He didn't deal with it, instead he allowed his mind to dissociate from the situation, in order to cope with it. As a result, it took time for him to play out different emotions.

It was still while he was trying to cope with that loss that he met and married again and had two sons and a daughter with this wife and though she obviously tried to be what he needed, it would never be. Emotionally tarnished there would be a divorce, a very nasty divorce.

When his son, died after having a seizure at the age of 16 it was too much to handle and Pete didn't even try. Instead he tried to find solace in the bottle and after being under the influence several times in court he eventually was unable to practice law.

He had been a good lawyer, now his drinking had lost him most of his clients but those who cared about him gave him jobs of looking up land titles and interpreting abstracts for them. I was one of those lawyers. I had known Pete forever and would never forget how he had given me moral support when I needed it.

All these memories flood to the surface as I sit looking out my office window and with them came the reality of the present. If I were to take on a murder case, I would be in court with Randall Walker. Though I knew I was a good lawyer, whenever I was around Randall I doubted myself. He had that way about him and as a result it usually ended with him winning. Well that would have to stop and here was an opportunity to do it. At this point the case became more interesting. If I say yes, this would be my first big murder case and a chance to best Randall Walker.

Chapter 3

"Good morning, boss."

I am so deep in thought I didn't hear her when she entered. "Good morning, Theresa."

"Did you have a good time golfing with your friend."

"Yes I did. It was relaxing and very enjoyable, so much so I didn't want to come back."

"Well, I'm glad you did, she said.

I left my perch at the window and turned to watch as Theresa enters her office and disappears from view. I know she is taking off her jacket and hanging it in the closet like she has done so many times before. I hear the sound of the Keurig she has in her office and soon she appears in the doorway. "Here, I thought you might like a cup of coffee."

"Yes, but I don't have much time." I go behind my desk and watch as Theresa leaves to return with her tablet. She sits in the chair in front of my desk and says, "I'm ready."

"Let's see. I have identified the cases that we need to consider further. See what you can find out about the two men arrested in connection with the car crash and shooting incident on Driving Park Avenue check the police records for Eugene Harden, 33 of Rochester and Joshua Latham, 24, from Pennsylvania. I also need more on the hit-and-run involving two vehicles that crashed into each other Saturday evening at Lyell and Whitney. Start with the man, Stephenson Brown, 63 and go from there."

"Finally, let's take a look at the details on the 14-year-old Georgia Clinman who was reported missing on Friday. I believe the parents live in Fairport and I'm sure they have filed a police report too."

I watch as Theresa leans over her tablet typing away and when she finally looks up I say, "By the way, did you hear about the murder?"

"Ah, no, I tend to enjoy my off days without thinking about cases and especially, murder." Theresa says, jutting her head forward in that way she does to emphasize the question is stupid.

"Well, you are starting where I am, except I did research this morning. I printed out documents that will help you catch up. I had a call from Mrs. Trapp and told her I will go see her husband at the Monroe County Jail at eleven today."

"Okay, I'll call downtown and let them know you're coming. Who should I say you are seeing?"

"Vincent Trapp. He was charged with murder and he wants me to defend him or so his wife said during our morning phone chat."

"I'm on it," Theresa says before returning to her office. I gulp down my coffee and follow Theresa to grab a set of the copies I have made. I then take them back in my office and open my briefcase. I keep empty folders inside so that in times like this all I have to do is grab one out and fill it with the papers.

Despite the rapid advancements of technology and the undeniable effects of internet-based and mobile technology on the business world, many lawyers have continued with business as usual, steadfastly maintaining that technology has minimal impact on the practice of law., but that's not me. I have done my best to keep pace with the rapid changes by learning about and implementing new technologies into my practice; sometimes it works and sometimes it doesn't.

Theresa is the one constantly pressing me into the technological mold. She is proficient at word processing, spreadsheet, telecommunications, database, presentation and legal research software so it is only right that I keep up if I ever want to locate files on my own and keep the staff level at two. I have a well-equipped briefcase that includes a PDA for keeping my calendar, to-do list, and contact information for clients, attorneys, and others. I have a digital recorder for logging thoughts, notes, and instructions along with a cellular phone headset, a notebook computer for quick lookups and picture taking, and a USB scanner to make copies.

Now as I ready myself I double check to make sure all of these are in my briefcase, then buzz Theresa to let her know I am on my way to the Monroe County Jail.

***

The minute I enter the County jail a depression descends on me. This is one of the largest county-run facilities of its kind in New York state and on any given day, the facility houses roughly 1,000 inmates, most of whom are awaiting arraignment, trial or sentencing in this green and more green interior. I know that they say green is the color of balance and harmony, providing equilibrium between the head and the heart, but not this much green, which is only broken up by unpainted areas of gray concrete walls and steel bars.

I remember the first time I visited a jail. It was a stressful experience. There are a lot of guards, a lot of locked doors, and a lot of rules and being unprepared can add to the stress and detract from the quality of the client meeting. It wasn't a great experience for myself or my client. But now I know what to expect and prepare appropriately.

That first time I forgot my bar card. Big mistake. I had to talk the front desk officer into taking my business card, Google me, and then call my office to confirm. They eventually let me in, but it was quite a production.

I make my way to meet up with Jeremy Sexton, the prison officer who does everything by the book. Jeremy has only a few more years to go before his retirement.

I approach him now and say, "Good morning Jeremy. I'm here to see Vincent Trapp, Jeremy," "Okay, but I need to see..." Jeremy starts, even though he knows me, but I am already taking out my Bar license and my photo ID to show him.

"Thanks, Mr. Dandridge." What do you have in your brief case."

I open it and watch as Jeremy peers in at the contents, holding up items for explanation before putting everything back and in order.

"Oh yes," I say, pulling out my cell phone, "I have this as well."

Jeremy walks with me to the lockers and offers me a quarter, which I take. I put everything in there except a pen and paper and the folder containing the printouts of the case since my electronics are not allowed beyond this point.

Jeremy explains that I have come at a good time and should not be stuck in lock down during any meals or inmate counting periods. This is important to know since I will be meeting with my client face-to-face and that is simply a better way.

"Mr. Dandridge," Jeremy says, reaching in his desk for his keys. "Do you want to see him in his cell?"

"No, is there a visitor's room available?"

"Sure," Jeremy said, "Follow me."

I walk beside Jeremy and wait as he pauses to unlock the entrance to the visitor area. We walk down the center hall and pause two doors down where he opens the door, steps back and says, "Sit tight," I'll be right back."

I listen to the sound of Jeremy's shoes echoing down the hallway. For our own safety, attorneys are shut inside with their clients in "professional visit cells," which are perhaps 6 feet by 8 feet in size so I can't leave the room. I take this time to review the personal information on Mr. Trapp to gain some insight into his character.

It seems Vincent Trapp is an avid outdoorsman, camper, and hiker. He has extensive camping experience in Africa. He also enjoys boating, golfing, swimming, jogging, tennis, and skiing. I read further and learn that Vincent Trapp enjoys working out several times a week and is a licensed amateur pilot who learned to fly in Botswana, Africa. He has an American Studies degree from Yale University and a Master's Degree in Italian from Middlebury College in Vermont. He is known to read extensively and may have kept a diary or journal.

It gets a little more intense at this point. A longtime insomniac, Vincent Trapp reportedly has been under psychiatric care in the past and has used medication for depression. I take my pencil and underline this before continuing on.

He drinks scotch and wine and enjoys eating peanuts and spicy food. Lt. Trapp is described as intense and self-absorbed, prone to violent outbursts, and prefers a neat and orderly environment. I underline most of this section as well.

I have to smile. This is not necessarily neat, but it is an orderly environment. I continue to read the report. Vincent Trapp was born August 1, 1967, his hair is Brown. He is 6'1 and weighs

180 lbs. He is a white American, and a retired army Lieutenant. who is currently The Under Secretary for Intelligence or USD. I don't need to underline here. Instead I now look over the print out on this job position and write, "stands to support his character."

"The positon of USD is a high-ranking civilian position in the Office of the Secretary of Defense within the U.S. Department of Defense that acts as the principal civilian advisor and deputy to the Secretary and Deputy Secretary of Defense on matters relating to military intelligence. The Under Secretary is appointed from civilian life by the President and confirmed by the Senate to serve at the pleasure of the President. The Office of the Under Secretary of Defense for Intelligence is principal staff element of the Department of Defense regarding intelligence, counterintelligence, security, sensitive activities, and other intelligence-related matters. With the rank of Under Secretary, this is a Level III position within the Executive Schedule with an annual rate of pay of $565,300. I double underline the pay rate.

In a few I hear footfalls and soon the door is unlocked. Jeremy enters behind a man who matches the description I have just read. "Mr. Dandridge, this is Lieutenant Vincent Trapp."

I look at the man before me now and find myself disliking him at first sight. I sensed an ego of self-love clinging to him like a cloak and I had to control my tolerance and sense of fair play so that I could be objective.

"Hello, there," he says, as he reaches out to shake my hand which I supply promptly. "I've been waiting for you."

I can sense an annoyance in his tone. "Yes, sir," I said. I nod my head to allow Jeremy to leave and wait until we are alone in the room.

We sat facing each other in the visiting room on uncomfortable metal chairs. I consider what to say and decide to get right down to business. I need to know his possible defenses to a charge of murder.

Vincent Trapp turns his attention elsewhere with an air of cool detachment. I watch as he looks slowly around the room and I follow his gaze. The room is battleship gray walls, ceilings with a gray trimmed dirty window and gray cement floor. Stuck against the far wall is an eye chart to test vision which snags Lt. Trapp's interest and he begins to read line 10 accurately.

"Well," I said with what I hope sounds like a jest, "There goes one possible defense out the window."

Vincent Trapp turns toward me now, his dark eyes boring into mine. "What's that?" he said.

"I'm afraid," I say dryly, "that you can't very well claim that your shooting was a case of mistaken identity."

Lt. Trapp grunts unsmilingly and resumes his cool survey of the room. I now knew that this defendant did not like to joke about the fix he was in.

"Before we talk about your case, Lt. Trapp, suppose we talk about you," I said. "This will help me get a better feel for a defense. It's what psychologists sometimes call a frame of reference."

"I wouldn't know," Lt. Trapp says."

I ignore that and ask, "How old are you?"

"Thirty-nine."

"How old is your wife?"

"She's forty-one."

"The newspapers said she was thirty-five."

"No, she's forty-one."

I make note of this. "Is this your first marriage?"

"No."

"Suppose you tell me your marital details."

"Is all this necessary?"

"Suppose you let me be the judge of that."

"It's my second marriage."

"How did the first one end?"

"We were divorced."

"Did you or she ask for the divorce."

"What the... Seeing the look on my face he decides to answer. "She asked for a divorce."

"On what grounds?"

"Cruelty, but not what you think. It was stupid, unimportant petty things." He pauses and adds, "The grounds were she'd found another man while I was busy doing important governmental things. I did not fight the case and gave her a divorce."

"I see. So, were you in the service?"

"Yes."

"Did you serve in the Iraq war?"

"Yes"

"Did you see any action?"

"Plenty. I was there when the U.S. forces invaded Iraq on March 20, 2003, because the country allegedly possessed weapons of massed destruction. I remained until December of 2011 to fight an insurgency against the U.S. occupation and the newly formed Iraqi government."

So, I might have a genuine military hero on my hands; one who was not only modest but reticent as hell, too. And wouldn't he look nice in court all decked out in his ribbons and decorations? "What," I went on, "what brought you to this neck of the woods?"

"Well, after I retired from military duty I came back to the States where I shifted between several jobs, unable to find anything of interest. I currently have a civilian position in the Office of the Secretary of Defense within the U.S. Department of Defense, but Paige doesn't like that."

I shake my head and then ask, "Who's Paige?"

"My Wife."

"Tell me about your wife,"

I notice a mere flutter of his eyes. "What do you want to know?"

"Was she married before."

"Yes. I'm her second husband. She divorced her first."

"Did you know her first husband?"

"Very well. We once served in the same outfit."

"You and he were buddies?" I asked.

There was a moment pause. "You might say that."

"I see," I said. "Suppose you tell me how you came to marry your buddie's wife.

"He died in Iraq."

"Sorry, my condolences." I pause briefly. "And where were you and his wife at the time."

"Both in New York State."

"Do you have any children from previous marriages?"

"No."

"From this one?"

"No"

"Any future plans to start a family?"

His voice is tinged with savageness. "Not unless that dirty bastard Arietta knocked her up!"

This was a sudden step on dangerous ground, very dangerous ground. In a case like this there were legal danger points and I wasn't ready to delve into this right now so I abruptly veered away.

"What kind of weapon did you use on, Arietta?"

I saw his eyes gleam. "A luger. It was a war souvenir."

"Let's see, that's a semi-automatic pistol, fairly equivalent to our semi-automatic Colt .45?"

"Yes," he replied.

"The cops have it now?"

"Yes, I gave it to the state police."

"Tell me where you got this pistol."

"Is that necessary?"

"Yes, it is?

"Want the long or short version?"

"The long, if you please."

Vincent Trapp sat up straighter. His dark eyes clouded and he seemed to be far away. "Well," he started, "it was at the battle of Alasay on March 23, 2009. The French and Afghan troops defeated the Taliban insurgents in the Alasay Valley. It was dusk and I was leading about a dozen men out on night patrol. The area had been badly shelled and there was very little cover. Intelligence told us the Taliban were in full retreat, that the way was clear. They were wrong. Anyway, there was shots fired and one of the injured had a luger pistol clutched in his hand. I took the pistol as a souvenir."

I needed a moment. "Excuse me," I said, rising. "I'll be back shortly."

"Sure, no problem."

I pressed the bell near the door and in a few minutes, Jeremy returned. He unlocked the door and I stepped out.

"Jeremy I need to make a call. I shouldn't be long."

"Sure Mr. Dandridge. Just wave when you're done," he said, then turned and walked away.

I thought about what I knew and this new revelation would do great in court if I could figure a way to get it told. But reality took over. I was not going to take this case anymore because Randall Walker was planning on taking the case. I was taking it because it was going to prove interesting. I found my way back to the locker and took out my cell phone and placed a call to my office.

34

"Theresa," I said, "it's kind of looking like I might be defending Lieutenant Vincent Trapp in his murder case."

"Good," Theresa said. "But what's he going to pay you with? Professional soldiers never have a dime? I was married to one."

I gulped and swallowed like a kid caught raiding a cookie jar. "Not this one. We haven't discussed it yet. All I'm after now are the facts. "

"Well you better discuss your fee before you get too involved.

"Sh…Not over the phone, Theresa. I'm supposed to be the successful, defense lawyer. I only take cases out of my sheer love for the law. My heart bleeds for the underdog."

"Sure. While you're on the phone, tell me, what'd you do with the retainer for the Earl Field Trial

"I bought a few necessities."

"What necessities?" Theresa persisted.

"Only a little booze and a much-needed jacket. My old one won't do. Oh, yes, and a nice surprise for your birthday. Look, I called to tell you I won't be back this afternoon and you spend my time lecturing me. You need to cancel any appointments and I'll finish up on the mail tomorrow."

"There are no appointments," Theresa says. "People are beginning to think you have moved away and I'm beginning to think that maybe they're right. The only contacts have been Pete Adams who came in and, oh yes, an airmail special delivery from your mother and that's it."

"What did Pete want?"

"He wasn't feeling well and probably wants some money. Will you be back this afternoon?"

"No, I'll work here and then I'm going golfing later."

"Golfing," Theresa said, "You just had a long weekend of it. Look, boss, enough is enough."

"Tell you what, if you've nothing better to do than brood over my check book you can leave early."

"I just may take you up on that," she said and then hung up the phone.

I disconnect the call, turn and wave at Jeremy to have him let me back in. When I enter, Lt. Trapp is standing by the door. "Don't worry," he says, "I'm not going to bolt. It wouldn't help anyway."

Time is passing and I decide the moment to discuss the case has arrived. Without preamble, I begin. "This morning after talking on the phone with your wife, I went online to read about your case," I said. "Tell me, have you read the online details?"

"Sure, naturally."

"Are they correct reports I'm reading?"

"I think so, yes."

"So we are clear, what I read is that you walked into the Founders Café and Bar and confronted the building owner, Noah Arietta at around quarter after twelve midnight Friday, or Saturday morning; whichever way you care to look at it, and shot him five times. Is that correct?"

"You're telling it. Go on," Vincent said.

"So then you drove your car back to your home in Pittsford, called the Pittsford police and told them you had just shot Arietta. The dispatch office in Pittsford called the Rochester State Police and you waited in your home until the officers arrived. Is all this true?"

"Sounds about right."

"I checked out several online papers and they all say that the officers took you into custody and brought you to this jail. Your wife accompanied you here and she told the officers that earlier that evening Noah Arietta had raped her in the Great Embankment Park and then Arietta later beat her up. Is that what she said and what happened?"

"Go on."

"The police officers than called in the rape and two uniformed officers came to take a report, and gather evidence, then drove her to Highland Hospital on South avenue for further evidence collection and to complete a rape kit. They had her bring a complete set of clothing because the clothing she was wearing at the time of the assault was collected as evidence. The Rape kit exam was an hours-long medical forensic exam to collect evidence from your wife's body to preserve possible DNA evidence and receive important medical care. Procedures were complete and by the book. Correct?"

"I guess so."

"Only problem is that the doctor from Highland called with the results of the exam and the rape kit was negative for sperm. It was his opinion that your wife had not been raped." I paused to let this sink in. "Shall I continue?"

"Sure."

"Your wife volunteered to take a lie-detector test to proof she was telling the truth and that test was given, but the results are undisclosed. Right?"

"Yes."

"Online at several newspaper sites it says that you have refused to elaborate on your original oral statement to the officers that you shot Noah Arietta. Is that right?"

"Yes."

"Have you made or signed any other statements with the police?"

"No."

"All right. So far so good. Now we need to talk about some details that may or may not have been reported in the papers online. Did you see Noah Arietta rape your wife?"

"What?" For the first time there is a reaction visible in Lt. Trapp's expression. His eyebrows raised up and curved and the skin below his brow stretched with horizontal wrinkles across his forehead. I can see his eyelids are so wide open that the whites are showing above and below the pupils. Lower on his handsome face I see his jaw has dropped and his teeth are slightly parted. "No," he said softly.

"Did you see him beat her up?"

"No."

"Did you hear her shout out, as she claimed?"

"No... Well, I heard some shouting but wasn't sure. It wasn't until we packed up and headed toward home that she told me."

"So the first time you learned of the attacks on your wife by Noah Arietta was when she told you about them?"

"Yes."

"What did you do then?" I needed more than a yes or no answer from this man.

"I tried to calm her down. She was a wreck with one eye nearly swollen closed, her face badly bruised and her arms were showing bruises as well. Her skirt was torn, her panties were missing, she said, and, and..."

He stopped suddenly and that same expression appeared on his face.

"Please, go on," I said.

"And there were marks on her thighs." The venom in his voice could not be mistaken.

"What, if anything, did you do?

"I told her to clean herself up. After she was done, she put on her clothes from the day before and I took the other clothes and stuff out back and burned them in the barbecue pit."

"Before the police arrived?"

"Yes, immediately."

I paused, keeping my eyes down. "Did it occur to you that this would have been pretty conclusive evidence that the man had raped her?"

I looked up and saw anger written all over his face. His mouth was firmly pressed together with the lips drawn down at the corners. He didn't want to admit he did something so stupid.

"Well, did it," I repeated.

"Did it what?" he said heatedly.

"Did it not occur to you that you were destroying the best proof that Arietta had raped your wife?"

"I didn't think of that," he blurted. "I couldn't stand the sight of her looking like that."

"Now, answer honestly, did this happen before or after you shot Noah Arietta?"

"Before, of course."

"Hm…How long did you stay with your wife before you went to the Founders Café?"

"I don't remember."

"This is important. I suggest you try and remember."

"Maybe an hour," After a pause, Vincent said.

"Maybe more than an hour?" I asked.

"Maybe? Vincent replied.

So maybe less than an hour?" I added

"Maybe."

I needed to think. If I took his case, I knew at the get-go his case at this point was legally defenseless. So, I stop now and beg off and let some other lawyer worry over it or I ask him the fatal questions. I look at him and wonder if he realizes how close I had him to admitting that he was guilty of second degree murder. He had willfully and with malice murdered Mr. Noah Arietta. Yes. As the defense attorney, I would be ethically bound to zealously represent my client, the guilty as well as the innocent and a vigorous defense is necessary to protect the innocent and to ensure that judges and citizens and not the police have the ultimate power to decide who is guilty of a crime.

As the defense attorney, I had to change my way of looking at this because as the defense attorney one almost never really knows whether the defendant is guilty of the crime he or she has been charged with. Just because the defendant says he did it doesn't make it so. The defendant may be lying to take the rap for someone he wants to protect, or may be guilty, but guilty of a different and lesser crime than the one being prosecuted by the district attorney. For these I must deal with the facts to put on the best defense possible and leave the question of guilt to the judge or jury.

I remember the motto. 'Asks not, what did my client do?' but rather, 'What can the government prove?' No matter what the defendant has done, he is not legally guilty until a prosecutor offers enough evidence to persuade a judge or jury to convict. But this was Randall Walker I tell myself, not some first timer like myself.

I continue my silent review. There is that fact that a criminal defense attorney may vigorously defend guilty clients, but they risk committing professional suicide by doing so. So why would I even consider the case. Was it because I saw a chance to win and at the same time beat Randall Walker? Or was it because it was my big chance to win a tough case and finally knock Theodore Sampson off his pedestal as the leading criminal defense lawyer of Monroe County. That was a good argument but then there was the bigger one of running for District Attorney against Randall and this would be my opportunity not only to beat him, but to show my capabilities. As I continue to mull this over, it came to me that there was even a better way of looking at this. This would be an opportunity to defend a war hero that might just give credence to the case.

Jeremy opened the door and pulled me out of my reverie. "It's noon", he said. "Time for lunch. You can join us if you want."

"No," Jeremy, "Thanks for the offer, but I have a luncheon engagement. I looked over at my prospective client and saw he was smiling.

"Well done, Counselor," he murmured. "Hope you enjoy your lunch."

"More importantly, hope you enjoy yours," I said. "See you at two."

Chapter 4

Before exiting the jail, I stopped at the locker room to gather my things and headed out. Once outside I looked around and found there isn't a restaurant in walking distance to the jail and I didn't want to take a chance of losing my parking space so I found a quiet area where I could sit and review my files. Surprisingly, this Lt. Trapp was an odd bird and I needed as much ammunition as I could gather to keep a step ahead of him or he would try and take the lead. The problem with that was that if he did, he would lose the case for me. I could find nothing that showed he had a record, but the way he acted made me think he had experience with the law so I continued to dig and sent an email to Theresa to do the same. I was deeply into my internet search when I glanced at the corner of the screen and saw that it was time I was getting back to the jail. I shut down the computer and deposited my stuff in the locker. I soon was with Jeremy who took me to the Visitor's area and then went to get Lieutenant Trapp.

While I waited, I pulled out the files and reviewed what we had covered earlier. The file was getting bigger and I was feeling quite sure I knew this man. So now I needed to be careful what I said and how I said it because counseling is one of the most important tasks of a defense attorney. As the advocate, I knew I was expected to champion my client's case, but as counselor, I must advise my client about the possible legal consequences involved. It was my job to evaluate all the strengths and weaknesses of the prosecutor's case and assess the success or failure of various legal scenarios. It was my job to weigh the likelihood of conviction or acquittal and it was my job to interpret the law to my client because in most cases the client was not well versed in what the law considers important and what the law will demand. On that wave link, I concentrated on handling Lt. Trapp.

As if on key, the door opened and I hear, "Hello, Mr. Dandridge, back again. Hope you had a better lunch than I did."

"Hello, Lt. Trapp."

"Have a seat," I said. I arranged the papers I had on the table while Vincent took a seat.

"I've been thinking about your case," I said.

"Yes, so are you going to defend me?"

"Before I answer that, I need you to understand that in order for me to be an effective advocate and counselor, I must know all the facts of the case. That is why the legal system protects attorney-client relationship so that the facts can be discussed without penalty. Anything you say to me is considered privileged communication that the law protects against forced disclosure without your consent. This protection extends to any work product I do in order to represent you. Do you understand?"

"Yes."

"Getting along with a client is important, but not necessarily easy. It will help if you try not to irritate me by refusing to cooperate, deceive me or be dishonest. I am not an idiot so don't tell me implausible stories, invent alibis, or withhold any key information. Do you understand?"

"Yes," he replied.

"Fine. Now I know there are many questions still I need to ask, facts we will need to discuss. I am not prejudging your case, but as things stand, I must advise you that in my opinion you have not yet disclosed to me a legal defense to this charge of murder."

"Okay..., I don't know what you want." Vincent Trapp blinks and rubs his forehead. "Are you advising me to plead guilty?" he asks.

"I may eventually, but that is not what I am saying. I just want you to understand where everyone who will be involved in this case will be and know how important it will be to not think they are dimwitted and don't know anything about homicide and the alternatives."

"So, what are the alternatives."

"Well, homicide is conduct which causes the death of a person and is classified under manslaughter or murder."

"So what is classified as manslaughter."

"Simply put, murder is a form of criminal homicide; other forms of homicide might not constitute criminal acts. These homicides are regarded as justified or excusable. For example, individuals may, in a necessary act of self-defense, kill a person who threatens them with death or serious injury, or they may be commanded or authorized by law to kill a person who is a member of an enemy force or who has committed a serious crime. Typically, the circumstances surrounding a killing determine whether it is criminal. The intent of the killer usually determines whether a criminal homicide is classified as murder or manslaughter and at what degree."

"What's the worst-case scenario." Lt. Trapp asks.

I give it a moment and then tell him, "Murder in the second degree and aggravated murder are both class A-1 felonies, which carry the maximum sentence permitted by the law. They would be the worst-case scenario."

I can almost see the wheels churning as Lt. Trapp picks apart what I have told him. "So what legal defense can be used against the crime."

"Several come to mind. Manslaughter, as opposed to murder, may be charged in those cases where a person acts with a mental state of lesser culpability. Thus, where a person intends only to inflict another person with serious physical injury, but does not intend to kill them, a prosecutor may decide to charge that person with manslaughter in the second degree, rather than murder. Another mitigating factor that may downgrade a charge of murder to manslaughter in the second degree is whether the person acts under extreme emotional disturbance

"I don't quite follow what you're saying. Can you expand a little more?"

"Well, first-degree felony murder requires the defendant's intent to kill a victim. Second-degree felony murder requires only the defendant's intent to commit one of the predicate felonies. A person charged with first-degree felony murder must have personally caused the victim's death or commanded another to do so; on the other hand, a person may be guilty of second-degree felony murder as an accomplice of the actual killer." I pause. "Does that help?"

"Yes it does." Lieutenant Trapp got up and walked around, then turned to me and said, "So what are the possible defenses for a murder charge."

I cautiously said, "Defenses to second degree murder charges can be extreme emotional disturbance, assisted suicide without the use of duress or deception, mental disease or defect, self-defense, or defense of another person."

I could see a look of scrutiny on his face as he rambles, "I do understand. So, what about Arietta raping my wife? How does that play? There is no death penalty in New York State, is there?" What are the possible sentences here?"

"Whoa, slow down, we aren't there yet. Let me just say that normally the sentence can be life imprisonment without parole or imprisonment for a term of 20 to 25 years."

I watch Vincent Trapp absorb this information, staring down at his hands a moment, then looking about at the bleak gray-painted room. "I'd sooner die than spend any more time in a place like this." He said.

"Well, I can honestly tell you it won't be like this, it will be worse, much worse. This is merely a way station, but prison is Hell."

"What does the law say about a man who kills another because the man raped his wife? Isn't that a whole new matter?"

"No, you have the right to prevent the rape or if you are able to catch him, to prevent him from escaping."

"It doesn't seem fair."

"Life isn't fair." I responded.

I need to get down to business and guide the conversation on to his case. "At this point it is known that the death of Arietta was not a suicide or accident, and that you did it. There isn't an alibi or a case of mistaken identity to consider since you were seen at the Founder's Café Bar."

"So what you are saying is that I should just plead guilty because there is no justification or any excuse acceptable in the eyes of the court," Vincent said.

"No, that's not what I'm saying. You see, legally a man is not justified in killing a man for raping or beating up his wife. Morally, though, it has some righteousness to stand on."

"What do you mean," Vincent asked.

I needed to paint him a picture. "The Hebrew word for "murder" literally means "the intentional, premeditated killing of another person with malice and malice is a form of evil intent that separates "murder" from "killing". When a killing lacks evil intent, they are given exceptions in the murder laws of the United States."

"So you are saying there is a defense?"

"Well if one of the following conditions is met it is possible. If a person kills someone accidentally or a person is trying to defend him or herself and prevent his or her own murder this is self-defense. Then if a person is trying to prevent someone from entering his or her house to commit some violent felony or a person is trying to prevent the murder of someone else that is seen as protecting an innocent. In these situations, killing is actually legal and justifiable."

One look at Vincent Trapp and I knew what he was thinking before he said it.

"Maybe…," he said. He pauses to choose the right words and then continues. "Maybe I did see Arietta in the act. I didn't tell the police one way or the other. I never really told them I was or wasn't there."

"Listen Lt. Trapp there is more to this and you need to understand it all. I need to understand it all if I am to defend you. Whether you told the police or not, you did tell me and there is the time element to consider. You would need to have murdered Arietta right then and there and not an hour or so later. If, and I stress 'if' you caught Arietta in the act and murdered him then and there you would have some justification. But you didn't and so to the court your shooting of Noah Arietta is a thoughtless, malevolent act. That is exactly what they are charging you with."

Seeing the worried look on his face, I add, "All I am doing here is trying to help you see what you're up against, not trying to tell you how to plea."

"So what do we do?" Lt. Trapp asks and from the sound of his voice I could tell that I was now in command. He was ready to follow my lead.

"Well, in your situation, Lt. Trapp, whatever happened to your wife was over and done with when you learned about it. It was too late for you to save her because her danger was past. If Noah Arietta raped your wife he could have faced a rape charge in court and a rape charge would have given him a sentence of life in this state, but not death. Because you took action, murdered, Arietta you usurped the law and at your hand, gave Noah Arietta a death sentence. You broke society's law and that law now seeks punishment for your action."

There was silence in the room as Lt. Trapp pondered what was said and I wondered what he would ask me to do next. I kept my head down and glanced at my watch. The second hand kept going around, one, two, three times and still not a word is spoken. I want to think about if I wanted this case and if I did, how would I lay out a defense to win. Just how did I plan on doing that. Finally, Lt. Trapp spoke.

"Can't the jury just let me go, no matter what the damn law states?" Lt. Trapp asks forlornly.

I sat quietly with my head still down looking at my watch as if it held the answer. I looked up and directly at Lt. Trapp. "Yes, the jury can," I said. "And juries often do but you need to think about the jury process and the effect it can have. Five days a week, Monday through Friday, the County Courthouse buzzes with prospective jurors running between the waiting room, the cafeteria and the courtroom. They fill the elevators with small talk about how slow their cases are going, the books they brought with them to read between sessions or whether they can beat the rush-hour traffic home. Then after the court interrupts their life, many of them are never picked to sit on a jury. Most who are chosen end up hearing civil lawsuits or minor criminal cases but a handful eventually end up listening to the evidence in a murder case. For those few, say judges and jurors alike, jury duty is an experience never forgotten and not easily left behind because the emotional toll of a murder trial can have a profound effect on a juror. When something means that much, it is going to be approached prudently and precisely"

I need a moment to think and phrase my words in a way that Lt. Trapp will understand and accept. "The evidence often is psychologically shocking, and the strain of a decision that could relegate a person to life in prison can be devastating. Because of this mental anguish and overall exhaustion, betting on a jury is like playing the horses. As things now stand in your case, the law would be against you. The judge would be virtually forced to instruct the jury to convict you".

I take a moment more than say, "Don't you see? A jury would find it hard to let you go; they'd have to really work at it because from a legal point of view your situation presents a classic one of premeditated murder."

I could tell by the look on his face, Lt. Trapp understands and it humbles him. "You don't want to take my case, then?" he says.

"I am not saying one way or the other at the moment. I need time to sort it out and you need to give it a lot of thought too. I am not willing to enter the court without a sound and plausible legal defense in your case."

I pause thoughtfully as something occurs to me. "There's one other possible alternative."

"What is that," Lt. Trapp says excitedly.

"Well, you can get another lawyer. I haven't tried a murder case in a while. I know that a winning defendant extols all of the efforts of their lawyer, no matter how devious and slimy, and the loser blames the incompetence of their counsel and the weaseled ways of their opposition for their loss. In other words, everyone wants a shark to represent them, but nobody wants a shark on the other side of the courtroom. I am not a shark."

Lt. Trapp doesn't say a word as he stares directly into my eyes and I genuinely feel sorry for him. "So, who would you recommend."

Now it is my turn. "Well, there is this guy Theodore Sampson". Mr. Sampson is well known in the legal circle and is notorious." I pause. "Let me read you something that he said. 'A famous murder will arise if an individual who is in the limelight is prematurely killed at the hands of another individual. Although the death of the victim is publicized, the attached punishment does not typically waver from a regular murder case. In addition to the victim being regarded as a public figure, a famous murder case can also place the famous individual as the aggressor or defendant'. That's a great statement. Now, let me cite one of the notable cases that he won. "Decorated Air Force officer charged with Rape. Client was facing 30 years in prison and would have been registered as a sex offender. The client would have lost everything from a distinguished 20-year career in the military to all his benefits and any future jobs. He even would have been limited on where he could live. Their team of attorneys put together a solid and aggressive defense, with experts and private investigators along with other critical resources to prove their client's innocence. They took the case to trial and they won. They got a Not Guilty verdict on all counts!"

I sat down and stared straight ahead. "What I am saying is that Theodore Sampson has the manpower, the experience and the notoriety to win what can be perceived as an unwinnable case."

"Funny you should mention Mr. Sampson. I tried to get him but he was just diagnosed as having lung cancer and is trying to take a moment to breathe between making the decisions for treatment and getting a second opinion. I know him, so he was quite open with me that he needed to pick his battles and simplify his time now. That is why he turned me down."

"Cancer," I said. "Old Mr. Sampson has cancer? I didn't know." I felt a sudden wave of sympathy for him.

"So now what?" Lt. Trapp said.

"Well, let me be honest with you. When I take on a case to defend a man before a jury, I want to have a fighting chance of getting an acquittal. That includes having a chance to move for a new trial or to successfully appeal. You may think you morally had the right to murder Noah Arietta and I can understand that. But in court I prefer to leave the judgements to the jury. The main reason I hesitate to take you case as things now stand is my fear of losing it because your case would do better with a team of lawyers and a history with murder cases and that I do not have."

"I can understand that," Lt. Trapp said. "Do you have any other recommendations for me."

"Not just yet," I said. This would require a valid legal defense, if one exists. What Noah Arietta might have done to his wife before he killed him may present a favorable circumstance but it simply isn't enough. I paused. "What I know so far is not enough for me, anyway, to give you an answer."

I need to stretch my legs so I get up and walk around as I tried to figure out what the next move should be and I had an idea. It was a little idea, but at least something to consider. Wouldn't it be true that if Noah Arietta actually raped Paige Trapp he would be considered a felon at large at the time he was shot by Vincent Trapp? So, what if that is true? "Hm…" I said.

"What are you thinking?" Have you come up with an idea?"

"Nothing…, it's nothing." I was not ready to share this just yet so I reverted to a second alternative that had come to mind. "You could plead insanity."

The Lieutenant's head swiveled quickly to face me and he surprises me with his words. "So tell me what that entails."

"Okay." I wasn't prepared to get into this but I opened the gate. "When a defendant pleads not guilty by reason of insanity they are admitting that they committed the crime, but seek to excuse their behavior by reason of mental illness that satisfies the definition of legal insanity. People who are deemed to have been insane at the time they committed a crime are neither legally nor morally guilty."

Lieutenant Trapp sat down in the chair across from me and I could see a twinkle in his eye. "I see. So, what happens if I am found not guilty because of mental illness?"

I needed to lay it down straight forward. "When you are found not guilty by reason of insanity you most likely will not be set free. Instead, you may be confined to a mental health institution." I pause for emphasis or just to make sure he is hearing me. "You probably will remain confined for a longer period of time than had you been found guilty and sentenced to a term in prison if the jury decides you are insane and not just suffering from temporary insanity."

The Lieutenant shows no reaction to my last statement, but instead says, "How long can it take to get me out of there?"

"You will be confined until you can convince a judge that you are no longer legally insane. If you claim you were insane at the time of the offense but are sane at the time of the trial and possible acquittal, it may take months, maybe a year but more importantly you need to consider that a lifetime of mental illness hardly makes an insanity defense a sure thing." This I say referencing the fact that he has been at some time under psychiatric care. "The jury needs to be convinced that you were sick that evening and that you did not understand the consequences of your actions or that what you did was wrong. The standard is so difficult to meet that few defendants who use the insanity defense in New York win at trial."

Lt. Trapp rose from his chair and went to look out of the window. When he turned, he looked directly at me and said, "Maybe I was insane when I shot Noah Arietta."

"Why do you say that?"

"Well, I can't really say I remember what I did. I must have blacked out because I can't remember beyond going to his place and then coming home. In between is a total blank."

"You are telling me you don't remember shooting him?"

"Yes, that's what I'm telling you."

"Do you remember driving home?"

"No."

"Do you remember threatening Arietta?"

"No."

This was crazy; or was it. But maybe it could work. It was not an open and shut defense, yet, but it was a start. As I continued to mull it over, I saw the first loophole.

We were both standing near the window when I turned to him and said. "You mentioned to more than me the fact that once you returned home after shooting Noah Arietta, you called the RPD and told them, I just shot Noah Arietta." Isn't that a fact?"

Lt. Trapp replied steadily. "That's right,"

"So, tell me how come you could tell the police you had just shot Noah Arietta if you had really blacked out and didn't remember a thing? Did someone tell you?"

The silence in the room is thick as I wait for Lt. Trapp to give me his answer. I can tell that he is taken aback as he continues to stand in silence. Then it hits him. I see his shoulders draw back and his head lean backwards on his neck as he pulls his jaw upward.

"It's becoming clear now. Noah Arietta was the last man I saw before I blacked out. I know that when I arrived at the bar my gun was loaded but when I returned home, I saw it was empty. Don't you see, that is why I figured I must have shot him and so called the police."

It was the only plausible explanation he could have made. "I see," I said thoughtfully, aware that this would still require some careful reflection. I glanced at my watch and walked back over to the table. "That's enough for today," I said. "I'll see you tomorrow."

"Does that mean you are taking my case?"

"No, I'm not sure yet. We still have other details to go over."

"But, do you think we have a chance? Did my calling the RPD spoil things?"

"I don't know. I have an appointment so I must go now."

"Okay, Mr. Dandridge, Vincent Trapp said. "I'll see you tomorrow."

Chapter 5

I was in for a sleepless night. After talking with Lt. Trapp there was now a possible defense hanging out there. It was a dangerous one to consider, but what else did I have. He had admitted killing Arietta and there were witnesses to prove it. Now I needed to do more research and study the hell out of an insanity plea. A defense strategy is not as simple as telling the truth in a way that shows the defendant's innocence or lessened legal culpability. I needed time to design a case along these lines that would be convincing and find provable facts to support it.

As I drive my mind works diligently. Lt. Trapp has been charged with murder and he has told me his story, which he also confessed to the police after being arrested. Apparently, he was identified by an eyewitness shortly after the murder took place. The witness is not certain of the identification, but is "pretty sure". Lt. Trapp now says that although he was present at the scene of the crime, he did not remember committing the crime.

I look up and realize that I have driven myself home instead of to the office. As I pull into my driveway, I stop, thinking I really needed to go to the office and check out facts. But what I need to do first, is decide whether or not to take the case and I can do that without cracking a book. That resolved, I pull the car up further in the driveway and turn off the ignition.

Once inside I am astonished at how calm I feel. This decision could have a major effect on my career, yet I am not worried. I know it's not because I am confident in winning this case. Not by a long shot. This will not be easy-- that's if I even consider representing Lt. Trapp. I shake my head and head toward the kitchen.

I enjoy cooking. I move around the kitchen gathering the ingredients and then turn on the stove and put a pan on the burner to warm up as I prepare slices of onion and garlic. It takes my full concentration as I slowly add tomatoes, peppers and diced chicken to the pan. When everything is cooked just so, I go to the refrigerator and retrieve a baggie that contains precooked pasta; a trick I learned from my mother who would say, "I like to cook, but boiling pasta is not my idea of cooking." In minutes my meal is ready and I take it to the kitchen island and turn on the television before fixing myself a dish and pouring myself a glass of wine.

With a good meal and a little wine my mind drifts to the matter at hand. Do I want to take the case? I ponder this and start with the basics. I know now that Lt. Trapp is a man who has served his country and has been decorated for his accomplishments. He will therefore receive the respect of the jury members who will decide his fate. He is handsome, and comfortable in a position of being judged by others. I pause unable to think of much else at the moment so I go on to what might be points against him. I know even from our short conversations that he is intelligent and makes sure those he meets know it. And, he has a way of looking stern.

I'm comfortable with the pros and my ability to overcome the cons. I pour myself another glass of wine and think about our conversation. I know the basics of that legal option and it is that a defense can only establish that the defendant was suffering from a bout of temporary insanity by comparing the actions the individual engaged in at the time with the actions the individual took both before and after the crime. I don't have enough information one way or the other, but I do know that the challenge is exciting.

I clean up the kitchen and make my way upstairs to climb into bed. I sleep well that night and the next morning I am up and about early, eager to get to the jail. I know what I want to do.

***

"Good morning Jeremy," I said when I arrive at the jail.

"Good morning Mr. Dandridge."

"Jeremy, I got us coffee. Do you have a few minutes to spare?"

"Sure. Do you mind drinking it in my office?"

"No, that's fine." I follow him as he leads the way and once we are seated, I wait patiently as he performs the task of taking the coffee cup I hand him and carefully lifting the cover as he turns the cup around slowly in his hand. Once the lid has been removed, he holds it over the top of the cup and gently shakes it before laying it on the desk. I watch his motions with interest. Rumor has it that Jeremy's meticulous nature is what halted a jail break.

As the story goes, several years prior Jeremy had noticed something odd in that a prisoner named Adam Reed was visited by his girlfriend, Melanie Peters, or at least that is how she had signed in. The first time she visited Jeremy hadn't thought much of it, but on subsequent visits she seemed nervous and at sorts, drawing his attention. Later a woman who looked suspiciously like that woman Melanie had come to visit another prisoner named Danny Lincoln. As far as Jeremy knew and those he mentioned this too, these two prisoners did not know each other. Jeremy had brought this to the

57

attention of his superiors stating that he didn't know for sure, but something was going on. His superiors told him he was probably wrong. He tried again to bring the matter to their attention and they again put him off. The register showed the woman who visited Danny to be a Marilyn Walker and not this Melanie Peters but Jeremy was sure they were one and the same. He couldn't shake the feeling of something going on so he decided to search the prisoner's cells and taking extreme care about minute details he examined everything. He found a sheet of paper in Adam's cell that had a date on it and the words, 'safe and sound'. In his search of Danny's cell, he found a piece of paper with the same date and the same words. He put two and two together and told the authorities in time to block the escape. The attempt was kept hush hush as would be expected, but Jeremy was compensated for what was reported as 'his persistence'.

Now as I watch him I know he is the person to talk about my situation. Finally, Jeremy leans back in his chair and while he takes a sip of his coffee I ask, "Jeremy, were you on duty the night they brought Lt. Trapp in?"

"Yes, I was. I surely was."

"Jeremy, Lt. Trapp wants to hire me as his lawyer, but I don't know. I just don't know." I pause and then continue. "Do you know what kind of woman Mrs. Trapp is?"

"Oh, she is a nice person, very nice. She is very pretty and well endowed, if you know what I mean."

I have to smile at that. I feel a tinge of guilt trying to pump him for information so I need to just come out with it. "Jeremy I 've got to ask you a question. Do you know whether Noah Arietta raped Paige Trapp?"

"Why are you asking me, Mr. Dandridge," he says, glancing away and then back again. "How can I know. I wasn't there, but that lady was. Why not ask her?"

"I don't want to involve you, but I have to decide whether I'm going to take this case and I have to make a decision this morning. If I decide to take the case I want to win it and to win it, I need to know if Noah raped Mrs. Trapp. If he did, I maybe can win it."

Jeremy is uncomfortable. He glances furtively around the room before saying, "I think maybe he did rape her."

"Why do you say that?"

"They gave her a lie detector test and she passed it."

"Are you sure? She passed the lie detector test, Jeremy?" I pressed him. "I have to be sure."

"The State police told the sheriff and the sheriff told me," Jeremy said. "I shouldn't be telling you this, but since you are thinking of being his lawyer, I think it is all right."

"Thanks Jeremy, you've been a big help. That's all I want to know. I feel better already. "Jeremy leads me to the visitor's room and unlocks the door. He leaves to get Lt. Trapp.

While Jeremy is gone, I review what I have learned. The lie detector test showed Mrs. Trapp was telling the truth about the rape. Was the prosecution going to sit on the results? If they were, how was I going to get them before the jury? Especially since the results of these tests were inadmissible in court? Yes, that was a stumbling block but I'd have to face that matter later. For now, I knew that Mrs. Trapp was telling the truth about the rape.

I also knew that the polygraph test that she took and passed would be thorough. It would cover every detail of the case including the rape and the scene that took place in the park where Noah had allegedly beaten her up, and that would eradicate Lt. Trapp of any suspicion that he had beaten his wife up in a fit of jealous rage, which was one way that the jury might look at this. It also would support the truth of Lt. Trapp's story of his movements after his wife had entered the house. Now I not only knew these things were true but I knew that the prosecution also knew them to be true. While all this still did not afford Lt. Trapp an open-and-shut case, I knew what the People knew. Then it came to me that they probably didn't know that I knew. That was priceless. Perhaps I could lure the prosecution into trying to hide the results and… I am interrupted.

"Good morning, Mr. Dandridge," the familiar voice said.

"Good morning Lt. Trapp."

"You seem deep in thought this morning."

"I am. Shall we get started."

Hearing me say that, Jeremy left the room, locking the door behind him.

"Lt. Trapp," I said, I've decided to take your case."

"Good. I'm glad to hear that. I couldn't sleep last night, worrying if you were not going to defend me. Thank you, thank you so much".

"You are welcomed, but there is still my fee to discuss," I said.

"No problem. So, what is your fee?"

"Although most lawyers technically bill by the hour, it's common for private defense attorneys like myself to lump-sum fees for their services. A relatively straightforward murder case that requires just one or two witnesses to prove the defendant's innocence is liable to be inexpensive by most lawyers' standards but this is a more complex case. Before I give you that figure, you need to remember that first-degree murder is a very serious crime that carries stiff penalties. Defendants who plead "not guilty" and lose their cases during the trial process face the near-certain prospect of a long prison sentence. As such, a defendant who lacks faith in his or her lawyer's ability to secure an acquittal should strongly consider pleading "guilty." But, on the other hand, defendants who believe that they can successfully fight their charges should consider the costs and benefits of retaining a qualified lawyer who will pull out all the stops and win the case and that will be me. Knowing that I will do everything in my legal power to win."

I pause and then continue. "For a serious felony crime I charge by the hour for all services, at the rate of $300 per hour. To hire me you must pay an up-front fee called a retainer. I will deduct that hourly rate from the retainer as the work is done. When the retainer is gone, you will be billed for any additional payments".

Again, I pause, looking across the table at my perspective client to get a reading on how he is taking this news. His face does not give anything away and I can't tell if he likes or dislikes what I am saying. In any event, I continue. "To take on your case, the retainer is $25,000."

Now I wait silently for his reaction.

"That is fair enough. I rather thought it might be more."

I try to keep the look of shock off my face. "I will need you to sign this form verifying that you agree with my fee."

I watch as Vincent Trapp looks over the form and signs it. He pushes it back across the table and I look it over.

"You've just brought yourself a lawyer and I seem to have a client. Now, we need to get down to work. There is plenty we need to cover."

"Okay, where do we start?" Vincent asks.

I need to find out so that I can explain to you the case that the prosecution is using and when I do, I need you to include important pieces of fact in their testimony. For example, if they say that a key part of the prosecution's case is that the you were in a certain location at a certain time, you need to remember to tell a version of events that does not put you at that location at that time. On my part I need to tell you about various pieces of information on the prosecution's case so that you know what kinds of evidence they need to produce. We are now a team and we can have no secrets from each other.

Jeremy arrived and opened the door. I watched as he took Lt. Trapp to his cell and then made my way out the front door feeling quite pleased with myself.

Chapter 6

The outer jail door opened and in strolled Sheriff Lincoln Simpson a character straight out of Criminal Minds. His thick head of silver gray hair and twinkling gray eyes drew attention to his impressive features before noticing the tailored pin striped dark gray jacket and matching deeply creased suit pants. He wore a sparkling white shirt and a purple and white print tie that set off his eyes to a tee. Eventually one focuses on his prominent nose that appears to have been broken at one point as it tilts to the right, giving his features a flaw that makes him more approachable. Sheriff Simpson earned his post by obtaining a degree in Criminal Justice from Monroe Community College a business degree from Roberts Wesleyan College and word had it that he just recently completed his Master's Degree in Security Studies from the Naval Postgraduate School Center for Homeland Defense and Security.

Knowing of his background as well as his character I treat this as a solemn moment and I restrained an impulse of grabbing his hand and shaking it. I am so glad to see he is back at last from his vacation, but not because of any inadequacy at the jail. It is because talking directly with him I can feel him out. I watch as his keen gray eyes restlessly searched the room and finally rest upon me, lighting up as if glad to see me.

"Hello, Richard, he says. He walks toward me and reaches out to grasp my hand in both of his. "I am so glad to see you. Is Jeremy treating you and the Lieutenant agreeably? I can feel his other hand as he slaps me lightly on the back and I think, what a long way he has come from being the stanch man of his early years. Now he has an unsuppressed gift for camaraderie. He strives to always make those he meets feel important, no matter what their political parties. I like him just as much as I did before his position called for such personable responses to everyone. I had always liked him.

Now as we greet each other, I am not the least bit surprise he is aware I am there to meet with Lt. Trapp. Unlike myself, whether away or at home, the Sheriff is always kept informed of any activity within the town.

"Hello," I say. "Yes, Jeremy has been a big help to me and my client. How have you been."

"Oh, so you are taking on the case. I thought you might, but then…" He paused a moment in reflection before saying, "I'm doing just fine, Richard. Good to see you." Sensing he is ready to retreat, I move aside.

His attention shifts from me to Jeremy. "Any calls, Jeremy?" I hear the Sheriff say.

"They're on your Surface Pro," Jeremy responds. "I may not be a fan of the technology, but my writing is getting worse and I have to admit this is better."

"Of course, of course." Seeing me still standing there, the sheriff asked, "Is there something I can do for you Richard?"

"If you've got a minute, I'd like to have a chat with you."

"Sure, no problem." He speaks with Jeremy then turns to give me the signal to follow him as he makes his way to his office. Once we are both inside, he points toward the chair in front of his desk. This is his environment so I take a seat and wait for him to let me know when to speak.

The Sheriff picks up his phone and dials. "This will just take a minute," he says, turning his back to me as he speaks softly into the phone. "Hon, I'm going to be late. Can you meet me at the kickoff dinner for the Blue Cross tonight? There is a pause. "Good. See you then."

The Sheriff puts the phone back on the cradle and then looks across his desk at me. "Sorry about that. Now, I'm all yours," he says. "What can I do for you Richard?"

I didn't want to just blurt it out, but I didn't know how else to ask, except to be direct. "Well, I would like to know the results of Paige Trapp's lie-detector test."

I wait patiently for his reply, knowing that he may not want to share this with me because the information shouldn't be coming from him. I know he knows the results because he has friends in higher places that would have filled him in on what they already knew. I just hope beyond hope that friendship will prevail.

"Oh, I wish I could tell you my friend, but the test was done by the State Police. It would be better if you went and asked them."

Did he know? Of course, he knew. Disappointed I said, "Sure, you're right. I should ask them directly for the results, but, I have a feeling that they won't tell me… so why waste my time." I pause for affect. "The results aren't admissible in court anyway so forget I asked."

I stand up and lean across the desk to shake his hand. "Thanks for your time, Lincoln, it was worth a try. Good to see you."

The Sheriff nods his head as he lifts his phone to make another call. This is the signal that it is time for me to leave. I hear him say, "Hello, this is the Monroe County Sheriff, returning his call."

I pause and turn around at the door to look once more at my friend, wondering if I should have handled the matter differently. As I stand at the doorway, instead of looking at Lincoln my eyes travel around the wall of framed photographs behind him that I have seen many times before. I know his history very well and for the first time I wonder why there are no pictures showing him receiving an award or in the act of duty or even just with a local peer. Instead as I stare beyond him I see pictures of him shaking hands or hugging some well-known local celebrity or famous person. Interesting, I think as I watch Lincoln continuing his conversation on the phone for a moment more. Very interesting. Finally, I turn and walk out of his office.

Chapter 7

From the accused's point of view, an arraignment is really about bail - whether or not the judge will set bail, and if so, how much. Although other things happen at an arraignment, the most obvious and significant thing from the perspective of the accused and the friends and family of the accused is the judge's decision to set or not to set bail. I think about this as I arrive at the jail on a pleasantly warm early Monday morning in August to meet with my client before taking him before the judge. I have been meeting with Lt. Trapp for some time and am aware that he sees himself as smarter than the average person and tries to manipulate situations. Knowing this about the man and what he thinks of himself, I do not want any surprises so talking to him is a priority.

At the jail, the first person I see is Jeremy who gives me a hardy welcome and shows me to the visitor's room before going to get my client. Knowing how the Sheriff sees Jeremy as his confidante, I wonder if maybe it was the sheriff who told Jeremy the results of that lie detector test. I tell myself to get on topic and let it go for now.

A few minutes' pass and Jeremy returns with Lt. Trapp in tow.

"Good morning counselor," Lt. Trapp says.

"Good morning. Take a seat, please, we need to go over a few things before we go before the judge." Sensing the urgency in my voice, Lt. Trapp reacts quickly and takes a seat. I wait until he is seated before I begin. He needs to hear everything I say so I must have his undivided attention. I begin.

"For starters, as we discussed earlier, you were arrested on the spot without an arrest warrant so the officer had to submit a warrant request to the prosecuting attorney and it was issued. This is fine. The police can make a lawful arrest if they have probable cause to arrest, or a valid arrest warrant. For probable cause, it requires that they had either direct observations or hearsay information provided by others to the police.

"So, what were the charges submitted?"

"At that time it was murder in the second degree." Seeing his reaction, I quickly add, "But wait, that's normal and nothing to worry about just yet." I see his shoulders drop as he lets out his breathe. I give him a minute before continuing.

"I know that you spoke with a court representative and I have the information that you shared and what your wife told them about your background and the personal circumstances of the case. Those reports were filed with the judge and copies given to myself and the prosecuting attorney." I let it sink in, then add, "Because you confessed, it makes it difficult."

"I know, I know, I wasn't thinking," Vincent Trapp says.

What's done is done. "Confessing is certainly one option. But it would have been wiser to consult with an attorney and follow his advice. There are, after all, legitimate reasons for pleading "not guilty" to something you have technically done."

"What did the report say?" Lt. Trapp asks.

"This is where it can get sticky if we don't handle it right. It is normal for the judge in a murder case to refuse bond which would mean you would be incarcerated until the case is decided. But because this is a first offense and because you are well known in a good way in the community, I am sure we can get bail if we play our cards right."

"What do you mean by 'play our cards right'."

"Well, you have to enter that court and look as though you are sorry for what happened and that you are willing to face whatever the court decides. Plus, you need to accept whatever bail is set without a whimper. I know it will be high so expect that."

"How high?"

"I think it will be somewhere in the vicinity of $200,000."

"Two hundred thousand! What, is the judge insane?"

"See, that's the type of talk that will get your bail denied. You need to think of the alternative. Bail, or no bail and stay in jail."

"Okay, fine, fine. I'll keep my mouth shut and pay it," he says with a scowl.

"I think we're ready, so, let's get this show on the road," I say.

"Oh, wait a minute. While we are in front of the judge, I will be referring to you as Lt. Trapp. It may give us some pull. You were a lieutenant in the army, right?

"Right."

I ring for Jeremy, who arrives with the court bailiff to escort us to the court room where the proceedings will be held. As we advance down the corridor that connects the jail to the court room I keep praying we get a sympathetic judge, or any hope of getting Lt. Trapp out on bail will be difficult or impossible. This I do not share. I remind myself that it will be important to remember to call him Lt. Trapp instead of Mr. Trapp from this point on.

Once in the court room, we take our seats at the table in front of the judge, and stand when the bailiff says, "All rise," the Honorable Judge Ben Remick presiding." We stand until the judge is seated, then take our seats. We are in luck. I have requested bail in front of this judge on many occasions and walked away with success. We may just have a chance.

"My name is Judge Ben Remick I am the judge of the Monroe County Court. I am here to give you the warnings required by Article 510 of the New York State Code of Criminal Procedure. At this proceeding I am to inform you of the allegations made against you, the range of punishment for the crime with which you have been charged, and to make a decision on bail for you. This is not a hearing or a trial, and I cannot hear your plea or hear any testimony regarding the alleged offense. That will take place later."

There is a shuffling of papers and then Judge Remick continues.

"Will the defendant please stand." Vincent stands up.

"Are you Mr. Vincent Trapp?" There is silence.

I nudge Lt. Trapp. "Yes," he replies.

"Is that your true and correct name?"

"Yes, Your Honor."

"You are alleged to have committed the offense of murder in the second degree. Defined by this court, murder is the killing of another human being without justification or valid excuse, and it is especially the unlawful killing of another human being with malice aforethought. First-degree murder constitutes a very serious crime and as such a conviction results in a very serious punishment. In New York State a conviction for first-degree murder can result in life in prison without the possibility of parole and under some circumstances a lesser sentence." Judge Remick pauses before continuing.

"Do you understand the allegation against you and the full range of punishment for this offense?"

"Yes, I do, Your Honor."

"You do have rights under the New York Penal Code, Article 125 § 125.25 Murder in the Second degree and they are if you are a foreign national, you have the right under the Vienna Convention to contact your national consulate and the right to consult with them concerning legal representation in this case. You have the right to remain silent and not make any statements, and any statement made by you may be used against you. You have the right to hire a lawyer to represent you, to have a lawyer appointed to represent you, if you are indigent and cannot afford a lawyer, to have your lawyer present during any interview with peace officers or lawyers representing the state, and to terminate any interview with peace officers or lawyers representing the state at any time. These are your rights."

"Do you understand these rights?"

"I do," Lt. Trapp replies.

"Do you have any questions about any of these rights?"

"No, they are perfectly clear, Your Honor."

"In that case, please sign this document acknowledging that I have explained your rights to you and that you understand your rights. This is not a plea of guilty or not guilty, but merely an acknowledgment that I have read these rights to you in your presence."

The judge hands the paper to the bailiff who brings it over for Lt. Trapp to sign. I watch as Lt. Trapp looks the document over and then slides it across the desk so that I can read it before he signs. I nod the okay and he signs the document.

"Lt. Trapp, is this your lawyer?"

"Yes, Your Honor."

"Good morning, Mr. Dandridge, good to see you. You are representing Lt. Trapp?"

"Yes, your Honor, I am representing Lt. Trapp." I see a slight rise of the judge's eyebrow when I say, Lt."

"I need to ask you some questions so that I can set bail. Please answer honestly."

"Where do you live?"

"I live at 14 Epping Wood Trail in Pittsford, New York."

"How long have you lived there?"

"Almost 5 years, Your Honor."

"Do you have family in Monroe County?"

"Yes, I have my wife who lives with me."

"Where do you work?"

"For the Government, Your Honor. At the present time I am The Under Secretary for Intelligence."

There is another lift of the judge's eyebrow. "Have you ever been arrested before?"

"No, Your Honor."

There is a pause while the judge stares down at the paper in front of him, making his decision on bail. When he lifts his head, he stares directly at Lt. Trapp.

"Your bail is set at $250.000. You will need a personal bond or bail bond or a cash deposit in lieu of the bail bond. If you pay cash bail to the court, meaning you paid the full bail amount, you will have that money returned to you after you, Lt. Trapp make all required court appearances. If you do not show up in court, that money will be forfeited and you will not see it again. And if you are arrested again while out on bail, no refund will be given. "

"Do you understand?"

"Yes, Your Honor."

"If you are found not guilty, the bond is discharged; if you plead guilty, the bond is discharged at the time of sentencing."

"I understand, your Honor."

"You must adhere to the following restrictions or risk being put back in jail until your trial. From this point on you cannot travel outside the county. You must refrain from excessive use of alcohol or any use of narcotic drugs. You cannot have a firearm in your possession and you must refrain from contact with the family of the victim. Can you agree to all of this?"

"Yes, Your Honor," Lt. Trapp says.

In the case of murder bail is often denied, but because this is a first offense, and because of your position, I am incline to allow you bail so you are free to leave, once you have paid the bail."

I am admittedly proud of my client for not wavering when the Judge announced the bail would be $250,000 and Lt. Trapp was released. I follow Jeremy and the officer back to the jail and wait while Lt. Trapp is processed before driving him home.

***

The drive to his residence is made in silence. I can only imagine what is going through his head at that moment. Even though the bail hearing went smoothly, I am sure at any moment he will blurt out that he was being charged unfairly and that there were mitigating circumstances behind the murder. This must have been very hard for him accepting his fate not knowing if they are aware he did what he did because his wife was raped.

I get on I-490 East and head south for a little over ten miles before taking Exit 27 to NY 96 that runs along Bushnell's Basin. With the warm weather and clear sky, this is a nice drive along the Basin which is a hamlet running along the Erie Canal within the town of Perinton. I enjoy watching the sun leaving diamond patterns on the calm water surface as we make our way pass this scenic view before making a left on Thornell Road in the town of Pittsford and then another quick left onto Epping Wood Trail. I pull into the driveway of number fourteen.

We open the doors of my car at the same time, to stand in the driveway, feeling the warm sun as it shines down on us. There is the smell of the many flower gardens on his property and one can barely hear the distant hum of traffic in this quiet neighborhood.

"Mind if we take a walk by your gardens before we go in?"

"No, that would be a welcome change from what I've been seeing," Lt. Trapp says.

"By the time August rolls around many flowers have finished blooming and others are beginning to look a little ragged around the edges, but our gardener with the directions of Paige have managed to keep our flower garden looking fresh from late summer into autumn. Here we have. garden mums, and over there are I believe what is called, yellowbells or hardy yellow trumpets. They are native to Central America and the American Southwest; or at least that is what the gardener told us."

We walk a little further and Lt. Trapp points out rose, lavender, pink and white china asters that have flowers resembling the garden mums, but only larger. "Now here are more china asters, but of a different variety."

"How long do they bloom," I ask.

Well, they begin blooming in August and continue until the first frost. These are my favorite. Look at the colors."

We continue along the side of the house where there are what he calls sweet autumn clematis because they have a sweet scent, then we slowly work our way back to the front of the house and step up to the front door.

I step back and wait while Lt. Trapp opens the door to what I learn later to be a 5000-sq. ft. house. I remember thinking to myself that it must be impossible to keep in touch with one another in such an enormous structure. I could not, nor would I ever want to live in such a massive building. Lt. Trapp tells me there are five bedrooms, four full bathrooms and a powder room. Those I did not see as our tour began and ended on the main floor. Up until this point I was already in awe of the property. This oversized home sat in the middle of a two-acre estate on a private wooded cul de sac lot that will be forever wild. It was like living in the midst of a park, and ironically, there was a park adjacent to their property.

My mind wonders as he explains that this is a custom Ketmar home, whoever that is and as I step over the threshold and enter the two-story high ceilinged foyer the feeling that came over me was 'cold'. Can't explain it beyond that.

I am like a trained seal following my client who is indeed in charge as if leading his troops into battle. He guides me to the left into what he mumbles is the family room and I take in the cherry built-ins and soaring coffer ceilings above rich gleaming hardwood floors, thinking that the room looks unlived in and unloved. The only homey feel comes from looking through the glass in the French doors running along the wall, that reveal a handsome stoned patio.

Lt. Trapp then takes an about turn and through the foyer we again go to enter another massive room that mimics the family room interior except in here the cherry built ins are bookcases filled with books and art, giving this room a comfortable feel. It is here that Lt. Trapp ends the tour.

"Take a seat, please. I need to wash up a bit and will join you shortly."

"Take your time," I reply. I watch him as he walks away and then I go over to the bank of French doors in this room. I try the door handle and find it is unlocked so giving myself permission I open the door and step out onto the patio that continues along this side of the house. This I find is more than a patio as it meanders around the length of this massive structure. Though I feel as though I am intruding I cannot stop myself as my feet take me forward along the patio, to a walkway and finally to the back of the house where the real glamour begins. Here the patio is wide with levels and stone walls separating the designated areas. There is a swimming pool with waterfalls, a hot tub with lounge chairs, but what impressed me was the outdoor gourmet kitchen and fireplace area. Now this is something to envy, I think. I want to stand here forever, but after a bit I force myself to return the way I came until I am back at the office entrance. I step inside and am greeted by my host.

"So there you are!"

I felt like a little child caught with his hand in the cookie jar. "Please, I am so sorry…"

"No problem," Lt. Trapp says, "shall we get started?"

Chalk it up to embarrassment. "We'll need a psychiatrist," I say bluntly, shocking even myself. I shouldn't start our talk with that sentence. I give it a minute to see if I need to apologize. Luckily I do not. Being direct is Lt. Trapp's forte so this does not annoy him in the least.

"Why?"

"A person accused of a crime can acknowledge that they committed the crime, but argue that they are not responsible for it because of their mental illness, by pleading "not guilty by reason of insanity. In New York, the "extreme emotional disturbance" defense works like this. First, the defendant must prove he was more than just angry. Doubtless, anyone who fatally attacks another is angry. He must prove that he was so emotionally disturbed that he actually lost control. Second, the defendant must prove that there was, in the words of the New York penal code, a "reasonable explanation or excuse" for his emotional disturbance. What's reasonable is determined from the defendant's viewpoint."

"Are you insinuating that I am crazy?"

"No, that's not it at all. The insanity defense reflects a compromise on the part of society and the law. This means that on the one hand, society believes that criminals should be punished for their crimes; on the other hand, society believes that people who are ill should receive treatment for their illness. The insanity defense is the compromise: basically, it reflects society's belief that the law should not punish defendants who are mentally incapable of controlling their conduct.

"So, can't you just develop a case on what you know and just have a doctor in our pocket if we need them? It is you that suggested an insanity plea so you must know what to do."

I needed to set him straight before we go on. "No," I say, "I merely mentioned to you what the possible legal defenses were and with facts that you shared with me I could see that someone could conclude that you may have been insane." I had to be sure that he understood this was his idea and that I didn't lead him in that direction.

"Fine," Lt. Trapp replies. "I chose the insanity plea."

"In any case, we can't just have any doctor because our defense would be weak. We need a psychiatrist if we decide to go this route. A man trained in this science who can offer explanations to whatever the defense throws at us. So, we know what to do and what way to go."

"Not sure I'm following," Lt. Trapp says.

"It's not just one way here. For instance, there is an important distinction to consider. "Not guilty because of insanity" or "diminished capacity" Although a defense known as "diminished capacity" bears some resemblance to the "reason of insanity" defense in that both examine the mental competence of the defendant, there are important differences. The most fundamental of them is that, while "reason of insanity" is a full defense to a crime -- that is, pleading "reason of insanity" is the equivalent of pleading "not guilty" -- "diminished capacity" is merely pleading to a lesser crime. That's what I know of the defense at this time and rest assure that the prosecutor knows this too."

"But how would they know?"

"How would they know what?" I ask.

"How would they know we are going to plea insanity?"

"They will know because the law says that we must tell them. There is a little thing called, 'discovery', a procedure designed to allow disclosure of information between Plaintiffs and Defendants. It's a fact-finding process that takes place after a lawsuit has been filed and before trial in the matter so that the parties in the case can prepare for settlement or trial."

"That's stupid. We have to lay all our cards in front of them?"

"Yes, basically that is true. Discovery is based upon the belief that a free exchange of information is more likely to help uncover the truth regarding the facts of the case."

Lt. Trapp is quiet, then says, "So we let them in on it later. What about that?"

"Sorry, can't. There are deadlines and guidelines for filing discovery requests and submitting answers. A failure to timely or properly answering a discovery request may lead to fines and other sanctions."

"That's so asinine. We want to win and to win we must tell our game plan. That's just stupid."

"It does seem that way, but it goes both ways. Who knows what the defense is turning up and planning to use. If they didn't have to disclose their ammunition, we would be fighting blind and that would put us at a disadvantage."

"So," Trapp. says, "how do we go about finding the right psychiatrist; one who will agree that I am crazy."

"We shop around until we find one which won't be easy. I'm sure once the defense hears our plan, they will go after the obvious choices. They won't take into account that the field of psychiatry and the profession of mental health is both an emotionally and mentally stressful job and sadly, there are times when the professionals in the field are so overworked, burned out, and fatigued that the people relying on the professionals may not be given individual attention. That's the case of the obvious choices they will make. They will go after those connected with public institutions of some kind because they will cost less."

"What do we do? What do you have in mind?" Vincent Trapp asks.

"Well, first you accept the fact that this is going to cost you."

"Fine. I'm fine with that."

"Or," I start thinking out loud. There is one other alternative we could check. I would think you would suggest it."

"What is that?"

"Well, you admittedly have connections. I know you were a Lieutenant in the army and now you are The Under Secretary for Intelligence."

"Where is this going," he asks.

"You might be able to get a psychiatrist from the United States Army," I reply.

Lt. Trapp thinks a bit. "I don't know whether the Army would."

What about the government since you are the USI."

"That is less of a chance. I don't want to lose my post. It may be already lost, but I don't want to force the hand that feeds me."

"That makes two of us but you can probably tell me where and who to see about this. We need to be clear that at this point your only legal defense is insanity and to prove this we need a psychiatrist."

"Give me some time and I will see what I can come up with."

"We don't have the luxury of time. I need to get the wheels spinning right away and I plan on doing it tonight."

That put a fire under him and Lt. Trapp went to his desk and began rummaging around.

***

I wandered to the bank of front windows and looked out at the expanse of the well-manicured lawn. I watch as a black sedan comes up the driveway and as it gets closer I recognize it to be a Volvo S60, a fifty-nine-thousand-dollar automobile. I continued to stare as a woman gets out of the car, followed by a small Yorkshire terrier. This isn't just any woman. She wears dark framed large sunglasses and as she floats across the lawn toward the house, I am mesmerized at how in high heels she keeps one foot in front of the other as if walking a tight rope staring straight ahead with her viewable features focused and poised. As she draws closer I watch the sun dance around her russet color hair that bounces back and forth in a ponytail that has a slight flip at the end, appearing and disappearing with each step. Her figure is trim and in balance as she advances. I immediately find myself thinking, so this is the woman that my client killed Noah Arietta over.

No longer in my range of site, I hear the key turn in the lock, followed by the door softly closing, followed by the tap, tap of heels as they move from the foyer to the office.

"Your home, darling. Your finally home." The woman travels the distance until she is standing in front of her husband. I quietly wait until the welcome is over. "Honey, why are you cooped up in here with the sun shining so warmly outside. I would think you had enough of indoors for a while."

Ignoring her words, "Hi, Paige," Vincent said to his wife and then added, "How's our little Enzo," With all the major introductions done Vincent Trapp finally turns to me and says to his wife, "Paige, this is Richard Dandridge. He's taking my case and has arranged for my bail. We are in here because it is easier to work on the case in the office."

"Good to meet you Mr. Dandridge," Paige Trapp says, extending her well-manicured hand while smiling cheerfully. "I hope you can help my husband out of this terrible mess I've got him in."

I reach out and take her hand. "I will do all I can to help him, Mrs. Trapp. If all of us do our part, I think there is a good chance to win his case. "

While we are acknowledging each other, Lt. Trapp kneels down to pet the little dog who yips in ecstasy. It is easy to tell that the dog, loves his owner and is glad to see him. I remember reading somewhere, 'Folks will know how large your soul is, By the way you treat a dog!'

"Enzo missed his daddy. He hasn't seen him since…, since that awful night." Mrs. Trapp says.

Something about her words have me asking, "Mrs. Trapp, when did you last see your husband?"

"Sunday afternoon. Why do you ask?"

"No reason, really, I was just wondering." I paused. "So when can we talk. I need to hear what you have to say about this, um, situation too."

Mrs. Trapp looks at her husband and then back at me. "Why, any time is fine with me. We could talk now if you are finished with Vincent."

"That would be convenient for me," I say. "Do you think it will be fine for all of us to talk together?"

There is an awkward pause before Mrs. Trapp responds. "It doesn't matter to me," she says. "Whatever you and Vincent think is best is fine with me."

Lt. Trapp is still kneeling and petting Enzo. "What do you think, Lt. Trapp?" I ask.

Vincent looks up at me sideways. "Suppose you call the shots, Mr. Dandridge? What do you think is best?" At that moment I glance over at his wife and I think I see her shake her head.

I make up my mind and say, "I think it may be better to talk alone, at least for now." I don't know if it is real or my imagination, but it feels as though they both are relieved by my final decision.

"There's something else," I say. "We are going to be seeing a lot of each other from now on and it would be much easier if you would give me permission to call you by your first names. I hope you will not hesitate to call me Richard. Apologetically I add, Sorry, but I don't go by any nickname."

"That's perfectly fine, Richard. You can call me Vincent. I do go by a nickname. Paige, on the other hand doesn't go by a nickname either."

"Okay, Richard, Vincent says, rising from his crouch position, "I'll leave you and Paige to talk." He looks at his wife and says, "I'll see you later, Darling." As he heads in the direction of the foyer, he pauses and says, "come on Enzo. It dawns on me that

Vincent and Paige Trapp have not touched each other during the whole encounter.

***

Alone in the study, I ask, "Paige will you please remove your glasses."

"No problem, I can do that." Slowly she lowers her head and with both hands, removes her glasses. When she raises her head, I am in shock. "Good Lord!" I say out loud. In my line of work, I have seen wounds that were open and bleeding freely, gunshot wounds, deep cuts caused by sharp objects, lacerations cut or torn open, but this is worse. This is indeed a case of blunt force or trauma to the eye sockets that has resulted in obvious burst capillaries and probably some hemorrhaging. The eyes she reveals are swollen and both black and blue in color.

"Did Noah Arietta really do that?"

Her eyes within their discolored frame are green and seem to look right through me. Even with all this bruising I can still see a very attractive woman who knows how to use her attributes. She is the type of woman who wears her sexuality like a badge and for the opposite sex it is hard not to respond. So, this is what Noah Arietta must have felt and what lead him to do what he did. If, of course he did rape her.

Slowly I watched as she attempts to raise her eyelashes and regard me solemnly. She nods her head and says, "Yes, Noah Arietta did this to me."

"I think you had better put the glasses back on," I say, hoping my voice does not betray the way she activated my feelings.

"Sure," she says. The light does bother me. I wait while she replaces the glasses before I toss out my next question, "Are you planning on being at the trial in support of your husband?"

I could hear her surprise. "How can you ask that Mr. Dandridge? Why wouldn't I stay by his side?"

"I'm sorry, Paige, I don't mean to offend, but I have to ask as your husband's lawyer. It's important that I know so there are no surprises. You are a key witness in this case and if you don't plan on helping, it will be hard to win this case. Right now, it is about fifty-fifty he can beat the charge. So, bear with me and please, you still haven't answered my question."

Now, I wish I could see her eyes because it would help highlight whatever comes out her mouth. "Are you with him or not?"

I see a slight shake of her hands as Paige Trapp turns to me. She remains silent and just as I thought, there is something amiss between her and her husband. Just as I am about to urge her on she said, "How much did Vincent tell you. I don't mean about the case, but about our personal life."

"Nothing, Paige, about any personal matters between the two of you," I said truthfully.

"Well, tell me, what gave you the impression that I would not help my husband?"

"It was a routine question, Paige, just routine and not based on any observation." Forgive me if I was too blunt about it.

"Be truthful with me. We are not very affectionate so is that what made you think that. I will do what I can for poor Vincent."

Strange set of words I think, but say, "I have to admit that yes, I did notice the lack of affection. If I notice it, others will too. This is a small community and I am sure each and every one of them are aware of the murder. I don't want any nasty rumors to begin so you need to be aware of how you and your husband react to each other.

"Okay, I understand, but don't mention this to Vincent, please."

"Why not?"

"Well, because...; just don't. I'll handle it."

"Okay, then you've got my word on it."

Chapter 8

As I was leaving the Trapp residence I couldn't help wondering about what I was up against. There was definitely a lot I still needed to learn about my client and about his wife. I wondered how much hearsay was already out there and how much more was developing from just around the case. By the time I reached my office I had worked myself up into a frenzy.

Once I parked my car, I anxiously hurried toward my office knowing that I would be wise to seek help on this case if I wanted to win. To add to my frustration, I run smack into the prosecutor, Randall Walker, standing at the entrance to my office, the wrong entrance, I might add.

Randall is about the same age as myself. He is wearing a light tan suit with a golden yellow shirt that shows off his summer tan. He has added a splash by wearing a polka dot tie of many colors. As he turns and smiles at me the sun glints off his Lugano Diamond Sunshades, so fittingly appropriate on his handsome face and his wall street hairdo.

I say nothing about the fact he is at the wrong door as I walk up to greet him. "Well, Richard," Randall says, "Lincoln tells me that you're handling the Trapp case. If that's true, we're going to be in court together."

I could hear the notes of humor lacing each syllable. I watch as he checks himself by adding, "I couldn't pass this one up."

"Me either. It is a doozy of a case, Randall," I reply. "Murder, rape and I just found out it also has a little dog named Enzo."

Randall is quick on his feet as he says, "Alleged rape, don't you mean, Richard?"

"Sure, that's what I meant. I just got involved with the case and haven't gotten beyond taking the case on." I add, "Why don't you come in and we can talk further."

I open the door and show Randall into my office where he immediately picks a seat. I am hoping that this encounter will be a sharing of information; especially details of the lie detector test.

Once seated, Randall says, "Just got involved, you say, well, then you will agree with me."

"Agree with what Randall?"

"A continuance," Randall says. "What do you say to our agreeing to a continuance on the case and not put it on the September calendar."

"What are you thinking," I ask.

"Wait until December. There are lots of reason this will benefit us both. We're into the Congressional election for one and Judge Jasper will be available in December who I know I would like to have on the bench and assume you would too."

I had to agree with what Randall was saying, especially about wanting Judge Jasper as he was the most qualified judge to hear such a case. Personally a delay would benefit me so that I could find a competent psychiatrist and in time to rehearse Lt. Trapp. Of course I am pretty sure my client wants this over with as fast as possible, but isn't this what is best for him. As much as I want to go with Randall on this, I seriously can't.

"No, Randall, I'm afraid we can't agree to a continuance, though I would like to. You raise some valid points." I pause and add, "But even if we move to December, I don't think Judge Jasper will be able to sit. He's been sick and I have a feeling he won't be handling cases now or in the future."

"So, okay, what about agreeing on a plea to second degree murder for 25 years?"

I think about it for only a minute knowing that it will either be 15 or 25 to life he will be facing and knowing Randall he is not offering bargains.

"No, Randall, I can't do that. Lt. Trapp could get a sentence of life for that and I can't risk it. But, what about dropping the charge to manslaughter?"

"Are you kidding, Richard! The charge has to be murder."

"Fine, but if I were the D.A. and knew that Noah Arietta had raped Mrs. Trapp I think I'd seriously consider lowering the charge since you have the results of a lie-detector test that backs me up on this point. Of course, if you still think the rape is 'alleged,' I would agree with you not to lower the charge.

I had hoped to throw Randall off his game and possibly get him to share the results of the test, but he doesn't budge an inch or have a change in his expression that I could read one way or the other. Instead he clears his throat and says, "I guess we better get to work for a September trial. I thought we could reach an agreement, but no dice. Your lieutenant murdered Noah and there were witnesses to the shooting."

"So, what are you saying, there is no defense? If that is what you are thinking you are wrong. It won't be easy, but I believe in my ability to defend my client, more than you must believe in yourself to win the case."

This time I get satisfaction. The look on Randall's face is priceless with the redness showing through his tanned complexion and his pursed lips clearly conveying his irritation. I hide my amusement as I watch him get up from the chair and say guardedly, "See you in court, Richard."

"So long, Randall. Let me walk you to the door."

I swing open the door and Randall turns to shake my hand. As he turns back around, we are face to face with Paige Trapp, who is standing at the office door. I am surprise to see her as we haven't set up an appointment.

"Am I interrupting something?" She says. "Can I come in?"

"I wasn't expecting you Ms. Trapp, but please come in."

Paige glides across the threshold and into my office, openly inspecting the interior. "I'm surprised; this is not what I imagined. This is nice."

"Well thank you. Glad it meets with your approval. Tell me what brings you downtown?"

"Who was the man who passed me on the steps?" she asks ignoring my question.

"That was Randall Walker, the Prosecuting Attorney."

"Um," she says. I can tell by her expression that she liked what she saw.

"Paige, what brings you here," I ask again.

"Well, I want to make sure you didn't take it wrong; me saying not to mention to my husband that you thought I wouldn't be on his side."

"I don't think I took it wrong. I am trying to understand and I think I know. He is jealous of you. Am I right?"

Paige looks at me thoughtfully. "Yes, he is jealous and always has been. I thought it was cute at first, but now, I don't know."

I look at her and decide to take a gamble. "Are you afraid of him, Paige?"

"I'm not sure how to answer that except by saying no, I am not exactly afraid of him, but afraid of his thoughts. Does that make sense?"

"I'm not sure I understand," I reply.

She walks across the room and then returns to say, "Vincent is protective, very protective of me and in some instances, what he thinks turns out bad for the situation."

Not exactly sure, I say, "Does Vincent have any reason to be jealous." Then cautiously, I pause before adding, "Have you done anything that warranted his jealousy?"

"No, never. Sure, I will admit that there have been opportunities, but I have never acted on any of them. I could say it is not my fault, but I know I am pretty and I do play it up like any woman would. Only problem is that when you truly are pretty it is looked at differently."

I can't help myself. "Paige you are not just pretty. You are beautiful."

She pauses and grants me an imposing smile, "See, you too. I like fun and gaiety and I do like hearing that I am beautiful, but so does every other woman. I would venture to say that Vincent is probably jealous of even you."

That throws me back a bit. Here she is in my office and probably he doesn't know she has come. That might play wrong in his mind if he is truly that jealous of her. That would be bad, very bad for me and for our case. What good has come of this is that I am now pretty sure that Paige is being open and honest with me.

"Well, we need to make sure that Vincent doesn't feel that I am a threat."

"He's really a great guy, but he's strangling my feelings for him. The way he acts and the things he says makes me think he sees me as nothing more than a cheater, a street walker, someone who doesn't know how to conduct herself. I think he was jealous of Noah Arietta."

"Why would you think that he has such a, um, low opinion of you."

"He doesn't, you see, but when he thinks someone is looking too passionately in my direction, we argue and he says things that he later apologies for. Only the more he does it, the harder it gets to forgive; at least right away."

"I see. What do you mean you think he was jealous of Noah?"

"Well, we ran into Noah on several occasions. It's not like it was planned, but he would go to the same places we did and of course, we went to the Founder's Café a lot. Since Noah is the manager and owner of the building there, of course we would run into him. On several occasions he tended to compliment me on my hair, or my clothes and that irked Vincent."

"Was there any incident or scene after any of these chance meetings?"

"No, never. Vincent would make me hurry and finish my lunch and then whisk me out of there as fast as he could."

I needed to know this, but I also needed to know if anyone else knew as much. "Have you mentioned any of this to the police or to anyone else?"

"No. I told them about the, the incident that took place that day, but I said nothing more. I told them what happened because I didn't have anything to hide."

"You have to be sure of this, so I ask again, think back to the conversations you had with the police or anyone else."

"I shared nothing other than the details of that night."

"You mean you told them about the sexual attack made by Noah and the details leading up to the attack and what happened afterwards."

"Yes, in great detail."

"Did you go into all of this as well during the lie-detector test?"

"Sure, of course,"

"Now, I need to ask you, who suggested that you take a lie detector test?"

"Why, I did. I'd heard about them somewhere."

"Did they share the results of the test with you?"

"No, I haven't heard the results, but I didn't ask about it. I figure if the machine is any good there would be only one result. I passed."

I did not plan on telling Vincent or his wife that I knew the results, or I knew the results that Jeremy shared which could be right or wrong. I didn't want to get Jeremy in any trouble so I had planned to keep it too myself, but now I had second thoughts.

"Paige, you did pass," I said. The results say that you were telling the truth."

"Great, she said," Did that handsome young prosecutor tell you that."

"No," I said. I heard it from another source." As I tell her this, it dawns on me that Randall did know the results and if it had shown that Paige was lying he would have shared it to get me to agree to his plea to second degree murder. His not sharing just verified what Jeremy had told me.

"Does Vincent know I passed?" Paige asks.

"No, not yet. I wasn't going to tell him, but I've decided that I will." I think it will help him and you as well if he knows this. Plus, if as you say he is jealous of me now, he might not think that.

Paige, I would appreciate it if you did not tell a soul that you know the results of this lie detector test. If anyone asks, simply tell them you don't know. It could be vital that you do this so will you promise me that?"

"Sure. No problem. I hope I have helped you to understand more clearly."

"Yes, you have helped me a lot."

"Don't think I shared any of this to criticize Vincent. He is a loyal and tender man in many ways. He'd do anything to protect me."

I can't help myself. "Would he kill for you?"

Paige buried her face in her hands and doesn't reply.

"Listen Paige, I know you want to help Vincent and I want to help him too. That's what we need to focus on so anything I say, or you say is to help the case. Okay."

"Sure," Paige replies.

"Now, you should go home and be with your husband. You need to start now to be open with your emotions for him. It might be a good idea to go out to dinner so that people can see you together. As for me, I need to get to work. I would like for us to get together again in the morning."

Paige smiled and thanked me as she walked toward the office door. "Good evening, Richard.

"Good evening Paige. Keep your chin up.

Chapter 9

It is going to be a long night for me. I begin at the beginning. I pull out the paper that Vincent Trapp wrote down information on who to contact at the Army for a psychiatrist. I tap in the number and wait. It is a recording that refers me to the Veterans Administration where I listen to another recording that informs me what to press to get to the person I need to speak with.

"This is a waste of time," I say to myself and hang up the phone. I need to find someone and like I predicted, the army psychiatrist is probably a good one, but overworked. I know it will cost, but it is the best route to explore elsewhere and find a psychiatrist who will be able to dedicate himself to the case. So I begin a search online, not wanting to call other lawyers and take the chance of setting up alerts to the prosecutor.

My first search brings up details about the types of psychiatrists that I read with interest. "Lawyers and law enforcement professionals utilize the expertise of forensic psychologists and psychiatrists when working on both criminal and civil cases. In criminal investigations, these mental health professionals assess whether a person involved with the case is mentally ill, and if he or she can stand trial." After reading this I now have to question exactly whom do I need. Do I need a psychiatrist or psychologists?

I do another google search to get that answer too and come up with a decision. We are not dealing with a serious kind of mental health problem here, such as depression, bipolar disorder, or schizophrenia, nor are we looking to have my client medicated. That means I don't necessarily need a psychiatrist. I ponder the matter, examining my findings to come up with the best choice. I review other cases that have used forensic psychologist and those who used forensic psychiatrist. Both help attorneys, courts and other parties determine an individual's mental competence. They both also act as expert witnesses during a trial or other court proceeding. In some cases, they ask forensic psychiatrists or forensic psychologist to weigh in with sentencing recommendations.

I have jotted down the names of several individuals and do a search on them to make sure they are reputable and well thought of, then I look over the fees, because now it seems to be the only way to make a decision. It doesn't take long to find out that psychiatrist can make more than double what psychologist do. Forensic Psychologist salaries were ranging between $59,000 to $190,000 a year. Most of the forensic psychiatrist though get paid by the hour for their work with the hourly rate charge being around $85.00.

My eyes are tired from staring at the screen so long so I get up and walk around thinking and I make a decision. I will share what I found with my client and show him the names of the psychiatrists and psychologists that I would recommend. It will be his choice who to use. I call the Lieutenant.

While I wait for him to connect, I go over what I will say. I don't have to wait long. "Hello Vincent, this is Richard. I want to run something by you. Is this a good time?"

"Sure Richard, what is it."

I tell him what I have learned and wait for a decision on what he wants to do. I can hear him typing in the background and know he is conducting a search of his own. I hear papers ruffling as if he is rummaging through his desk and then finally he says, "Well, I think we need to go with a psychiatrist since we only pay the hours they work."

"Yes, I think that is a smart choice."

"There is a pause and then Vincent says, "I think we need someone that has a reputation as an active clinician and expert witness. Someone who is a specialist in Forensic Psychiatry and who has a record as having a major impact in high profile cases where he has served as a witness." There is a thoughtful pause. "I am looking at Milo Goodman, and see he has not only local credentials but seems to be quite well known. Yes, he has been recognized by Delaware Today Magazine as a Top Doc three times in a row and as a Top Psychiatrist in America by the Consumer Research Council. He is Board Certified in General Psychiatry, Geriatric Psychiatry, and Forensic Psychiatry." Another pause and then Vincent adds, "Not bad, he has held licenses in New York, Delaware, New Jersey, Pennsylvania, Massachusetts and Maryland, North Carolina and Virginia. He is Assistant Professor of Psychiatry and Human Behavior at The Thomas Jefferson University College of Medicine and a Special Guest Lecturer at Widener University School of Law. Yes, he looks like our man. What do you think of Milo Goodman?"

"I agree, he seems well qualified and has expertise in the important areas of your case. Is that who you want me to contact.?

"Yes, let's go with him."

"Okay, I will take care of that right away. Let's hope he is free. If not, I'll call you and we can consider someone else."

While talking with Vincent I have pulled up information on Milo Goodman and I find a picture of him. Knowing what I know about the Lieutenant now I wonder if Dr. Goodman would have been his choice if he had seen a picture, too. Milo Goodman is an extremely handsome black man whose sex appeal is apparent even in that professional psychiatrists pose. There is something about his eyes that seems to draw you in and hold you captive. I'm sure that his looks along with his history has played a part in his success.

As soon as I hang up with Vincent, I call the office of Milo Goodman, hoping he just might work late too. There is no answer, but I leave a message on his service and then as a backup I click on the email address link on his website and begin writing to him, giving him as much information as I can to peak his interest and make sure he is aware of the urgency of the matter. I look the email over and I am satisfied. I click Send.

That handled, I open another word document. Success at trial does not happen by accident. It takes time and preparation, and that commitment of time and effort starts right now. I study the file of notes and papers I have been accumulating. I take out the police report and read it through, then review the evidence provided in the case file. I take notes of people I need to interview to clarify questions and information contained in the file and jot down any additional investigative work that needs to be done.

I want to go home, but I can't. Instead I decide to stay in my office apartment so that I can do as much as possible and if I am to stay alert I'll need coffee. I go into Theresa's office and start a pot and stand by the counter waiting impatiently for the pot to fill up. It seems to take forever so I retrieve the pages I have sent to the copier and when I return, the 'ready' light blinks on and I pour a cup. I carry it with me to my desk and push aside some of the papers that are accumulating at a rapid pace.

I open another Word document and look over the evidence and weigh it against the possible options I need to be clear on the level of offense and the filing criteria. Whether I plan to or not, I review the possibility of a plea bargain and how the prosecutor will attack it. Will they charge high and plead down or will they shoot straight to the point. I need to be prepared with any options that I plan to accept.

By my third cup of coffee I am finally getting to the procedural stuff that needs to be addressed. I will need to look over the filing charge papers, looking for any 'smoking gun' evidence that the prosecutor may present and how I will be able to manage to have it tossed out. I deliberate on this for some time before feeling I have covered every possible angle.

I am getting very tired, my eyes want to close and my shoulders ache from leaning over in my chair so I get up and walk a bit more, taking my coffee with me. It helps and when I sit back down I open a fresh word document and write a letter for Theresa to sign for me. I send an email to Theresa asking her to tell Pete Adams that I need to see him at my office tomorrow evening. I think hard and check over my notes to see if I am missing anything.

Finally, I feel I can stop. I am so tired and my eyes refuse to focus after sitting in front of the screen for so long. My brain is totally exhausted and I know I cannot force another piece of information into it. I take a minute to shut down the system then stand up, moving my shoulders about and bobbing my head forward and back to relief the pressure of being in one spot for so long. I stretch then allow myself a big yawn before going to turn off the coffee maker and returning to my office, I lock the door. A quick look around and I am finally able to drag myself upstairs to fall into my unmade bed.

***

The alarm on my cell phone breaks through my sleep. I am momentarily disoriented then remember that I stayed at the office overnight. It takes a bit of an effort to get my body off the bed and into the bathroom where I look in the mirror. I need a shave, my hair is tousled every which way and there are bags under my eyes. I look like a zombie. I quickly climb into the shower and begin to vigorously wash my wayward hair and scrub my body until I begin to feel alive again. The bathroom is steamy by the time I reach out and grab a towel to wrap around me and step out to bravely face the mirror again.

I wipe the steam off the mirror and begin preparing myself to face the morning. By the time I've shaved and organized my hair I feel like myself. I go into the closet and when I emerge I have on a clean shirt, pants and a jacket. In front of the mirror again, I put on my tie. One last look and I hurry downstairs to put all the papers back in my brief case, check to make sure I have my Surface Pro and swing the strap over my shoulder. I pick up my cell phone and slip it into my breast pocket. I am ready. I grasp my keys then head for the front door making sure it locks behind me.

Outside the early morning air is crisp and the street hasn't begun to hum with traffic as I make my way to my car, hesitating for a minute to place a call to my client.

"Good morning Vincent," I say when he answers. Hope I didn't wake you."

"No, I'm awake, have been for some time."

"Well, I am on my way over to your house and should be there in about twenty minutes," I say.

"I'll put the coffee on." Vincent pauses, "Should I wake Paige and have her join us."

"No, that won't be necessary. I want to talk with you first."

I guide the car out of the parking space and head toward the Trapp residence. It is a nice September morning and this early it can be enjoyed without concentrating on the traffic. I turn on the radio and hear the newsman say, "On September 11, 2001 a series catastrophic events occurred in New York City, New York. Al-Qaeda planned strategically conducted events, known as suicide attacks. Nineteen al-Qaeda members hijacked four commercial airplanes, including United Airlines Flight 93, American Airlines Flight 11, American Airlines Flight 77 and United Airlines 175. Two of the planes purposely crashed into the World Trade Center buildings. In addition, another plane crashed into the Pentagon in Arlington, VA. and the fourth plane crashed in Shanksville, Pennsylvania. There are several events planned...."

I had forgotten that this was the anniversary of 9/11. Each year of remembrance is like that was the day the world changed and nothing will ever be the same again. It hits home that there are people out there who want to absolutely destroy America and it is something we should never forget. Only now I don't want to fill my head with this so I turn off the radio and try to enjoy the fact that the sun is shining, the air is warm and I am alive. It is in that spirit I pull into the driveway of the Trapps.

I was just about to ring the doorbell when it swings open to reveal a wide awake Lt. Trapp standing in the foyer.

"Come on in Richard, I have the coffee ready. I hope you don't mind having it in the kitchen."

"No, that's fine," I say as I follow him into the gleaming white kitchen with its stainless steel appliances. There are stools around the island and I settle on one and watch as Vincent gets two cups of coffee ready. "Do you take cream or sugar?"

"Just black," I say.

"Yeah, me too."

When he joins me at the island, I start the conversation. "I came to tell you that your wife passed her lie-detector test. She was telling the truth."

There is silence. I can sense and see the change in my client as he stares back at me with his eyes squinting as though gazing into the sun and his jaw dropping at least an inch. His voice filled with emotion he finally says, "How do you know this?" At that moment I know that Vincent had suspected his wife of lying about what happened that night.

"I can't tell you that, Vincent, but I know it is true." I wait while he absorbs what I have said. "It's true that she was attacked and it's true that she was raped."

The relief on his face told the whole story. Until this moment he had thought that maybe she had lied about being raped so that he would do something to this man. He might have entertained the idea that Noah Arietta had not been totally at fault as she might have encouraged or even solicited him.

"There is more and this is important. You can't tell anyone that we know the results of the lie-detector test"

"Sure," that's fine with me, but why not? "

"Because it gives us a slight advantage. They know the results and now we know the results so that if they try to make it seem as though she didn't pass, we won't react in the wrong way." I wait a bit and then say, "Now I need to talk alone with your wife."

His whole image changed in front of me again. He looked like a man who was possessed as he squeezed out the words, "You talked with her yesterday, so why do you need to talk with her alone again."

"Yes, I did speak with her yesterday, but I have more questions for her." I added, "We are fighting to get you from spending the rest of your life in jail so you don't have time for all this ill-placed jealousy, Vincent. You need to keep focused on the important things now. Paige is a loyal wife to you so you don't need to worry. Understand?"

I held out my hand and waited while Vincent slid off his stool and stood frozen in front of me until finally he relaxed and took my hand. "Yes, I know you are right. I'll go get her."

***

I looked around the gleaming kitchen at its orderliness and wondered if a full meal had actually ever been prepared in this room. As we say, the kitchen is the heart and center of the home. This beautiful, well lit room seemed as though it was a mere pass through. Sure, we were here having coffee and leaning on the island marble counter top, but everywhere I looked each item in this room appeared new and shining. How can that be. A clean, spotless kitchen, that is an oxymoron It was just so neat and so white. In the midst of my reverie, I hear the sound of Paige's heels as she hurries to join me in the kitchen with Enzo at her heels."

"Did you tell Vincent I passed the lie-detector test?" she asks before barely entering the kitchen. "How did he take it?" At first I am puzzled, did her husband not come and get her? At that moment I felt as though I was working with kids instead of two grown adults and it scared me.

"Yes, I told him, and he was glad to get the news. I also told him not to tell anyone that we have this information. That is important. It is imperative that we keep it quiet. So now it is time to hear your story. I want you to tell me everything."

Paige stared at me with those soulful green eyes that still showed the bruising from the beating she had taken. "Okay, let's go out in the garden and sit. You can get another cup of coffee to take with you and I'm going to make myself a cup of tea."

"Sounds great," I say as I go to the Keurig and fix myself a second cup. Purposely I allow a few drips off my cup to fall on the counter; just because it needs a little mess to make it real. When I turn around, Paige already has her tea prepared and guides me out the French doors, onto the patio.

The air is even warmer now and I feel comfortable as I sit across from her taking in all the landscaping that surrounds the patio and beyond. I love the sound of wind chimes, birds, waterfalls and plants gently rustling in the wind and sitting here these sounds combine. It's really amazing as I find myself relaxing and taking in the sights of the garden. There is color everywhere – bright color, subtle color – pinks, reds, yellows, oranges, purples, greens – you name it. "Do you want me to tell you everything and tell you just as I told it to the police." Paige asks, pulling me back to the matter at hand.

"Yes, please, just as you told the police. Give me a minute while I turn on the recorder." I quickly check to make sure that the microphone device on my Surface Pro is set properly. "I need to get this word by word. I have to know all that they do and more so don't leave anything out, including your feelings and those of Mr. Arietta."

"Where do I begin," she said musing.

"Start at the very beginning, where you feel it actually began."

***

Paige Trapp takes a deep breath and then begins her tale.

"I had worked in the garden most of the afternoon, what I tend to do most days not only because the gardens need attention, but because I love doing it. Anyway, Vincent returned home from a meeting much later than he usually did. It was about six o'clock in the evening on the night…the night of the shooting."

She pauses to sip her tea and I take the time to ask her, "Do you know what the meeting was about?" That would speak to her involvement with her husband and may prove valuable later.

Paige looks absently at me and say, "Yes, actually I do. It concerned Russell Frost of Wichita. This man had spent more than a decade as a private contractor in the Middle East and during his last contract in Iraq, he and two other Americans were taken captive by a militant group and held hostage for 31 days. That's all he could share on the matter."

I was listening but also took the time to appraise her wardrobe. Paige is wearing a tight sweater and black slacks that I noticed as she walked out to the patio, hugged her curves. I make a note that I might want to speak to her about what she wears in court and for that matter, during the trial; period. As an afterthought I think that maybe I should ask Theresa if she would handle this for me.

"Anything else?"

"Yes, I told the police that I think that Vincent might have stopped off for a drink before coming home. In any case, when he arrived home he was sleepy and hungry."

"He had been drinking?"

"Yes," I think so.

"Was he drunk?"

"No, just feeling relaxed, not drunk."

"I see," I say. "did you tell the police about him being sleepy and not drunk?"

"No, I didn't because they didn't ask me."

"Okay," I say. "Go on. I just wanted to have this clarified."

There is a pause while Paige tries to get back on the topic. "So Vincent took a brief nap before dinner; then he ate, um and then he took another nap. When he woke he asked me to fix him a drink, but I found we didn't have any more of the whiskey he likes. I told him as much and he said he would settle for a beer, but when I checked, we didn't have any beer in the house so I asked if we could go out, and it being so nice I thought maybe going to the park would be fun. We could pick up some wine on the way."

"So what did he say?"

"He didn't exactly say anything, he just grunted and stretched out on the sofa and soon fell back to sleep."

"Okay, and what did you do"

"Well, I tried to entertain myself, but I eventually got bored so I woke Vincent up and told him I wanted to go to the Founders Café for a drink and would he like to join me. He yawned, looked at me and said, why don't I just stay home and we can go get something later. I told him it was already late and later would be too late. So he just said, I need some rest."

"Is this normal behavior for him?

"Well, let me just say, think about how draining it is for you to setup a defense for a client. Now multiply that by one hundred and you've got the stress that most of Vincent's meetings this year have caused. So, I would say that this was definitely normal for him this year."

"Okay, what did you do then." I asked.

"At first I decided I would wait, but then I thought about it and it being such a nice evening I could take Enzo out for a walk, so at around nine o'clock or shortly before, I left the house with Enzo in tow. We walked through the woods, just over there," she pointed toward the far side of their property, which I do many times because it is shorter that way to get to any place and Enzo could do his business without me having to stop and pick it up. I then brought Enzo home and checked on Vincent. He was still sleeping so I left again, walking in the same direction as before."

Before continuing, Paige stretched her arms above her head and took a sip of her tea. "When I got to the Founder's café it was almost deserted. There were a few customers that I recognized as locals and some I didn't. The only other people there was Hamilton, the bartender and a blonde waitress named Mary something or other, not sure of her last name.

"Where was Noah Arietta? Wasn't he there when you arrived?"

"No, he wasn't. He came in later. I ordered a glass of wine and took it over to play the Frogger video game."

"Wait a minute, you played the Frogger video game?" I looked at her and the thought seemed incredulous.

"Yes, Frogger is a classic video game that can be played by one or two players. The game's objective is to move a frog from the bottom to top through a road full of traffic first and then a river." Paige smiles. "When you are moving your frog through the traffic, you have to face speeding cars, buses and many other obstacles on your way which must be avoided to safely transport your frog to the other half. It's a blast."

"I know the game. I guess I didn't pin you as a Frogger player; excuse the pun."

"I didn't know that you had to be a type to play Frogger, but whatever."

"Sorry, go on," I said.

"Any way I had been playing for a while when Noah Arietta walked in. I didn't see him enter and only knew he was there when he came up to me and challenged me at a game of Frogger. The winner had to buy the other one a drink. Sounded innocent enough so I took the challenge and won the first game. Noah signaled Mary and she served us drinks at the machine.:

"Wait a minute, what shape was Noah in?" I asked. "How did he act to you. Did he seem drunk or, did he make any kind of a play toward you?"

Paige thought for a moment before saying, "He seemed to be sober and he acted like a gentleman the whole time we were in the Founder's café together. We laughed and talked about nothing in particular, you know, the fact that it was most days still like summer outside and about the Corn Hill Festival that was held in July. Other topics along those lines. As for him making a play on me, I am sensitive to advances of that sort and I didn't sense anything in that way."

"Did the police ask you about his attitude toward you at the café?"

"Yes, and I told them the same thing." That is exactly what happened and I told them he was friendly and courteous the whole time we were there."

"What happened next."

"Well, Noah and I played several games and then had a few drinks at the bar, I switched to a scotch and soda and had maybe two or three of them, but I was not intoxicated. I felt more relaxed and I was enjoying myself. Then I noticed it was almost eleven so I asked Brook, that's the bartender, Hamilton's first name, if he could sell me a six pack of beer. Brook said he could and when he gave it to me, I prepared to leave. It was then that Noah asked if he could give me a ride home, but I told him that I would be fine and would welcome being in the open air for a bit. I told him I had a flashlight so I would be able to see my way home. I thanked him and excused myself to go back to the restroom before leaving. This also gave me an opportunity to use the side door and leave without being noticed."

I made a note to myself wondering why if Noah was acting nice, Paige tried to avoid him.

"Once outside I turned on my flashlight and that is when I saw a shadow at the side door. It was Noah. He was standing there with his car motor still running and expressed concern about me walking home that late at night. He asked again if he could give me a ride home. He was still courteous and seemed sincere in fearing for my safety so not wanting to appear rude, I finally agreed to let him take me home. It was just a short distance anyway."

I must have frown or something as Paige asked, "What's wrong?"

"I looked at her and said, nothing. Please, continue."

"Well, at first we were heading in the right direction, but then he turned and sped up pass the house and turned into what I think was a driveway; a dirt road or driveway that I hadn't noticed before and that was when I began to be anxious. I asked him where were we going, but he didn't answer me. Instead he grabbed my arm and kept driving. I don't know how far we went when he suddenly stopped the car and turned off the headlights."

I could see the worry on her face as she paused to pull herself together before continuing.

"As soon as the car stopped I tried to get out, but he had a hold of my arm and pulled me back in. I tried not to show any fear; thought I could possibly control the situation. I asked him what did he think he was doing and he grimaced at me and tightened the grip on my arm. The more I fought to break free, the tighter his hold became and I knew, knew I was fighting a losing battle. He was too strong for me. He leaned in toward me and I lifted my right arm up to slap him, but he was fast and He got his face up close to mine and said he was going to rape me." There was a catch in her voice as she said the word, rape. I gave her a minute to recover.

"He used those exact words?"

"Yes, those are his exact words. Then he said I'd better not give him a hard time or I'd never get out of the car alive. All the time he was talking he was groping at me, trying to pull me closer, but I kept trying to fight him off."

"Did you scream?"

"No. I knew we were not near any place where someone could hear me. We were in the middle of nowhere and I couldn't help thinking that he meant it, that he would kill me as he threatened to do."

"What happened next," I asked.

"He kept groping at me and beating me on my knees with his fists to force my legs open. I fought, I fought as long and as hard as I could, but I could feel myself getting weaker and finally said to him, hoping he would stop, that my husband would kill him if he didn't let me go."

"You told him that?" This could be a problem if she had shared that with the police.

"Yes, I was desperate and I thought by saying that I could scare him off and maybe he would come to his senses."

"Did it stop him?"

"No, it only made it worse. He laughed at me and said Vincent didn't have the guts to kill him and if he tried, that he, Noah would kill him first. He ranted on like a madman and I could barely understand his words as I kept trying to get away. I remember screaming that if he did rape me, Vincent would hunt him down and kill him dead over and over again. That's when he moved back a little and I felt his fist make contact with my face, hard, very hard.

He was swearing at me, yelling, take that you bitch amongst other things as he continued to force my knees open. I felt my panties being ripped off me and I struggled trying desperately to stop him. He was out of control acting like a crazy man, hitting me and squeezing my thighs, but by then I was too weak to give him much of a fight."

All the time as she spoke I watched her closely. She didn't weep or hesitate, but told her story as though she were telling me about some bad dream. "And then what happened?" I asked.

"Well, he came."

"Are you sure of that?"

"I knew he had entered me and he came. I could feel it. I was just glad the nightmare was over. I felt the full weight of him on top of me, trying to catch his breathe. I must have fainted because the next thing I remember is the car moving again."

"Did either of you speak?"

"No, nothing was said. Noah was still breathing deeply, trying to catch his breath. He was making funny sounds as he struggled to breathe. It was almost like he was about to cry. I don't know why it sounded that way, but that's the best way I can explain it."

"Go on," I said.

"Well, he drove back to the main road and when he slowed the car, I tried to open the door, but he grabbed my arm and pulled me back. He was talking like a madman again as he tried to rip off my sweater and I knew he planned on raping me again and that seemed to give me the strength I needed to wrench my arm away and get out of the car. I ran, but he caught up with me. He tripped me and then started kicking me after I fell down. He continued to hit me with his fists, hard, all over my face and body. I think he was trying to kill me with his bare hands and I felt as if I was going to faint. That is when I screamed. I think I screamed two or three times with all I could muster. I was so busy trying to scream it was a while before I realized I was alone. I managed to lift my head up so that I could look around. It took all my energy to just get into a sitting position before taking a deep breath and getting myself on my feet. I had to get away because he wasn't acting rationally and might just come back. I started to run, well not exactly run, but at the fastest pace I could muster. I didn't care what direction I was going, just so long as I was able to just keep going was all that mattered. Finally, I stopped to catch my breath and let out a sigh of relief when I saw the lights of my home just ahead. It was at that moment the fear I had felt was replaced with anger. Who did he think he was doing this to me?"

"You didn't see Noah at all after that?"

Paige closed her eyes and shook her head. "No, I didn't see him again. Not alive or after he was dead. I made it to the front door and just as I reached out for the door handle, Vincent opened it, scaring the bejesus out of me. He seemed only half awake but he told me later he'd dreamed he heard me screaming and it woke him up. All I could do was fall into his arms."

We have been at it for some time now and I could see she was exhausted. "Do you want to take a break?" I asked. Even if she didn't, I did.

"No, no, she said, and then she smiled as she observed me, "but perhaps you do.'"

"You're right. I could stretch my legs for a bit. I need to just walk around, if you don't mind.

Chapter 10

Paige's words haunt me. "Vincent will kill you." Did she say this only because she knew her husband well. Did Noah really think that Vincent would do nothing. I can believe that Paige knew just how angry he would be and that he would not hesitate to kill Noah or anyone for that matter who hurt or raped his wife. As I walk around I think that if Vincent had been insane that night then Noah must have been stark raving mad. He knew her husband and most likely knew how jealous he was when it came to Paige. He had to be an idiot to rape her and beat her and that fact cast doubt on her story. What in the hell did Noah Arietta think would happen to him? As I stroll around the property it comes to me that I am not done researching this case. I had to find out who Noah Arietta was and find answers to some very baffling questions.

'Vincent will kill you,' that is what Paige said and that would be a fatal phrase to overcome as the defense lawyer. I had to deal with it because my hands were now tied. The words were out and the prosecutor would be stupid not to use it against her husband. Just like a magician I needed to manipulate forces for my own purposes. I had to be a skilled performer and make believers of the jury. I need to be well versed so that I can employ the right psychology and misdirection methods to achieve my goal in making my theory seem reasonable and believable.

So how can I do that? What Paige said was natural enough but it would be taken in a different light in view of the outcome, plus it would put up stumbling blocks for our insanity plea. From the other side it could be viewed as a warning from Paige to a deliberate killing in a fit of rage by her husband. I need to know if she told the police what she had said to Noah. I need to know if she told Vincent what she had told Noah. If she had it would seem that she suggested to Vincent that he go out and kill this man and that my friends would lead to Paige being an accessory to murder. Paige would be seen as knowingly promoting or contributing to the crime. In other words, she would be seen as aiding or encouraging the offense deliberately, not accidentally. The court would call this an accessory before the fact because she is someone behind the scenes who orders a crime.

With determination, I walk back to where Paige sat. "Paige, did you tell the police that you told Noah, Vincent would kill him?"

"Yes, I did. I told the police everything that happened; at least everything that I could remember that was said or done. Wasn't that the right thing to do?"

"No, I mean yes, of course." I couldn't put her on the defensive or scare her. "And did you tell Vincent what you told Noah that he would do to him?" Now, I held my breath.

"Yes, he was the first one I told what I said."

My heart sank. This might present a gigantic problem in that it would make it hard for the jury to believe the insanity plea and just as bad, it might cancel out our psychiatrists supporting an insanity plea. Vincent was my client and I must concentrate on his case and not the possibility of Paige's. I have to get an angle. In order to think it is right to kill another person you must be insane. Sounds reasonable till analyzed it says therefore all murderers are technically insane. Can a sane person commit murder? I could cast doubt in this way? Insanity can be viewed as something that only happens in the heat of the moment or a person can be insane for hours, days, weeks or even a lifetime. Shake it off, I tell myself. This gets me nowhere until I have time to put it all together. And that thought makes me wonder if there could be more. I had better get all the bad news at once.

"Did you tell the police that you had already told Vincent that you told Noah he would kill him?"

"Yes. It was as we were driving to the jail in the police car that I told Vincent so the officers undoubtedly heard me. Then later I told them, the officers, again.

Oh my goodness. I almost said it aloud as I comprehended what Paige just explained. I could hug her, but instead said, "You are saying that the first time you told Vincent about telling Noah he would kill him was after the shooting and not before?"

"Why, yes. Why would I tell him that before? I said it to scare off Noah. I know my husband and I know that his reaction would be to kill Noah. He'd think that on his own. Besides everything was happening so fast that night with calling the police and going to the station, and of course, the rape itself…"

"Do you remember what you were wearing that night. Were you dressed as you are now." Secretly I hope not, but I had a feeling this was Paige.

I watch her pretty face as she tries to concentrate on the question. "Well, I was wearing a sweater, much like this one," she said pointing to the one she was wearing that was low cut and hugging her breast. "I had on a peasant skirt…" Seeing my puzzled expression she adds, "Which is a full skirt that goes to the ankles, underwear and sandals."

"Did you have on a bra?"

"Yes, and panties, which I mentioned that Noah tore off me."

"Do you know where those panties are now? Do the police have them?

"We gave the ripped skirt to the police. Later they took me to the spot where they think Noah stopped. It was determined it was the place where he raped me because there were tire tracks from a car turning around, but they didn't find the panties. They even scoured the woods around the area with no luck. They did find my glasses though and they were intact."

I had been jotting down notes when she made this declaration. My head popped up. "Glasses?" I said. "You're telling me that you were wearing glasses through all this?"

"No, not wearing them, I was carrying them in their case. "I'd been holding them in my hand and I guess when I first tried to get out of the car I must have dropped them."

"Why aren't you wearing them now?"

"Well, right now I'm afraid I still need my dark glasses. Anyway I only use them for reading or when I'm doing anything close up. I had carried them with me when I went to the Frontier café since I knew they had a Frogger video game." She let out a nervous laugh. "I'm glad they found them. I can't even read a headline without my glasses."

Glasses, I meditated. Another small score for our side. It was going to be hard, at best, to tone down this sensual woman, but I would have to try. Now as I thought ahead, wearing glasses would help. I made a note to remember to tell her that she needed to wear her glasses in court.

"What else can you tell me?"

"Well we have had to lock the gate going up to the house and ever since that night I have been surrounded by all kinds of people like I am a two-headed monster or something. Every time I dare to go out the door, there they are, gawking at me. Even when I take Enzo out for a walk in the woods there are people with cameras, some even bold enough to want to ask about the details of the case. Such morbid curiosity." She shook her head in disgust.

"The price of fame, my lady," I said. "But you haven't seen anything yet. Just wait until the trial. Morbid curiosity is not confined to just the locals because once it becomes known, everyone will want to know. It's the nature of the beast."

"Do you think the court will be crowded during the trial?" She asked anxiously.

"No doubt in my mind. Your case has everything to draw attention. A rape, murder, even a little dog." I see her body frame stiffen and decide to change the subject. "So what you've told me so far is exactly what you told the police?"

Paige nods her head. "Yes, exactly the same thing."

"Well you have told it very well and very effectively. It has the ring of truth. I only hope you can do as well in court."

"Thank you, Richard. I will certainly try." I watch as Paige finally allows herself to relax. It's as though she is able to let it all go once the story is told.

"There is one more thing and it is important."

"What's that? She asks.

"You understand that when we're in court during the trial, the prosecutor will get to question you when I am done."

"Well, that is what happens on television and in the movies," she says.

"Well on cross examination, the prosecutor can't ask argumentative questions. These are questions that don't seek information, but rather challenge you in order to persuade the judge or jury. An example of an argumentative question is, *You don't expect the jury to believe that, do you?* That you would not answer. The prosecutor is not allowed to scream, curse, or ask about inadmissible evidence. But, as long as they follow the rules of evidence, the prosecutor doesn't have to be cordial and might hope that a confrontational style will fluster you or expose a nasty character trait. For example, he might take a harsh tone with the goal of creating an inconsistency in your testimony or displaying your temper. When they question you, they will be trying to shake you up and confuse you, or try to bring out something that we might have overlooked. I can't really predict what they will do, but I just want you to understand. Do you?"

Paige nodded her head. I know I am ahead of myself, but I feel it necessary. Paige may never be called as a witness during the trial, but I have to make sure she is prepared so I share all that I have mentioned earlier to her husband.

"What you need to remember is to always tell the truth, like I believe you have been doing, but Randall...I mean the prosecutor, may try to dig deeper into areas we have not covered and try to get you to lie or soft-pedal around instead of answering. Don't. When in doubt tell the truth and let me worry about how to handle it. We have a good case if we play it right. I know we do."

"You really want to win, don't you Richard?"

"Yes, I do and I think we can. I want you to do one more thing for me and that is to have photographs taken of your injuries. I want them done by a photographer friend of mine, a Gerald Powell. He will know how to handle it. I can see that the bruises are already healing so I will call him right away and get you an appointment for today. Can you do it today?"

"Yes, if you think I need to."

"I know him to be not only good, but he won't try to make the bruises look worst or better. Plus, we are not looking for glamour, so don't get all dressed up with makeup, and fancy clothes for this. I will inform him to take full body shots and check for bruises that you may not know you have. So you can't be modest about this."

Okay, I'll do that."

"Paige, I know I am asking a lot of you at one time, but it is important. When you are done with the photographer, I want you to come to my office." As I say this to her, I hand her a card for the photographer.

"Fine, I guess I will see you again today. I'll come looking like a hag right after my pictures."

"Sure, you look like a hag," I said. "That would take some doing." I smile. "Tell your husband I said goodbye."

Paige walks beside me down the sidewalk from the patio to the front of the house where we say our goodbyes and I climb into my car. I see her standing there as I look out my rearview mirror.

Chapter 11

As I drive back toward my office, I feel anxious to get started, but I haven't eaten since last night and need some food in my stomach so I force myself to drive to the Genesee Brew House since I know it opens for lunch at eleven. Having lived here most of my life, it amazes me how the Brewery transformed this 100-year-old building into a stunning space with interactive exhibits, a gift shop, a pilot brewery and a pub-style restaurant situated right behind the main plant. As I pull into the parking lot, I am glad I am here early. The lot is almost empty and I have my pick of spaces. I maneuver the car into a close spot, climb out and walk the short distance to the building. Once inside, I forego checking out the shopping area as I take the steps up to the second floor where the restaurant is located.

It is quiet up here with only the employees chatting amongst themselves as they get ready for the crowd that usually starts drifting in around eleven-thirty. Seeing me there, the hostess comes over with a menu in hand. "Where would you like to sit, sir. You can sit at a table, or over at the bar," she says with a sweep of her arm in each direction.

"I'll take a seat near the windows overlooking the Genesee River"

"No problem," she says and then guides me to the table that gives me the best view of the river and the cross over bridge.

"This is perfect," I say. I watch her as she returns to her station at the head of the stairs, then stare out the window, but I am not seeing anything as my mind drifts.

"What can I get you from the bar."

"Excuse me!" I am momentarily taken aback, having the silence invaded and my mind far away thinking about the case.

"Sorry, I didn't mean to scare you. I will be your waitress and I wanted to get your bar order, if you are ready, of course."

"Sure. Don't apologize, I was just thinking about something. I'll take a Brew House IPA for starters."

She leaves to get my beer and this time I pick up the menu and look over the offerings so that I will be ready to place my order when she returns. That done I stare out over the water and the walkway bridge feeling myself relaxing and by the time the waitress returns I am calm. I order an Asian Ahi Tuna Salad, thank her and stare decisively out the window again.

This is exactly what I need. Now as I feel the pressure of the morning receding I take a few deep breaths and a sip of my beer wishing I could remain in this state forever.

I didn't see him as he entered and didn't see him as he stood by my table. "Well, look who's here."

Startled, again, I look up and as soon as I recognize the intruder, I smile. "Hello Travis. Good to see you. What brings you to my neck of the woods?"

His appearance causes a stir at more than my table as he stands there like some Greek god. His blue eyes sparkle in his tan face. His laugh lines appear as he smiles down at me, and the slight brush of a beard and mustache accentuates his wide mouth and white teeth. That look, that swagger can't help but draw attention.

"Well, the Genesee Brew House is a client of my marketing firm and I just finished meeting with them and thought I would catch a bite to eat. Can I join you?"

This is wonderful. "Sure, have a seat."

Travis is the perfect distraction as he is not one to talk business. "Good to see you, Travis, done any golfing lately?"

"Matter of fact, I have. I was out on the course yesterday, but I am up for a game at the Genesee Valley Golf Course on East River Road if you're interested. That was Travis, never thinking that anything but a lack of interest will stop a golfer from any opportunity to swing the clubs. "I haven't been there and I hear they have an 18-hole North course that covers over 6,300 yards of golf from the longest tees for a par of 71."

"Yes, I know the course, it has a pretty good rating. I could use the distraction. Want me to call for Tee time." I ask?

"No, I can do that". The waitress comes and Travis says, "Give me the same as my friend, here." As soon as she leaves he picks up his cell and in no time he has located the phone number for the course. He places the call and while waiting asks me, "What time shall I tell them?"

"Well, give us an hour to finish lunch and then about a half hour to get there. Let's say, to be on the safe side, we can make a 1:00 p.m. tee time."

Travis relays this information as soon as he is connected, then we chat about nothing in particular. Because we are early for the lunch crowd, we are in and out in no time and taking our individual cars, drive to the course and get in a good game of golf before parting to go our separate ways.

As I again drive toward my office, it comes to me that I need to talk to a doctor about the swab that had been taken on Paige. I have doubts that this was done properly because I feel sure she was raped. Only, I don't know the procedure well enough to question it. I take out my cell and place a call and the doctor's office tells me to come in. I work on my questions as I drive to Doctor Augusta Ryan's office. This is an imposition on the doctor so I need to be sure to get what I need in the shortest period of time.

I sit impatiently at two lights before finally making it to the parking lot at my destination. I park the car, grab my briefcase and hurriedly make my way up to the entrance and into the waiting room. I panic as I survey the room in front of me. The room is a sea of pregnant woman waiting with a sprinkling of men. One couple discuss names for their future child. Another woman is reading an old parenting magazines left in the waiting room. A couple so young they seem out of place here, are taking selfies and catching me staring say, "Really, what else are you going to do?"

As I make my way to the receptionist window I hear someone say, "This sucks. I hate doctors' offices." And I now feel like an intruder who is about to make their wait even longer. I lean into the reception window and in a very low voice say, "I'm here to see Doctor Augusta Ryan. I'm the person who called earlier.

"Sure, Mr. Dandridge, Doctor Ryan will be with you shortly. Please take a seat.

I look around the waiting room and decide to stand and look as inconspicuous as possible. I hadn't experienced it firsthand but I know emotions during pregnancy are heavy-duty and usually involuntary. The strong hormones fueled by the human fetus take over the mother's body and sometimes her minds. A smile can easily switch to hurting words and who knows what else. I was admittedly afraid. This could end up being a room with lots of anger, resentment and bitterness if they knew I was delaying their appointment time. By the time the receptionist signals in my direction I have worked myself into a frenzy. Sir, she says, "Can you come to the window for a minute."

I go up to her, feeling all eyes taking the journey with me. "Yes, what is it?"

"The doctor will see you now."

I try not to make eye contact with those waiting as I go to the entrance door and make my way to Doctor Ryan's office. It isn't until I am in the room, do I allow myself to relax.

"Hello Richard. This is a surprise. It's been a long time since I've seen you out on the course."

"I haven't gotten in much golf lately. I can see you are busy too so I won't take up much of your time.

"No more than usual. What can I do for you?"

I get right down to business. "I'm defending Vincent Trapp on his murder case and I need some information. I'm sure you have heard about it by now because it has been in all the papers that Vincent Trapp's wife Paige was raped by Noah Arietta."

"Yes, I've heard about the case."

"Well, unfortunately, Mrs. Trapp showered and changed her clothes before going to the jail so Doc Pierson only took a vaginal smear instead of performing the full rape kit tests because there was in his words, no evidence of clothing fibers, hairs, saliva, or blood to gather; just semen or body fluid."

"Did the smear show sperm."

"Doc Pierson reported that the test was negative for male sperm."

"He most likely did other tests. Most physical injuries are relatively minor, but some lacerations of the upper vagina are severe and he probably reported on this." He pauses. "If patients seek advice before medical evaluation, they are told not to throw out or change clothing, wash, shower, douche, brush their teeth, or use mouthwash; because doing so may destroy evidence."

"Unfortunately that is not the case here. I think she did all of the above." I add.

"Well they probably examined her mouth, breasts, genitals, and rectum closely. The common sites of injury include the labia minora and posterior vagina. They may still have performed the examination using a Wood's lamp to detect semen or foreign debris on the skin. Colposcopy is particularly sensitive for subtle genital injuries and some colposcopes have cameras attached, making it possible to detect and photograph injuries simultaneously."

"So, there may be more information than just the sperm report. "Is that what you're saying?"

"Well the routine testing includes a pregnancy test and serologic tests for syphilis, hepatitis B, and HIV; if done within a few hours of rape, these tests provide information about pregnancy or infections present before the rape but not those that develop after the rape. Vaginal discharge is examined to check for trichomonal vaginitis and bacterial vaginosis; samples from every penetrated orifice are obtained for gonorrheal and chlamydial testing. If the patient has amnesia for events around the time of rape, drug screening for flunitrazepam, the date rape drug, and gamma hydroxybutyrate should be considered." Again Doctor Augusta Ryan pauses. "Testing for drugs or abuse and alcohol is controversial because evidence of intoxication may be used to discredit the patient."

I am rapidly writing down what he is saying along with recording his every word. I take the pamphlets he offers sporadically as he talks on the subject. "So Paige will need to go back for further testing?"

"Yes, in six weeks for gonorrhea, chlamydial infection, human papillomavirus infection, syphilis, and hepatitis and in ninety days to check for HIV infection, six months for syphilis, hepatitis, and HIV infection. However, testing for STDs is controversial because evidence of preexisting STDs may be used to discredit the patient in court."

Thoughtfully I ask, "Was the way this was handled correct?"

"Well, let me say, that is not the way I would have handled it."

"But, was what Doc Pierson did medically accepted in a case of rape?"

"No, I would definitely say it is not."

"So, what do we do now," I ask.

"If the vagina was penetrated and the pregnancy test was negative at the first visit, the test can be repeated within the next two weeks. Patients with lacerations of the upper vagina, may require laparoscopy to determine depth of the injury. In our state evidence of a rape can be collected up to seven days after the rape. We are talking about DNA testing and that this will identify the assailant and that evidence may still be present."

"Will you examine Mrs. Trapp?"

There is a slight pause. "Ah, when were you thinking?"

I hesitate at first and say, "This afternoon?"

The doctor ponders the question and then says, "It doesn't matter, yes, send her in and I will perform a full rape kit exam on her."

"One more question. When they do an autopsy on Noah Arietta can they find out if he had intercourse shortly before his death and reached a climax?"

"There is?"

"How?"

"There will be stains on his body and clothing." I watch as he goes to the back wall of his office and pulls out a book. He opens it and shows me the page that describes the details of an autopsy.

"Interesting," I reply after reading the section. "Who would have thought."

"Has an autopsy been performed on the deceased?" the doctor asks.

"I am assuming so," I reply. "Isn't that the only way the People can prove the cause of death.

"Did they examine the body and clothing for the things we discussed and what you read there?"

"I don't know, Doc. That's one of the reasons I came to see you because I am not well-versed in this area so I need information so that I can ask the appropriate questions and gather the necessary information."

"I understand."

Now I needed to pose the question. "Doctor would you be willing to testify for the defense on these things, if it should become necessary?" I pause. "I should say that it will probably become necessary." Now I wait for his reply. He is a well-known, well respected doctor and I haven't a clue how he is taking all of this. Yet I had to ask. I need him, but out of respect I say, "I understand if you say, no."

"Well, yes, if it becomes necessary, you can count on me."

"Thank you, doctor. Thank you so much."

As I am led out, I realize that I have gotten my doctor, the one I had wanted and whose opinion will go a long way in court. He has never been known to sell out and I know there are many who would. I feel somewhat elated, but keep my face stolid as I maneuver may way through the waiting room and to the front door, eyes always forward. At that point I can relax. I take out my cell phone and immediately call the Trapp residence.

"Hi Vincent, just want to let you know that I am supposed to be meeting with Paige this afternoon. There has been a change in plans though. She needs to go to Doctor Augusta Ryan's office for an examination first so please tell her to go to his office instead of coming to mine. Do you have a pencil handy?"

"Yes, I do. Write down this address. I share the address of Doctor Augusta Ryan's office with him. "Take down the phone number just in case..."

Silence. "Did you get all of that Vincent?"

There is still silence, then, "Richard, Paige has a doctor."

"Yes, I know she does, but I trust this doctor and I need to have her examined by him."

"Why don't you trust her doctor."

"I don't know him and I need someone who will examine her and then will be willing to defend her in court. Not only that, but the doctor needs to be well known so that what he says will not be questioned. Does that make sense."

"Yes, I guess so. So when do we get together? Tomorrow."

"No, I am working on the leads right now. I need to get to the Frontier café and do a little detective work."

"So when will I see you again?"

"Probably the day after. I hope to be able to share some information with you about the case by then."

Chapter 12

When I finally make my way to my office I see my old friend Pete Adams dozing on the couch across from my desk. He hasn't changed, nor do I expect he ever will. This is him now and this will be him hence forth. Pete wore his dirty blonde hair long and parted in the middle. He had a somewhat neat mustache and a small sprig of hair under his lip and before the hair growing on his chin. He wore tortoise shell color glasses with a slight tint that kind of hid the puffiness under his eyes. At his throat he wore a scarf tied to the side, an open collar blue shirt with purple stripes and a black pinstripe suit. His shoes spoke volumes as they were scuffed and untidy.

I watch my old friend for a bit not waking him. I walk over and leaned down to smell his breath and am happy to know he is apparently sober. I sniff again for assurance and as I move up I am greeted by Pete's open eyes. "What do you think you are doing?"

"Nothing," I say sheepishly. "Nothing at all. Just making sure you are with the living is all."

"Where have you been I might ask? You told me to come and I came and you were nowhere to be found. I asked Theresa where you were off to and apparently you didn't tell her either." He stops reprimanding me. "So, I guess you called me in about the case so what are we waiting for. Let's get down to business."

I know that Pete is not looking for an explanation of my whereabouts so I sit down and taking my briefcase, I lay the papers out on my desk. I loosen my tie and motion for Pete to come over and join me and I begin my story, leaving nothing out and making sure he knows what information I question and what information I believe.

"So, you are telling me that Vincent Trapp, a retired army lieutenant who is now ah,"

"Under Secretary of Defense for Intelligence," I interject.

"And lives in Pittsford, murdered Noah Arietta, the owner of the Academy Building on Marsh Road."

"Yes, also the place where the Founder's Café is located on the first floor."

"Let me see, this gentleman, Trapp, claims, in his defense, that the victim had raped and beaten up his wife Paige, but the doctor ah,"

"Doc Pierson."

"Yes, Doc Pierson found no evidence that she had been raped. But that is not the case we are actually working on. Our efforts are to be for the charge of murder on Vincent Trapp. A man you have witnessed firsthand to be extremely possessive and jealous when it comes to his wife."

"Correct."

"In any case, the inclination will be that Paige and this Arietta guy had a physical relationship, possibly for some time and that she might have been angry with him and forced her husband to get revenge."

"I agree and so I have to find my way around that." I pause to organize my words. "So, my client Trapp doesn't remember the actual act of shooting Arietta, but he knows that he did kill Arietta. The killing was prompted by Arietta's alleged rape of Trapp's wife, Paige. At the present, there is no physical evidence of that act beyond her black eyes, torn clothing and bruises."

"So how have you told the Trapp's to react at this point."

"I've told them not to tell a lie to me or in court, and that I want Vincent Trapp to plead not guilty due to temporary insanity after hearing that Arietta had raped his wife. His wife, Paige told Arietta that her husband would kill him and that, of course, we know to be the outcome. But, and a big but is that Paige told Vincent that she had told Arietta he would kill him, on the way to the precinct, in the police car' So after the fact."

From his recitation I know that Pete has been alert with his mind racing over the details. It felt good having him here and I could feel some of the confusion and uncertainty that had bothered me earlier in the day being dissipated by the simple act of hearing the facts and then having them analyzed and repeated by Pete.

As we sat comfortably in my office, I could hear the drone of the traffic lessening outside my window and I knew without looking at the darkness that the day was drawing to a close. Sure it had been my intention to sit and go over my notes and I hadn't really done that, but in a way I had. In a way I was further along just by talking with my old friend Pete Adams.

"Well, Pete, you have sat as a prosecuting attorney and from what I have told you, do you think that I have a chance of pulling this off."

I watch as Pete sits silently, knowing that he is running through the whole story and analyzing each detail.

"So do I have a chance of winning this case?" I repeat.

"Of course you've got a chance. You wouldn't be working it so hard if you thought you didn't have a chance, now would you. It is quite a case; I can see that already. It has all the elements for attention and all the elements to draw you in. It draws me in," he sighs.

That was what I was hoping to hear. "I want you to work the case with me. All you need to do is say, yes. What do you say?"

Silence permeated the room. I want to stand and stretch but I don't want to interrupt this silence because it is Pete's way of making his decision.

Pete finally speaks. "Let me get this straight. You didn't call me here for advice, but instead you called me here because you want me to work the case with you. Is that right?"

"Yes, Pete. I want you and I admit, I need your help. I want to win this case, but I cannot do it alone. I need you as a partner on this case."

"No, I can't do it as a partner, but I will do it. I have to have your word that I will work the case behind the scenes. I stay in the background and not even your client can know I am working with you. No one except Miss Theresa, of course." He pauses and then adds, "Did Theresa ever tell you her favorite saying?"

"She has many. Which one."

"The one from Mia Wasikowska. You never choose the way that you're raised, it's just the way that you were raised, but you do get to a certain age where you're in a position to question the expectations of you and the way that you've been formed by your surroundings." That's how she explains her choices in life.

"But Pete, this could help you get a leg up."

"No, it can help you get a leg down. If I sat in the court at the counsel table, you would have just one more strike to overcome and I don't want that to happen. No, I do not have any hopes of entering the legal field beyond what I am doing now and that is how I want it to remain. If you agree, then I am in."

"I don't like taking all the credit when you deserve some too."

"Well, that is the way I want it. Besides, I know you are capable of winning this case. Look how much you have done so far and the angles you have pursued. You just need a sounding board and I want to be just that for you." He pauses, smiles and then leans back in his chair. "I want you to win this case and I want it to be solely your victory."

I think about it and say, "I will accept your terms on one condition."

"What is that."

"We share the fee equally between us!"

"No, I can't take your money like that."

"Yes, you can. I want this because whether you know how important you are to me on this case or not, I know."

"Well, if you insist. Okay, we share the fee. Now I have a question to ask. Did the fact that Randall Walker was the Prosecutor have anything to do with you taking this case?"

No sense in denying it I say, "Yes, I have to admit that at first, the thought of going up against Randall played a part in this, but now it's more than that. I got the bug. I am attracted to high-profile cases for public interest and private gain. I no longer mind, and sometimes even welcome, public scrutiny because I know it establishes my reputation and my firm's credibility. In high-profile cases the publicity is worth more than you can imagine, because if I am successful, the case will bring in business and I won't have to go out and pursue it."

"I'm proud of you Richard. You have learned a lot over the years and it has all been good."

"Thanks Pete. I'm glad to have you on the team."

Chapter 13

The day had all but disappeared as we sat together in my office feeling comfortable with each other. I am relieved that I no longer have to worry if Pete will help me and I am sure that Pete feels comfortable knowing that I thought enough of him and his legal talents to want him to share equally in the proceeds. He is not one to admit it, but he doesn't have to. Yes, friendship is nice, but when you put the money where your mouth is, it seals the deal of how you really feel about a person.

While I have been thinking about our arrangement, Pete has been concentrating on the case itself. Pete says. "If I were the prosecutor, I would go for the juggler on this one point. Trapp took a gun to go see Noah Arietta. If the defendant Trapp did not take a gun and go to Noah Arietta's office solely to kill him, why in hell else did he go there? Members of the jury, I would say, here is a man who deliberately takes a loaded pistol as he goes to the business establishment where the man, Noah Arietta resides and works. He goes there because the man, Noah has been accused by his wife of raping and beating her. He pumps the man full of lead. He kills him, which is what one would do with a gun. Can you explain any other course for his actions?"

Pete pauses his brown eyes glowing and alight. "Does defense counsel concede any merit in this argument. How, my resourceful friend, do you propose to get around that?"

"I see your point, but there is more. Hit me with all of it and then I'll try to fight back."

"Yes, there's more to it." Pete continued thoughtfully. "In connection with this same line of argument, and also to dispute your claim of insanity, I would educate the jury on the fact that, immediately after the shooting, the defendant returned to his home and called 911 to say, "I just shot Noah Arietta." In other words, "Take me in, Mr. Policeman, my mission is accomplished; I went there to get Noah and by God I got him: Are these the actions of a crazy man, of a man who didn't know what he was doing? Why, even his wife, who knew his jealous nature, predicted he would kill Noah.

"Objection, Pete," I said, "No fair on that jealousy business. That's inside information I hope the prosecution doesn't and won't have. But otherwise you've been hitting me where it really hurts."

"Objection overruled," Pete continued coolly. "This Walker fellow is inexperienced and all, and perhaps no great heavyweight as a prosecutor, at least yet, but he's not stupid. Just from her statement alone, which she did share with the police, he will know that jealously played a role in Trapp killing Noah and if he doesn't think so, the jury probably will anyway".

"I won't pretend her statement can't hurt us, Pete," I said. "You know it's got me worried. But I would argue that Paige, in a desperate attempt to ward off her assailant said the first thing that came into her head. In the grip of anger, frustration or in this case, physical danger, someone threatens to kill someone else, often by yelling it at the top of their lungs or by simply saying it calmly. The words don't matter because they are often used as a threat. If there's no realistic chance of it being carried out, this is also quite a straightforward example of Ineffectual Death Threats. Unless said target dies, in which case they'll be near the top of the suspect list."

"So, what then. The target, Noah, died. So what do you have to say for yourself?"

"Well, once they are thinking about how common the phrase has become, I will remind them that this is a man who is well-respected and lives by the letter of the law and Paige made the statement but that is hearsay, not fact. What is fact is that she told her husband what she said to Noah, after the fact and that we can use, somehow."

I pause in reflection. "So, what I need to concentrate on is the defenses to second degree murder charges and they fall into two major categories: claims that the defendant did not commit the killing in question, which we know won't fly, and admission that the defendant committed the killing, but did not commit second degree murder. So, since Lt. Trapp admits to killing Arietta I can assert defenses that he was justified in doing so in self-defense, which may or may not have value, or that he was somehow incapacitated and thus not legally liable."

"Fine," Pete says, "but these defenses require the defendant to put forth proof to support his defense."

"Well, how's this. Second degree murder defendants also may simply argue that the prosecution has not proved all elements of a second degree murder charge which typically are that the defendant killed willfully, deliberately and with premeditation. Though the defendant may support such an argument with evidence, he is not required to do so, as proof of all elements of the crime falls on the shoulders of the prosecution."

"That's good. What else can you come up with."

"The insanity defense to second degree murder since the insanity defense, for purposes of determining criminal liability, states that the defendant is cognitively unable to appreciate the quality of the act being committed, or unable to realize that the act is wrong. There is also the volitional aspect to "insanity" giving some defendants with disorders being able to claim impulse control as the basis for the insanity defense."

"Good Richard," Pete said, nodding. "Yes, a fairly good answer, young man. Did you just think of it?

"I guess I've been brooding about it all the time. But there's still a lot of work to be done. I've barely scratched the surface. For one thing I've an enormous amount of law to look up. I simply haven't had time to get at it all because I haven't really thought through the angles much, until now."

"We've got a lot of work to do for sure." Pete said reprovingly. Between the two of us, we'll come up with the perfect defense for our client."

After that announcement Pete and I kicked the case around, planned strategies, rejected them, substituted others, pondered how we might get in evidence of the rape, how the prosecution might block it, how we might try to bring out at least the fact of Paige's lie detector test. We kept at it until Pete checked his watch.

"Lord help me; I haven't been up this late in a long time. This is enough for tonight, Richard. We need sleep if we're going to keep sharp. We will be battling the common law legal system which places great value on deciding cases according to consistent principled rules so that similar facts will yield similar and predictable outcomes, and observance of precedent is the mechanism by which that goal is attained. Which brings me to another question. Is Judge Jasper sitting on this case? I sure hope so."

I shook my head. "No Pete, I'm afraid not. He's taken ill and from the last report there was hope he would be on the bench again in December, but that now seems unlikely."

"Who then?"

"I haven't the foggiest notion. And if Randall knows he isn't saying. We're going to need a judge with a real lawyer background. By the way I'm driving to the Frontier café to have a look around and then going the route possibly taken by Arietta. Want to come along?"

"You bet. But now it is time to turn off the brain and get some rest. It is after midnight and I can't think any longer.

"So what time do you want to meet in the morning."

"The earlier the better. Let's head out by eight."

"That sits well with me. Eight it is. I'll meet you here at the office."

***

It had been sometime since I had played detective and I hoped my skills weren't too rusty. Normally I would have someone gathering the information for me but if I was to stick to the plan, it had to be Pete and myself doing all the leg work so that he would not be discovered.

My mind was relieved by what we had accomplished this evening. I knew I should take a run by my mother's house and then go home, but I was too tired to think of going out so instead, I went up to the apartment and fell instantly asleep. I dreamt. In it I was wandering in a warehouse that was or at least seemed to be vacant, but I kept hearing an extremely loud punching noise and saw giant bellows of steam floating above me. I listened carefully and finally went over to a window that was inside the building but when I looked out what I saw was darkness and it was raining. I felt myself tensing and I wanted to pull back but couldn't until a lady touched my shoulder and as I turned to see her I woke up. My alarm was going off and from the light coming in the window of my apartment, it had been ringing for some time.

Chapter 14

My situation was clear to me as I went about getting ready for the morning of detective work with my new silent partner. Neither one of us can claim to know the intricate details of being a better than average detective which is what this case would require, but I didn't have a choice in the matter since I had promised Pete this partnership would not be revealed so while in the shower I tried to lay out a plan for the day.

First on the agenda will be to go to the bar in back of the Founder's café where the shooting took place. And because Noah lived there, it might be wise to check out the Academy building apartments and its residence. I wasn't going to fool myself into thinking we would find something at the crime scene since it had been gone over quite thoroughly before I came on board, but there was always a chance. For me, I grinned, it would be a big chance since I wasn't sure what I was after, only that I needed to see the scene for myself.

I knew Pete would have a better idea of how we should proceed so I wasn't worried. By the time I was dressed and ready, I literally danced down the stairs to my office. I am in the process of gathering papers when Pete enters.

"Ready to go," he said as if he had a long luxurious evening of restful sleep."

"Yes, I'm ready," I said not mentioning I wasn't well rested. We walked side by side to the parking garage and climbed into my car. As I pulled out of my parking space I thought about stopping for coffee, but once within the confines of the car with the windows up, I could smell coffee on Pete's breath. At least one of us had breakfast already, or at least some of that precious amber liquid.

When we were on the road, Pete says, "I don't think we take advantage of what there is here in Rochester."

"What do you mean, we. You don't know if I'm not doing Rochester things."

"Okay, did you go to the lilac festival in Highland Park, or the Jazz festival, hm?"

"No, I was busy, I think."

"So, what did you do to enjoy Rochester."

It only takes me a second to come up with a reply. "I golfed." Seeing Pete getting ready to interrupt, I add, "Did you know that Rochester is one of the ten best golf cities in the country. It is the only city in the U.S. to host both the PGA championship at Oak Hill Country Club and the LPGA championship at Locust Hill Country Club. At least that was the case until recently. So you see I have enjoyed what the city has to offer."

"Okay, I guess that counts."

"You bet that counts," I said as I turned and smiled at Pete. "Something else I enjoy is the traffic isn't so bad. Typically, it takes about 20 minutes to get to any place in the County. The expressways are never really crowded and you can often fine alternative routes via side streets.

Pete shakes his head in agreement as we continue on our way to the suburb of Pittsford known for its large beautiful homes and money. "Pete", I say, "It just goes to show that rich or poor, murder has no boundaries."

"You ask me, if I was going to burglarize a place or have a motive for murder, I would pick the richest suburb." Now it's my turn to shake my head in agreement. That makes sense.

Just ahead is our destination and I begin looking for a place to park and find one in walking distance to the building. When I turn off the car, Pete says, "Why don't you go to the Café and nose around while I go to the Academy apartments and see what's what."

"But," I start, then remember, we cannot be seen together nosing around a crime scene, not if we're supposed to not be working together. "Gotcha," I answer as I open my car door and watch as Pete climbs out and goes into the building that house both of the locations we plan to investigate.

I press the car door lock button and walk over to the back entrance of the Café. It's locked. I rattle and pull at the doorknob but it does not give at all so I walk toward the front and enter through the same door that Pete did, only I walk through the lobby and continue down the hallway to the back area.

"It just isn't my day," I say to myself, on finding the door to the café is locked here too. I look around and see a sign that says *'Founder's Cafe open for business'*. I peer through the glass. The place is dim and there is no sign of activity. I wasn't going to give up right away, so I walk down the hallway further to another window and peek in hoping to get a glimpse of the bar and the Frogger video game, but no luck. I sigh and move into the Academy apartments entranceway.

Unlike the café, the lobby is well lit with gray and white marble tiles on the floor, echoing each step I take making it impossible for one to secretly enter. The area is quite large, more the size of a meeting room than a lobby with tan and white marble rectangular wall tiles that surround me. The lobby is deserted but this time I notice a door inset at the left end of the lobby. I missed it the first time. It looks as though it might be an entrance to the café so I go over and try the knob. It turns and I gingerly entered the bar area of the café.

At first I feel I am alone as I wait for my eyes to adjust. I step forward and look around. The Founders cafe and bar harkens back to a time in the eighteen hundreds with the high ceilings, dark wood paneling, and the unbelievable wall carvings. The room is long and wide with floor to ceiling framed windows allowing lots of light to penetrate the dimly lit interior. From the dark wood plank floors and the simple décor the atmosphere is one of calm.

I check out the mahogany wood of the tables gleaming naked about the interior while the chairs are stacked off to the side. I can just about make out an inset of tiles ahead that must be the designated dance space. I spot Paige Trapp's Frogger video game in the corner to my left, standing between an upright piano and a dark paneled antique jukebox. Adjoining this and nearer to me are the wash rooms.

I advanced slowly into the room. To my right about thirty feet from the street door I had just tried to enter, was the bar itself. I am startled for a moment when I see, standing motionless behind the bar, is a man holding a towel and glass in his hands and intently regarding me. He is wearing a blue dress shirt with the sleeves rolled up to reveal several colorful tattoos and his eyes were squinting at me above his tight pressed lips.

It takes me a moment to find my voice. "Hello," I said advancing. "I'm Richard Dandridge, Lieutenant Trapp's lawyer."

"Yes, I know," he replies, averting his eyes, busily polishing his glass. "What can I do for you, Mr. Dandridge? I'm Hamilton. I'm the bartender."

"Well," I said smiling, "for starters, if you have any, can I have a bottle of water?" I watch as Hamilton turns and reaches somewhere under the bar and sets a bottle of water in front of me. "Thanks." I take a moment to open the water and take a sip before continuing. "So do you mind answering some questions," I ask not waiting for answer. "Were you…" I am interrupted.

"I was here," he says evenly. "Just like it said in the newspapers."

I ignore the innuendo. "Maybe we could talk a little about what happened."

"Maybe," he says, inspecting the glass by holding it so that the overhead light reflects off it, then begins polishing it once more "And then again, maybe not."

"That's okay. You have the right to remain silent. It's not a crime to refuse to answer questions, but refusing to answer might make me or anyone else suspicious about you." I give him a moment to absorb what I said.

"Look, Mr. Hamilton, whether you choose to clam up or talk is a matter of considerable indifference to me. I'll have my crack at you in court, where you'll bloody well have to talk and plenty. It's up to you. Tell me now or later in court. In any case I will get my questions answered."

I can see I hit a nerve when Hamilton stops polishing the glass. "What do you want to know?" he asks

I shrug. "Oh, for starters, let's see". I put my hand under my chin and rest my head on it. "Where was Noah Arietta and Vincent Trapp; I mean Lieutenant Trapp, standing when the shots were fired."

"I didn't see any shots fired."

"Oh, I see. Where were you, then?" I ask.

"I was standing out on the floor talking with some customers at a table."

"Is it normal for you to step out from behind the bar during business hours?"

Hamilton thinks about this and says, "I hadn't been able to take a break because it was so busy so Mr. Arietta offered to relieve me so that I could take a break."

"Wasn't that odd?"

"No, not at all. He was thoughtful like that and didn't mind pitching in."

I am pensive for a moment, going over what Hamilton has said. Something bothers me and I can't put my finger on it at first and then it becomes clearer. Here was a tired bartender who was relieved by his boss, but that wasn't it. It was that he said he was standing out on the floor. So if he is tired why stand out on the floor and talk to customers. Why not go outside and get some fresh air or find a quiet spot to sit a bit. That just didn't make sense. I needed a step around to find out what I wanted to know.

"Who were these customers?" I ask casually.

"Fellow called Horwitz and his wife if that's any of your business. They had another fellow with them."

"Regulars?"

"No, said they had been out for a drive and decided to check this place out."

I made a note to remember the name. I wanted to ask him to spell the name, but I had a feeling he wouldn't know since they were not regulars. Instead I asked, "Where was the Horwitz's table located?"

"Out on the floor."

"Naturally," I said. "but where on the floor? Over by the Frogger video game? The stairs? The piano?" I paused, pointing suddenly sure it was by none of these. "Or was their table over by the outside door there?"

Without hesitation, the bartender replies, "Yes."

I pause in retrospect. Seems to me that anyone standing by the window near the door would have an unobstructed view of any one approaching the door from the outside, like Lieutenant Trapp for instance. I tread carefully, not wanting to make the bartender suddenly stop talking, but knowing I need more information. I find an angle.

"How come, you didn't sit down when you chatted with the Horwitz's? Aren't there usually four chairs at a table?"

I witness the slight lift of one side of his mouth as he sought quietly for an answer and found it. Triumphantly he replied, "they had a package on the other chair."

Good, I thought, he is good, but I wasn't going to let him off that easily. I decide to have a little fun.

"So, you were too tired to pick up the package and put it on the table? Or, you could have drawn up another chair to sit on, don't you think."

Hamilton scowled at me, but said nothing as he glanced at the stairway.

"Cat got your tongue, Mr. Hamilton, or was it that you didn't understand the question."

That set him off. "What are you driving at?" he demanded angrily. "Sitting or standing, what difference does it make?"

There was a hint of apprehension in his voice now and I knew that he knew I knew. Only I wanted to keep him on the hot seat for a while longer.

"No reason to get upset. These are only questions." I added, "So Noah Arietta was alone behind the bar when Lieutenant Trapp came in. Is that right?"

"I've already told you he was."

"Was he sitting or standing?"

"Standing. He always stood when he was at the bar."

Carefully now I ask, "How long had it been that he relieved you, standing there alone behind the bar?"

"Oh, for upwards of an hour I'd say."

"An hour."

"I said upwards of an hour."

"Okay, upwards of an hour then. And what time was it when he relieved you at the bar?"

"Around midnight, I guess it was."

"Ah, what time was the shooting?"

"At twelve forty-six exactly."

"How would you know that?"

"At the first shot I wheeled around and looked at the clock."

Why would he do that; look at the clock. I wondered if the bartender had been surprised when he saw that the wrong man had been shot? I looked behind the bartender and noticed the clock behind him. "Did you witness any of the other shots fired, Mr. Hamilton?"

His hand trembled ever so slightly as he sidestepped the question. "I saw Lieutenant Trapp standing up on the bar foot rail, leaning over and pointing at something down behind the bar."

"Something behind the bar?" What does that mean. Why would he say 'something'?

"Sorry, I mean at the time I wasn't sure, but later I found it was Mr. Arietta he was looking at."

"Where at the bar was the Lieutenant standing?"

The bartender sidled over and pointed. "Near the middle, there, right behind those two service rails."

I looked where he was pointing and asked, "What are they for?"

"To separate the bar area from the service areas. It keeps the customers at the bar from blocking the waitresses access to the bar counter."

"So what happened next."

"The Lieutenant turned and left almost as soon as I'd turned around and I ran out the door after him." Then as if taking an opportunity to make be the blunt of a joke said, "The same door you just tried to enter."

I take the bait. "Oh, so you saw me out there. Thanks a lot." I paused and then turned the conversation back on track. "What happened then?"

"When I got outside he wheeled around and faced me and said. "Do you want some too, Buster?"

I winced, but continued bravely.

"What did you do?"

"I said, no sir: and hurried back inside."

It was me on the hot seat now as I know that the bartender would be questioned by more than me and anyone hearing these parting words would put doubt on Lt. Trapp suffering from shock and grief did not have his wits about him. I take the time to turn the page on my pad allowing me time to pull myself together and go on.

"Is your first name Buster?"

"No, Brook is my first name.

"Okay, can you tell me if Noah was still alive?"

"No, he'd apparently died instantly. Five out of the six shots got him." The bartender stops, then adds, "The man didn't have a chance."

"You mean a chance to fire a shot himself?"

I catch just a glimpse of shock on his face before he quickly says, "I mean a chance to live."

I let it go. "To your knowledge did either man speak?"

"No, but someone told me later that Noah said, good evening to the Lieutenant."

"What about Lieutenant Trapp. Did anyone say he said anything?"

"No, apparently he didn't utter a word, but several people said they talked to him, including one of our waitresses."

"What's the waitresses name?"

"Mary Taylor."

"Did you go over and look at Noah?" I asked.

"Yes."

"Did you examine his body?"

"Yes, later after I'd cleared out the stragglers and locked the place."

"Do you know what time that was?"

"About one o'clock."

"Anyone give you trouble when you tried to clear them out?"

"Nobody did. Most fled right after the shooting."

"So then you were left all alone with the dead body from one o'clock?"

"Well, yes, somebody had to wait for the police."

"Who called them?"

"I did."

"When"

He hesitated and to urge him on I said, "It will all be a matter of record, you know. I will find out either way."

"I was just trying to think," he said. "I believe it was about one-fifteen, I should say."

"How come you waited so long to notify the police, Mr. Hamilton?"

This threw him and he stumbled about trying to find an excuse. "Oh, well, all the excitement and all. I guess I just forgot to make the call until then."

"Hm," I say looking at my notes. "Your boss is shot to death at twelve forty-six and in all the excitement you manage to note the exact time he is shot but later the excitement keeps you from calling the police until a half hour after the fact because it didn't cross your mind to call them.

"Yes, that's right," he snapped.

I took a drink of water and watched as Brook Hamilton picks up the same glass he had before and begins polishing it again. I notice that his hands are now shaking and he tries desperately to hide it. I am sure that he knows much more than he is telling and because he is on guard now, he probably won't tell me what he is concealing, or for that matter anyone else. Yet, from what he has said, I am convinced that Noah Arietta had been waiting for the Lieutenant. That is one reason why he had relieved his bartender and the other was because being behind the bar gave him protection not only by the bar, but the people who stood around it. But there was one problem with this and that was the waitresses service station area. It was the opening that became a fatal flaw in his plan. I am pretty sure that Noah was armed and think maybe I can get more information.

"When did the police arrive?"

Hamilton thinks for a minute and says, "Shortly after two."

"Okay, so you were alone with the body for over an hour." I add matter-of-factly

"Yeah, I guess that's correct," he says keeping his eyes on the glass that he continues to polish. He doesn't look at me at all.

"Of course it's correct, you just told me that," I said and again I pause. "Would you mind greatly putting down that glass, Mr.

Hamilton? It makes me nervous watching you do that and besides, I like to look at the people I'm talking with."

To my surprise he makes no objection as he puts down the glass.

"Thank you," I said. "Now was it sometime during this period you were alone with the body that you removed the firearms from behind the bar and got rid of them?"

I again struck a nerve. Hamilton was seething and I could tell it by the look in his eyes. He makes no loud, explosive outbursts, but it smolders in the background seeking self-justification. This kind of 'quiet anger' can be particularly insidious and harmful, and I would have backed down except I also sense he is afraid. Wide eyes, raised eyebrows and a mouth pulled back toward the ears tells me that he is off his game.

When he speaks his voice is coated with angry hostility. "What pistols," he says, trying to control himself. "I don' know what you're talking about. Who said anything about pistols?"

He tries to calm himself. "I think you need to leave. I have work to do."

I give him a minute then say, "I said firearms. I didn't say anything about pistols". I lean in closer and say, "So what did you do with the pistols?"

All the color leaves his face and as he grasps at straws he says, "It makes sense you meant pistol because a rifle is not the usual gun kept behind a bar".

"I wouldn't know," I said. "But you called them pistols, I didn't. It will be wise to remember that when it comes to the trial."

"Is that all?" he says coldly. "Is that all you wanted to ask me?"

"No, there's more. "Had Noah left the place during the evening?"

"Yes."

"When?"

"Around eleven, shortly before Mrs. Trapp left."

"When did you next see him?"

"Around midnight, shortly before he took over for me."

I think about what he said. "Which way did he enter, from the street or the apartment stairs?"

I can sense his hesitation as he replies, "He came down from the apartments."

I try not to show my excitement at his response. That means that Noah had the time and the opportunity to change and cleanup. Then I remember one more thing. That also gave him the time to get rid of Paige Trapp's missing underwear. I rush on.

"Did Noah change his clothes?" The bartender has caught up with me. I know this because he doesn't answer. So I ask again. He still doesn't answer.

In case you have forgotten the question. "Did Noah change his clothes?" Don't lie because I can ask someone else if you don't tell me."

"Why don't you ask the others, then?" he demands hotly. "Why do you keep firing away at me."

"I can only talk to one witness at a time and right now that witness is you." I shrug my shoulders. "But if you want it that way..." I turn as though to leave. "You don't have to answer anything. Perhaps you'd prefer me to bring it out in court that you wouldn't answer that simple question. It's your choice."

He almost spat his reply. "He changed from a white shirt to a sweatshirt. He, often did that so it's no big deal. Beyond that, I don't know if he changed anything else. I don't have a habit of checking out what everyone is wearing."

It was time to put the cards on the table. "Perhaps the sweatshirt gave him more freedom to lift a glass, say, or even a gun? Weren't you surprised when you wheeled around and saw the Lieutenant still standing and not Noah?"

Hamilton plastered a frozen smile on his face. "Suppose, you try checking that one out with the other witnesses."

He is smart in his attempts to only share what he knows anyone could tell me. He knew more, but those 'secret' things he wasn't about to open his mouth and share. There was no sense in trying to push it. I knew that so I said, "At any rate, Noah comes down in his sweatshirt and replaces you at the bar."

"That's correct. Everybody saw that." He feels confident that it is safe to tell this without helping the defense. But I want the other facts, the ones that will help our case and this is the man who knows those facts. Why is he being so evasive and hostile, I ask myself. It has to be because he knows what I need to know and he's keeping it back.

"Was it Noah's regular practice to relieve you behind the bar?"

His eyes flickered. "Occasionally."

"How often had he relieved you, say, during the last two weeks before the shooting?"

"Well it wasn't always at the same time, but he had relieved me lots of other times."

"How often during the entire last month then?" I asked.

"I don't remember."

"I don't think a jury would like that answer. They might even suspect you of being evasive or something. Suppose you try again."

"Okay, okay, he didn't relieve me."

It was beginning to all fall in place. "Ah, now we're getting somewhere," I said. "Noah just happened to relieve you the very night he also just happened to have raped and beaten up Paige Trapp."

It was time to aim for the heart. "Look, Mr. Hamilton, let's be honest with each other. Didn't Noah tell you to move away from the bar so you wouldn't get hurt. And didn't he order you to stand by that window for nearly an hour so you could spot the Lieutenant coming and warn him?"

What I said seemed to fly right over his head as the bartender acts as though he heard for the first time that Noah had raped Mrs. Trapp. "Who said Noah raped her?" he demanded.

If this was a game, I was going to play along. "You doubt it?" I said.

"I wasn't there."

"I know you weren't there. But I just asked you if you doubted that he'd raped her."

I could hear defiant in his voice and manner. "Yes, I doubt it. If he had sex with her which I also doubt, it would be with her consent. You can tell by the way she dresses and carries herself she wants the attention."

"Mr. Hamilton," I said, "you don't like being asked all these embarrassing questions and I really don't blame you, but somebody has to answer them and at this moment it is you. Unfortunately, I can't stop asking the questions as I need the answers in order to defend my client. You had a ring side seat at a murder and because of that a man's freedom and his future is in your hands. I know that you are not telling me everything, not even half. So, if you want this confrontation to end, you need to tell me what happened in glorious color or you will be sorry you didn't."

He flushed with hot anger and took a quick step back. "Is that a threat?"

"No, not a threat," I said. "but a promise. You need to start telling the truth right now. The truth is so easy, Mr. Hamilton; nothing to make up, no evasions, no entanglements, no inconsistent statements to try to explain away. Just the simple truth."

"You thing everything I've told you is a lie?" he demanded.

"Of course not. But you're holding back, you're not telling the whole truth. I know this because you aren't a compulsive liar so it's not easy for you to pull off. I told you early on that I need to look at the person I am speaking to and that is because I can tell by your eyes, your posture and nervous ticks when you are lying if I have witnessed when you are telling the truth. I have been lied to a lot by many so I have had to develop the skills to recognize it when someone is lying to me."

"What are you saying?" He asks.

"You're leveling with me only on the things you know I already know or that others will testify to anyway. And you're being evasive, evasive as hell. A little while ago I asked you if it wasn't true that instead of replacing you so you could take a break, Noah actually did this to put you out of the range of fire and to have you watch to see when Lt. Trapp was coming. That question you did not answer. I guess you thought I would forget about it, but I didn't."

Brook Hamilton stood in silence. I could tell he was thinking about what I had said and could be weighing the pros and cons of what more he could share with me. What was his angle anyway? That I couldn't figure out. Why was he so loyal to Noah? Was it more than loyalty that he shields him. Did Noah mean that much to him or was it something Noah promised him. Maye it wasn't Noah that had him holding back. If so who and why. All these questions I add to my notes.

You still haven't answered me," I said.

He sighed and shook his head. His mind was made up. "He didn't send me away and he relieved me just like I told you. I wasn't watching for Lieutenant Trapp or anyone."

I still felt as though I almost had him so I tried once more. "Very well, you've chosen how you want to handle this and I have warned you, you will have to pay the consequences of your actions.

"I've told you the truth," he said sullenly, almost resignedly. The anger and defiance were gone from his voice and body movements or else he was hiding it. One thing was for sure, he wanted me to go away. I could tell I would not have any luck if I kept badgering him. Maybe if I did give him some space by temporarily leaving the room, it might help.

"Excuse me," I said. "I need to go to the wash room." Giving it a little more thought I add, "I'll expect to see you here when I come back."

Chapter 15

The interior of the bathroom was a stunning surprise. From the curved faucet over the stone vessel sinks sitting atop a thick solid wood block that seemed suspended by hammered metal legs, it was indeed a work of art. It felt like a high end bathroom with its modern design fitting perfectly into the old world charm of the building. As I washed my hands I can't help but admire the mirrors running all the way up to the ceiling in wood frames across the back wall of the sink. "Better than my bathroom at home," I thought as I turned for one more look before making my way back to the bar.

Hamilton hadn't moved an inch from the spot where I left him and he looked more resigned than before so I walked over and began immediately. "Tell me Hamilton, how long have you worked here for Noah?"

When he replied I could tell that he had decided to be cooperative and answer my questions. Maybe it is because he knows I won't leave until I have all the answers. "Eighteen months."

Short and to the point. I liked that. "Did you know Noah before you started working for him?"

"No."

"So how did you come by getting the job."

"I just came in and asked about bar tendering. He needed a bartender and I got the job."

This was going better than I hoped it would. "So, who are you working for now that Noah—Noah is no longer... Sorry, I don't know how to word this."

"That's fine. I am working for a woman now."

That kind of threw me back. It is not what I expected. "A woman? Do you know her name?"

"Sure. Her name is Tyra Pederson."

"Who's in charge of the apartments? Do you know?"

"That would be Tyra too. She's running everything now."

"What did she do before she took over?"

"She was Noah's hostess."

I think I hear a bit of hesitation when the bartender mentions her previous job description, but I am still in shock over the who scheme of things.

"Is she just filling in for now until the new owners take over or does she own the place."

"Why ask me. She's right upstairs and you can ask her yourself?"

"I think you know the answer and I am here with you now. I can check the probate court records online and even check to see who the liquor license is being transferred to. It's all out there and easy to fine since it is public record so save me some time and tell me what you know."

"Okay, okay, Noah left a will. I guess he left everything to Tyra, ah, Miss Pederson." I wait quietly I can see by his facial expression he is about to say more. "I know he did. It has to go through probate court but she is in line to get everything."

This is not what I expected at all as I try not to stare with my mouth agape. I have trouble believing what I am hearing, but I need to pull myself together because I can't stop now. "Was Tyra here when the shooting occurred?"

"No."

"Do you know where she was?"

Hamilton drops his eyes down and says, "I really don't know where she was at the time."

It may be true, but I decide to make a note to check this further. I look at the bartender. "Tell me, were you one of the witnesses when Noah made his will?"

I watch as Hamilton's eyes grow big and his mouth opens slightly causing the corners of his lips to droop. "How do you know that?"

"It is obvious, quite frankly since you know the contents. So when did Noah make the will that you witnessed."

"I think it was about three weeks before…before he died."

Three weeks before. So it was a recent development. That raises another question. "Brook, can I call you Brook, Mr. Hamilton."

"Yes."

"Brook, was Noah married?"

"He was married, but they divorced a long time ago." Without me having to probe Brook seems to like talking about Noah's previous life as he offers up that Noah lived on Long Island in a fancy house on two acres that had ocean frontage, but the wife got the house in the divorce settlement. Was it that Brook was comfortable talking about ancient history, or because this shows how close he was to his boss. Since Brook is more comfortable and willing to share all he knows I continue on this vein. "Are Noah's parents alive?"

"Both dead."

"Did Noah have any children?"

Brook Hamilton smirks and sensing this may be important; I note his reaction. It means to me at that moment, Brook's opinion of

Noah is that he was a womanizer and that will help my case. "I think he has a daughter," he says.

"Did he leave anything else to any other relatives?" I decide to reword the question, "Did any other relatives come to his funeral?"

"I don't know because he was buried on Long Island and I didn't go." I start to ask why Long Island, but there is something more interesting to ask before he decides he's said enough.

"Okay, but did you know of any other relatives besides a daughter?"

I watch Brook as he first glances toward the stairs and then lowers his head and scratches the back of his neck. "He has the wife he divorced, the daughter and there may be a married sister." He now slightly raises his head with his eyes still looking down as he takes is finger and begins biting his nail. For some reason, this subject upsets him far more than the actual shooting. I decide to share something with him this time.

"I only ask this because there are rules. The law is quite specific here. When a person dies without leaving a Last Will and Testament, it's said that they died intestate. When a person dies intestate, that person's property is distributed according to the law. Who gets what depends on who the living relatives are and their relationship to the person who died. The family members who are entitled to a share of the Decedent's estate when there is no will are called "distributees" and in New York, that law in the simplest terms states that a spouse inherits everything if there are no children. If there are children but no spouse, then the children inherit everything. If there is a spouse and children, the spouse inherits the first $50,000 plus half of the balance. The children inherit everything else. If there is no spouse or children, then the parents inherit everything and so on and so forth. So this daughter would inherit even if there wasn't a will. If there are any siblings but no spouse, children or parents, the siblings inherit everything and finally, if a child dies before the Decedent and had children of their own, then the Decedent would have grandchildren. Those grandchildren would step into the Decedent's child's place and inherit in place of the child."

I had noticed the perplexed stare as I explained all of this to him so I am not surprised when Brook says, "Sorry, but I can't follow all of that. It doesn't matter. I think I understand what you are saying, though."

"Good."

My mind continues along this path. The only way a stranger can inherit anything is if Noah willed everything to them and that would cut out the daughter. But if a relative or guardian were to contest the will and wins, then the daughter would inherit it all. This I review in my head. There are only four ways to contest and they are undue influence, fraud, improper execution and lack of capacity. A light dawns.

"Brook, who was the other witness to the will?"

"The night clerk upstairs."

"Do you have a name?"

"Connie, something. I don't know her last name."

I am just getting to know those around him, but I haven't gotten a good picture of who this Noah was yet and that was important. "Brook, was Noah a heavy drinker?"

Brook took a minute and says, "He drank some, like most people in the business."

"Did he drink maybe more on the day of the shooting?"

"No, just the same as usual."

"Well, how much is that?"

"If you are asking if he was drunk, he wasn't. Nothing more than usual."

"Okay, but what is nothing more than usual." I am growing impatient now.

"Oh, sorry, I thought you meant…A few shot glasses full a day."

"I don't believe that. I happen to know that he drank quite a bit with Paige Trapp that night, but let's drop that for now. Tell me about Tyra. What was she to Noah?"

Again that smirk on his face. "I think you need to ask her. She is nice and will answer your questions. I told you she was the hostess here." I see him glance quickly at the clock over the bar. "Excuse me, I've got to go unlock the street door. It's time to open."

I look at the clock and see that it is now 11:30 a.m. The sign on the door had said 12 noon. Brook was nervous and needed a distraction so he is opening early, or so I thought, but as I watch Brook as he comes out from behind the bar I follow his path. Brook heads toward the door, but instead of unlocking it, he quickly scampers up the stairs at the back; the ones that lead to the apartments. In my head I believe he is going to warn the heiress, Tyra Pederson, that I am here and asking questions about her.

I didn't mind much as I realize I am suddenly alone in the bar. I get up and walk behind the counter. On the floor in the middle of the bar is a large dark blotch that I envision being where Noah had fallen. I carefully study the bar and then kneel down and survey the lower areas of the bar. About six inches below the surface and near the bar service station, out of sight of those on the other side is a narrow wooden shelf about four feet long. I whistle softly and lean closer. The shelf is made of wood but inferior to that of the bar itself so I assume it had been added later. And to what purpose, I wonder as I see that right now it holds a collection of assorted salt and pepper shakers and mustard jars. I move them aside and see what I am looking for. The shapes of what use to be on the shelf is still visible. Carefully I put the items back in place.

I turn around to face the huge bar mirror and liquor shelf. The mirror seems intact but when I crane my neck over the rows of bottles and stand on my tiptoes I see a neat small splintered hole near the base of the mirror. If this was made by a bullet it would have gone through the person's heart at that height.

I stare at this a moment and think, at least one of the bottles should have been broken. I walk out from behind the bar and hear someone rattling the street side door, but ignore it. I look at the clock and realize that my friend the bartender has been gone for some time now. It strikes me that he and his new boss must be having quite a conversation. They must have needed to collaborate desperately for them to leave me alone in the bar. I plan on taking advantage of this time.

I walk over to the door and stand by the table where the window that Brook stood by was located. There is an awning over the door entrance that is obstructing my view and I stoop to what I judge to be the height of Brook who is shorter than me. The view is now fine. I can see outside and, turning slightly, I can also see the bar. This is a perfect spot for a lookout.

I turn my attention to the inside of the bar and on the wall adjoining the door on the other side of the room and closer to the bar, is a large bulletin board which appears to be covered with various papers. I quickly move over that way and taking my glasses out of my breast pocket, I put them on.

I find myself thinking of Sheriff Lincoln Harper, because like the board in his office, this board is dedicated to Noah Arietta. There are newspaper clipping, pictures, announcements and other items telling of his exploits. A quick survey and I know that he is an avid fisherman, hunter, expert marksman. But what interest me most is Noah is a marksman. One article tells of his winning the action shooting, a game measuring the speed at which a competitor can hit one or more targets, starting from a position in which the handgun is securely holstered. The targets may be stationary or moving. He placed second in silhouette shooting which is a shooting gallery on a grand scale. Scoring is simple: shoot to hit off their stands, metallic silhouette targets that are placed at different distances. The challenge is that shooters are permitted to use only one hand while engaging targets at ranges varying from 10 meters to 50 meters. Moving over to the end of the board I see another article that praises his precision shooting. Precision shooting ranks as one of the most popular recreational uses of the handgun today. Finally, there are several articles on his skeet shooting ability where the participants, using shotguns, attempt to break clay targets mechanically flung into the air from two fixed stations at high speed from a variety of angles.

"He was quite a man, wasn't he?" I hadn't seen Brook enter the bar and he startles me.

I collect myself and ignoring his comment I say, "Did you have a nice chat about me with Tyra Pederson?"

"Most satisfactory and to the point. She told me to keep my trap shut. No more questions and no more answers. Those were the lady's orders and she's the boss."

She may be a trifle late, I think. I start to not only wonder about her being the sole heir, but what she is like, but I decide to turn my attention elsewhere. "Well," I say, "if you can't talk to me, I might as well leave. It's time for lunch so it's a good time to take off. But I have just one more question and it's harmless," I say.

"If you will promise to leave, then I'll try and answer it."

"I point to a large glossy unframed photograph on the bulletin board. In it is a couple standing on a sandy beach. The man, who has bushy black hair and rich brown skin is clearly Noah. He is smiling down at a woman, a stunning looking brunette who is gravely regarding the camera. They make a nice looking couple and I would have guessed they were married or in love except for one thing—the age difference. I would guess Noah was old enough to be her father. Could it be possible that this fragile and well-bred appearing young woman was the scheming Tyra Pederson?"

"Is that a picture of Noah and Tyra?" I said.

"That's Noah and Tyra," he replies. "She's pretty, isn't she?"

"Yes she is," I say, trying to hide my confusion over this sudden new development. "Okay, I'm leaving like I promised, but one friendly tip before I go."

"What's that?"

"Don't remove the gun shelf from behind the bar. It's too late. I've already seen it and it'll only look worse if you take it out now. You should have done that before the police came at the same time you got rid of the pistols."

Beyond a surprising look that he checks immediately, there is nothing more that Brook adds. I walk away thinking that he might have been nervous but generally he is a smart person. I wonder what his cut will be if it all turns out okay. It didn't matter really because my only concern is how much his part would help or hinder my case. I had told Randall that this case had everything, but now I had more. Now the case had Tyra Pederson. This was going to be interesting.

Chapter 16

When I enter the lobby there is more activity going on with tenants leaving possibly to go to work and others coming in who from the looks of their attire, went for a run. As there is only one elevator and the only stairs up are inside the bar area, we all stand waiting for the elevator to descend to the lobby. A quick glance at those waiting and I know that if I want to be on the first load, I best move forward so I squeeze pass several people in front of me, ignoring their looks of disgust.

When the elevator reaches the lobby, I wait patiently for everyone to disembark and then move forward. Just as I am about to step over the threshold, someone behind grabs me by the arm, "What do you think you're doing? You need a key card to enter."

I had noticed each person, going over to the panel to the left before getting on the elevator, but I paid little attention. So now what. I start to step back when the man next to me says, "Aren't you a friend of Brooks? I saw you talking with him earlier." Thinking quickly on my feet I say, "Yes, yes I am." My new best friend takes my arm and we enter the elevator together.

The elevator is filled to capacity making it hard to move or have a conversation and that is fine with me When we arrive on the second floor, I squeeze forward keeping my eyes staring straight ahead until I am able to exit the elevator but before I do, I thank the man who has been the good Samaritan.

There in the second floor lobby I try my best to look like I belong but it's hard not to gawk at the décor that reeks of money and good taste. Somehow I manage as I make my way over to the desk next to the elevator. "Getting busy," I say to the woman sitting there watching the activity around her.

"Yes, it is."

Her smile is pleasant. As I smile back I see that her skin is wrinkled showing the advancement in her age, but her eyes are dancing behind her metal framed glasses. If I had to guess her age by her physical appearance it would be somewhere nearing eighty, but I am sure that her mental age will be a lot less or she wouldn't have put herself in a position with so much activity. I continue to size her up before I make my request. She looks like a person who likes her conversationalist to come to the point. I let my arms hang at my side and face her.

"Good morning, I look at her name plate; Ms. Dunbar."

"Good morning young man. Can I help you?"

I am direct and to the point. "Yes, I was wondering if you were on duty the night Noah was shot?"

Her appearance suddenly changes. I can see the orbits of her eyes narrow behind her metal framed glasses and her chin lowers slightly. I wait patiently and finally she looks up at me sharply. "Why do you ask?" she says.

"I'm Lieutenant Trapp's lawyer. My name is Richard Dandridge."

"Oh, sorry, everyone has been asking questions and I am getting a little annoyed with it. Since it happened it has been the topic of the day and the evening."

"I understand." I pause to give her time to adjust and when she doesn't answer I say, "But were you on duty?"

"Sorry, yes, I was on that night."

"Do you remember when Mr. Arietta came in."

"Yes."

I pause briefly to write her name down and seeing me looking at her name plate, Mrs. Dunbar says, "You can call me Mildred if you like."

"Thank you, Mildred. I was wondering if you remember how Mr. Arietta was dressed when you saw him. What did you think of his general appearance?"

Mildred Dunbar speaks with more animation in her voice. "Well, Mr. Arietta came running in at just about..." At that moment we are interrupted by a heavyset woman, dressed in an expensive suit who ignores me and asks, "Is lunch being served downstairs yet?"

I step slightly back so that the woman can fit in the space in front of the desk. I can't help but admire the patience noticeable in Mildred's voice as she says to the woman, "Yes, it is." The woman doesn't even say, thank you, as she walks away. Mildred waits until the woman is out of ear shot then turns to me and says, "Where was I?"

Before I can answer, we are again interrupted by another woman who walks with purpose toward Mildred's desk. "Excuse me sir. Mildred, Miss Pederson wants to see you downstairs."

"Sure, no problem." Mildred turns to say something to me.

"She wants to see you immediately." The woman says authoritatively.

"Okay." Mildred replies. I watch Mildred trying to move quickly, her aging joints slow to respond. As she presses down on the desk for support, she looks at me and says, "Sorry" before she is finally on her feet.

I nod my head in acceptance and then watch as Mildred surprises me with how easily she now advances toward the staircase. I think maybe she isn't as old as I thought.

So, Tyra Pederson has eyes on me. I pay no attention to the intruder because I am sure she is not important to my cause. Instead I decide to go find Pete and see what he has managed to learn.

As I move around the second floor I would have thought to see someone from the Government Foreign Service Office, the FBI or the Army, but if they were here I couldn't identify them or they had already completed their investigation and gone. I would have liked to talk to them, but maybe Pete ran into them and got information.

I continue searching for Pete when suddenly he comes charging into the upstairs lobby, his standard attire giving him a ragged look that is softened by the fact he is wearing glasses but lost on the people who now openly stare at him. Most likely they are thinking he doesn't fit in. His hair is disheveled and I can see he is unaware of the attention he draws. I walk forward, but then my way is blocked by the same woman who had interrupted my previous conversation with Mildred. This is one rude woman, I think as I manage to step around her and hold my tongue.

"Pete, I was looking for you."

"I was looking for you. Let's go down and have lunch." I know this is code for I have something to tell you so without a word we walk over to the staircase and take the steps down to the café.

As we enter the bar area of the café, a young woman comes forward to meet us. I catch my breath. First I notice that she is well endowed, then I take in her shade of mahogany hair. It flowed in waves to adorn her glowing, tanned skin. Her eyes, framed by long lashes, were a bright, emerald-green and seemed to sparkle. A straight nose, with high cheekbones and full lips - she appears the picture of perfection. Without being told, I know this is Tyra Pederson. She is breathtaking, prettier than her picture, with a tall, willowy figure.

"How many", she says.

"Two," I stutter.

As she leads the way I watch. She is all poise and confidence and I can't help wondering how had a character like Noah Arietta ever even had the gall to approach such a beauty. I sigh, knowing that in most cases it is not the physical appearance, but what the man has to offer that draws in someone like Tyra.

"Is this okay," Tyra asks as she stops at a table near the window.

"It's fine." I pause trying to gain some composure before saying, "Thank you."

"Hope you enjoy your lunch, Mr. Dandridge," she says smiling the smile of someone who has the upper hand and defeated another. For a second or two she stares directly into my eyes, then says, "Your waitress will be with you in a minute." Then she turns and walks away.

"Who's that," Pete asks, the admiration dripping off each word.

"That, my friend is Tyra Pederson. She used to be Noah Arietta's hostess or should I say, she is since apparently she is still on the job."

More interested in the person, my last comment is lost on Pete. "So that's Tyra. I never expected her to be so enchanting."

"So, you heard about her too," I said to Pete. "Tell me what you learned about her. There's something I'm missing here that doesn't add up."

"Well, for starters I heard that Tyra was supposed to have been Noah's mistress, but seeing her I don't think that was true. But,

169

I heard that she had come to Rochester several years ago with a group of friends and Noah fell for her like a ton of bricks and made her boss lady of the place over all the other waitresses who had been here for some time. As you can imagine, that kind of attention breeds enemies so I can't take their comments literally. He also paid her twice the amount he paid the other waitresses and then later he gave her the hostess position."

"I see." I watch as Pete's eyes follow Tyra as she shows another person to their table. "You seem to be falling under her spell too."

"It's that she reminds me of someone I use to know."

His statement and the change that comes over him makes me aware he is talking about his wife, Courtney. I didn't know much about her except that she had died of breast cancer a long time ago. When she had been diagnosed, Pete was beside himself trying to care for her. He had loved her deeply and became her main caregiver, spending every minute of his time either searching for a medical miracle or making her comfortable. He wouldn't listen when people told him that he needed to take care of himself because his physical, emotional and mental health was vital to the wellbeing of Courtney. And when she passed he was filled to the brim with stress, anxiety and depression. He was frustrated because he couldn't help her to live. With no alternatives left, Pete began drinking heavily and it helped a little, but it could not make him forget. 'Losing someone is hard to accept, but moving on is the most painful.' Pete had once told me.

I wait for him to pull himself together and then ask, "What else did you find out, Pete."

It takes Pete a moment to collect himself. "Well, I heard that Noah was half-crazed with drink when he met up with Paige Trapp and that she led him on. Then others say that he probably never raped her at all."

The waitress arrives at our table. "Are you ready to order, she asks?"

"Yes, I think so," I say as I quickly look over the menu. I'll have the Chipotle Turkey Avocado Sandwich and a be…., I begin and then change tactics. I mean, an ice tea with lemon. I didn't want to encourage Pete to drink. He has become quite valuable to me sober.

"And you sir?"

"Let me see. I'll try the Chicken Caprese Panini. That's with real oven roasted chicken breast and not cold cuts, correct?"

"Yes, sir, real chicken breast. What would you like to drink?"

"Just water. Add a lemon to that, will you?"

"Thank you."

We wait until she leaves the table before we continue our conversation. "Okay, continue," I begin.

"Well, I heard that Tyra had just recently taken up with an officer that works with Lieutenant Trapp, named Ian Solenhauser. Ian was one of those black leather jacket, hair all over his head type of guy and Noah tried to break it off."

"How?"

"I heard he offered to marry her, someone else said that he told her he would give her the café, but she refused his offers and would not stop seeing the guy."

"So do you believe it."

"I am having a problem with it, for sure. I don't know what is the truth and what is not. There is one thing that the rumors agree on and that is that Noah had been drinking quite heavily lately. Those who were around say that there was no doubt that Noah was drunk the night that Paige Trapp came to the bar and when she went to play the Frogger video game he was all over her."

"It doesn't make sense. Here is a man that is trying to impress this woman Tyra who works here and is aware of all that goes on, and he flirts and makes a play for Paige Trapp. Yes, Paige is beautiful, but she is no Tyra. It just doesn't make sense."

"That is a mystery. It baffles me too. The only thing I can come up with is that whatever was going on here, the Trapps were not part of it. They became part of it because they were just in the wrong place at the wrong time."

I thought about what Pete said and I had to agree. It made more sense that the Trapps were innocent pawns in some big, mysterious game. What this game was is the real basis for what happened that night.

Even as I think about this I wonder if it had anything to do with the defense for my client against the murder charge. Assuming we did find out what was actually happening that night, would it have any bearing on the case? Also, was it important to understand why Tyra Pederson was so bent on shielding Noah when she apparently was blocking his advances. It didn't make sense unless she was protecting her interest in the café, only she didn't act like a gold digger. Yes, her looks fit the bill but not her apparent personality.

"In any case, we need to get to the truth in all this."

Our meal was delivered and the table grew quiet as we enjoyed the food immensely. It was everything stated on the menu and it looked exactly like the picture. Even the tea was better than usual. It definitely was fresh brewed. When we finished, like clockwork, the waitress appeared and asked if we wanted to see the dessert menu. I looked at Pete, he looked at me and together we said, "No, just the check please."

We waited while the waitress completed the check and handed it to us. To Pete's objection, I put my credit card in the slot. When she returned, I signed the slip and took my receipt and credit card from the leather pocket and put it in my wallet. Seeing Pete's objection still apparent on his face I said, "Business expense."

Before leaving the café, Pete had asked why I didn't approach Tyra now that she was available and I told him that it would be useless. She was silencing the employees so the chance of her talking to me was next to impossible. Besides, I wanted to have as much of the story as I could uncover before I said anything to her. So to give him an idea of how powerful Tyra could be, I paused at the bar and tried to engage the bartender in conversation. It was hopeless. All he could say was, "I'm sorry. I need this job."

When I reply that he will have to tell me eventually and if not before, then in court, he says, "Will I?" then turns away.

I guess even before I turn around and see her, Tyra stands motionless in the doorway facing the bar. When she sees me looking her way, she smirks nods her head and then moves toward the dining room. Pete, witnessing this exchange gets the message. We leave, careful to appear like just old friends getting together.

We walked out and climbed into my car and soon we were on our way, Pete turned to me and said, "So, what did you find out, Richard?"

I told him how I had discovered the gun shelf under the bar and hit on the high points of my conversations with the bartender and the observations when he left me alone in the bar. I told him my theory that the bartender was serving as a lookout that night, and about the bulletin board that proved Noah was quite the marksman. I mentioned that once the bartender left and went upstairs, he informed me on his return that Tyra had told him to shut up, I had learned that she was the beneficiary in the will and would get all of Noah's estate, though, before he was silenced.

I look over at Pete and I can see he hasn't told all of what he knew. "Pete," I say, "I can tell you are holding back. What else did you find out."

Chapter 17

I've always respected and admired Pete Adams as my mentor, I was beginning to respect him even more for his tenacity. I have always known he was a great lawyer at one time before he sought solace in the bottle, but now I was learning he was also a born detective. He was shrewd and resourceful.

Just like myself, Pete had gotten off to a slow start in his investigation when the first person he approached clammed up and fled at the mention of his wanting to know about the fatal shooting. It being early, he was unable to get pass the lobby through he had walked all around the area looking for a way upstairs. Finally, he gave up and went out on the street. There were several establishments in the area that could possibly come up with some information so he started walking down the sidewalk and checking out each one of them. It wasn't hard because everyone was talking about the shooting and were more than willing to share what they knew. He had learned a lot about the life and times of the late Noah Arietta and one point that seemed to keep coming up was Noah's being an expert marksman.

"I didn't take down names or try to memorize faces because I didn't want to scare anyone into not talking to me. By the time I got to the last location several things had clearly emerged regarding the character and reputation of Noah."

"What was that?"

Pete continues saying, "first and foremost Noah was perhaps the most thoroughly disliked person in town. The general air of rejoicing over his demise was as shocking as it was obvious. This sentiment was based on those around him feeling he thought himself to be superior to them. He constantly bragged that he could outshoot, outfight, out love and out anything anyone else could do." Pete paused. "Only I also sensed that it was more than just dislike. I feel they feared him."

"Why? Why did they fear him?"

"It seems that the reports were right on about his abilities. Apparently Noah not only thought he was good at most things, he was. It was proven when a young man had come in to the bar and said to Noah, that he was going to kill him."

Seeing my mouth start opening, Pete added quickly. "No, no one seemed to know why this man was so angry at Noah. Anyway, rumor has it that Noah almost killed the man instead of the other way around. There were other confrontations too, but this gives you the gist of why I think people feared him.

"Go on."

"So, Tyra Pederson came to work for Noah. When she arrived there was something underhanded going on at the establishment, but Ms. Pederson changed that. Tyra managed to convince Noah that he had to clean up his act because whether he believed it or not he was playing with fire and might get burned. She knew that Noah would resist because she was talking about throwing out his patrons, the ones who made him money so she laid out the plan for him to add the café to the bar, turn the upper level into apartments and reap more money than ever from his establishment. So as the story goes, Noah put out an unwelcome mat to all of the 'regulars' and told them to get the hell out and stay out."

"There wasn't a fight or confrontation of any sort when he did this?"

"What do you think? Sure there was. Bitter resentment brewed until, alas, the inevitable results surfaced."

"What was that?"

"As fast as they come to the door, Noah threw them out. Those who wanted to fight, Noah fought and he did it as long as he needed so that eventually all the clientele whether part of the drug scene or not, were forced away."

"Drug scene? What are you talking about?"

"My finale. In coordinated arrests the FBI, ATF, U.S. Postal Inspection Service, and Rochester Police Department took eight people into custody in an alleged wide-ranging drug trafficking conspiracy. Members of the conspiracy maintained drug stash houses throughout the Rochester area and search warrants were served in Genesee, Wayne County, Lyons, New York, Canandaigua and Pittsford, according to information shown to me at one of the establishments. A statement from the agency said some of the drug traffickers conducted their deals at a Mexican restaurant in the South Park neighborhood, the Tempera restaurant and others, along with the Founder's Café. The defendants were scheduled to make initial court appearances on a Wednesday afternoon in U.S. District Court. The members of this drug trafficking conspiracy brought meth, cocaine, and heroin to our communities, preying on those with addictions to line their own pockets and the lengthy investigation also led to seizures of illegal weapons as well as street drugs."

"So how long was this investigation?"

"According to court records that one of the owners pulled up on his computer to show me, the investigation of the drug trafficking organization began back in November last year. Surveillance indicated the conspirators brought the drugs up from California and sold them at various locations ranging from auto wrecking yards in Auburn to outside restaurants at the shopping mall. Many of the drug deals were made in or around the Mexican restaurant. Members of the alleged drug conspiracy arrested Wednesday following their indictment by the grand jury for drug distribution included many of the names of patrons of the Founders' café. Right now the charges contained in the indictment and complaints are only allegations."

"Why is that…Oh yes, a person is presumed innocent unless and until he or she is proven guilty beyond a reasonable doubt in a court of law."

"You've got it. This was an Organized Crime and Drug Enforcement Task Force investigation and was led by the FBI's Safe Streets Task Force including officers and agents from the Rochester Police Department and the Bureau of Alcohol, Tobacco, Firearms, and Explosives and the U.S. Postal Inspection Service. The arrests also involved a number of law enforcement. The case is being prosecuted by Assistant United States Attorneys Henry Worthington and Katherine Watson."

"So what happened at the Founder's Café."

"A man named Chaz had been a frequent at the Bar and a man named Jason Owens entered the scene as an undercover cop. Later it was learned that Owens was following a lead from a confidential informant who told police Chaz was dealing drugs at the Founder's Café. During the investigation, detectives frequently observed people who visited the bar only stayed for short periods of time. Most of them also appeared to be drug dependent, according to the search warrant. Eventually, undercover agents purchased heroin from Chaz at the bar, which led to a raid. Police recovered $21,000, rubber bands, a handgun and a safety deposit key from Chaz's house. During the raid police seized 20 grams of heroin, and several thousand dollars in cash. Chaz is now out on bond until a jury trial scheduled in December."

"So didn't they suspect Noah."

"I think they did at first, but thanks to Tyra forcing him to throw out those patrons, she saved his butt. No one involved in the scheme would have thrown out these people and lucky for him he knew how to hold his own.

Chapter 18

We are silent for a bit as we drive toward home. Pete breaks the silence saying, "It's sad to see someone so beautiful stoop to such deception. I saw her signal the bartender, all right. I saw her shake her head"

"See, I told you. Whatever her motive, Tyra Pederson is as relentless a fighter as her late boss and she is suppressing the truth that we need desperately to build our case."

For now, we have all the information we can get from the Founders Cafe so we drive away and head towards the Great Embankment Park where the assumed rape and beating had taken place.

It is actually in walking distance from the Founders Café, and I note there are walking trails to follow in the park. I assume on one of these, Tyra began her walk to the Founders Cafe. We traverse over the Irondequoit Creek that runs through a tunnel under the canal and I take note of the two metal guard gates standing at either end of the embankment.

As we drive by the areas I see the denseness of the trees in the distance and the openness of the area around the canal. the parks naturally occurring, rolling fields become the highlight of the area as we drive even deeper into the narrow winding roadway. We pass three baseball diamonds currently being used by school age children. Further in we see the soccer and cricket field, also occupied and then we come to the familiar area to me, the golf courses. There are two of them and do not require membership to use so all types of people who love to play golf are able to use the course. There is a clubhouse with a pro shop and food concessions which draws not only the golfers, but many others to the area.

"This is a busy park," Pete says.

"Yes, it is. I like to golf here, but I can't say I have taken advantage of much else. I come sometimes and watch the boat competition. It's kind of fun to see some of those homemade contractions actually floating when they look like they will fall apart at any moment."

"That's because you're use to the more flamboyant type of water vessels." There is a hint of laughter in his voice as he makes this claim.

The road narrows even more and the foliage increases as we continue through the park. Here the sky is hidden behind a canopy of leaves and the sun provides less light than during the early part of our travel. It's beautiful, but in an eerie way as we endure the sound of the brush touching the sides of the car. Finally, up ahead we observe the yellow tape, marking our destination. We are in the rougher terrain of the park and here there are only dirt ruts making the passage for automobiles.

"This would be the road that Noah drove Paige down when he raped her. I'm sure they are done looking for evidence now, but keeping the tape up doesn't hurt."

As an afterthought I ask, "Pete, do you think it is strange that the café is open for business and that it is the site of a crime scene. Shouldn't it be closed down?"

"There isn't a standard time limit, nor is there a standard for how much area to protect. That is determined by the amount of evidence that needs to be collected, and the area that is required to protect the scene. At the café it was much easier to gather the evidence needed and I'm sure it was done efficiently but as quick as possible so that the café's business was not interrupted for longer than necessary."

I understand what he is saying. This crime scene is in the open air and covers a bigger area so it stands to reason it took longer to investigate. Here they had to investigate not only the site of the rape, but other areas which might yield valuable evidence such as driveways, surrounding yards, and pathways. I'm sure, like us, teams are returning as they go over their records and possibly think of something they might have missed.

We get out of the car and head toward the taped off area and start walking around, but outside of the tire marks and foliage pressed to the ground, there is not much else to see. I had hoped that maybe we could find the missing panties, but not such luck.

"Well, no panties. Pete, I wonder where they found the sunglasses?"

"Don't know," Pete replies and I don't think they will share that with you until they have to."

"Well, what to you say we go back?"

"Sure." We walk side by side mindful of the ruts so that we don't twist an ankle. "You know, Richard, I heard that Noah was quite the marksman and that he had a special display box behind the bar showing all his medals and ribbons he had won."

"I didn't see any such display case, Pete, and I looked around the back of that bar quite thoroughly."

"That doesn't make sense. The display case was there on the night of the shooting, because one of the people I spoke with mentioned it. Also, from what I saw at the park just now, there was only one way that Noah could have taken to drive Paige home and she knows the area so she should know that too."

"Interesting. Can you make note of that so that I can check it out. A missing display case and a question on Paige's ride with Noah."

"Also most of the people I talked with didn't especially care for Noah, but they liked Tyra Pederson. They thought her to be kind and sweet and couldn't understand what she saw in Noah."

"Yes, that's what I heard too and I wonder what connects the two them because it seems to me they were close."

"Well, I saved the best for last."

"The best for last?" I say. "What could be better than what you have already told me?"

"Well, most of the tenants at the Academy Apartments were approaching me or talking about what had happened and were anxious to share. I found that out just by hanging by the door of the Academy since I couldn't get upstairs. It so happens that one of the tenants of the Academy building said that they had recently stayed at a friend's house that was located near the Trapps' residence and she remembers waking up from what she thought was a dream. She heard screaming and looked out the window to see a woman shrieking at the gate. It wasn't a dream. Now she has nightmares about it".

"Wait a minute, Pete. She said at the gate?"

"Yes she did and she said that it woke her and she looked at the clock. It was midnight."

"Good work, Pete. Did you get the names?" My mind goes back and I remember that Paige had mentioned that ever since the incident they have had to lock the gate and that would make me think that the gate wasn't locked before that time.

"Yes, he says, patting his breast pocket. Yes, I did. I have their names and addresses. Of course, they already spoke with the police too so they know about this already."

183

"There's more," Pete says. "I also ran into a man who said he was having a conversation with a fellow and they began talking about the murder. This guy shared with him that he recently had a conversation with another guy who had been in the Great Embankment Park. He told the man I talked with that at the time he was there he saw a young man lying on the ground and standing some paces away behind a pile of driftwood, he saw a woman whom he recognized later as the hostess at the Founder's Café. He said he didn't know her name, just remembered her from there."

I am shocked and unable to say anything except, "So what did the man do?"

"He ran."

"Well, you know it could have been a mistake as it is quite dark, as we found even in the daytime. Besides I'm sure many couples go to secluded spots in the park."

Pete shakes his head. "Remember, I did find out that Tyra was going with some young man at one point and that Noah tried to stop her from seeing him. That peaked my interest in this conversation and so I asked a little more and found out that the couple was practically naked, which is probably why the woman was hiding behind the driftwood, probably heard him coming. This man said…"

"So what. How would this help our case at all. I can't see any use for this in our case."

"It isn't that. It isn't about them being in the park," Pete doggedly went on…"

"What then. I can't see the issue in all this."

"Well, Pete said, it seems that the man says the conversation just might have been overheard by the bartender because he turned to order a drink after he had shared this tidbit, but the bartender was no longer behind the bar. The bartender was heading up those back stairs."

"Are you saying that the bartender may have gone up to tell Noah about what he heard and that this was before Paige Trapp had come to the bar."

"Now we're on the same page. Yes, that's exactly what I'm saying. He told Noah before the shooting."

"Tell me, please that you got the names and addresses of the teller and the one who witnessed the scene."

"What do you think?"

"You are amazing, Pete. I thought I had played detective well, but you take the cake." I glance a look in his direction and see that he appreciates my statement though he doesn't respond. We drive the rest of the way to his apartment in silence. I couldn't help smiling as I pull in front of the building and wait while Pete gets out. "I'll be in touch." Pete just nods.

I pull away and head to my office feeling as though we have a good chance now of not running into too many surprises during the court case. This is a big case and it can help my situation if I win. I want to win and I think now that it is a good possibility. I pull into the parking area and get out and taking my briefcase with me head toward the office. When I enter, I realize for the first time I have been whistling and so does Theresa who stands in the office doorway. "Someone's happy," she says.

"Theresa, I want to run something by you and get your opinion."

"Sure boss, what is it."

I share the information that Pete had obtained trying not to let my ideas come into play and then wait for her to absorb it all. "So, what do you thing?"

Theresa walks into the room and sits in the chair in front of my desk. I can tell by the vacant stare and the pursing of her lips that she is concentrating so I remain still. Finally, she looks at me and says. "Well, as I see it, if the bartender did hear the conversation and told Noah about Tyra's being with this man in the park, wouldn't he go after this man, or even Tyra? Why would he rape Mrs. Trapp and force Lt. Trapp's hand?"

I threw up my hands. "Yes, that is the question and I don't know the answer. It seems the more I find out about this case, the more it wipes out any reasonable conclusions. If Noah did know about Tyra and the man on the beach, it wasn't that much of a surprise since he knew the man existed and that Tyra was seeing him. That's a given because Noah was trying to break them up. So, what if Noah was so mad at this man that he wanted to just hurt someone, anyone since he could not get her to stop seeing him. Or, maybe he figured if he knew about this man, then everyone knew and they were laughing at him and that Noah could not stomach.

"Now, that does make sense," Theresa said. "Go on.

"Well, when he saw Paige Trapp he just kind of transferred his hate and frustration at her."

That distant stare appears again as Theresa meditates over my findings. Then I see a slight raise of her eyebrow and her teeth cover her upper lip. I try to be patient, but can't wait and ask, "What, are you thinking."

"What I am thinking is that I can't give you any more answers right now and it's late so I am going to pack up and go home. You should do the same."

Disappointed that she hasn't come up with something for me, I know she is right. It won't happen just like that. It will take time to sort all of this out.

"You know; you're right Theresa. I need to go home and sleep in my own bed. Well, technically I own both beds, but I do sleep better at home than here at the office. Yes, maybe at the house I can let it go or even come up with some answers for myself." I think about this and then add, "Both Pete and I are very positive about what we see. He is certain that what he is seeing is true, and states the fact that it is true because that is what he sees. But looking at the it from many viewpoints we get a better picture. You can look at something from one point of view and you see what the answer is. But if you look at the subject from a different point of view, you will see something else and come up with a different answer."

Theresa adds to this saying, "This is how division comes about. I totally agree with you."

"Yes," is all I can say. "See you in the morning Theresa."

I watch Theresa as she returns to her office and pay attention as she prepares to leave the building. Lights are turned off and footsteps are heard heading toward her doorway. I hear the door close behind her and then wait for the click that I know will come as she locks the entrance. Then I listen attentively for the usual, jiggle of the door handles to make sure the lock is set. Then it is my turn. I gather up all the papers and without giving them a second glance, put them in my briefcase. I go upstairs to make sure all the lights are off and then return to the office for a final look around before I let myself out, lock the door and set the alarm.

All the way home I try not to think about the case, to just let my mind drift between maneuvering my car through the traffic and what I will fix for dinner. I am a good cook and I haven't fixed myself a meal in some time. But at that instance I think that I should swing by my mother's. I toy with the idea then let the thought pass. "Her house is fine; just fine," I say aloud in the car as I continue on my way home.

I can feel the relaxation of finally pulling up into my own driveway and parking my car. I get out and gather up my stuff and watch as the porch lights come on, illuminating my path and then finally I am on my porch and opening my door. This is a quiet neighborhood and there is no need for an alarm; especially since I have my neighbor who tends to see and hear everything that happens around here.

Inside I take a moment to look at the familiar surroundings before going into the kitchen and turning on the light. I put my briefcase on the island and go over to the fridge to see what I have that will make a meal. I start taking out containers, smelling the contents and sit them near the stove.

I look at the boneless skinless chicken breasts that I had cooked and stored from an earlier meal. I open another container and see that it has some penne pasta. The wheels are turning as I go back in the fridge and take out the sun dried tomato vinaigrette dressing and add it to the items next to the stove. I then go to the pantry and take out a small can of chicken broth, the garlic powder and grab a frying pan on my way back. I open the chicken broth container and pour half of it into the skillet and then turn the pan on. While it heats, I go to the fridge and take out a half package of cream cheese, a hand full of grape tomatoes and place them on the table before getting out a container of shredded parmesan cheese and a couple leaves of fresh basil that my Mother and brought over the week before. She had proudly handed them to me like a trophy saying, "See what you can grow if you take the time." Thinking of her makes me smile.

My final conquest is a bottle of beer. I twist the cap and open it and take the first swig, letting it help my mind to remain clear and untainted by office matters. I focus on cubing the chicken and adding it to the broth, along with a dash of the sun dried tomato vinaigrette dressing, a little garlic powder and pepper. I take another swallow of the beer and stir the mixture in the frypan as I add the cheese, and grape tomatoes. Slowly the ingredients begin to take on a creamy delicious appearance and the aroma makes me hungry. When the meal is finally ready, I take the frypan off the burner and go to the cupboard for a dish. I slowly pour the contents of the pan onto my plate, trying to make it as neat as possible without any stray juices around the sides of the plate. I then add the basil and the grated cheese, giving it time to melt while I clear the counter and then wash the pan.

As I carry my meal and the rest of the beer over to the island, I sit down and then call out to my new best friend, Amazon's Alexa and ask her to play Celine Dion. She does so immediately. And with the music, the calm, and my meal my body relaxes. I was in for a night of deep sleep.

Chapter 19

The next morning, I feel chipper, actually chipper as I take my time getting ready and leisurely make my bed before doing a Fred Astaire impression as I tap dance down the stairs. In the kitchen, I turn on the Keurig and get out a traveling mug and set it on the drip tray. Then my thoughts turn to work as I take my Surface Pro out of my briefcase and set it on the peninsula. I hear the final sputter as the Keurig finishes so I press the Surface button and head over to retrieve my cup. I smile remembering that saying by Richard Whatel, "Lose an hour in the morning and you will be all day hunting for it. How true, how true.

Back at the peninsula I sign on and sit on the stool, then I am lost as I surf the internet. As I reach across the peninsula to get a paper out of my briefcase my eyes glance my Fitbit and I see its time to go so I shut the Surface of and put it back in my briefcase, grab my keys off the hook near the door and take a final survey to make sure everything is turned off and what I need with me is back in my briefcase. Satisfied, I am on my way out the door.

In the driveway I feel the warmth of the sun on my face and stop to appreciate the autumn day. Up above the sky is blue, and the trees are painted with brilliant shades of red, yellow, orange and gold. I breathe in the air and think how Autumn is a perfect season for a scenic drive through New York, viewing nature and its colorful palette, but unfortunately I get just this quick moment to enjoy it. Resolutely, I walk down the drive and climb into my car, never once checking the time just knowing that no matter what time it is, I needed to use every minute.

There are not many cars on the road though it is nearing rush hour as I make my way and skate around the one way streets as I near the downtown area. I appreciate the lack of major traffic jams found in other cities, but at times it can be a little hectic, but not this morning. When I pull into my parking space and walk the short distance to the office, I am in the best mood ever.

I am barely settled in my office when Pete appears, even before Theresa and joins me. "Want a cup of coffee Pete," I ask.

"Sure." He waits while I go into Theresa's office and turn on the pot. Instead of going back into my office while I wait, I check the mail in the box and see a letter from the Government. I find Theresa's letter opener and slit the top. "Could have guessed," I say to myself. I quickly look over the rest of the mail and see nothing urgent. By then the coffee is ready and I press the button and watch as the cup fills, knowing that Pete, like me takes it black. I fix myself a fresh cup and juggling both of them along with the letter, I carry them into my office.

I barely set the cup in front of Pete before he says, "I've been thinking."

"Yes, me too. Here, take a look at this." I hand him the letter that informs us that the Army psychiatrist is a no go.

"Well, isn't that what you thought best since they are always too busy."

"Yes, I have contacted Milo Goodman but haven't heard from him yet. It would be nice to have a positive reply from the army to back us up if Doctor Goodman isn't available."

"So," Pete says, setting aside the letter and picking up a paper that he had laid on the sofa next to his chair. He begins to read out loud. "A criminal defendant who is found to have been legally insane when he or she committed a crime may be found not guilty by reason of insanity. In some cases, the defendant may be found guilty but sentenced to a less severe punishment due to a mental impairment. In states that allow the insanity defense, defendants must prove to the court that they did not understand what they were doing; failed to know right from wrong; acted on an uncontrollable impulse or some variety of these factors." He stops and looks up questioningly. "Did you share this with Lt. Trapp?"

"That and more. He's prepared, but I will make sure I go over the details again with him."

"I watch as Pete gets up and goes over to the draped area in my office. He pulls the drapes apart and searches through the legal books, I keep there. Once he locates the one he needs, he brings the book with him and sits, thumbing through its contents. He finds what he is looking for and reads out loud again.

"Code Of Criminal Procedure, Title 1. Code Of Criminal Procedure Chapter 46c. Insanity Defense Art. 46c.002. Maximum period of commitment determined by maximum term for offense. Subchapter b. Raising the insanity defense Art. 46C.051. Notice of intent to raise insanity defense. (a) A defendant planning to offer evidence of the insanity defense must file with the court a notice of the defendant's intention to offer that evidence. (b) The notice must: (1) contain a certification that a copy of the notice has been served on the attorney representing the state; and (2) be filed at least 20 days before the date the case is set for trial, except as described by Subsection (c). (c) If before the 20-day period the court sets a pretrial hearing, the defendant shall give notice at the hearing. Art. 46C.052. Effect Of Failure To Give Notice. Unless notice is timely filed under Article 46C.051, evidence on the insanity defense is not admissible unless the court finds that good cause exists for failure to give notice."

"Get what I'm getting at? We know they are going to rush this case and if they do, we need to have this all in place in a timely fashion."

I like Pete, but he can be overpowering at times, just like this and I feel as though he doesn't think I've done my homework. "Yes, I understand all of that," I say trying not to let my annoyance show. "I have put this off until I actually have word that Milo Goodman, or someone else, is willing to take the case for the insanity plea. I also didn't want to show our hand sooner than necessary to the prosecutors. But like you said. We need to meet the deadlines so maybe we need to do this now, even if we don't have a psychiatrist on board."

"Well, I see what you are trying to do, but it could backfire too. Here in New York State the burden of proof is on the defendant so we need to keep that in mind."

"I know this is true even if we are going for a temporary insanity claim." I pause as my mind goes over what I know about such a plea. "Okay, so simply speaking, the temporary insanity defense permits factually guilty defendants to escape both punishment and institutionalization so it is seen as the perfect defense." Something comes to mind. "So it is the jury that we need to convince because, successful or not, the temporary insanity defense has always been accompanied by a storm of controversy because it is often most successful in cases where the defendant's basic claim is that honor, revenge, or tragic circumstance – not mental illness– compelled the criminal act."

"That's right, but what about success rate or even cases that we can bring up to support our case."

We both get the same idea and head back to the books. I hear Theresa come in and ask her to bring her Surface pad so that she can take notes while we concentrate on gathering the information. I then join Pete at the back of the office and we both come back with something. Pete goes first.

"It says here that the law does not excuse such behavior, even though it recognizes the fact that it was committed under great emotional stress. While the law accepts the fact that the individual was unable to deliberate about it, and the law recognizes its impulsive character, the law classifies the act as a crime and describes a penalty for it."

I continue to look through the book I have taken off the shelf and share the following: "Though the insanity defense is rarely invoked in criminal trials, it remains a controversial issue. The need for such a defense is questioned by legislators and the public. Okay, this is an example. When John Hinckley successfully used the defense after shooting President Ronald Reagan to impress the actress Jodie Foster."

"That's good," Pete says. "Here it says that the public is given a distorted view of who uses the defense and how it is employed. Whew," he says after a pause. "I didn't know that about one percent of criminal defendants invoke the defense. More important though is that the criminals rarely beat the rap by pleading insanity." He walks around silently until he finds something to share. "When an insanity defense is employed, it means the defendant admits committing the criminal behavior and is now seeking a not guilty verdict on the basis of his state of mind. If the jury does not agree, the defendant will be convicted, and generally will serve a longer sentence than will someone convicted of the same crime who has not pleaded insanity."

Pete looks over at me. "Maybe we don't want to tell your client that."

"Gotcha." I turn pages and come across the following to read out loud. "Of the defendants who plead insanity, juries find in favor of about 20 percent of the defendants. This figure does not reflect the reality that many insanity pleas are the result of plea bargains." I flip through the pages and read, "Sixty to seventy percent of insanity pleas are for crimes other than murder. They range from assault to shoplifting. The truth is that the insanity defense is a risky one at best."

"That doesn't encourage us at all," Pete says.

"Yes, but remember they are talking about the insanity defense. We are talking about temporary insanity.

This is a little harder to find as we go back to the bookshelves. I peruse one and stand interpreting the contents, "The problem of temporary insanity assumes a practical significance in connection with court trials." I look down the page and read, "It is introduced by defense attorneys in the form of a plea with the avowed purpose to bring about a mitigation. As might be expected, it is used with preference in second degree murder cases with the intent of preventing a death penalty, or, in a no-death penalty state the mandatory life sentence."

I read silently and then look at Pete. "This is it," I say. "This is the way to go. I think we can make this fly in our case."

"What is it? What does it say."

"To paraphrase it says that it is usually alleged that, at the time of the crime, the defendant acted under such great mental stress and mental tension, that he was unable to know the nature and quality of the act that he was doing, or that the act was wrong. Immediately after the homicide, the tension and mental stress is eliminated, and the defendant is able to function like any other human being".

I finish and Pete adds to this, "How is one to differentiate the state of temporary insanity from those violent emotional explosions which precede and accompany the so-called crimes of passion?"

Pete is thoughtful. "People who commit the so-called crimes of passion are usually described as being in such a state of upheaval at the time of the commission of the offense that their acts are attributed to being positive. It is felt that these people, too, are not acting reasonably, but are motivated chiefly by overwhelming passion. In short, their mental faculties are considered to be inoperative; they are thought to be unable to bring past experience to bear upon the present. Hence, they are incapable of establishing the inhibition to impulsive acts which under ordinary circumstances they are able to do" Pete looks up and smiles. "I think we're getting somewhere."

"Yes, listen to this. The law classifies the act as a crime and describes a penalty for it. In contrast, a temporary insanity plea, if accepted by the jury, often brings about a not guilty verdict."

"So, it is safe to say that one can also show in most ordinary crimes of passion that once the defendant committed the criminal act, he calmed down and returned to a humbled, reasonable and remorseful mood. In short, he returned to his senses."

I walk back to my desk and sit down.

We have been at it for some time and Theresa has been recording most of our findings. As I lean back in my chair I add, "Nevertheless, the fact is that ordinary, run of the mill individuals still end up with some sort of prison sentence. On the other hand, financially well-heeled offenders who can resort to the best of legal talent for defense, including an array of prominent psychiatrists to establish a temporary insanity plea, many times get off scot-free through a finding of not guilty". I clear my throat. "I don't think that will play well here in Rochester, even though Lt. Trapp can afford the best legal talent and prominent psychiatrists. He can, but he wants to go with us. Go figure."

196

"Well, don't sell it short yet. Besides we aren't seen as financially and famous lawyers and we can't afford a so called array of psychiatrists. Let's wait and hear what Doctor Goodman has to say."

I turn to Theresa. "I need you to prepare your notes and then we will work on a combined notice and proof of service, along with three letters. We'll do all this when you're ready."

"Yes, boss."

As she leaves the room I turn to Pete and say, "Okay, we need to create a form of notice of insanity." I guide Pete over to the table in the office where we can spread out and converse easily. Together we prepare a draft copy of the notice in my Surface.

Chapter 20

Theresa joins us again. On the wall behind her chair is my favorite saying. 'The moment when you first wake up in the morning is the most wonderful of the twenty-four hours. No matter how weary or dreary you may feel, you possess the certainty that, during the day that lies before you, absolutely anything may happen. And the fact that it practically always doesn't, matters not a jot. The possibility is always there. ~Monica Baldwin'. I direct my attention to Theresa.

"Take a seat Theresa." I wait until she has her tablet ready and then proceed. "We need to get a copy of this to Prosecuting Attorney Randall Walker," I say as I reach across the desk to hand her a folder containing some paperwork. "He has to receive this in writing. And we need to file a copy of the same with the clerk."

I pause to give her time to make her notes. "Theresa we need a letter to Colonel Tammenden." I walk over and pick up the rejection letter from the end table and hand it to her. "You can send him a similar letter to the one we prepared when we asked for the army psychiatrist. Just fix it where needed so that it makes sense."

Theresa looks over the letter and says, "There is an email address here. We could send a copy by e-mail and then one by snail mail."

"Good. Let's do that. It might not be a bad idea to set up the other documents to transmit both ways too. That is if you can get email addresses."

"No problem. I'm sure I can."

"Well, that's all for now." I watch as Theresa gets up and leaves my office then turn to Pete.

"Well, I read that if we intend to introduce expert evidence relating to a mental disease or defect or any other mental condition of the defendant in connection with the issue of guilt or punishment, we must provide expert witnesses to verify this."

"Do we have expert witnesses?"

"Not yet."

"Any expert evidence?"

"No."

Pete stares at me. "Well, let it go for now. "

"So what do you want to do now?"

"Richard, I saw an article in Newsweek on the fascination with crime fiction, that said that the crime stories fill our TVs, theaters, cinemas, computer files and book shelves. We are so fascinated with stories of crime and it doesn't matter if they are true or fiction."

"Yes, I can see that."

"My question to you is that do you think that juries today are so well versed on how TV juries work and what cases require what type of action that they judge real life against this. If so, do you think this hurts us?"

"Good question. In my opinion, and only my opinion, it's not so much the court renditions, but more the forensics that influence the jury. Think about it. The most popular crime shows don't take place in a police station or courtroom. They take place in a lab with scientists. The cops and the lawyers are not the focus."

"I don't know about that, Richard."

"Okay. Consider CSI: Crime Scene Investigation. It is the most-watched TV show in the US and has spawned two popular spin-offs. Despite the fact that much of the science the show portrays, such as instantaneous DNA and foolproof fingerprint analyses is not true in real life, the show has those computer graphics to draw us in."

"Yes, that is true," Pete adds. "Think about the real-life shows like Forensic Files. The shows only profile cases that result in convictions and air only after all appeals are exhausted, presenting guilt as a scientific certainty. But that has been exposed with last year's scandal at the Houston crime lab in which widespread contamination of evidence and employee incompetence were uncovered."

"Interesting and true, Pete, but as a thought, if these shows guide the mind than a show with the outcome we want could help the jury accept the premise of an insanity plea and make our job easier."

Pete ponders this for a minute and then adds, "The best episodes of the forensics show lay all the evidence out on the table, challenging us to solve the case along with the scientist. There is one common thread through it all and that is people lie, but evidence doesn't. And the investigators are the protectors of a system that punishes the guilty and protects the innocent."

Theresa returns with the finished letters for me to sign and as I read and sign them, she puts them into the envelopes she has prepared.

"I'll take those, Theresa." She hands the sealed envelopes back to me.

"For the sake of Lt. Trapp, I hope we're guessing right, Richard." I can tell Pete is wondering if our choice of defense is going to be too hard to prove.

I look at Pete and say nothing as we walk out the door and to my car. When I pull out, Pete says, "why not give me the envelopes and drop me off at the courthouse.

Puzzled I say, "O-k-a-y…"

"You need to go over to Lt. Trapp's and bring him up to date on yesterday's findings and I need you to ask him a question.

"What's the question?"

"Ask him if he didn't intend to kill Noah when he went to the bar with that loaded gun, just what did he intend to do? It could be important so you need to ask him and to get an answer."

"Okay. Are you going to tell me what you're thinking?

"Not just yet."

Chapter 21

Pittsford is a semi-affluent suburb of Rochester located on the Erie Canal with the distinction of being the oldest suburb and like most areas of Rochester, tall stately trees are everywhere. It is a scenic ride as I drive down Main Street with its closely nestled stores lining the way and across the sidewalks the fancy light posts catch my eye.

I had thought of living here but then I saw Irondequoit it changed my mind and I never regretted my choice. Now as I travel to the Trapp home I have time to think about what I will say to the Trapps and what I hope to accomplish. Before I know it I am pulling up to the gate which is open so that I can drive down the concrete drive to their home. I park the car and reach over to get my briefcase on the passenger's seat before climbing out and heading toward the front door. Before I can ring the bell, the door opens and I am greeted by Lt. Trapp.

"Good morning Richard. Can I get you something to drink?"

"No, I'm fine for now, Lt. Trapp" I say sure my surprise is written all over my expression. When something is as beautiful as the Trapp home, you never get use to seeing it. From the entrance way to the scenery all around it, the estate is something to behold.

"It's Vincent, remember?"

"Sorry, you just surprised me. I usually have time to just admire your home and having the door open suddenly caught me in the midst of just letting myself settle into the ambiance here."

"Did you know that this is the oldest house in the Town of Pittsford."

"So the house has historical significant?"

"Yes it does. It was built in 1793 by the nephew of the town co-founder, Simon Stone, a lawyer like yourself, but unlike you he built a farm instead of spending his time golfing."

"Well, it doesn't look or feel that old."

"That wasn't always the case. The house and the acreage fell into disrepair before it was purchased in 1948 by a Doctor and Mrs. Clifford Ford. They restored the property and took great care in keeping with its historic character, though they added modern amenities. They lived here until their deaths. I heard about the property and my wife and I fell in love with it so we purchased it, developed the surrounding acreage and remodeled the home to its present style."

"You did a bang up job."

"Thanks Richard. I'm telling you this to give a picture of who I am. I am not a rich man who doesn't care about the area. I am not someone who sees himself as better than others." Vincent pauses and says, "Come here. I want to show you something."

I follow Vincent as he takes me through the house and out to the gardens. We walk to the edge of the lawn and he points. "I don't know if you are aware, but that area is where the walking trails start for the Great Embankment Park. It's right there, just steps from our door."

I look out at the treed area with tall grass and a few wild flowers still in bloom. Its beauty hides the truth of what took place not so long ago.

Vincent interrupts the silence. "But that's not why you came here; to get a history lesson." He turns around and I follow. We start our walk back to the patio behind the house and when we step onto the stone walkway, Vincent says, "What's on your mind, Richard."

"I almost forgot why I came. I enjoyed learning about the area. But you're right, I did have a reason for coming". I divulge what I have learned about the events leading up to the shooting from people in the area and some who had information communicated to them. I convey how I had gone to the location in the park and investigated as well as making a trip to the Founder's Café to see what further I could learn.

"Here, have a seat. You've been busy."

If you only knew, I said to myself. I tried to give him only the details that he really needed to know and nothing more. Information like what I learned about Tyra Pederson was not something I felt necessary to share, or the reluctance of some to tell me what they knew. In this way I might learn how he felt on the topics, plus that was not information that was proven to be true or necessary to share at this point. But there was something more to tell.

"Vincent, did you know that Noah Arietta was an expert shot?"

Vincent doesn't hesitate. "Yes, I'd heard about it and I saw his medals displayed behind the bar."

"Did you know or ever hear that he owned a lot of guns and pistols and that he kept some behind the bar?"

"Sure. It was common knowledge around the village that he owned quite a collection of guns and kept some at the bar."

"What else did you know about Noah?"

"Well, let me think a minute." I watch as his dark brows knit together. "Oh yes, someone once told me that Noah one night had a dispute with some guys who were getting out of hand. The way I heard the story was from a regular patron of the bar who was talking, quite loudly I might say, to his friend. He said that two middle aged men got into it inside the Founders Café Bar after the two participated in an argument over who was to be served next. The bartender admitted he did not know who had come in first and tried to get the men to cool off, but to no avail. The argument grew into pushing and shoving until the bartender had to signal for Mr. Arietta to come over. It seems that when Mr. Arietta came to his aid he joined him behind the bar. Mr. Arietta first tried to get the men's attention and since that didn't work, he yelled and told them to take it outside. When he got no reaction to that he reached down behind the bar and produced a semi-automatic weapon. I didn't know until then that he had heavy artillery. I thought about turning him in, but…"

"You knew about that confrontation the night of the shooting."

"Sure I did. I hear a lot in that bar."

"But you weren't there when it happened just heard about it."

"True."

"Did you ever see any of his guns yourself?"

"No, can't say that I have."

"Do you happen to know how I can get in touch with the guy who saw Noah produce the pistol?"

Vincent is thoughtful, his eyes mere slits, his heavy black eyebrows lowered. "Not for sure, but I could give you a possible lead if you need it."

"Good. Can you write it down?" I take out a pad and pen and pass it across the table to him.

"Did you know that Noah was also a trained fighter. I mean that he had taken lessons in defense."

"Noah was a bragger so I heard something about it, yes. Paige confirmed that when she told me he bragged to her about how he knew Judo."

"When did she tell you that," I ask.

"She told me that when I was taken to jail. Either at the jail or on the way there. Not sure which."

I take a moment to write down some details and then go on. "So, knowing that Noah was well trained in using guns and knowing that he was a trained fighter, you still decided to face him that night at the café bar."

Vincent hesitates. "Yes, he grudgingly admits, yes, I knew he was considered to be pretty good in both departments."

"Nevertheless, you had the guts-- the courage to walk in and face him."

Vincent looked at me sharply. "He raped my wife. No way I wasn't going to get revenge."

I could see and feel the intense anger coming from Vincent as he spoke and the use of the word 'revenge' made me hesitate at the moment to go further. I need to turn the subject away from this stressful topic. I remember that Pete wanted me to ask Vincent a question and I promised to get him an answer so I have to continue even though I don't want to upset the man.

"Vincent, if you didn't intend to kill Noah Arietta that night when you went to the bar with a loaded gun, what did you intend to do?"

"I don't know, but I knew he had guns so I wasn't going to take a chance of a face down with him. In my head all I wanted to do was grab hold of him, shake him up. Let him know I was angry and that he wouldn't get away with it."

"What do you mean exactly by grab him and hold him, or shake him up. You've had military training so you had a good chance of besting him."

"I can't explain it except that is what I wanted to do to him. I believe that this man had raped Paige, he needed to pay for it. Don't you see, it made me crazy to know what he had done and I thought about him doing it again to not just Paige, but some other women as well and it made me sick with fury. I saw red and I thought that he might be crazy enough to come after me too so I wanted to turn him in before he fled. I knew that was what this type of man would do. He would run like a coward."

Vincent is out of breath, his face red and his eyes mere slits. Cautiously I ask. "You were holding him for whom?"

"For the cops, I guess. All I know is that I had a feeling I had to go get him before he skipped town or got me. I simply had to protect myself and Paige."

"Did you mean to kill him?"

Shock replaced the anger as Vincent stares at me. "No, no. I didn't plan to kill him, only to stop him." He pauses. "If he had attacked me and I was threatened, I would have killed him."

"Did he? Did he try to attack you?"

"I can't say for sure," Vincent says as he scratches his forehead. "It all happened so fast. It's all kind of a blur."

"Just tell me what you remember. Think hard."

Vincent gets up from the chair and walks around the patio, then returns and sits back down. "Well, when I got to the Academy Apartment Building, I parked my car and stood by the side of it for a moment. Then I went into the bar. This, this Noah guy was behind the bar facing the mirror where the shelves for the booze were so his back was to me."

"I see him in the mirror and he stares back at me. We watch each other and it is as though we are the only two people in the bar. I move forward and when I am halfway between the door and the bar, he turns around quickly as if anticipating trouble. I watch him closely as he drops his left arm onto the bar, but I can't see his right arm. He keeps that down behind the bar. I stare at him and see his lips moving as though he is saying something, but I can't hear him."

Vincent is quiet while he takes a sip of water, "I guess I shot him then. I can't remember anything after that."

An uncomfortable silence fell as we sat there surrounded by the beautiful gardens and feeling the warmth of the sun. I think he has had enough, but there is something else pressing on my mind. "Vincent, if you felt you needed to hold him or to keep him from running, why didn't you take out your cell phone and dial 9-1-1?"

"I guess that would have been the smart thing to do. I know it would, but I wasn't thinking straight and never thought to call anyone."

"Thanks, Vincent for giving it to me straight." I wanted to say, thank you to Pete too for helping me solve one of our biggest headaches. He had given me the question that needed answers and now the pieces were beginning to fall into place.

"Well, look at the two of you!"

Startled, we both turn to see Paige Trapp with her little dog Enzo coming towards us. We both watch as she walks over and quickly kisses her husband and then comes over to shake my hand. She is wearing a full skirted A-line black dress, fitted at the waist below a deep V-neck bodice that is sensibly low instead of sexy. The dress covers her knees and she wears sensible black heels. As I watch her go around the table and take a seat, I think that this would be a passible outfit for court if we added in the glasses for a bonus effect.

"I'm glad you're joining us, Paige. You missed what I told Vincent, but he can tell you all that later. I have some questions for you too."

"I'd be shocked if you didn't."

"Well, I'll leave you two..."

"No, Vincent, you can hear what I have to say to Paige. Please stay. You might be able to help too."

With everyone seated again I begin. "Paige did you get the photographs and make the doctor appointment?"

"Yes I did. The pictures will be ready tomorrow and the doctor will let us know."

"Great. Now a question to you both. Have either of you ever met Tyra Pederson?"

The sun shines and reflects off the glass of the table, making it hard to see the expression on either of their faces. "Yes, we both have," Paige replies. "I found her to be charming." Vincent nods in agreement.

"Do you know anything about her. She worked for Noah, you know." I needed to know all that they did about their personal knowledge of Tyra.

"Well," Paige said, "I did hear stories about her and Noah." She looks directly at me and adds, "But as far as I know she is a perfect lady. There was a young man who was sweet on her, too."

"Who was that?"

"I don't remember". She looks at her husband. "Vincent do you know?"

I turned toward Vincent. "Yes, a fellow named Ian Solenhauser."

"Do you know about the relationship. Were the two of them serious?"

Paige and Vincent look at each other and they both shrug their shoulders. "Lord, I don't know, Richard," Paige says; "It could be just a summer flirtation or serious. I don't know."

"Vincent, what do you think?"

"I wouldn't know about the personal affairs of Ian or Tyra" he says.

"How about the bartender, Hamilton?" I ask.

"How about him," Vincent says. "He makes a great drink."

"He was always sweet to me," Paige adds. "He was thoughtful to us after the shooting."

I sat up straighter, sensing something important was about to be said. "How do you mean?"

"Well he came and offered to drive me down to the jail to see Vincent that first Sunday. I was in no shape to drive."

I listened attentively. "Anything else?"

"On the way he told me how sorry he was for Vincent and me and…"

"And what?" I say impatiently.

"And he said he could have told me that Noah was a wolf."

I look at her. "You mean Noah's bartender said that he could have warned you that Noah was a wolf? He used that exact word? He said, 'wolf?'"

"Yes he did, Richard. Didn't I tell you that before. He also said that Noah had been drinking heavily lately and that it was too bad we had come to the café when we did? Does that help anything?"

I think about what she said and then ask, "In what context did he share this?"

"Oh, sorry Richard. It was when I asked what type of man Mr. Arietta was. He first said that he was quite the man when sober, but he had a drinking problem like most bar owners did."

"It might help. Can you remember anything else?" When she shakes her head, no, I turn toward the Lieutenant, "anything at all to add Vincent?"

"Yes, the bartender Hamilton told me how sorry he was for my trouble and said that he wanted me to know that for his part the only thing he had against me was that when I shot Noah I broke a bottle of Jim Beam Single Barrel and that it was the best-selling brand of Kentucky straight bourbon in the world. One bottle cost thirty-five dollars."

"He used those terms?"

"About the bourbon?" I roll my eyes. "Sorry, couldn't resist. Yes, he said those exact words concerning the man."

"What happened next?"

"Well, the bartender left the bar saying he had to talk to some clients. Paige, as you know, stayed after I left because she wanted to play the Frogger video game. It's not something I enjoy doing."

"Have either of you seen him since." I feel I need to clarify, "I mean the bartender?"

"I look at Paige and see her shaking her head. I saw him once on the street near the café. Naturally I haven't been back in the café since it happened. He paused briefly and inquired about Vincent and then hurried on his way. That's the last either of us have seen or heard of him."

"Was there any more talk about Noah, when you met him on the street?"

"No, just as I've told you..." I could see her thinking and then she adds, "Now that you speak of it, it does seem he was sort of restrained and reticent. And in a hurry. About all he did was say hello, ask about Vincent and then he was gone."

This differs greatly from what I had learned and what I learned was after Tyra Pederson laid down the law. What had happened? Here was a man who'd gone out of his way to be nice to the Trapps at one instance and calls his deceased boss a wolf and Mrs. Trapp on the level of a floozy. Just what was the score here. How much was true and how much was fiction.

This seemed the right time to now share with the Trapp's that the army psychiatrist was not going to represent our case and that we needed to get a psychiatrist in time for the trial. I let them know that things were moving along and it looked as though the date for the trial would be set somewhere around September, 2016. That's not a lot of time.

To put it in perspective I let them know that from the date of his arrest on July 31st that was a year and a month before we would be in court so I would be actively working on their case from here on out. I assured them that I was currently looking for a psychiatrists and had several irons in the fire, but if they had any suggestions to let me know. I can't think of anything more to say.

"Do you have anything you want to cover?" I ask and when they are both shaking their heads, no, I stand up. They follow suit.

"Well that's all I need for now. Goodbye to both of you."

In unison they both say Goodbye and walk with me to the front of the house. I turn before getting into my car and take in the view of the two of them arm and arm and think, "That's a picture for the photographers".

Chapter 22

In the car I marvel at how great the weather is holding off the signs of the coming winter and lingering in the fall season. It uplifts me and makes me feel as though I can do anything as I drive to the main road and turn toward downtown Rochester.

There is still not much traffic on the road and taking Route 31 to 490 I pull into the parking area of the court house in downtown Rochester, fifteen minutes later. As previously arranged, my comrades had asked that I pick them up here since they planned on doing a little research on their own.

***

Begun in 1894, this is the third courthouse built in Rochester. It is a unique example of the Italianate style of architecture which is not what most would consider for a public building. Unfortunately, I am not here to marvel at the structure so I hurry to the entrance.

Inside the building I cannot help admiring the impressive staircase, and marble floors and walls as I enter the echoing hallways in search of Pete and Theresa. My shoes reverberate on the floors as I hurry from one place to another on the first level with no luck. I take the stairs to the second floor thinking I might find them there in either the library or the café so I travel the tangle of corridors to the back of the courtroom and enter the law library.

Leather bound books fill the recessed bookcases around the perimeter of the room while computer screen monitors glow at every wooden desk structure. The room is void of decorative touches beyond these books and monitors and at the moment it is almost deserted. I leave and peek into empty court rooms on my way back.

I continue down the empty corridors and come to the attorney conference rooms. Upon opening the hall door I find the front room is empty but I can see the entryway to the prosecuting attorney's office is open so I walk that way and peek in and see that the office is not currently occupied. I hesitate in the doorway a moment wanting to go in, but decide it would not be wise so I leave. I next check out the court stenographer's office and find it too is empty. Where can they be, I wonder and where is everyone else.

On chance, I go and try the heavy mahogany door of the judge's chamber and find it is unlocked. I push it open and step in. The door snaps shut making me jump in surprise. When my breathing settles down I realize I am alone in the chamber.

In all my years as a lawyer, not once have I wanted to be a judge knowing the extent of the job. It is not easy for judges. They have to preside over the proceedings and see that order is maintained. They need to determine whether any of the evidence that the parties want to use is illegal or improper. They are responsible to give the jury instructions about the law that applies to the case and the standards it must use in deciding the case. Then they have to sentence convicted criminal defendants. It is too much responsibility and would be very demanding for me. It takes me a minute to get my feet going again and I leave the room to enter the back of a court room.

Inside the cool interior, I take it all in from the back view. I look over at the judge's bench in the center of the back wall area flanked on the right by the court clerk and on the left by the witness stand. I stare out at the court reporters desk and the jury box and a distance away at the counsel tables, each with two seats behind them and I think, so structured, so powerful in its presentation that it takes my breath away. I have been in here for quite a while, but I can't help it. It's like the room hypnotizes me and I forget what I am doing. Finally, I gain control and leave the courtroom in search of my two lost comrades.

It's getting late as I decide to go downstairs to the lower level and see if maybe they found their way there. I hurry, hanging onto the railing until I stand on the floor below the entrance area. I take a step forward and stop. I sense this is where they are. It's the steel floored filing vault of the probate court. I lean into the entrance door and push. When it opens I allow my eyes to adjust before moving forward. This room is a vault since it encompasses all matters and proceedings. These records as well as the room is private. In many instances, the probate records are the only known source of relevant facts such as the decedent's date of death, names of his or her spouse, children, parents, siblings, in-laws, neighbors, associates, relatives, and their places of residence. Here one can also find information about adoption or guardianship of minor children and dependents.

I hear them before I see them. Pete is holding a paper and dictating stealthily to Theresa. They are so engrossed in what they are doing that they didn't even hear me enter. "Come on guys, we need to go."

"Give us five more minutes, please, and be quiet."

I wait for them to finish what they are doing and then we head out together. "What did you find in there?"

Neither one answers.

"Come on, share."

"Wait until we're alone, man. This stuff is hot."

I can't tell if they are pulling my leg or this is for real as we climb into the car and Pete is all apologetic. He explains that they were in luck and found the Noah Arietta file.

I could see it on their face that they hit pay dirt. They had dug out the probate records in the new file entitled: Estate of Noah Arietta, Deceased. The file had been set up the Monday following the shooting, the day I got the case. Tyra Pederson had filed the petition for probate of the Will, listing as required by law, a daughter, Bernadine Arietta, age sixteen, as the sole heir *at law*, living in Pensacola, Florida but the Will left everything to Tyra Pederson, and was dated as the bartender had said, about three weeks before the shooting. The next important paper had been an appearance and notice of Will contest filed by a Pensacola Lawyer on behalf of a Janice Arietta, individually and as guardian of the daughter, Bernadine, attacking the Will on just about all the classic grounds a Will can be attacked on, including undue influence and lack of testamentary capacity on the part of Noah Arietta on the grounds of his excessive drinking and alcoholism.

"Janice Arietta?" I said, "that would be the child's mother and Noah's divorced wife."

"Correct," Pete said dryly, "except that the lady does not concede to be the divorced wife; she has filed a notice and a collection of supporting affidavits claiming that the Pensacola divorce between her and Noah was void because she had never been served with process or received adequate notice of Noah's divorce action against her."

"Oh that's rich. We'll need to verify that. From what I do know filing for divorce means you have given your petition for dissolution of marriage to the clerk's office of the circuit court for the county where you are filing. The petition must be notarized before filing with the court and you'll give a copy of your signed and notarized petition to the clerk, along with the filing fee for a dissolution of marriage, and they should give you a copy with a date stamp and notation showing that it has been filed with the court."

I think about this and add, "We need to find out about the details on a Florida Divorce and a New York State Divorce if we find he issued his through New York. I'm sure he made a copy of the petition for himself, as well as an additional copy to serve on his spouse. What's her angle?" I went on, "Surely after all these years the woman must have known she was divorced."

Why in hell should she be trying to undivorce herself now?"

"Money," Pete answered, hugging his shoulders and rubbing his dry palms together. "Just the same old dreary love story, money. I found this," he says shuffling through some papers. "It says that effective July 7, 2008, the designation of your spouse as beneficiary of certain benefits is revoked if you get a divorce, annulment or judicial separation and the court receives written notice, unless you have a Domestic Relations Order (DRO) on file that specifies otherwise. The designation is revoked regardless of when the final decree of divorce, annulment or judicial separation was entered. Which means she doesn't have a case."

"Let's check into it though."

"No problem, but don't you see, Richard? If this woman can dump his old divorce and the Will, she will come in for her wife's share of Noah's property, the daughter getting the other share. If she can dump the divorce alone, even if the Will is sustained, she'll come in for her statutory widow's third and certain other loot, come hell or high water, even if the daughter is let out in the cold. And her Florida lawyer is' no slouch either. I checked him out already".

"Yes," I said, "but how can she expect to come into a New York probate court and attempt to make a collateral attack on a Florida decree of divorce? That's forbidden, isn't it, under the 'full faith and credit' clause of the constitution?"

"Generally, Richard," Pete conceded. "But she also alleges that she is initiating action down there to set aside the Florida divorce. Furthermore, if she claims to be Noah's wife, it seems to me that it might be up to Tyra Pederson to disprove it."

"Yes, Pete, now it looks like we're not only got Lieutenant Trapp's murder case to defend, but Noah Arietta's will and divorce as well."

"Pete smiled. "How do you mean, he said. "I figured you to say what's that to us?"

"Well you're wrong, Pete because this Will contest and divorce business are plainly affecting our man's chances to win this case. That's why Tyra Pederson and the rest of the Founder's cafe crowd have clammed up. Can't you see? It's to protect the Will, not primarily to hurt us. If they can protect their precious Will, Tyra Pederson will still get roughly two thirds of the loot, come what may, even if the former wife dumps the divorce, then Pederson will get everything if she can disqualify both the Will and the divorce. So that's why they can't allow Noah to be seen as a boozer and a womanizer."

"That's just what I figured, too," Pete says dryly.

That's why the bartender suddenly clammed up with the Trapps," I ran on. "That's why he's now willing to make Paige appear as a loose woman. That's why Tyra Pederson is willing to let our man possibly hang rather than let us get at the truth. This is a vexing problem to say the least".

"But what do we care about all this," Theresa said. "How can all this possibly affect our Lieutenant?"

"Because, I said, "this rape, is the golden key to our defense. Anything that sheds any doubt on that brutal fact hurts our case.

"I still don't get it"

"Look, one of the biggest areas of possible doubt in this whole matter is that who will believe that a sober man in his right mind would do what Noah did. To the extent that these people successfully picture Noah as a sober, god-fearing, un-pistol packing boy scout, and try to pull down Paige Trapp in the process, they will cast doubt on our story and at the same time build up sympathy for the late departed. What's more, it happens not to be the truth."

"I see, Theresa said frowning."

There is silence in the car. "What did you mean when you just said the bartender had clammed up with the Trapps?" Pete demanded. "When did that happen?"

"Things are breaking so fast I haven't had time to tell you". I enlightened Pete on what I had just learned from the Trapps about the bartender's expression of sympathy the day after the shooting and then the next time they meet, his sudden aloofness. "It's all tying in, now" I continue. "He's Tyra's star witness and her key man to sustain the Will. Lord knows what his slice of the pie will be." As an afterthought I add, "Probably a cut of the bar."

There is a moment of silence while each of us is in deep thought. Pete breaks the silence.

"On another subject, the records show that Bryan Atwater is Tyra Pederson's lawyer," Pete said. "As you know, Bryan is a shrewd probate and estate lawyer. He won't brief his case till he has to and unfortunately our trial will be over and done before this Will contest is heard. That's still another good reason why our murder case should be prolonged and by then the Will contest and all would be over and done. Then it wouldn't matter whether they win or lose, the heat would be off.

"There will doubtless be an appeal from probate whichever way it goes, so a continuance in our case is not the answer. God what a mess."

"But just think of the law Richard, the law," Pete breathed ecstatically. "think of all the sweet lovely law we've got to research. I can scarcely wait to get at it. Shall we go to the office and start now?"

"I'm with you. I won't object to getting a head start." I fumble with the keys in the ignition and remove one. "Here, Pete, we're partners so you should have access to the office at all times. This key opens the front door of my office."

"Thanks Richard," Pete said, soberly pocketing the key. "Thank you, my friend, I'll use it tonight."

"And there's one interesting subject you might start brushing up on right off the bat," I said. "The law of the right of a private person to make an arrest without a warrant for a felony committed out of his presence. Thanks to you, that subject is now right smack in the middle of our case."

Pete's eyes lit up with eagerness. "You remembered to ask him?" he said excitedly. "You asked him my question? Tell me what he said?" That's another one I dreamt up last night in my sleepless bed, Richard. Don't you see? It opens up vistas." He paused and blinked his eyes and shook his head. "Beautiful rolling vistas of lovely law and instructions.

At that moment Pete looked almost indecently happy. I envied him for here was one of those rare and lucky mortals whose main hobby, at least next to whisky, happened also to be his profession; the law. It was not just a job to him. It had become his life.

PART 2
PRE TRIAL

Chapter 1

There was no doubt that Pete Adams had changed. He smiles more easily and appears each day clean shaven, though he keeps is mustache, chin hair and that little bit of hair under his lower lip. His hair is still long, laying just above his shoulders, but it is now shiny and organized. It's hard to believe that this man use to drink his way through each day and seemed to enjoy being a loner. Even having been friends for a long time, I can't remember ever seeing Pete so relaxed and, yes, happy.

From the minute he heard the Lieutenant's response to his question, Pete was anxious and couldn't wait to get started researching the case. I had to force him to get something to eat, told him to try and sleep and we would have at it early the next morning. Resignedly he agreed, but whether or not he would actually do it, I wouldn't know because I, aware of how we would proceed from here, am anxious to get some sleep too.

After saying our goodbyes, I showed my comrades to the door, locked up the office and headed home feeling as though something was about to change only I couldn't identify what or how. On the way home I stop by my mother's. Everything is quiet at the homestead so I continue on my way. I put a CD into the player and allow the music to soothe me and by the time I enter my home I am more than ready to sleep. I lock the door behind me, leaving my briefcase and keys on the entry way table and head up the stairs. In minutes I am asleep.

The alarm goes off and I feel happy as I sit up and stretch before going about my morning rituals. By the time I am ready to leave I am feeling refreshed and anxious to start the day.

The weather has taken a turn and the air has a slight chill as I make my way to the car. As I back out of my driveway and head toward town, the weather reflects my mood with the sun streaming through the leaves of the trees and warming the side of my face. I open the sun roof cover just so I can let as much light in as possible. I feel great. I turn the car radio to a news channel and hear the weather report. It is more for sound than for listing as it doesn't matter what the weather will be since we plan on spending the day in the office doing research. With my law books and the internet there is no need to go out and in the privacy of the office, we can discuss issues at length.

I am earlier than usual as I make my way to the office and am not surprised to find Pete already in the office when I arrive.

"Started the coffee," Pete says.

"Great. I didn't make a cup this morning or stop off to get one," I said. "I can see you are already hitting the books".

"Yes, I am. I thing we need to start at the base and work up, not taking anything for granted. I have been reading this New York Penal Law §125.25 for Murder in the second degree and it states that second degree Murder is an unlawful killing that is both willful and premeditated, meaning that it was committed after planning or 'lying in wait' for the victim."

"Okay, I guess we're starting," I said then in response to his reading added, "Sounds about right. It would be second degree if Vincent Trapp went to the park and found Noah Arietta raping his wife and then the next day he goes to the Founders Café and seeks out Noah, shoots and kills him. So, in our situation though Vincent did not witness the rape, he did hear about it and then later went to find Noah and shot him. Second degree, no doubt."

"Right, Richard. It also says that there is a case for felony murder if a person commits first-degree murder during a felony such as arson, burglary, kidnapping, rape and robbery and a death results during a felony."

"Okay," I say, giving it some thought. So, I can't see this working for us at all." I pause and start walking around the office. "Let's see, State laws categorize murder into first, second and possibly third degrees. Generally, second degree murders include three basic elements: willfulness, deliberation and premeditation. "

"That's right," Pete says as he flips through the book he has been carrying around with him. But remember it is not always cut and dry. He finds what he is looking for. "It says here that in terms of willfulness, second degree murderers must have the specific intent to end a human life. This intent does not necessarily have to be focused on the actual victim. A murder in which the killer intends to kill but kills the wrong person or a random person would still constitute second degree murder."

He continues to turn the pages and reads more. "Whether a killer acted with the deliberation and premeditation required for second degree murder can only be determined on a case by case basis. The need for deliberation and premeditation does not mean that the perpetrator must contemplate at length or plan far ahead of the murder. Time enough to form the conscious intent to kill and then act on it after enough time for a reasonable person to second guess the decision typically suffices. While this can happen very quickly, deliberation and premeditation must occur before, and not at the same time as, the act of killing."

"Okay," I add having turned on my computer and opened up the internet to a legal site, "And then there is malice aforethought where perpetrators of second degree murder must have acted with malice which generally includes an evil disposition or purpose and an indifference to human life."

"I think we are getting somewhere here."

I leave the office and get a cup of coffee and sit down at my desk, then remembering, I get up and walk over to the book cases.

"Hey Richard, listen to this. "Defenses to second degree murder charges fall into two major categories: claims that the defendant did not commit the killing in question, and admission that the defendant committed the killing, but did not commit second degree murder."

I stop what I am doing and listen carefully to Pete. "It goes on to say that defendants admitting to having killed the victim can assert defenses that they were justified in doing so for example in self defense, or that they were somehow incapacitated and thus not legally liable. These defenses require the defendant to put forth proof to support his or her defense." Pete pauses and looks over the top of the book in my direction. "That might be interesting for us."

"I think you might have something there, Pete. Mark the page". Here use this paper clip." I hand him a paper clip and watch as Pete puts it over the edge of the page."

"There's more too. It says second degree murder defendants also may simply argue that the prosecution has not proved all elements of a second degree murder charge typically that the defendant killed willfully, deliberately and with premeditation. Though the defendant may support such an argument with evidence, he or she is not required to do so, as proof of all elements of the crime falls on the shoulders of the prosecution."

"That's right, I know. We can count on arguments of proof from all angles from the prosecutor for sure so we have to have our rebuttals in order."

Pete shakes his head in agreement and continues looking through the book. "Something here about mistaken identity."

"That doesn't fly. We know who murdered Noah and the prosecutor knows because Vincent admitted he killed him.

"In your discovery did you come up with any argument for justified homicide, because it says here that not all homicides are crimes, let alone second degree murders. The most common legal justification for a killing is self-defense or the defense of others."

"Yes, Pete," I say thoughtfully. "Because Noah's hand was kept out of sight behind the bar and the fact that the guns had a shelf in that vicinity Vincent could be seen as shooting to preserve his life or in self-defense, but he would have to know that Noah had the guns there and Noah would have had to aimed the gun at Vincent. Plus, it would be hard to prove that Vincent didn't instigate the threatening situation and as for defending his wife the use of force must be timely and proportional to the threat faced, and the perceived threat of death or bodily harm must be reasonable."

I pause and like Pete I continue searching while talking and eventually find what I am looking for. I share it with Pete. "The Insanity Defense as a charge of second degree murder. It says here being cognitively unable to appreciate the quality of the act being committed, or unable to realize that the act is wrong."

"That's it. It seems the only way to go with this. Temporary insanity." Pete goes over to his desk area and searches through some papers. He finds what he is looking for and adds, "Temporary insanity in a criminal prosecution is a defense by the accused that he was briefly insane at the time the crime was committed and therefore was incapable of knowing the nature of his alleged criminal act."

Somewhere along the way, Theresa has delivered a pizza and bottles of water that we eat between discoveries. The books pile up on our desks and the copies printed off the internet are delivered to us by a silent Theresa as we continue our research until Theresa tells us it's time to stop, go home and get some rest.

The days run into one another without change as we go over and over our findings making sure that when we reach a decision, we have made the right choice for our client's defense.

***

Days turn into weeks and weeks into months before we settle on the defense. In between times we have talked with the Lieutenant and his wife to help solidify our defense.

"I think we can make it work. Temporary insanity is claimed as a defense whether or not the accused is mentally stable at the time of trial." I do a search on the internet and see something encouraging.

"Listen to this Pete, "The Twinkie defense is a derisive label for an improbable legal defense. It is not a recognized legal defense, but a catchall term coined by reporters during coverage of the trial of a defendant named Dan White. Dan White murdered San Francisco city Supervisor Harvey Milk and Mayor George Moscone. White's defense was that he suffered diminished capacity as a result of his depression. His change in diet from healthful food to Twinkies and other sugary foods was said to be a symptom of depression. Contrary to common belief, White's attorneys did not argue that the Twinkies were the cause of White's actions, but that their consumption was symptomatic of his underlying depression. White was convicted of voluntary manslaughter."

Pete jumps in, "Yes, I've heard of it and the fact that most see the Twinkie defense as a gross miscarriage of justice. The main focus of the defense's case was diminished capacity -- that White had suffered from periodic bouts of depression, amounting to "a major mental illness. The truth be told, Dan White was an angry young man who should have received the death penalty but instead was convicted of voluntary manslaughter and got a meager sentence of less than eight years and with time off for good behavior, he would end up serving a little over five years."

"I see what you're saying here. He got a lighter sentence and the case was based on blaming food. Hm, we have a better case than food to support the Lieutenant's actions, but Pete, we don't have the same ingredients. Dan killed a major and a gay politician back when that was not something you announced. Our case is less flamboyant, for lack of a better term."

"That's not it. The similarities to look at is that there was no question, like our Lieutenant, that Dan White was guilty and if we are lucky, the prosecution, like then, may think it is such a clear-cut case they don't do their job, because that is what got Dan White a lighter sentence."

***

There was so much data to makes note and eventually like each day before, the information we have uncovered has been given to Theresa to prepare for our files which are growing by leaps and bounds. Lucky for us, Theresa organizes the pages making it easy for us to find what we need.

Some days the topics run together and others end with a possibility or a need to thing, regroup and attack from another angle. On one of our bull sessions I go back to the Dan White case and say, "The picking of the jury will be very important. It says here that when the jury listened to Dan White's confession, some of them wept. That would mean that we need to make sure we fill the box with sympathetic jurors maybe that recognize our clients service history and the fact that he is still involved in keeping our country safe. That may be as good an image as we can get since we can't count on getting in the rape."

"I agree wholeheartedly, that and keeping the topic on task or it could turn and bite us." Pete pauses. "The Lieutenant went to Noah's business with a gun that he emptied in his victim and we want them to declare he suffered from diminished capacity and depression when his actions reek of premeditation. At least unlike White, the Lieutenant didn't reload his revolver. Lucky for White the jury was mindful that they had to take into account "reasonable doubt," or they may not have given him the lesser charge."

I am typing away as I listen. "Temporary insanity is difficult to prove, as it requires the defense to demonstrate to the court a credible reason the accused was insane when the crime was committed, but is sane at the time of the trial." Pete is thoughtful. "Since any psychiatric evaluations on the case can only occur after the incident, it can be difficult to obtain credible medical testimony on such matters."

"That's why we hired Doctor Milo Goodman."

Pete is pensive, then looks at me questioningly. "Tell me about him Richard. Tell me why you think he is our man."

I don't take offense since I know how important this choice will be. "Well, for starters I knew we needed a forensic psychiatrist since they focus on the interface of law and mental health. We also wanted him to be able to handle psychiatric consultation in a wide variety of legal matters and provide expert testimony. That was my starting point."

I could tell that Pete approved so I continued to the not so obvious points. When I had looked up the doctors online, I found several who posted their pictures along with their credentials. Dr. Goodman was one of them. "I also liked that he had lots of experience in all these areas. I went to my Surface and started going through my files until I found what I wanted. I carried the Surface over to Pete. "Here, read this."

I waited patiently as Pete reads about a recent case that Dr. Goodman had successfully convinced the jury and the judge that the man, a one time offender, had murdered his wife. Pete reads, then aloud mouths the highlights of the case. "…Hennessey was charged with killing his wife Vanessa by stabbing her 26 times with a kitchen knife… It should also be noted that Hennessey was the one who called the police reporting an attempted burglary though the police found no signs of a break in. The case drew much publicity in New York not only for the heinous crime, but because it was a case of homicidal somnambulism, or simply known as sleepwalking murder." Pete pauses and looks up at me before continuing. "The defendant was not in his normal state of mind when he committed the act. Sleep walking is a parasomnia manifested by automatism; as such, harmful actions committed while in this state cannot be blamed on the perpetrator… Hennessey claimed he did not remember the crime and was sleeping at the time, hence the murder while sleepwalking. Not only that, he did not deny the fact that he murdered his wife. In his criminal trial, the jury found him not guilty on the grounds that he was temporarily insane when he committed the crime. Although Hennessey fabricated the story about the intruders, he walked away as a free man. Members of the jury were also quoted later to saying they were aware that they were releasing a killer but he was not criminally responsible for his actions."

There is silence as Pete, looks as though he is in a trance. "Wow," he says, "Wow." I walk over and pull up another file that has a picture of the Doctor. "There are several cases like that one he has help win recently, but I think this one supports my choice. Also," I add, going over and opening another file, "Here's a picture of him."

There is no doubt he is an extremely handsome black man, but that wasn't our focus. We had both read the study that appeared in the journal *Psychology, Crime & Law* that said there were certain facial features that make an individual look more trustworthy — higher eyebrows, more pronounced cheekbones, rounder face. Our guy had it all, plus more. "We also need an image of someone who though successful and rich, doesn't look the part so that the jury can concentrate on the case."

Puzzled, Pete says, "I don't get it."

"Well, Pete, when a man like Vincent Trapp is brought before a jury we need a buffer. Vincent is rich, privileged, handsome and flaunts it…"

"I see what you mean. So what is his credentials?"

"Glad you ask." I open another file and start reading. "Milo S. Goodman M.D. is an active clinician and expert witness. As a specialist in Forensic Psychiatry, his testimony has had a major impact in high profile cases. Doctor Milo S. Goodman, is Assistant Professor of Psychiatry and Human Behavior at The Thomas Jefferson University College of Medicine and a Special Guest Lecturer at Widener University School of Law. He completed a residency in psychiatry at the Albany Medical Center Hospital and Syracuse. He completed a fellowship in forensic psychiatry at Syracuse University College of Medicine. He has been an Expert Reviewer for the United States Department of Justice Special Investigation Unit and a Member of the Delaware Governor's

Advisory Committee on Mental Health, Alcohol and Substance Abuse. He has been recognized by Delaware Today Magazine as a Top Doc three times in a row and as a Top Psychiatrist in America by the Consumer Research Council. Doctor Goodman is Board Certified in General Psychiatry, Geriatric Psychiatry, and Forensic Psychiatry. He has held licenses in New York, Delaware, New Jersey, Pennsylvania, Massachusetts and Maryland, North Carolina and Virginia. He is an active clinician in private practice in Wilmington, Delaware and has evaluated over 10,000 patients."

"Hmm, that smart and handsome."

"He has a good track record to boot." Pete looks at me with a few stray strands of his longish hair hanging over one eye giving him a rakish look as he lifts one side of his mouth in a half smile.

I had talked to the Doctor and once he had agreed to consider our case, he gave me a list of what he needed in order to make his decision and to get to know our client. It took some time, but eventually I had the data collected and called him. We set up an appointment and I personally delivered a copy of the case file to him so that I could witness firsthand the man behind the credentials.

From the first hand shake, to the hour he set aside for the meeting, I found him to be charming and easy to talk to. I was confident that he was our man and Pete seemed to be in agreement.

***

When you love your work, it's like peeling an onion. There are always more layers to discover and explore. Our problem definitely wasn't staying busy and on task and getting going each day wasn't an issue. There was always another thought that needed to be explored. Several weeks later and we were still trying to cover the loopholes in our defense pattern.

"So how do they determine if the person was temporarily insane, Richard."

I had read enough to know the answer. "They question the offender about the events surrounding the crime. They also question family members and other contacts who observed the behavior of the offender prior to the commission of the act."

"Okay," Pete says, making a note. "So what did you give the Doctor in the case file?"

"Well, everything. Dr. Goodman said he required a copy of the files for the case so that he could prepare for the meeting with Lt. Trapp and determine the plea is indeed warranted. He asked that I make sure the file included the exact legal insanity standard we were looking at. This information he wanted to review before the evaluation because the records may contain critical information about the defendant's mental state shortly before, during, or after the offense that we may or may not have perceived. He also asked me to check the file to make sure it included victims, witnesses, and police detailed statements, and any video of Lt Trapp's interrogation. He said that such evidence is a rich source of information about the defendant's mental state at the time of the offense. Sometimes just from the video he can surmise that the defendant was behaving bizarrely, intoxicated, hallucinating, or delusional at the time. Finally, he asked me to check to see if Lt. Trapp had at any point seen a psychiatrist or been committed at any mental facility. This he said Lt. Trapp may not have shared with us, but he needed to know so that he had all the data regarding his sociodemographic characteristics, his criminal history, and his mental health history."

"Wow. Does our client know all this too."

"You bet. I not only prepared a file for the good doctor, but also left one with Lt. Trapp."

I look at Pete and he is shaking his head in wonderment. "I think the Lieutenant will know how to handle this, but it won't hurt to put a list together, you know points to emphasize and ways to react appropriately. That will be our job."

Pete chuckles. "Look at us. Well versed lawyers having to hit the books for a murder case. If we need help, so will our client. So, to start let's make sure that Lt. Trapp realizes he must have suffered from the mental defect at the time he committed the crime and because of the mental defect, Lt. Trapp was unable to control his actions, exempting him from liability, even if he understood that the act was wrong."

I can't believe how much I have learned as I go over to the law books and pull down the one I need. I take it over to my desk and then find the paper clipped page and begin reading out loud. "In criminal law, irresistible impulse is a defense by excuse, in this case some sort of insanity, in which the defendant argues that they should not be held criminally liable for their actions that broke the law, because they could not control those actions, even if they knew them to be wrong." I pause and look at Pete. "This part is a section of the irresistible impulse insanity defense, which is not commonly used in modern U.S. law, but is the plea we are going with."

Pete has been listening, but also searching through his notes. When I finish he says, "You know Richard it says here that the number of not guilty by reason of insanity pleas across the nation is very low."

"How low?"

"Well, one study says the insanity defense is used in about 1% of all court cases and is only successful in about 26% of those cases. So, only approximately one quarter of one percent of cases in the U.S. judicial system end with a defendant being found not guilty by reason of insanity."

"So, we have a good psychiatrist and know how to approach the case and that leads me to believe we will be in that 26%."

"Okay, that's good to be confident but of those attempting an insanity plea, success in being acquitted is even more rare, at about 0.26%. Most defendants, about 70%, who have initially entered an insanity plea withdraw their plea after a court-ordered evaluation finds them legally sane."

I look at Pete. "So you're saying we have a chance." Pete looks up and smiles. "Yes, we have a chance."

Theresa peeks her head into the office. "You guys have been at it for quite a while. Can I get you anything?"

I glance at the clock on the mantel and realize it is after one in the afternoon. "I don't believe it! Where did the time go?"

"Obviously into those books", she says pointing at the ever growing pile on my desk. "Give me your orders and I will go pick up some food for you."

"What about a pizza? We could get it delivered, it's easiest to eat while working?"

"Sure, Theresa says, I can order you a pizza."

Chapter 2

It was like global warming had taken control of the area and with it the crime level increased, keeping me busier than ever. The unheard of weather fluctuations was making it hard to distinguish between the end of summer, the start of autumn or for that matter winter. The longest warm weather spell happened during the end of November and continued through mid-December with temperatures in the mid to upper 80s and people keep switching in and out of winter garb. But it would take a drastic change when winter finally settled in with a vengeance and the temperatures in January of 2016 went from 3 degrees to below zero.

I was now balancing several cases at the same time. I had two high profile cases that I could not turn down. The first was an explosive racially motivated crime in the city — an attack on three black men in Chili, New York, by a gang of white teenagers, who chased one man onto a highway, where he was struck and killed by a car. The two other men and their lawyers refused to cooperate. Then came the Hughes assault case where Hughes assaulted his girlfriend Melanie Harr by slashing her in the face with a piece of glass. Hughes took Harr to Strong Hospital the night of the incident, and she received between 20 and 40 stitches to the laceration on her face. During the trial, emergency room doctors testified that Harr told them early that morning that Hughes struck her with the piece of glass during the fight. When I found out that the prosecuting attorney was going to make the case at trial that Hughes was bringing an intoxicated Harr a glass of water in bed when he stumbled, and the glass struck Harr, I couldn't turn my back on her and took the case.

Pete shouldered half the load on these cases so that there was littler interruption on the Trapp case progress that was still ongoing and taking up large chunks of time in our day.

Trying to find examples that fit our case proves to be challenging as we go through law books, surf the internet and even try our memory at cases we might have heard about. We look up as many as we can and usually find that they don't fit the bill. But we can't give up as each day we work harder to find what we are looking for, just like Thomas Jefferson said, "I find that the harder I work, the more luck I seem to have."

Then, one day like all the days before, Pete and I are surrounded by piles of books when suddenly I come across what seems to be the answer to our prayers. "I think I have something Pete. Damn, I should have recalled this one right away."

"What is it Richard." Pete says as he walks over in my direction.

"John Wayne Bobbitt vs Lorena Bobbitt - Not Guilty by Reason of Temporary Insanity. John Wayne Bobbitt born March 23, 1967 in Buffalo, New York and Lorena Bobbitt née Gallo, born October 31, 1970 in Bucay, Ecuador are a former American couple, married on June 18, 1989, whose relationship made world-wide headlines in 1993 when Lorena cut off her husband's penis with a knife while he was asleep in bed. The penis was subsequently surgically reattached. During questioning, Lorena told police that her husband was selfish and did not care about her sexual needs. When the trial commenced, both John and Lorena revealed details about their unhealthy relationship and the circumstances that led to the crime. Lorena claimed that John repeatedly abused her during the course of the marriage, was unfaithful, and even forced her to have an abortion at one point. Her defense team claimed that his constant abuse and infidelity caused Lorena to live in constant fear of her husband, and to suffer from clinical depression, which eventually led to her actions that night. Expert witnesses for both sides were presented and Lorena's attorneys argued that this pattern of abuse and rape created an 'irresistible impulse,' to protect herself, which qualifies as temporary insanity. The jury deliberated for only seven hours, then returned a verdict of not guilty by reason of temporary insanity. Lorena was ordered to undergo a 45-day mental evaluation at the state mental hospital, and was released shortly thereafter."

I read every word and when I came to 'irresistible impulse,' I spoke the words louder. I couldn't believe it, just couldn't believe it. There must be something in the air leading us now because I am not the only one with a revelation.

"Great. Here's another one," Pete says, "It's that first criminal use of temporary insanity plea. It took a while to find the details, but here it is. Daniel E. Sickles, vs. James Gordon Bennett complaint for libel. Daniel Edgar Sickles, a commander at the Battle of Gettysburg, successful author, college-educated attorney, U.S. minister to Spain and England, and U.S. senator and Congressman, had a reputation as a ladies' man, and married a woman roughly half his age, she was 15, and he was 33. Although Sickles was known to associate closely with a known prostitute, and was reprimanded for bringing her to the Senate, and for taking her to London, where he introduced her to Queen Victoria, after leaving his pregnant wife at home. He was undone by his anger over learning his young wife was having an affair with Philip Barton Key II, District Attorney of the District of Columbia, and son of Francis Scott Key. After Sickles found a letter giving away the affair, he confronted his wife, and forced her to write a confession. The following day, Sickles saw Key, and followed him, shouting profanities, and claiming he must die. Sickles then shot at Key, the bullet missing its mark. Key then attempted to fight off Sickles, but Sickles pulled out another gun, and shot Key in the groin, and finally in the chest, killing him. Sickles immediately turned himself in, and was charged with murder. During his trial, Sickles made the first plea of temporary insanity the U.S. had ever seen. Sickles' attorney, Edwin Stanton, argued to the jury that Sickles had been driven insane by his wife's infidelity, and so he was out of his mind when he shot Key."

"That's good too, very good." I say as I continue my search. We have finally located the right listing of cases online that reference details we can use in our defense. I am giddy with excitement. "Here's another that gives us the background, sort of, of our case and results in manslaughter for the accused which too is better than life!" I pause and begin reading, " Jennifer Levin vs Robert Emmet Chamber, Jr. Nicknamed the "Preppie Killer" by the media, he pled guilty to manslaughter in the death of 18-year-old Jennifer Levin. He killed her in New York's Central Park during the early morning hours of August 26, 1986. Levin's strangled, half-naked corpse, covered in bruises, bite marks, and cuts, was found by a bicyclist beneath an elm tree on a grassy knoll near Fifth Avenue and 83rd Street, behind the Metropolitan Museum of Art. Her bra and shirt were pushed up to her neck, and her skirt was around her waist. The city Medical Examiner's office said that Levin had died of asphyxia by strangulation, and police officials had said that there were numerous bruises on her neck, both from the strangulation and from her own fingernails as she clawed at her killer's hands. Later, Chambers watched from nearby as police officers investigated the scene. The investigators had found Levin's panties some 50 yards away. Police were given Chambers' name by patrons at the bar, who had seen him leaving with Levin. When authorities arrived to question him at his home, he had fresh scratches on his face and arms, which he initially said were cat scratches. He was taken in for questioning. Chambers changed his story several times: his cat had been declawed; he didn't part from Levin immediately upon leaving the bar; she had parted from him to purchase cigarettes. It was later discovered that Levin did not smoke. In the final version of his confession, he claimed that some time after he and Levin had left the bar, she had asked him for rough sex, tied the 6'5" Chambers' hands with her panties, and hurt his genitals as she stimulated him, and that she had been killed accidentally when he freed his hands and pushed her off him. Confronted with this explanation, Assistant District Attorney Saracco said to Chambers he had been in this business for a while, and he was the first man he'd seen raped in Central Park. The rape scenario was considered to be highly unlikely in light of the fact that Chambers was more than a foot taller than the 5'4" Levin, and at 220 lb., he was almost double her weight. Before booking, Chambers was permitted to see his father, to whom he said, that the fucking bitch, wouldn't leave him alone. The media had labeled the crime 'The Preppie Murder'. Chambers was charged with, and tried for, two counts of second-degree murder. His defense was that Levin's death had occurred during rough sex. He was defended by Jack T. Litman, who had previously used the temporary insanity defense on behalf of Richard Herrin for the murder of Yale University student Bonnie Garland. The defense sought to depict Levin as a promiscuous woman who kept a sex diary, however, no such diary existed. With the jury deadlocked for nine days, a plea bargain was struck in which Chambers pleaded guilty to the lesser crime of manslaughter in the second degree, and to one count of burglary for his thefts in 1986. He was sentenced to serve 5 to 15 years, with the sentence for burglary being served concurrently."

I look at Pete and say, "I think we can pull from all of these and not only get a defense but see what the prosecutor may use and how to fight against what they come up with."

"Your right. We can study these cases further and be in tune to them so that no one opens up a rebuttal that we are unaware of.

"Well, I think we have just about exhausted the angles so maybe we should review the possible defenses for second degree murder."

"Right with you friend," Pete says as he returns with another law book in hand. "Defenses to second degree murder charges include Extreme emotional disturbance, Assisted suicide without the use of duress or deception, Mental disease or defect, Infancy for persons under 18 years of age, Self-defense, and Defense of another person."

"I wish it would be as easy as using the 'defense of another person' option, but it was not done while Noah was raping his wife." I add this, just thinking out loud. "I think we can both agree that its temporary insanity or nothing."

"I agree."

We have been at it for most of the day and well into the evening when I suggest we go get something to eat before we continue. It is not a question of where to go to eat as we climb into my car and head toward the Founder's Café.

Our reception is almost as cold as the air has turned outside, but politeness reigns as we are shown to our seats and handed our menus. Now, sitting here, we are both feeling extremely hungry until Pete says, "Do you trust them not to put something in our food?"

"Aw Pete, why did you say that. Now I can't think of eating here. Come on let's go." No one stops us as we leave the café and once outside I look at Pete and we double over with laughter. We can't seem to stop as we make our way to our car and drive away.

"So where to?" I ask Pete.

"I don't have a preference, but maybe we shouldn't look around out here in Pittsford. Maybe we should go somewhere, ah, friendly...."

Not sure where to go, we head back downtown toward the office and find ourselves parking at the Dinosaur Bar-B-Que. I look at Pete and he nods in agreement. We get out and are both smiling as we enter the restaurant.

The light no longer filters into the room from the large windows at the front of the office as evening descends. Inside, I walk back and forth as we continue our transfer of information and in one pass by the switch I flip on the recess lighting.

"Pete, I've got the Penal Code S 130.35 Rape in the first degree. It says a person is guilty of rape in the first degree when he or she engages in sexual intercourse with another person by forcible compulsion; or a person who is incapable of consent by reason of being physically helpless and that rape meeting these criteria is a class B felony. There's more, but it doesn't pertain to our case."

"Well, Noah isn't around to pay the cost of his action legally, but what would the sentence be?"

I flip to Penal Code S 130.92 Sentencing. "When a person is convicted of a sexually motivated felony and the felony is a violent felony offense, the court shall impose a maximum term. A class A felony, the term shall be life imprisonment; For the following the term shall be fixed by the court; class B felony, not exceed twenty-five years; class C felony, not exceed fifteen years; class D felony, not exceed seven years; and class E felony, not exceed four years."

"That doesn't do us any good Richard since Noah is dead but, we should take note of it, just in case we can somehow use it. What do you think?"

"True, but... No, you're right. Let's bring this issue up with the psychiatrist or hold off until after we meet with him and hear what he has to say, since it is my determination it can only help our plea for temporary insanity."

"Wait, are you telling me we have the psychiatrist, Richard?"

"Oh sorry, yes, I got his call. We didn't get the army psychiatrist, Thomas Caine which is fine with me except when it comes to the fee. Yesterday evening, I got a call back from Doctor Milo Goodman and he has agreed to take the case."

"So that is one off the check list for now. Good job Richard."

"Thanks Pete."

We felt good. We had accomplished a lot that day and left the office feeling much lighter. We decided to work on other cases and in between them write up our findings in a logical order that we turn over to Theresa to type. Our plan is to come back to this case in a couple of weeks.

Chapter 3

I didn't see much of Pete in the coming days as we work on different cases and only consult one time before finally we are able to get back to the Trapp cases.

"Okay, so what do we need to work on now."

"The Will dispute." Pete says. "Let's just do some surface checking for now and if we need to go deeper I will."

"I like that idea."

Pete goes back to the law books in search of Will disputes and I search the internet. I come up with something first. "Pete, it says here that as any New York Will contest lawyer will tell you, winning one can be a challenge."

"We know it's a tough call, but we may have no other choice here but to brush up on this. Besides, we are not going to handle the will dispute, just get up to par so if it happens to come up in court we can talk sensibly."

I watch Pete as he pores over a book and I look at the screen, wondering if he will ever let go and use the internet. It is amazing how much information is here and from so many different sources so that one can see the legality angle as well as the personal and professional individual angles. Soon I find something.

"Pete, it says here that by presenting solid evidence and proving the underlying facts one can be successful in a Will contest. We need to see what they may be looking at and be ready with a rebuttal."

Pete looks up and adds, "It says here that the basic grounds to overturn a Will would be if Noah was determined not well enough to make a Will."

"Well, that won't fly. He was well. That choice would involve proving that he was not well enough to make a Will such as he was suffering from dementia or mental illness or in the late stages of Alzheimer's."

"Wait, here it says that it is also applied to Wills of decedents who are in such a weak physical state that it can be claimed that they lost their mental capacity. Claims are also sometimes made that the testator was under the influence or medicine or illicit drugs, or was drunk during the Will execution."

I look up. "Okay, that sounds very interesting." I input a search in google and read the following to Pete. "The most effective strategy for this Will contest ground is to obtain medical records, go through them and see if there are any notes that point to incapacity. Some people, as they get older, may drift in and out. A contestant of the Will is going to try to win by proving that the Will was executed during the testator's unsound time, not during the lucid moments." I look up at Pete with a smirk on my face. "They have already made a point of mentioning Noah's consumption of alcohol."

"I'm sure your right. I think that's what they will go with too," Pete says. "We need to get Noah's medical records." I stop what I am doing and look at Pete and at the same time we say, "Dead Man's Statute !"

Pete watches as I find my way on the internet and come up with the Statute. He leans over and reads the screen.

"The legislative concern at the time was over perjury: that self-interest would prevail when a person testified in a civil matter involving conversations with a now-deceased person where the witness had a pecuniary interest in the outcome of the case. That concern persists today and is particularly evident in the area of Wills and trusts. New York's Dead Man's Statute is intended to protect the decedent's estate against claims of conversations or interactions that cannot be verified. What a Dead Man's Statute does is make a witness legally incompetent to testify about conversations that the witness had with a deceased person in a case where s/he could benefit financially if the trier of fact found that evidence to be materially determinative. Since the deceased/legally incompetent person's lips are forever sealed, so must the lips of the other conversant with respect to the matter in contest. In New York, the statute has been invoked in cases involving such matters as bequests in Wills; trust provisions; requests for specific performance; and lack of testamentary capacity. There are also interesting cases where the Dead Man's Statute intersects with the competency of a witness exception of the Federal Rules of Evidence (FRE) Rule 601, at which point the Dead Man's Statute supplies the state law . At times, the Dead Man's Statute serves as a statutory exception to the hearsay rule. At other times, the hearsay exception in the Federal Rules trumps the Dead Man's Statute. Establishing pedigree for either the witness or the decedent in a Wills contest is one such example (FRE 804(b)(4))."

I wait until Pete finishes and then go to see what the exceptions are. "It says here that in New York, there are three exceptions to the Dead Man's Statute: in a tort action for negligence involving a car, boat, or plane, an interested witness can testify to the general facts and results of the accident; in estate cases where the estate "opens the door" by offering evidence or questioning an interested witness about conversations or transactions with the deceased; where the estate of the deceased does not lodge a timely objection during a Wills contest or trial, then the estate waives it right to object based on the Dead Man's Statute."

"Sounds good, but I think it's the last two fit our needs here. The first exception is an important one in vehicular negligence actions because New York does not have a guest statute. Thus New York's interest is to allow a New York State domiciliary the right to recover damages against a negligent driver. The next two exceptions can be triggered during an estate contest, for instance, where a substantial gift is concerned."

I quickly send an email to Theresa to get a HIPAA form filled out for Noah's medical record. Pete suggest getting a complete copy of the ME's report which might suffice. I add this to the email.

Okay, but we can't stop there. Remember the first rule of a detective is, to go where the evidence leads, so what else does it say, Pete."

"Yes, so another contest would be Pressure to Make a Will."

I enter the words in google and come up with the following that I share with Pete. "This involves proving that the people that Noah trusted took advantage of him and pressured him to make the Will to their benefit. A common strategy of people challenging a Will based on this ground is to prove that the proponent of the Will had a confidential relationship with Noah. That makes it easier to show that the proponent of the Will was in a position of influence and had the opportunity to pressure the Will maker."

"That's a good one too. That person of influence would be Tyra Pederson or one of several other choices, like the bartender." Pete pauses and says, "The next is Forgery which involves proving that the signature on a Will is forged or imported from another document, or the text is manipulated such as the pages are replaced or the text is changed."

"Right with you Pete. For Forgery it says the way to win a Will challenge based on forgery is to bring a handwriting expert and to present evidence of other handwriting samples of Noah comparing them to the handwriting on the Will and saying that it's not a close enough match. This usually becomes a battle of the experts for the Will proponent and the objectors."

"So, Richard, we might need a handwriting expert. I'll make note of it." I also make note of it on the Surface Pro and send it to email for Theresa.

"Moving right along, the next is Fraud", Pete says.

"Fraud can mean misleading Noah about the Will itself, such as slipping a Will under a guise of a different document or such or mischaracterizing what is in the Will and having him sign it. Fraud can also mean misleading Noah about circumstances outside of the Will, such as misinformation about friends and relatives."

"That is a sticky wicky, Pete says. Fraud is challenging to prove, but possible if the right evidence can be found. We can't assume they don't have forged evidence to use. Anyway the next is Improper Execution."

"Okay, to be valid, a Will has to be executed in accordance with New York Will execution formalities. The most common Will challenges are problems with witnessing the Will and with the testator declaring it to be the last Will and testament to the witnesses. This challenge is more plausible when the Will was executed without the supervision of an attorney, such as a Will printed out from the internet or filled out in a store-bought form."

I make a note to check and find out who was the attorney for the Will; if there was one and also about the fraud issue.

"The final one is a Combination of Factors…I guess it's good we didn't stop and kept going."

"Why, Pete, what does it say?"

"It says that when it rains, it pours because it is rare that a Will challenge is presented with only one ground. In fact, in the beginning stages of a Will challenges, every possible ground is usually pleaded with the hope of finding one that sticks at later stages of the case. If there is an allegation possibility of the decedent not being well enough to make the Will, an allegation will also be made that this diminished mental state made the decedent vulnerable to being misinformed or pressured to make a Will a certain way. It will also be claimed that the Will was made in a hurry and was not properly executed. "

We look at each other and I shake my head. Pete gets up and stands by the pile of books on the table. I notice he has put markers now in many of the books and several pages each. "So what now."

Well, I will send the file I have built in the computer to Theresa and you can put those books on her desk. Guess who she will appreciate more?"

"Come on Richard, don't do that to me. Tell me you recorded this session."

"Yeah, I did, but I wanted to see your face."

"So two points that may be of interest is The Existence of a Later Will and if that Will be validly executed the later Will wins if it wasn't overturned. Then Improper Execution of the Will such as it not being executed with all of New York's formal requirements will not be valid. This might make the job easier and the chances of winning much better."

As usual Pete is following along and adds, "The formal requirements are: (1) The Will must be signed by the testator or in their direction in their presence, (2) the signature must be at the end of the Will, (3) signed in the presence of each witness (4) testator must communicate to the witnesses that they are witnessing a Will (5) two witnesses are required (6) the entire ceremony must be completed within 30 days of the testator's signature. If the Will was not executed in compliance with New York's formalities, it will not be valid."

"Well, that may be hard to find since we both are known by the people involved. It might come to getting a warrant, but if we do, we can't let them know we are doing it or; poof goes the evidence."

"One more thing is that the validity of the Will is decided in a trial. The estate will not be distributed until the trial finishes. If the Will is found to be invalid, the court will not admit the will, only admit a portion of the Will, or admit an earlier Will in its place, or not admit any of the Wills, and distribute assets among Noah's relatives as if there was no Will."

"There's a reason to have all your ducks in a row," I said. "Ooh, wait, it says here the time to contest a Will may pass once the Will is admitted to probate. Probate is sought by the Executor of the Will following the death of the Deceased. Once Probate is granted, a Will may be challenged if a person believes they have been treated unfairly or inadequately, or that they may have missed out entirely on part of the inheritance. A Will may be successfully challenged if the Claimant can establish that the Deceased had a responsibility to make provision or a better provision." I pause and look down further and add, "A valid Will may only be contested for up to six months after the granting of Probate."

"Well, they will meet the time period, unless it does drag out."

It's getting late and our brains are fried as we stare across the desk at each other. "Let's call it a night and meet early in the morning."

"That sounds like a good idea. See you in the morning Richard."

"See you Pete."

I walk to the door with Pete and see him out, then went about shutting off lights and making sure the other doors are locked. I started to gather up the papers and books, but decide to leave everything as it is and instead just put my Surface Pro into my briefcase and turning on the alarm service I exit through the front office door.

Chapter 4

My mind is happy. I finally feel good about where we are on the case and that every possible angle has been covered. Over the months I have met with Lt. Trapp and his wife to make sure we are all on the same page. It hadn't been easy. Lt. Trapp's version of events had to include explanations for incriminating evidence, motivations, the timeline leading up to the murder, and every possible statement the prosecution may present. At first he was difficult, but then as time passed he realized I was on his side and we finally had that open and collaborative communication between us and we had our overall defense strategy. There was no denying that the Lt. shot and killed Mr. Arietta. The shooting had been witnessed and he himself admitted he had done the crime but just because I know a crime has been committed, and that my client did it, doesn't mean that something can't be done. Sometimes there's a little, sometimes there's a lot.

I know that people see it all differently when they ask how can I defend someone I know is guilty. I have to face the stigma of people thinking it takes moral depravity on my part to undertake such a task but on the up side my client, especially the person who is facing incriminating evidence, the need to post bail, and find a lawyer, sees it all in a different limelight. The question on the tongue of my client is 'What can you do for me?'

All of this runs through my mind as I make my way to the office. This is an important day for the case and I feel confident it will be a good day as well.

At the front of the office door, I sit the cups of coffee I brought from home on the railing and take my key out of my pants pocket to open the door. I lean inside and put the code in the alarm then using my foot to hold the door open I grasp the two cups of coffee.

Inside it is quiet and quite dark since the light timers have shut off the inside lights. I walk carefully over to my desk and sit the coffee mugs down and in doing so, the strap of my briefcase slides off my shoulder and I allow it to rests next to the cups. I then head back to the front to open the blinds and the first thing I see is Pete hurrying down the sidewalk. I pull the cord on the blinds and go to the door to let him in.

"Good morning, Richard."

"Good morning, Pete? I brought you coffee."

I watch Pete as he sits down behind his pile of books on the front side of my desk and I think that maybe I need to get him a table or something that is all his own so that he has more space to use. Who am I kidding, so that I have more space to use. I smile at the thought. As I go behind my desk instead of leaving the briefcase on the top, I sit it on my chair and begin unloading my Surface and placing it on the first open space I see on the desktop. I then try and find two safe spots to put the coffee. That done, I clear my chair off and sit down.

Pete looks up. "So, the agenda for today," he says looking at his notes. "We need to draft questions for the psychiatrist, set up the appointment with the psychiatrist, and prepare for the preliminary hearing which I feel we have a good start."

"Sounds like a plan."

I begin by placing a call to the psychiatrist and I look over at Pete, about to say something when I am stunned by the voice on the phone. It is not a recording; it is not a service or anything like that. It is the doctor himself answering the phone.

Pulling myself together and giving Pete a raised eyebrow look of puzzlement, I manage to say, "Good morning Doctor Goodman, this is Richard Dandridge. I spoke to you briefly about examining my client, Lt. Vincent Trapp."

There is a rustle of papers and I know that the doctor is getting out the file before he responds. "Yes, Mr. Dandridge, Good morning to you. I have had a chance to review the information you sent me about Lt. Trapp." There is a slight pause and then the doctor says, "I can see him soon. How does September 27, at say ten o'clock in the morning work?"

My lips pressed firmly together, forcing my cheekbones to rise is enough of an expression for Pete to lean forward to catch what I say next. "That's great, Doctor, I will contact Lt. Trapp and if there is a problem I will call you back. Otherwise, assume that Lt. Trapp will meet with you on September 27 at ten."

I hang up the phone and see Pete looking at me. "Well that went well. I can't believe we are getting an appointment that soon."

"Yeah, that took me by surprise. I thought we would be rushing to get the results at the last minute, but now it will be in plenty of time."

Not wasting a moment, I call Lt. Trapp and when he answers I give him the details of the appointment with Doctor Goodman and ask if he wants to meet beforehand.

"Sure, if you think it's necessary. I can drop by your office this morning. I have an appointment downtown so it would not put me out of the way."

"That works for me. See you in a bit."

255

Pete speaks before I can say a word. "Tell you what, I will grab my things and go upstairs to the apartment to work while you meet with the Lieutenant. Just let me know when it's safe to come down."

We use the time to go over what I should discuss with the Lieutenant and because I know using my office door seems preferable to visitors, Pete then gathers what he needs and disappears. Shortly after he leaves, Lt. Trapp walks in.

***

We talked. I begin by sharing with Vincent that a claim of temporary insanity in a criminal court case is related to a defense claiming that the act was a crime of passion and his case would qualify. But crimes of passion and temporary insanity defenses are very difficult to prove because temporary insanity can only be found by evaluating the actions in hindsight. A defense can only establish that the defendant was suffering from a bout of temporary insanity by comparing the actions the individual engaged in at the time with the actions the individual took both before and after the crime.

Because I know that it will be hard for Vincent to expose all these personal feelings I must stress it. Actually this session with the psychiatrist is like a practice run for the courtroom. I continue making sure that Vincent knows he needs to bring up the rape and all the details he shared with me.

It is not in his nature to be flustered or show it. Trapp is intense and self-absorbed, prone to violent outbursts, and prefers a neat and orderly environment. I know this about him, but I also know that the prosecutor and the psychiatrist will not 'comfort' their words and he needs to control his temper, his words and his actions and not take anything as a direct attack. Now as I listen to what he will be saying to the doctor and watch his expression as he speaks each word, I feel good. I feel confident he'll do okay.

Not putting words in his mouth, but more reminding him I say, "Lieutenant, you should tell how you went to the bar and your intentions, in your own words, were to grab the man, not shot, not kill, but grab him." He shakes his head in agreement. "And don't forget, knowing about Mr. Arietta's love of guns and shooting them you thought he was reaching for something behind the bar before you shot him. It's important because it shows that the tables could have turned and you might have been the one killed. A threat against your life will make it easier for all parties to consider that you do not deserve to be prosecuted."

The Lieutenant sits rubbing the back of his neck, not making a sound, but when he lifts his head and I see his furrow brow I know he is about to attack. In an instant he is standing, pacing back and forth as he says, "I don't believe you or any of them. The man raped Paige. He raped and beat my wife and because he is dead he is being 'protected'? Sounding as though he just completed a marathon, he puffs, "I stood there in front of that drunken animal and knew he probably did it before to another woman and would do it again. That sicken me and I saw red."

I go into Theresa's office and pour him a glass of water. When I enter my office he is still pacing around the room so I wait quietly. Finally, he goes to the window and stands stiffly in front of it and I think of an oak tree with roots deep in the ground, unmovable.

"Here, Lieutenant," I say as I walk over to him and hand him the glass of water. Thankfully he takes it. Minutes pass and I watch his hands relax at his side and his face softens. I know he is ready to go on. Cautiously though I explain to him that when talking with the doctor he needs to tell how he couldn't be sure what he had done.

"You mean that the only way I knew I had killed him was that my gun was empty and I knew it had been loaded?"

"Yes"

"I think that's it. Unless you have something you want to go over?"

The Lieutenant looks directly at me. "No, I think we did good." I hear a little chuckle in his voice. "Thank you, really. I feel good about this and understand what you have told me." A few minutes later we are shaking hands and I see him out the door. Before he has made it down the front steps, Pete appears and I go over what we have discussed, though I have a feeling he heard the majority of our conversation.

Before we part for the day, I say to Pete. "I am confident that the Lieutenant will do good. He will be telling the truth in his own words and that is what we want."

***

I drive in an unsettling daze feeling as though I need to put in more time for debate but know that I am mentally drained. When I pull into the driveway I begin to relax a little, but when finally, I am ready for bed, I fall into a fitful doze, waking at several intervals for a drink of water and then go back to bed to toss and turn until the alarm goes off.

Chapter 5

The next morning there is not much time to do anything, let alone worry about the upcoming preliminary hearing. I first drive to Lt. Trapp's home and am greeted by Paige who, even this early in the day looks like a million bucks. "Come in Richard. Vincent will be down in a minute." As if on key, Vincent suddenly appears and we are soon on our way.

My next stop is my office and I am not surprised to see Pete is ready and waiting which I take that to mean he is as anxious as I am.

"Good morning Pete. I would like you to meet Lt. Trapp."

As we had previously discussed, Pete says, "Good morning, Lieutenant, my name is Pete Adams and I have been working as Mr. Dandridge's investigator on your case."

After the acknowledgements are concluded we take the short ride to the courthouse in silence. I park the car in the court house parking lot and we climb out. Pete closes his door and walks over to the sidewalk. Lt. Trapp follows him while I open the back to get out my briefcase before joining them. We nod at each other and proceed toward the entranceway.

This is not my first time taking a case to court, but it sure feels that way as I nervously make my way to the entrance hoping that this feeling leaves me before I enter the courtroom. My briefcase feels as though it weighs a ton as I pull at the handles to relieve the pressure of the strap as it lays heavily on my shoulder. I start taking deep breathes to calm myself, but once I step inside the courtroom the weight of the moment descends and by the time we are seated at the defendants table it is like a brick has been placed on my shoulders.

I can see that my client is anxious as he sits perfectly still at the table so I step in front of him and reach out and offer my hand. We shake and at that moment my fears move backward allowing me to smile and say, "Don't worry, lieutenant we've got this," then take my seat next to him.

"All right. Let's go on the record in Case No. 22015SU044891, People versus Lt. Vincent Trapp," Judge Nicholson said. "The Charge is murder."

I slide my chair back and stand then turn and nod at the Lieutenant. I wait until he is erect and facing the judge. The Lieutenant stands straight with an assertive and correct posture of the military with his chin up, chest out, shoulders back, stomach in. His arms are fixed at his side; his eyes face front with his head locked in a fixed forward posture. Below the level of eye view, his heels are together, with the toes apart. His uniform is freshly pressed and I take a moment to adjust my suit hoping I look as put together as he does.

Judge Nicholson reviews briefly the delays in the preliminary hearing before commencing. "The State is present through District Attorney Randall Walker. The defendant is present and in person with his attorney, Richard Dandridge." He nods his head at each table. "At this hearing, it is the prosecutors job to show that the State has enough evidence of the crime to warrant a trial." Mr. Walker is that man and right now he stands off to the right holding the information document and looking over at me expectantly. I can read that look and know that he is wondering, would I insist upon his reading the long information or give him a break?" The Judge pauses, looks over the top of his wire rimmed glasses at the prosecutor, then continues.

"Appearances?" the Judge asks.

"Richard Dandridge for the defendant," I clear my throat and reply.

"Very well," He says and turns toward Randall. "You may proceed with the reading of the information, Mr. Prosecutor."

"In Case No. 22015SU044891, People versus Lt. Vincent Trapp, Rochester, New York, Attorney for the defense, Richard Dandridge will be representing former Army Lt. Vincent Trapp who is charged with the murder of the Founder café owner Noah Arietta. Lt. Trapp states that he doesn't remember the actual act of shooting Arietta, but he admits to knowing that he did indeed kill Arietta and that the killing was prompted by Arietta's alleged rape of Lt. Trapp's wife, Mrs. Paige Trapp. There is no physical evidence of that act beyond Mrs. Trapp's black eye. The accused, Lt. Vincent Trapp is pleading not guilty as a result of temporary insanity. Evidence for the defense states Mrs. Paige Trapp returned home to tell her husband, Lt. Vincent Trapp she had been raped and as a result, Lt. Trapp did admit to going to the Founder's café and shooting Mr. Noah Arietta. He claims, in his defense, that the victim had raped and beaten up his wife Mrs. Trapp. Although Mrs. Trapp supports her husband's story, the doctor who examined Mrs. Trapp could find no evidence that she had been raped. During the course of interviews, it became apparent that Lt. Trapp is violently possessive and jealous and there is reason to believe that Mrs. Trapp may have had an affair with the deceased, Mr. Noah Arietta."

"Mr. Dandridge, how does your client plea?"

"My client, Lt. Vincent Trapp pleads 'not guilty'."

"Are both sides ready for trial?"

"The defense is ready, your Honor," I said.

Judge Nicholson turns to face Randall, looking at him inquiringly. Randall is frowning, his eyes not visible as he stares down at the floor in front of him. The judge clears his throat.

"Sorry, your Honor," he says. "We may need to move for a continuance," Randall says.

Judge Silas Nicholson remains still as he looks down from the bench, his navy blue eyes peering over the top of his metal framed glasses. He lifts one grey eyebrow as he stares intensely.

Finally, I say, "Your Honor, the defense is ready for trial. We have received no formal notice of any motion for a continuance and will be obliged to resist one if it is made."

"Back to you, Mr. Prosecutor," Judge Nicholson says.

"The other side has filed a notice of the defense of insanity," Randall says, "but it still hasn't furnished us with the name of the psychiatrist who by law should appear on the witness list."

It's my turn as Judge Nicholson peers over the top of his glasses at me. "Mr. Dandridge?"

"A copy of the notice of insanity was served on the prosecutor nearly six months ago. The original is on file with the clerk. It contains the names of the witnesses then known to us. Mr. Walker's copy was accompanied by a letter explaining that I could not then give him the name of our psychiatrist for the simple reason that I did not know it, and that I would do so as soon as I had a name. With leave of the court I am now prepared to do so, having learned his name only late last night."

A frown appears on the judges face as he looks in my direction and for a moment I am worrying whether this is going to be a problem. Quickly I add, "Your Honor, once the psychiatrist was contacted, I had to wait until the psychiatrist had a session with my client and informed me if he would be willing to take the case. He has." Finally Judge Nicholson says, "Leave is granted."

I step forward and hand the Judge the original of the supplemental notice containing the name and address of Milo S. Goodman M.D. I then walk over and give Randall a copy. The Judge looks at Randall. "Do the People still press?" he says.

Randall, not used to being out done, now pauses and finally speaks. "I still feel that we are entitled to a continuance."

"Do the People after nearly six months' notice of the defense of insanity now claim to be surprised that the defense retained a psychiatrist to support their claim? If you need a minute to review the excellent qualifications of Doctor Milo Goodman before you respond, take it now."

"No, Your Honor," Randall replies sounding embarrassed, "We believe the psychiatrist we have already retained is fully able to refute the defense's, but a continuance is simply being requested on the grounds that the defense hasn't followed the State statute."

"Mr. Dandridge, how do you respond?"

I have to control a smirk from appearing on my face, as I lean over and reach for my brief case to pull out a volume of the New York State statues. In the next chair, Pete sat with his hand over his eyes. "If it pleases the court, I wish to read first Penal § 40.15 Mental disease or defect. In any prosecution for an offense, it is an affirmative defense that when the defendant engaged in the proscribed conduct, he lacked criminal responsibility by reason of mental disease or defect. Such lack of criminal responsibility means that at the time of such conduct, as a result of mental disease or defect, he lacked substantial capacity to know or appreciate either 1. The nature and consequences of such conduct; or 2. That such conduct was wrong."

I pause and look for the next paper clipped page and proceed. "Rule 12.2 Notice of an Insanity Defense; Mental Examination (a) Notice of an Insanity Defense. A defendant who intends to assert a defense of insanity at the time of the alleged offense must so notify an attorney for the government in writing within the time provided for filing a pretrial motion, or at any later time the court sets, and file a copy of the notice with the clerk. A defendant who fails to do so cannot rely on an insanity defense. The court may, for good cause, allow the defendant to file the notice late, grant additional trial-preparation time, or make other appropriate orders. (b) Notice of Expert Evidence of a Mental Condition. If a defendant intends to introduce expert evidence relating to a mental disease or defect or any other mental condition of the defendant bearing on either (1) the issue of guilt or (2) the issue of punishment in a capital case, the defendant must—within the time provided for filing a pretrial motion or at any later time the court sets—notify an attorney for the government in writing of this intention and file a copy of the notice with the clerk. The court may, for good cause, allow the defendant to file the notice late, grant the parties additional trial-preparation time, or make other appropriate orders."

I wait for this information to sink in before I proceeded. "The statute requires that when it is filed and served the notice of insanity shall contain the names of the defendant's witnesses, 'known to him at that time.' I submit we have fully complied with both the letter and intent of the law."

"Thank you Mr. Dandridge," the judge says before turning to Randall. I believe that Mr. Dandridge has more than explained his position, though we should all be well aware of the law. In any case, "Mr. Walker, I gather that the People have also retained a rebuttal psychiatrist?"

"We have, your Honor."

"And have you told Mr. Dandridge who he is?"

264

"No, your Honor. His name is endorsed on the information along with the other witnesses. Opposing counsel will get his copy directly."

The judge puts the tips of his fingers together and rocks in his chair. He seems to be studying the clock on the wall. "Hm..." he says, "The defense doesn't know the name of the People's doctor and the People have just learned the name of the defense's doctor. That makes things pretty even, doesn't it, Mr. Walker? Perhaps, at this moment, even slightly in your favor?"

Randall's embarrassment shows on his handsome, boyish face. "Yes, your Honor," he concedes.

The Judge smiles not unkindly. "Then I think perhaps we'll just leave it that way. To the extent that the People have made a motion for a continuance it is denied. Now we need to determine how much time will the trial take? I'll also entertain the suggestion of counsel as to when we might get underway."

The judge turns his head so that he is looking directly at me.

"Counsel has handed me a copy of the information," I said. "I have already counted over thirty People's witnesses. I would guess that four days to a week might be closer. Starting Wednesday morning is agreeable with us."

"In quite a few years of experience on the bench,'" the Judge says, "I have found it a pretty safe practice to at least double the estimates of counsel." He smiles. "Lawyers are far too modest in that they do not seem adequately to realize their enormous talents for consuming if not wasting time. In any event we will mark this case one on the trial docket and hope it will end by Christmas."

Judge Nicholson pauses to consult his calendar on his phone. "The trial will commence at nine a.m. this Wednesday. Will counsel approach the bench?"

Randall and I move forward and the judge lowers his voice. "Counsel will please confer with me in chambers after the call of the calendar. That will be all, you can step back now."

As Randall and I return to our tables to gather our belongings, I turn around and address Pete. I tell him the judge wants to see me in chambers. I then turn to Vincent and thank him. "Pete, here will take you home." We shake hands and I watch them leave the courtroom. I then sit quietly in the back of the court as the Judge continues his calendar scheduling and the next counsels take over the defense and prosecutor tables.

Up front, the judge consults his calendar and then looks up. "People versus The State of New York, Respondent, v. Ramona Santora and Martha Schloss, Appellants, et al."

"Your Honor," The case counsel says.

I am only half listening, knowing that the Judge will be tied up until he clears his calendar. This time I take a seat in the back and watch the proceedings. I hear, "Defendants were arrested for violating Penal Law § 245.01, exposure of a person, when they exposed that portion of the breast which is below the top of the areola in a Rochester public park. The statute, they urge, is discriminatory on its face since it defines "private or intimate parts" of a woman's but not a man's body as including a specific part of the breast. That assertion being made, it is settled that the People then have the burden of proving that there is an important government interest at stake and that the gender classification is substantially related to that interest. This is covered in Mississippi University for Women v Hogan, 458 US 718, 725. In this case, however, the People have made no attempt below and make none before us to demonstrate that the statute's discriminatory effect serves an important governmental interest or that the classification is based on a reasoned predicate. Moreover, the People do not dispute that New

York is one of only two States which criminalizes the mere exposure by a woman in a public place of a specific part of her breast."

Sitting there I am relaxed almost to the point of falling asleep as the cases continue to be heard until I realize that Judge Nicholson has completed his calendar and is leaving the bench. I get up and head toward the judge's chambers.

I meet with Judge Nicholson and Randall Walker in the chambers. Judge Nicholson turns around as he takes off his judge's robe and hangs it in the closet and with his back still to us, says, "I can feel tension in the room. Gentlemen, relax, I've eaten my quota of lawyers for the day. Just relax."

Trying to show calmness, Randall says, "It's a nice day outside for this time of year."

"It is," I add.

Judge Nicholson turns around and moves over to his chair behind the desk and smiles. "Nice attempt." He regards us thoughtfully. "Let's get started shall we. As you have undoubtedly heard, I can be a bear in the courtroom. I think it lends dignity to the work at hand. I also find that lawyers and the public are both apt to construe too much indulgence in a judge as a sign of weakness. But I am a reasonable man so let's see if there is anything you can do to facilitate the case."

"Well," Randall says, "I'd like to put on our pathologist first, if I may. It's somewhat out of order, I know, but he's a busy man and his time is valuable."

Judge Nicholson looks at me. "I have no problem with that. I think it is a sensible suggestion, Randall."

"Anything else, gentlemen?"

"I'd also like some seats set aside for the People's witnesses," Randall says. "There's quite a few, as Richard has observed, and if they don't have reserved seats the crowd may freeze them out and..."

"How many do you need?"

"I estimate three benches will do," Randall says. "At least for the first day or two."

"I see no problem with that," Judge Nicholson says, "Unless the defense disagrees." I shake my head, no.

"Anything else?

"I would like to suggest having a twelve-man jury with six alternates. That will save time if for any reason we need to dismiss a juror or someone gets sick."

The Judge looks at me and says, "Excellent idea, Richard. Randall? Any problem with that?"

"No, none at all." Randall continues with his next request, "We've made a chart of the Founder's café and also of the Trapp home and the area between his house and the woods that we would like to use in court."

"Who made them, Randall," I ask.

"Det. Sgt. David Heide sent over the measurements that the police made during their investigations. These were given to SWBR Architects & Engineers PC over on East Main Street.

I had worked with Det. Sgt. Heide on several occasions and had no problem with him whatsoever. "We won't have any problem with the charts, Randall," I said.

"Anything else gentlemen?"

Randall smiles and replies, "I can't think of anything else at the moment, Your Honor."

I glance quickly at the Judge who says, "And you, Mr. Dandridge? You haven't said very much."

"Nothing to add. Besides, wouldn't it be a pity if all of us gave away our surprises beforehand."

Instantly I can tell that this did not set well with the judge. "An interesting point, Counselor, but only up to a point." He gives me a look over his glasses, his eyes piercing mine. "A lawyer sometimes lures the court into error and thus often deceives only himself. And I say to both of you men that anything you may feel you can legitimately confide to me, to expedite the correct resolution of this case, will be treated in confidence. Now I don't mean that either of you should come running to me the moment the other's back is turned. I don't propose to try this case in the hallways or in chambers. Remember, I said 'legitimately confide.'" He pauses and again says, "anything else, Mr. Dandridge?"

I had hoped for a shrewd and perceptive judge and it seems my wish was granted. "Instructions," I said. "If either side should have any requests for instructions, might the court allow counsel to submit them to him before the end of the trial?" The theory of our defense was wrapped up on the request for instructions that Pete and I had polished and toiled over for so long. I had not intended showing our hand on them until we had to but here was a judge plainly asking us to give him a clue, telling us that he could be trusted. Why keep him in the dark, indeed?

"Not only will I entertain your request for instructions, I want them," the Judge says. "when lawyers sit on their law and strategy as long as they can, perhaps to confound and mystify their opponents they may complement the judge's erudition and clairvoyance, perhaps, but they just as often risk mystifying him as well. I don't claim to be a mind reader nor do I claim to know all the law. Do you have any requests to submit now?"

"Not quite yet, Your Honor," I lied whitely, glancing at Randall. I did not want Randall to know, if I could help it, that I planned to request any instructions. I knew that it must be a written request to the court for instructing the jury. "But perhaps, who knows, we'll have one or two later on. If so would we have a chance to amend or supplement our request in the light of development at the trial?" As an afterthought I added, "I suppose counsel should not be held to pre-trial clairvoyance, either."

The judge just grinned and nodded, he had seen my quick glance at Randall. "Certainly you can amend and supplement your instructions when the time comes. Or start over from scratch, though I wouldn't recommend it. I would treat any preliminary requests more in the nature of a confidential trial memorandum for the sole assistance of the court so any time at all Mr. Dandridge and the sooner the better."

"Speaking of trial memos," I say, "They would also of course be treated as confidential?"

"Certainly, Mr. Dandridge, unless counsel choose to exchange. And all this of course goes for you, too, Mr. Prosecutor. The court plays no favorites."

"Yeah," Randall murmurs absently glancing at his wrist watch, as he had done several times during the Judge's and my exchange. I felt sorry for the poor guy, and could imagine the sweat he was in, faced with his first big murder trial, with thirty-odd subpoenas waiting to get dated and served, with his phone doubtlessly clanging and cops and lawyers running in and out of his office on this and all his other cases. Not to mention people endlessly clamoring to get at him. "Please, Mr. D.A., this will only take a minute," they would say, but of course it takes more than a minute.

"Very well gentlemen," the Judge said. "I think our meeting may have already proved mutually profitable. And I thought it wise that we should get to know each other a little better if we must practically live together during the busy days that lie ahead."

"Thanks Judge," Randall said, edging toward the door. "Real nice to meet you." He shakes the judge's hand. "Well, I think I better get going. Lots to do…"

The Judge broke in and waved us out the door. "Good day gentlemen, good day, it so happens I've got a few little odds and ends to take care of myself."

"Yes, I can imagine," I say sympathetically as I shake his hand and leave his chambers.

"Nice old guy," Randall said, as we stand outside the judge's chamber together.

"He'll do fine, Randall," I said. "He'll give both sides a fair shake." I turned and walked away.

***

Yes, I thought, this judge would certainly do.

I hurried outside and saw that Pete was there, at the curb waiting for me. I climb into the car and as we drive away, I pull out the printout I had Theresa give me. It was Judge Nicholson's dossier. He grew up in Watertown and graduated from West Irondequoit High School. Graduated magna cum laude with a Bachelor of Arts degree from the University of Rochester and received his Juris Doctor degree from Syracuse Law School. After law school, worked at Bond, Shankle & King PLLC Law in Rochester, and became a partner in the firm. He is a past president of the Monroe County Bar Association and named to the New York Super Lawyers list three times. Beyond his business qualifications he is very active in the community, a past vice president of the Pittsford Youth Soccer Association and a member of the parish finance council at St Boniface Parish. He is married to a woman named Kim and has five children.

I look over at Pete and though I have all the confidence in the world for the judge, we two would now have to face the uncertain and fateful battle of "irresistible impulse."

Chapter 6

The next day we were busy. With Pete, we began our search and review of all possible cases where the plea was temporary insanity. There were many and that boosted my belief that we could win this case. As we pulled out case after case, the pile of books grew larger, while the sites I visited I stored in my history. It was important to fine sensational cases won as well as the less prominent ones so that we could identify methods and pertinent details for the successful outcome.

We were careful to take note of not only the case and its outcome, but also when we could find details study the type of jury makeup used. The first case was that of Richard Lawrence, acquitted in 1835, an unemployed house painter in his 30s who fired two pistols at U.S. President Andrew Jackson as Jackson walked through the Capitol Rotunda during a funeral procession. Both pistols misfired, and Lawrence was quickly apprehended. The jury acquitted him by reason of insanity after only five minutes of deliberation, and he spent the rest of his life in an asylum. After only five minutes of deliberation, the jury found Lawrence "not guilty by reason of insanity.

"Okay, so details that supported the insanity plea was what?" Pete asked.

"Says here at his trial, Lawrence was prone to wild rants and he refused to recognize the legitimacy of the proceedings. At one point he said to the courtroom, 'It is for me, gentlemen, to pass judgment on you, and not you upon me'. After only five minutes of deliberation, the jury found Lawrence "not guilty by reason of insanity." There was speculation also that the toxic chemicals in his paints were a contributing factor to his irrational mental state."

"Does it say why he did it?" I asked.

"Yes, it does. Lawrence convinced himself that his lack of work was inconsequential because the U.S. government owed him money, and that President Jackson was personally preventing him from receiving it. He was confident that as soon as he obtained the funds, he would be able to begin his reign as the King of England. Lawrence also held the president directly responsible for killing his father in 1832. Never mind that his father had died about a decade earlier and had never set foot on American soil."

"Nothing on the jury members that I can find." Pete shook his head in agreement.

There were indeed lots of cases of which the most known were Anthony and William Esposito, ,Daniel Sickles, Steven Steinberg, Andrew Goldstein, John Hinckley Jr., Jonathan Schmitz, Lorena Bobbitt, Jeffrey Dahmer, John Wayne Gacy, and Ed Gein.

"Great, but most of these are serial killers. We are not dealing with a serial killer." I say more to myself.

"Well, Bobbitt wasn't a serial killer. Lorena Bobbitt argued she was temporarily insane when she severed her husband's penis with a kitchen knife and a Virginia jury agreed; she was released after three months of psychiatric evaluation."

"Okay, let's keep going."

Pete reads aloud, "There was Daniel Sickles, acquitted in 1859, charged with murder after he shot and killed U.S. District Attorney Phillip Barton Key in broad daylight, within full view of the White House. At his highly publicized trial, Sickle's lawyer argued that he committed the murder in a state of temporary insanity, brought on by the enraging knowledge that Key was sleeping with his wife. The all-male jury accepted this argument, and Sickles was acquitted." He picks up another volume and reads, "John Schrank, institutionalized For Life in 1912. He was a New York bartender who shot Teddy Roosevelt at close range in Milwaukee, Wisconsin. Schrank was immediately arrested, and offered no reason for the attempted assassination. Later accounts reported that he said William McKinley had appeared to him in a dream and told him to kill Roosevelt. Before his trial began, a panel of doctors determined that Schrank was insane, and he was sentenced by a judge to life in an asylum. Ah, not what we hope for."

It went on and on as we studied each case for relevance and results so that we could pull this off without having Lt. Trapp sent to an institution or life imprisonment. We were looking at similar circumstances that matched our case and found some after going through many others like Ezra Pound declared Incompetent in 1946. He was declared unfit for trial and committed to St. Elizabeth's Hospital, a federal asylum, for the next 12 years. John Wayne Gacy convicted, 1980, pled insanity. The jury rejected the plea, and Gacy was convicted and sentenced to death. John Du Pont, convicted, 1997 and described as "the wealthiest murder defendant in the history of the United States was found guilty but mentally ill in his trial for the 1996 murder of Olympic wrestler David Schultz. In January 1996, du Pont had driven to Schultz's house on the estate and shot him dead in the driveway, in front of his wife. At trial, psychiatric witnesses for both the defense and the prosecution agreed that du Pont was mentally ill. The jury rejected the insanity defense and convicted du Pont of third degree murder. The guilty but mentally ill verdict meant that du Pont would serve his entire sentence in prison, but that he would be able to receive psychiatric treatment during his incarceration.

Those were the famous cases that Pete shared with me, while I searched for recent cases of not so well known individuals and when Pete concluded I read him my findings. "Court of Appeal, First District, Division 1, California. The People, Plaintiff and Respondent, v. Lashaun Harris, Defendant and Appellant Defendant. LaShuan Harris who took her three children and dropped them one at a time over the low railing into chilly San Francisco Bay. Harris later told psychiatrists. Passersby said she seemed dazed, disoriented. Defendant initially pled not guilty to all charges and denied the special circumstances allegation. She later entered additional pleas of not guilty on all charges by reason of insanity. After defendant waived a jury trial for the sanity phase, the court found her not guilty by reason of insanity. The trial court sentenced defendant to three concurrent 25-years-to-life terms on the murder convictions, and three concurrent 15-years-to-life terms on the convictions for assault resulting in the death of a child under age eight. The court further ordered defendant committed to the Department of Mental Health at Napa State Hospital to serve these terms."

I stop and take a drink of water, then continue. "In 1981, Steinberg was charged with killing his wife Elena with a kitchen knife. Elena was stabbed 26 times. It should also be noted that Steinberg was the one who called the police reporting an attempted burglary gone awry, though the police found no signs of a break in. The case drew much publicity in Arizona not only for the heinous crime, but because it was a case of homicidal somnambulism, or simply known as sleepwalking murder. Steinberg claimed he did not remember the crime and was sleeping at the time, hence the murder while sleepwalking. Not only that, he did not deny the fact that he

276

murdered his wife. In his criminal trial, the jury found him not guilty on the grounds that he was temporarily insane when he committed the crime. Although Steinberg fabricated the story about the intruders, he walked away as a free man. Members of the jury were also later to say they were aware that they were releasing a killer but he was not criminally responsible for his actions."

"Hm," Pete said.

I continued. "Kenneth Parks, a 23-year-old Toronto man with a wife and infant daughter, was suffering from severe insomnia caused by joblessness and gambling debts. Early in the morning of May 23, 1987 he arose, got in his car and drove 23 kilometers to his in-laws' home. He stabbed to death his mother-in-law. Parks also assaulted his father in law, who survived the attack. He then drove to the police and said "I think I have killed some people. Because he could not remember anything about the murder and assault, had no motive for the crime whatsoever, and did have a history of sleepwalking, his team of defense experts (psychiatrists, a psychologist, a neurologist and a sleep specialist) concluded Ken Parks was 'asleep' when he committed the crime, and therefore unaware of his actions. On May 25, 1988, the jury rendered a verdict of not guilty. Subsequently Parks was also acquitted of the attempted murder of his father-in-law."

I couldn't help getting excited as I came across cases that covered the areas of our concern. "Scott Falater Case in 1997 was accused of murdering his wife. On the night of January 16, 1997, his neighbor saw Mr. Falater hold his wife's head under water and called the police. The police arrived to find Mrs. Falater dead with 44 stab wounds. He denied any knowledge of the brutal murder and thus began his celebrated sleepwalking defense. According to the prosecution, the defendant changed clothes and placed his bloodied clothing along with the murder weapon in a Tupperware container.

He then put the container in a trash bag with his boots and socks and stashed the bag in the spare tire well in trunk of his car. He was found Guilty of Second degree Murder. On January 10, 2000 Scott Falater was sentenced to life imprisonment with no chance of parole."

Okay, that one bought me back down to earth.

"Pete, there is a lot about this sleep walking defense in these cases. I don't know much about it, but I don't know if we can use it so I am going to make note of this to run by the psychiatrist."

"Good idea. I have a few more questions for him too."

Chapter 7

Several days later I leave the office and head out to see the Lieutenant. I want to have him elaborate on his sessions with Doctor Goodman. I drive up and after ringing the doorbell for several minutes, I make my way to the back and find the Lieutenant and his wife seated there.

"Come on over, Richard," Lieutenant Trapp says.

"Yes, join us: Paige adds. "Can I get you something to drink?"

I continue forward until I am at the patio. I shake hands and sit before finally saying, "No, I'm fine."

"So what do we owe this visit to, Richard."

"I've come to see how you're doing, of course, and to find out how it went with the psychiatrist."

"Well on the first part, I am doing as well as can be expected and on the second part, I believe the sessions with Doctor Goodman went quite well. What bothers me are the media at the gate; always at the gate."

I nod my head in sympathy. "Care to elaborate on the sessions with the doctor?"

I sit back and listen as Vincent tells me everything that he can recall from his sessions with Doctor Goodman. I interrupt him at intervals to get further information on the topic he is covering and to add additional topics that I hope the Doctor had fit in. When he finishes, he says, "I was probed and every inch of my body examined for what reason I don't know. Then I had at least three intensive sessions with the good Doctor himself and when it was over he summed it all up perfectly for me."

I am about on the edge of my seat knowing I will get the results, but anxious to hear it now. "So.."

"So, the verdict is that there is no mistake, it all adds up to "irresistible impulse."

I let out a burst of air, only then realizing I have been holding my breathe. As I recover I ask, "I take it you told him about blacking out and all, and that you saw Noah with his right hand hidden from view behind the bar?"

"Yes, I told him everything that I shared with you and probably more. He had a lot of questions and I supplied a lot of answers."

"Did he get to going over the draft questions I sent?"

"He did and he told me that they were indeed helpful in making his diagnosis."

"So what next, Richard."

"I'm not sure, but I believe that the other side is getting their own psychiatrist and may want to have you examined by them. If they approach you, give me a call first."

"And, Paige," She looks up in my direction. "I want you to wear your glasses during the trial and only tops that are not tight. It might be advisable to wear shorter heels and a longer skirt too."

"I see. You want me to look like an old maid. I can put my hair in a bun too."

"No, that's not it and you know it. I am just asking that you not be, hm, flashy. Is that okay?"

"Yes," she smiles a real smile. "That's fine."

"Well, I must go. There's still a lot of preparation on my part that I need to get to."

"It's this 'irresistible impulse" plea that is bothering you, isn't it?" Vincent asks.

"No, not really," I said smiling bravely. "I want you to relax, Vincent. I'll see you tomorrow if possible, if not I will phone you to keep you informed. Wednesday is the big day."

I walk around to the front alone, thinking about all the work ahead of me and what I need to get to Theresa as soon as possible. I know that she will make the details mesh together from Pete and from myself. I climb into my car and head toward the office, but I make one stop and that is at the site where the rape took place. I pull over and get out of the car.

Every blade of grass in the field, every leaf on the trees are changing. The bright summer has passed away, and the foliage has been losing its freshness through the month of August. I can see yellow leaves appearing like the first gray hair that will continue into September while dahlias and marigolds will add to the landscape. Now as I step carefully along the dirt road I look closely, even kicking aside leaves as if I think something may have been missed, but I uncover nothing. Finally, I get back in the car and am on my way.

At the office Pete is still at it and I say, "I feel as though this judge can be trusted and I actually like him," I add.

"I have to agree and I don't know him as well as you might since the private meeting. But I read his dossier that Theresa prepared and I like his history."

"Yes, and the way he handled Randall on the continuance business showed that he wasn't arrogant like a lot of judges are apt to be."

Once I had settled in, Pete went over the list of the People's witnesses endorsed on our copy of the information. "There are thirty-seven witnesses," he says, 'and guess what?"

"What"

"Tyra Pederson's name is not on the list."

"You're kidding," I reply as I hurry towards him and read over his shoulder. "I don't believe it." I add as I walk back across the room, "What's the psychiatrist's name?"

"Hm, Pete says, "Let me see." I watch as he pores over the list of names. "There are three doctors listed. A Doctor Kindleworth who I think is the pathologist who did the post on the late Mr. Arietta and a Doctor Pierson"

"Doctor Pierson is the doctor who did the rape kit on Mrs. Trapp."

"Okay. And there is a Doctor Anderson,... Mason Anderson."

"That must be their psychiatrist, Pete," I said. "I have never heard of him. We need to check him out but right now we need to make a decision here. Let's check out the insanity plea more and think about that sleepwalking claim." I pause. If we want to go with 'sleepwalking' we will need a sleep specialist as part of our defense expert team.

That night shortly before midnight Pete and I separated across Grandma Dandridge's old dining-room table, giving us the space we needed as we continued our chase through the law books for information on the 'irresistible impulse' plea.

Pete stands up and says, "I think I have something here. "It says that when a child kills a parent, or a parent kills a child who is incurably ill, or a husband kills a man who is having a romantic or sexual relationship and especially a secret or improper relationship with his wife, there is reluctance to apply the penalty of murder. In order to dismiss the offender of criminal responsibility, the plea of temporary insanity is frequently entered."

"So how do they defend it?"

"It is usually alleged that, at the time of the crime, the defendant acted under great mental stress and mental tension, that he was unable to know the nature and quality of the act that he was doing, or that the act was wrong"

"Makes sense to me. So how do they eliminate the person being committed as totally insane."

"Well, they state here that immediately after the homicide, the tension and mental stress is eliminated, and the defendant is able to function like any other human being. The defendant reached such a state of emotional disorganization and personal breakdown just preceding the act that he actually arrived at the pathological state designated as insanity."

"I like that. Any problems that you can see."

"Well there is one. How to differentiate the state of temporary insanity from violent emotional explosions which precede and accompany the so-called crimes of passion?"

"Crime of passion," I repeat, as I search through the pages. "Here it is. People who commit the so-called crimes of passion are usually described as being in such a state of upheaval at the time of the administration of the offense. In short, their mental faculties are considered to be inoperative; they are incapable of establishing the inhibition to impulsive acts which under ordinary circumstances they are able to do."

I browse a little further and start reading again. "The law does not excuse such behavior, even though it recognizes the fact that it was committed under great emotional stress. The law accepts the fact that the individual was unable to think about it, the law classifies the act as a crime and describes a penalty for it."

"So," Pete adds, "a temporary insanity plea, if accepted by the jury, often brings about a not guilty verdict and it's not so for the crime of passion. Right?"

"Yes, Pete. In both instances the accused confronts behavior which is purely uninhibited and impulsive, and contains features of the so-called "irresistible impulse". Yet the one is put down as insanity and the other is not. The one is viewed as satisfying the requirements of the McNaghten rule of inability to assist counsel owing to impairment of ability to differentiate between right and wrong, and the other is considered as outside the confines of the McNaghten requirements."

"So Richard, the question is how do psychiatrists arrive at the differentiating point which would in the final analysis make the difference between acquittal and imprisonment?"

"I think that's why Doctor Goodman was so thorough in questioning and examining Lt Trapp about the events surrounding the offense, and talked with Mrs. Trapp who had opportunity to observe his behavior prior to committing the act."

Pete is quiet, thinking and then says, "There can be no question that pleas of insanity are unsound. In a criminal case, the accused has to be found guilty "beyond a reasonable doubt". If there is one grain of doubt, then he must be found "not guilty".

"So what are you saying, Pete?"

"I'm saying that there is no doubt that he committed the murder. That is a fact that we need to dispute. But how? I don't know where to start on this one other than plea temporary insanity and then hold our breath.".

"Your right Pete. But there is one thing and that is our client has money. Where the ordinary run of the mill defendant, who is unable to hire a high-class criminal lawyer for his defense, who is unable to pay the high fees of psychiatrists brought in for expert testimony, usually winds up with a prison sentence. Yet, and I can't help but wonder why, Lt. Trapp could have hired a high-power attorney and yet, chose me. He can also afford an array of prominent psychiatrists to establish a temporary insanity plea, but wants me to make the call on that." I pause in contemplation. "With the right representation, the Lieutenant would guarantee himself a ruling that would set him free, yet...."

In desperation Pete and I again began to reread all the old landmark cases and the new ones we had come across hoping to find a needle in a haystack. I picked up volume after volume from the stacks, my eyes heavy and my sight blurred from closely looking at every passage and then I saw it. "If the defendant was not capable of knowing he was doing wrong in the particular act, or if he had not the power to resist the impulse to do the act... that would be an unsound mind."

I read it again and then pushed the book over to Pete to read himself. When he finished he looked around the table and finally found what he was looking for. "This is it. This is the case that will fuel the fire. Supreme Court of New York State. People of the State of New York, Plaintiff-Appellee, v. Blake Blazor, Defendant-Appellant. Decided: June 12, 2001.

I am searching the Internet at the same time and we both start reading; Pete from the paper and I from the screen. Not a sound breaks the silence in the room as we devour the contents of the case, knowing this is what we have been looking for. We finish almost at the same time and look at each other. Slowly Pete's face breaks out in a smile and I follow suit.

Chapter 8

We are less than a week away from trial and preparing for the pick of our jury. Between then and now Pete and I had done our research and had the questions prepared for jury selection and the guidelines we wished for the jury members. But Pete takes it a step further, and my love for this man is apparent in my willingness to take his advice seriously. Pete had a hard life and along the way had lost everything. Now, I see him as working his way back and doing a good job of it.

Pete is a nice-looking man who flaunts his individuality. He wears his dirty blonde hair long and parted in the middle. He has a somewhat neat mustache and a small sprig of hair under his lip almost touching the hair growing on his chin, which makes you wonder if he had problems shaving. His tortoise shell color glasses with a slight tint give him mystery and the scarf he usually wears tied around his neck speaks loudly of his individualism. If there is one thing I have learned by knowing Pete it is not to judge a juror by their 'cover'.

Pete would say to me, "Amongst the twelve in a jury box are all degrees of alertness, all sorts of ideas, and a variety of emotions; and the lawyers, too, are important factors in the outcome. They are closely observed by the jurors. They are liked or disliked; because of what they say, or how they speak, or pronounce their words, or part their hair. It may be that a lawyer is disliked because he talks too little or too much, more often the latter. More importantly a lawyer must not seem to be above the juror, nor below him."

I know this is true and because Pete is not sitting at the defense table, I need only think about what opinion they have of me.

As for my opponent, Randall, I recently learn that he has a partner, a Jean Larson of the Attorney General's staff. I could see exactly why he has chosen this woman to sit at the table with him as she has the appeal of being motherly. Jean looks to be about sixtyish with chin length straight, no nonsense hair, frameless glasses that allow full view of her thin eyebrows and pale blue eyes. She has a pink complexion and a broad smile that pushes back her cheeks increasing the wrinkles that appear in that area. Her voice is surprisingly loud, which adds to the feeling of confidence she exudes.

Pete and I checked up on her and find her to be quite well known due to the cases she has won and how expertly she can pick and read a jury. She would be one to contend with, but in his heyday, Pete had been known for great jury picking too.

I am not fooling myself. Picking the jury for this case is not an easy task as a murder case calls for one type of jury and a rape case another. We needed to focus on the murder of Noah Arietta, but make sure we consider the fact of the rape of Mrs. Trapp.

I take advantage of Pete's knowledge on jury picking and though he will be sitting off to the side I need to display confidence in my choices or As I stand ready, I remember what Pete told me earlier and that was that a wrong pick can mean I threw away our case before it even got started. I knew that the jury picking was important but from the viewpoint of Pete, it was the most important part of the trial. So we spent hours outlining the characteristics of each person we wanted to sit on the jury. My only goal is to pick the chess pieces to beat my opponent. Thus we had a game plan in place. We wanted at least one minority female whose culture frowns upon women who call the police to handle a family issue and at least one who would react in our favor to rape being an inexcusable crime. We needed jurors who served their country in the service or those who were sympathetic to what a serviceman faced during combat and by all means, choose a man or a woman who laughs. A juror who laughs hates to find anyone guilty.

We did not want to take a wealthy man on the jury. He will convict, unless the defendant is accused of violating the anti-trust law, selling worthless stocks or bonds, or something of that kind. Since we were defending, it would be important to have imaginative jurors. If a person is instinctively kind and sympathetic, take them.

These were my objectives. Now if I could translate their body language, their personal style and their words correctly, I would have a good jury for my case.

Judge Nicholson has supplied us with a stack of completed questionnaires filled out by potential jury members and they detail that address a variety of aspects of the potential jurors' lives. Other questions that appear include how much the potential jurors are aware of the case and if they've heard about the case and what they may recall about it. There are other questions that ask how they feel about the presumption of innocence and what do they think of a defendant that doesn't testify in their own behalf. Additionally, they have been asked if the State proves this case beyond reasonable doubt would they have any moral qualms in convicting the defendant and how did they stand on the issue of a defense of temporary insanity.

The potential jurors completed the questionnaire upon arrival for jury selection and I have had time to review most of them. Our game plan is that while I question the juror, Pete will be observing them from the moment they enter the court room.

As the potential jury members file in I look at them and then pull the page from the file that details the jury we want. Further down my list it says to remember to think that a juror will tell you the truth about themselves is naive and will do our client a great injustice. So it will be important to look closely at the juror when asking the questions and to listen very closely to the answers they give because this is the only opportunity I have to interview the jurors and identify the ones who will potentially let our client go free. I tell myself that I must treat this like a job-interview and read between the lines.

God help me. I lower my eyes and pray and when I open them I am shocked to see that some 200 prospective jurors have been summoned to the U.S. District Court in Rochester, New York. "We're going to be here all day," I say to Pete. Pete shakes and gives me a thumbs up.

Judge Silas Nicholson begins, "Good morning Ladies and Gentlemen. The constitutions of the United States and of the State of New York guarantee defendants in criminal trials and litigants in civil trials the right to a trial by jury. The New York State Judiciary Law states that all litigants have the right to juries selected from a fair cross section of the community and that all eligible citizens shall have both the opportunity and the obligation to serve. Each of you have received a copy of the Trial Jurors Handbook which will answer most of the questions you may have about the procedures followed during the case. You should have this in your possession at all times. In addition you were asked to fill out questionnaires and they have been given to myself, the prosecutor and the defendant's lawyer."

The Judge begins by asking the prospective jurors questions to ensure that they are legally qualified to serve on a jury and that jury service would not cause undue hardship. Several potential jurors raise their hands; one is a college student who might miss critical exams, another few have upcoming surgery scheduled, some more are lost due to being a sole caretaker of an ill or elderly family member.

Judge Nicholson then informs the prospective jurors that in order to serve as a juror, a person must be a U.S. citizen, over the age of 18, live in the court's jurisdiction, and have the right to vote. No one raises their hands. He continues. "You must be able to physically sit through the entire trial as well as hear and understand the trial testimony." This causes several hands to be raised and they are dismissed.

Waiting until those who have been excused to leave the court room, Judge Nicholson says, "Each of you must also be mentally aware enough to comprehend and apply the judge's legal instructions. Any person who doesn't meet these criteria will be dismissed 'for cause'."

"I have one more question to ask you. Can each of you put aside your feelings and apply the law impartially—that is, without actual or implied bias. Anyone who feels they are incapable of doing this, please stand." Several individuals stood either because this was true or they saw this as a possible way to get out of jury duty. In any case, they were dismissed.

The field of perspective jurors dwindles and is manageable. "Those of you remaining have responded to the court as being able to serve and you have been qualified as a juror of this court. In a few minutes the prosecutor and the defendant attorneys will be asking you questions to help them in choosing the jurors for the case of Lt. Vincent Trapp vs the State of New York, Murder In the Second degree. We will need 12 jurors plus six alternates. The first juror seated will become the foreperson who will be responsible for reporting the jury's verdict to the judge. Because an alternate juror may be asked to take an excused juror's place, it is important that alternates pay careful attention to the proceedings. Does everyone understand what is being said." Heads shake

He waits and when no one says anything to the contrary he adds, "Okay, if you're ready attorneys, let's begin.

It is our turn. Both Randall and myself get a chance to question the potential jurors about their biases and backgrounds, as well as any pre-existing knowledge they might have about the case. Questions I have on my list are often covered by questions of Randall, making it easy to get through all of them.

I keep a record of each juror and the results of the questions that are designed to uncover characteristics or experiences that might cause a potential juror to favor either the prosecution or the defense. Everything is open field except for overly personal questions, and asking the jurors how they would decide the case in advance.

The questioning continues with Randall dismissing jurors who are otherwise qualified, but appear likely to favor the defense and I do the same when I feel the juror is leaning toward the prosecution. We argue our challenges and when Judge Nicholson grants the challenge, that juror is struck from the jury panel.

Once the challenges are completed and there are 12 jurors plus the 6 alternates left, we take our seats and Judge Nicholson has the floor as the 12 jurors file into the jury box and take their seat. The remaining alternates are guided to the front and stand before the judge.

"Your Honor," I say, "The defense is satisfied with the jury."

"Your Honor," Randall says, "The People are satisfied."

I let out a sigh. We had selected a jury in a murder case in less than half a day. I knew from pass experience that this process alone could take days to complete and what was more, neither side had mentioned insanity or rape during the jury selection.

Judge Nicholson turns toward the jurors and says, "Members of the Jury, you will rise, hold up your right hands, and be sworn to try this case." They all stand, including the alternates. "You, as jurors, are the judges of the facts. But in determining what actually happened–that is, in reaching your decision as to the facts–it is your sworn duty to follow all of the rules of law as I explain them to you. You have no right to disregard or give special attention to any one instruction, or to question the wisdom or correctness of any rule I may state to you. You must not substitute or follow your own notion or opinion as to what the law is or ought to be. It is your duty to apply the law as I explain it to you, regardless of the consequences. However, you should not read into these instructions, or anything else I may have said or done, any suggestion as to what your verdict should be. That is entirely up to you. Do you understand?"

"Yes your Honor", they reply in unison.

"You are excused until Monday morning at nine o'clock and if there are any delays, you will each be notified. In the meantime, please do not talk about the case among yourselves or with others. If any persons attempt to discuss the case with you, report it to me immediately. Do you understand?"

"Yes your Honor" each juror responds.

Judge Nicholson lowers the gravel and says, "This court is adjourned."

I wait for the courtroom to clear and then walk up to the Judge's bench, noticing he has his cell phone laying on his desk. Now, I know the law and because in my briefcase is my Surface, there is no way I am going to say anything.

"Judge Nicholson, here are my requests for instructions and a trial brief". I reach over the bench and place a manila folder in his hand. Here are the exhibits prepared by us along with the exhibit list and witness list as well."

"Thank you Richard. Are their three copies in the folder of the lists?"

"Yes. I assume you have received the same from the prosecutor?"

"Yes, I have. Thank you, Mr. Dandridge." He looks down at this cell phone and then looks over the top of his glasses with his lips slightly parted in a smile. I know the General Order states that Personal Electronic Devices are not allowed in the court room and I adhere to the Order, but, court is not in session."

"No," I laugh, "It is not, nor would I care either way. As far as I am concerned, it is none of my business."

I watch as his ruddy complexion flushes even more and hear the Judge laughing as I turn and walk away.

I see Randall and Jean Larson engaged in a huddle over at their table and as I pass them I say, "See you soon." They barely look up or show any signs they have heard me and I think of the quote from Mahatma Gandhi, "First they ignore you, then they laugh at you, then they fight you, then you win."

* * *

Taking my time now, I exit the courtroom feeling proud of myself. Choosing the jurors went well. My eyes are tired from all the staring that began with Judge Nicholson informing the candidates of their duty and providing a brief synopsis of the case they would be trying. I watched their faces and their body language closely and saw no one blinking fast, licking their lips or flashing a quick grimace before they smile. That was a good sign. It was a miracle too that I didn't have to use all my allotted six challenges to eliminate any jurors selected. It was like we were all on the same page giving and taking... No, I am not going there. I am confident that this was the ideal jury for both sides. I wanted a jury that will decide the case on the evidence and law given to them by the judge, even if they disagree with the law or the evidence personally and that's what I got. Right down to the Foreperson who was the first juror chosen I felt confident. Later when I talk with Pete, he smiles and says, "You made the right choices. No question about it. This is the right jury." That cemented the deal.

Chapter 9

After the jury selection, Pete and I planned to meet up for dinner so that we can discuss the case. The schedule is that I will drive over to his apartment and pick him up and we will go to the restaurant in the Irondequoit Country Club where I am a member. Pete, not being much of a golfer anymore, agrees when I ask if we could play a couple holes before dinner. I think it will relax us and freshen our minds for later.

I hurry home to change and then back into the car to drive downtown. I pull up in front of Pete's apartment building and don't have to wait long before he comes out to join me. He has changed into his usual attire of jeans, unbuttoned collared shirt with a neck scarf, but has put on a sports jacket to fancy it up. Not that I have stayed in my suit either. I have opted for a sports jacket too, and wear a casual open collar shirt tucked into my dress pants.

Barely in the car, Pete asks, "So, Richard, you belong to a country club?"

"Well, yes, I do. I joined because it is where my father use to be a member. "

"Hmm", Pete says and I immediately set his mind at ease. "I know what you are thinking. It must be high class, but it's not. It has an understated elegance that is relaxing. It's not going to be too crowded there either and even though the sun is streaming through the leaves of the trees, it will not be too much longer that I can enjoy a game of golf."

When we pull into the parking lot at the club, Pete and I get out of the car. He waits while I go up to the club house to make the arrangements, only to learn that there isn't an open tee time. Sadly, I return to the car and give Pete the news.

"Sorry, Richard," he says. I sense that he doesn't really mind at all as we lock the car and make our way into the club house for dinner.

Once we are seated at the table, we place an order for our drinks and make ourselves comfortable. "Richard," Pete says, "I'm falling in love with that judge. He seems a perfect replacement for Judge Jasper. Though he hasn't shown it yet, I think he might have a little humor in him too. He's got the attitude that will allow him to consider our requested instructions."

"I agree, Pete."

I lean back thoughtfully, "I wonder what he will think of our newest instructions on the private arrest and irresistible impulse?"

Pete had handled putting this section together on his own and I don't expect an answer from him. It was his baby, it was good and I knew he was proud of it.

"What do you think of Ms. Jean Larson?" Pete said archly. I can feel his dark eyes penetrating mine through his dark glasses, and a lock of his long brown wavy hair falls forward covering one eye and giving him a rakish look.

"Well," I say, I would have picked her too. She's perfect for the case with the gray hair, calm eyes, and that broad smile that makes you think of a warm kitchen with the smell of cookies in the oven. Who doesn't side with their grandmother, is all I can say"

Pete is smiling, his white teeth gleaming. "I think she is going to make it interesting indeed, but I don't think that she will sway our jury." He sobers and adds, "But I am worried about the relationship that you and Randall have going?"

"Why?"

"It's not about the case…it's the future, if you know what I mean. I think you need to concentrate on the here and now and not see Randall as competition, except in this court case. Know what I'm driving at?"

"Yes," I respond.

I gaze out the window over the rolling acres of perfectly manicured lawns and let my mind drift. I know what Pete is thinking and he's right. I could easily let the upcoming election for district attorney cause me to fight a battle that does not exist. I must keep focus.

The waitress comes to take our meal requests. We both order a half pound pure Rib Eye Steak, cooked to perfection, medium rare, with freshly steamed broccoli, carrots, cauliflower and beans plus a delicious mushroom sauce. Between bites we talk.

"Pete, I remember what you said when we first went over this case."

"I said a lot."

"Yes, you did, but what sticks in my craw is when you said that here is a man who deliberately takes a loaded pistol as he goes to the business establishment of Noah Arietta where he resides and works. He goes there because the man, Noah has been accused by his wife of raping and beating her. He shoots Noah and he kills him"

"That's good, Richard. I meant for you to keep that foremost in your mind as it is where the hardest explanation lies."

"I'm glad you decided to work with me Pete," I say, turning the conversation around. I hope you know that and know too that I'm sure the prosecutors will see you as a legal representative for the defense."

"Yes, once you had me sitting near the defense table I knew they would know, but we can't make it official or my past might cause the case harm. Remember, I am proving myself here."

At that moment, the waitress returns to our table. Neither one of us is interested in dessert so we spend the rest of the evening thoroughly reviewing our case over cups of coffee.

Outside the earth has turn away from where the sun is shining and goes into shadow, marking the beginning of night, but we are deep in thought, refreshing our memory on all that we have covered so many times before along with trying to identify every possible angle that the prosecutors will present."

"I think we have beaten this horse to death, Richard. What say we call it an evening and get some rest."

I signal the waitress and she brings us the check. Knowing it would be useless, I allow Pete to contribute to the bill and then we leave.

Outside the air has taken on a chill that has me pulling up the collar of my jacket as we make our way to the car and once inside we sit with the motor running giving the car time to warm up a bit.

I drive the short distance back to Pete's apartment, with neither one of us engaging in conversation. It is a comfortable quiet that we maintain until I pull up in front of his building and wait while he gets out. I roll down the passenger side window and say, "Good night Pete."

"Richard, I'll take care of getting the Trapp's to the courtroom Wednesday."

"Pete...."

"Yes, I know Richard, I will make sure that Mrs. Trapp is dressed appropriately."

I smile, roll up the window and ease the car onto the road, heading home. The quiet of the evening matches my mood and by the time I reach my driveway, I feel the first pangs of exhaustion overtaking my body. There is only one thing I wish to do now. I enter my house and climb up the stairs, going directly to my bedroom. I undress quickly throwing my clothes on the side chair then enter the bathroom to brush my teeth and run a wet washcloth over my face. Back in my bedroom I climb into bed where I instantly fall asleep.

PART 3
THE TRIAL

Chapter 1

On Wednesday morning, September 15, I look at myself in the mirror, noticing how deep-set my eyes appear under my thick eyebrows and my hair, even kept short, manages to still look tousled. I stare at my image making facial expressions in the mirror so that I see what the jury will see. I have been told on numerous occasions that I can look stern and I can't risk it in court. It will be important to make them like me and believe in me and that will come from how I appear to them. Painfully I pluck a few eyebrow hairs and stare at the results. "Not the best, but it'll have to do," I say to my image.

I'm nervous. Pete and I exchange text messages and talk on our cells. I think he senses how I am feeling and tells me not to worry it will be fine. I thank him, when he says he'll have the Trapps at the court on time and then we end the call. I need to go in early for a meeting in the judge's chamber to cover some last-minute instructions.

I hardly notice what kind of day it is as I drive to the court house as my mind goes over all the things I need and I hope I haven't forgot anything. If I have, it's too late to rectify it now. When I arrive at the judge's chambers Randall and Jean are already there. I walk over and shake hands with Jean first, taking in what she is wearing. She has chosen a teal suit with a double-breasted jacket that has flap pockets, with shoulder pads over a white silk blouse. Her skirt is long, stopping calf length making her appear thinner than she is. It is a very flattering outfit that goes well with her silver gray hair and I say as much. "Thank you, Richard." Jean says her voice ringing pleasantly in a sincere tone that I will probably not hear again today.

I turn toward Randall and inconspicuously look him over. He wears a tailored dark blue suit jacket that has a two-button front entry with notched lapel over a white shirt with a teal tie. The rest of his ensemble includes matching vest and slacks. I can tell that this is Italian made and tailored to fit his physique. But, I think, I am no slough in my three-piece navy pin striped off the rack suit that I set off with a white shirt and a red tie. I had read somewhere that you can't go wrong with a solid charcoal or navy suit. As for indulging in expensive designer suits, it's just not my thing.

Before I can make the gesture, Randall reaches out and shakes my hand. "Good morning, Richard."

"Good morning Randall," I reply and then turn slightly in the direction of the judge. Good morning Your Honor.

Judge Nicholson looks us over in one sweeping glance, nods and stands shaking out his robes. "I have heard from the Courtroom Deputy Clerk that she has received the exhibits prepared by counsel along with the exhibit list and witness list. Is there anything more either of you wishes to add?"

We both nod our heads no. "Then come on gentlemen", a side look and he adds, "ladies. Let's get started." We fall behind the Judge as he leads us down the short hallway to the courtroom where we part company and enter from the side hallway doors. We are barely at our tables when the judge enters the court room.

The Bailiff says, "All rise." Everyone in the court room stands. "Department One of the Supreme Court Of The State Of New York, County Of Monroe is now in session. Judge Silas Nicholson presiding." There is silence until Judge Nicholson says,

"Please be seated." The room fills with the rustling sounds of fabric as everyone prepares to takes their seat.

"Good morning, ladies and gentlemen. Calling the case of the People of the State of New York versus Lt. Vincent Trapp. Are both sides ready?"

Randall stands and says, "Ready for the People, Your Honor." He sits back down.

I stand and say, "Ready for the defense, Your Honor." I take my seat.

Judge Nicholson says, "Will the clerk please swear in the jury?"

Finn Landon stands and moves over to the jury box. "Will the jury please stand and raise your right hand?" He waits patiently until each member of the jury is ready. "Do each of you swear that you will fairly try the case before this court, and that you will return a true verdict according to the evidence and the instructions of the court, so help you, God? Please say "I do".

One after the other the jurors respond saying, "I do."

"You may be seated." His part done, Finn returns to his position on the left side of the court room.

"Deputy District Attorney, are you ready to give your opening statement."

"Yes your Honor," Randall says. All eyes are on him as he walks toward the jury box. "I am District Attorney Randall Walker for the prosecution for the case, Lt. Vincent Trapp versus the State of New York, the County Of Monroe. Serving as my associate will be Assistant Attorney General, Jean Larson." He turns toward the prosecutors table and Jean stands lowers her head in a bow and modestly smiles at the jury, He waits for her to be seated. "Good morning ladies and gentlemen of the jury. What the State intends to do is fairly present the evidence against the defendant, Lt. Trapp whom you see sitting at the defense table." He turns and points toward our table. "We will build our case brick by brick, witness by witness, until the wall that adds up to the guilt of Lt. Trapp is complete."

Randall walks to the middle of the front courtroom area as if gathering eyes on himself. He pauses, looks around and then moves back to stand in front of the jury.

"On July 31st, 2014 Noah Arietta was at his business establishment, The Founder's Café in the Academy Building on Marsh Road where he resides and works. This is a family type establishment known for its good food and great atmosphere. It is the type of establishment where one feels comfortable and safe. On the evening in question, as he has done numerous times, Noah Arietta fills in for the regular bartender so that he can take a deserved break in his work day. It is at this precise moment that the man, Lt. Vincent Trapp enters the bar and shoots and kills Noah Arietta. The defense will claim that the defendant, Lt. Vincent Trapp was temporarily insane at the time of the fatal shooting, but we will prove that he was sane and that what he did was done in the heat of passion and anger. We further plan to show that the killing was premeditated and the result of a predetermination to commit an act without legal justification or excuse. In other words, ladies and gentlemen of the jury, we will prove that the defendant, Lt. Vincent Trapp is guilty of the crime of murder." Randall allows his eyes to sweep across each juror and then says, "I thank you."

Randall's opening statement is good; it is clear, it is brief and contains no less than it should. It is well organized and I suspect that Jean Larson has prepared the majority of the content, but Randall pulls it off as he is known to do. His hands seem to emphasize each word that comes from his mouth while his open arm gestures seem to draw each juror into the conversation. As I have anticipated,

Randall has made no mention of rape or the taking of any lie-detector tests, but kept focus on the murder and the fact of the defense going for an insanity plea.

I watch Randall as he walks confidently to the table not unaware of getting admiring glances as he takes a moment to run his hands through his straight, short blond hair giving it a slightly tousle look that is attractive on any level. When he reaches the table, Jean congratulates him on his opening statement and whether her words can be heard by the jury, it doesn't matter because her body language says it all. That sideways tilt of her head and the warm admiring smile can easily be read. Motherly image or not, at that moment I would love to smack her really hard.

"Mr. Dandridge," the Judge says. "Do you wish to make your opening statement now?"

I am deep in thought and hearing the judges voice startles me somewhat, but I recover quickly. "If it pleases the court, Your Honor," I say as I stand at the table, "the defense would like to reserve its statement until later."

"Very well," the Judge says. He then turns and looks at the prosecutors table. "District Attorney Walker call your first witness."

"The People call Doctor Paul Kindleworth," Randall replies.

There is a silence in the court room as Doctor Kindleworth stands and walks with a lofty proud gait toward the witness box. He takes his time and when he finally reaches the front, Finn Landon walks purposely toward him. "Doctor Kindleworth, please raise your right hand." Finn pauses and waits until the good Doctor Kindleworth has his right hand raised before he begins the oath.

""Do you swear to tell the truth, the whole truth, and nothing but the truth, so help you God?" The seriousness that Finn Landon takes this job is prevalent in the punctuation of the words that spill from his mouth, making a somewhat short sentence expand in length. I wonder if he would take it just as seriously if he had to pronounce the Cambodian oath.

That thought lingers in my head and soon the words come to mind. 'If I am home, let fire destroy my house for 800 reincarnations; if I am in a boat, let it sink for 800 reincarnations; when I become a ghost, let me eat bloody pus, or swim in boiling chili oil for 800 reincarnations.' I almost laugh out loud but catch myself in time.

"I do," Doctor Kindleworth replies and takes the witness chair. Doctor Kindleworth looks the part of a person who could stare at a dead body without flinching. I wonder if it has to do with the fact that he has seen so many dead bodies, or because he doesn't think of the body as a human, but rather a cadaver. I continue to watch his progress noting that his ears stand out away from his head, uncovered by his hair worn short and neatly arranged. When he finally takes a seat, his small eyes, seem to gleam with malice as he stares with skepticism and I think here is a man who doesn't care what people feel about him.

I know the doctor's reputation. He is a pioneer in the field of pathology and helped establish a laboratory for teaching the use of forensics. He is indeed a highly competent pathologist and mentally I salute Randall for this witness choice.

"Please say your name for the court." Randall says.

"My name is Doctor Paul Kindleworth."

"What is your profession, Doctor Kindleworth."

"Medical doctor."

"Do you have any specialty in the medical field?"

"Yes, I am a pathologist at the University of Rochester, here in the city." The doctor demonstrates uneasiness as he tries to sit up properly with all eyes focused on him.

"How long have you practiced medicine, Doctor?"

"Over twenty years, not including residency training after I graduated from NYU School of Medicine".

"I'm sure most of us here are not aware of what a pathologist does. Can you describe your typical day?"

There is a pause as the doctor's demeanor changes to that of one in deep thought. Then he speaks. "Let me give you the short version," he starts. "As a pathologist my schedule closely follows the surgical operating room schedule. During the day, I am often called upon to examine surgical specimens in the operating room. This may range from opening a uterus to identifying the disease process, to opening a segment of intestine to ensure that the surgeon has taken adequate margins. As a pathologist it is also my job to perform autopsies."

"Thank you Doctor," Randall says quickly seeing that his recitation has disturbed the jurors and most everyone else in the court room as they picture in their minds their interpretation of his words.

"Did you have the occasion to perform an autopsy on the body of Noah Arietta?"

"I did."

"Can you tell the court when you performed the autopsy and where."

"Sure, on Tuesday evening, August 4 at the Strong Memorial Hospital located at 601 Elmwood Avenue, Rochester NY."

"Who requested the autopsy on Noah Arietta?"

"That would be Coroner Jennifer Pfeiffer"

I had an occasion to meet Jennifer. She was a young curly redhead woman who wears her bright red curly hair back, off her face emphasizing her high forehead, wide spaced eyes, straight nose and thin lips that are always pulled back in a smile. She is pretty as well as smart and definitely not what one would consider a coroner to look like.

"Do you remember who was present during the autopsy?"

"Well, let me see, there was Ms. Pfeiffer and Detective Sergeant Kent of the state police." He pauses, concentrating before adding, "There were two or three other officers but I don't recall their names, and of course myself."

"That's fine, Doctor." Randall says. "Can you tell me who identified the body?"

"Yes, the officers did. He had his driver's license in his pocket and the staff was able to verify the body as Mr. Arietta."

"Upon examining the body of Noah Arietta, what were your findings."

Doctor Kindleworth has with him an envelope that he now opens and takes out several pieces of paper. "This is the report that I prepared for the autopsy of Noah Arietta. As you can see it is quite long. If it is okay, I will summarize my findings, covering the important points of the report. If not, I will gladly read the report verbatim." Doctor Kindleworth leans back on the chair and waits

I stand and look first at the Judge and then at the jury giving them what I hope is a sympathetic smile. "The defense will agree to a summary of the autopsy report, if it pleases the court," I say.

Randall turns and glances at his assistant, Jean Larson. "The people agree," she says. "go on, Doctor, and can you please put it in laymen terms." She stops, but then decides to add, "and not too descriptive."

Not wasting another minute, Doctor Kindleworth begins. 'On August 4th at the Strong Memorial hospital in the coroner's office I performed the initial external body exam of the Deceased. The body was observed lying in a supine position on a small table in the receiving processing room. The Deceased was light skinned, of mixed race, African American, with tight, curly black hair, and blue eyes. His reported age was forty-five years old. He has a thin mustache and chin hair. The body had been transported from the crime site to the hospital via ambulance."

The Doctor pauses and takes a drink of water. "Can we show the visual chart now."

There is a flurry of activity and then the Clerk appears with a tripod holding up a marked diagram of a body. He places the diagram at a tilt so that the audience as well as the jurors and see it.

Doctor Kindleworth continues. "The Deceased has multiple penetrating and perforating wounds on the body like that made by a bullet entering at one point and exiting at another. One bullet entered the front of the right shoulder and emerged on the back side of the shoulder. Two other bullets entered at the right collarbone and came out at the spine. Another bullet went through the heart and the right lung and emerged at the right upper back midway between the anterior and posterior axillary folds. This resulted in a massive hemorrhage in both pleural spaces."

Randall interrupts the doctor saying, "Sorry doctor, can you explain this last part."

"Sure. This area is where there is an accumulation of fluid in the space between the membrane encasing the lung and the lining of the chest cavity. The normal pleural space contains only a small amount of fluid to prevent friction as the lung expands and deflates. If, however, there is a disturbance in either the production of this fluid or its removal, the fluid accumulates and threatens to collapse the lung."

"Thank you doctor. Please continue."

"The fifth bullet perforated the abdomen two inches below the level of the umbilicus, I mean belly button, and passed through the paired midline abdominal muscles, known as the rectus abdominis muscles. From there the bullet emerged about four inches to the left of the mid line."

The doctor picked up the glass of water and downed its contents quickly as though he was afraid he would not be given enough time to quench the dryness in his mouth.

"Were you able to determine the cause of death?" Randall asked.

"I was."

"Can you tell the court, what you found to be the cause of death."

"In my opinion the wound through the thorax and heart was the immediate and major cause of death. The other wounds of course I must admit did contribute to death."

"Thank you Doctor."

Randall turns to the jury and says, "As it appears on the listing previously submitted to the court, this copy of the autopsy report is marked as People's Exhibit 1 for identification,". To avoid the search process at trial, Randall has prepared individual CDs beforehand for each day's presentation. Now he projects the autopsy report by clicking on the title of the document on the screen and the system retrieves the exhibit and projects it.

The court reporter busily goes through folders on the desk. Exhibit cover sheets and labels are divided by yellow for plaintiff or blue for the defendant. There are also exhibit labels to affix to pictures or diagrams. Somewhere in the midst of all this are the large bulky items with exhibit label placed on tie tags or on the plastic bag containing the item. As has been done earlier, the Courtroom Deputy Clerk was advised which exhibits were needed for each witness. Now as the trial advances I can sympathize with the Deputy Clerk. I understand the need of placing the exhibits loose in folders so that the exhibit may be pulled out of the folder during trial and the need to get everything turned in at least 8 hours in advance of the trial. This had all taken time but now I understand why it had to be done.

"The People's Exhibit 1 has been received and marked," Judge Nicholson says.

"Your witness," Randall says to me as he goes back to his table.

I take a minute to glance at my list of questions I wish to ask the doctor and then walk slowly to the front. "Good morning Doctor Kindleworth. I will keep this as brief as possible." I walk a little closer. "Doctor, did it appear to you that Noah Arietta had been shot-- you said five times?" I ask.

"It did."

"And it appeared that each shot had gone through him and come out on the other side?"

"That is correct."

I pause for emphasis. "Then I take it you did not find any bullets?"

"No. I mention that in my report."

"Yes, but your conclusion that the wounds were caused by bullets was more or less of an assumption, then, was it not?"

"Well, in a sense…." The doctor pauses. "Yes."

"Would you say that your results were also influenced by the knowledge you had of the case and the men who requested and were present at the autopsy?"

"Yes." I could hear the hesitation in his voice as he wondered what I was getting at.

"You understood when you performed this autopsy that the subject had been shot by the defendant in the bar area of a café?"

"Yes."

"And this and certain other information had been supplied to you by the officers?"

"Well, yes. From them, the news on TV, the internet and by reading the newspaper, of course."

"But the officers gave you certain background information before you did your autopsy?"

"That is correct."

Someone was walking softly behind me and I turned around to see Jean Larson, rocking on her heels and trying to look innocent. I turn back to the witness. "So that to some extent your explorations were suggested by information you had received from them?"

There is a slight pause before the doctor responds. "Yes. But my primary purpose was to determine the cause of death. And I did determine it. I didn't need any information from anybody to do my job."

"Of course not, Doctor Kindleworth," I said. "You have made it very plain that the deceased was shot."

Wanting to make sure that the jury is aware that I am not trying to cast any doubt upon the evidence that my client, Lt. Trapp had shot Noah; I say this with determination because right now I am gunning for bigger game and the clever Jean Larson is perhaps smelling a rat so I go for the jugular quickly and deftly.

"Tell us then, Doctor Kindleworth," I say, "tell us how come you checked to determine whether spermatogenesis was occurring in the subject's testes?"

"I object!" Jean Larson says is a shrill voice, almost directly in my ear.

"On what grounds, Ms. Larson," the Judge inquires mildly.

"On the grounds of the findings being irrelevant," she said. "The People have called this witness to show the cause of death. He has shown it. Cross-examination should be confined to that issue.

Surely the question of whether the man was capable of... of spermatogenesis or what not would have no bearing on the issue."

"Mr. Dandridge?" Judge Nicholson says as he turns to address me.

"That is precisely why I asked the question, Your Honor," I said. I turned and picked up my copy of the autopsy report. "I now read from that portion of the doctor's report called General Findings on the top of page five, and it says, Spermatogenesis was occurring in both testes. That is part of the People's autopsy report. That report has now been officially entered as evidence in this case and I think I am entitled to inquire into anything that is on this report."

"The objection is overruled," the Judge said. "Doctor, you may answer the question."

"Sorry, can you repeat the question. I am not sure what I am to respond to."

The Judge turns toward the court reporter and says, "Please read the question to the witness."

I wait while the reporter looks back through his notes, locates the question and says. "How come, Doctor, you checked to determine whether spermatogenesis was occurring in the subject's testes?" He looks up with an inquiring expression and I nod my head in agreement.

I turn to the doctor, "Please answer the question, Doctor Kindleworth."

"Because they asked me to," the doctor replied.

"Who asked you to?"

"The officers present at the autopsy?"

"I see," I said. "Now did you know when you made that examination that another doctor had taken a vaginal smear from the defendant's wife and had reported it negative for spermatozoa?"

"I did."

"Objection," Jean Larson yells. "Based on hearsay, irrelevant." All eyes have turned toward the defense table and I am betting they are putting two and two together.

"You're a little late, Ms. Larson," the Judge said calmly. "the question seems to have been answered."

"Then I move that the answer be stricken from the record and the jury instructed to disregard both the question and the answer."

The Judge's voice seemed to rise a trifle. "The motion is denied. Please proceed, Mr. Dandridge."

"Now the primary purpose of this portion of your examination was to determine whether or not the seminal fluid of the deceased contained sperm?" I continued.

"Correct."

"And that inquiry had nothing to do with determining the cause of death?"

"Nothing whatsoever."

"In determining death you would ordinarily never make such an examination on a body that had so obviously met death from gunshot wounds?"

"That is correct."

"And you made this particular examination solely because you were asked to do so by the prosecuting officers?"

"I did."

"Now, doctor, if a question ever arose as to whether a man had intercourse with a woman who claimed that he had, and her smear for sperm showed negative, whereas the tests on the man were positive for seminal sperm, it might be said that he had intercourse, might it not?"

"Objection," Jean Larson shouted.

"Overruled," the Judge said.

"Yes," the witness answered.

"So, to clarify, the absence of sperm in a woman's pap smear might be the result of the absence of sperm in the male."

I turned around and looked at Jean Larson, jerking my head sideways as though ducking a snowball, and the courtroom chuckled while Jean Larson regarded me stonily. I turned back to the witness.

"I suppose that is true," he said. "I assume now that was the main purpose of their request."

"Objection; the witness assumes," Jean Larson persist.

"Objection sustained," the Judge ruled.

"Move that the answer be stricken and the jury instructed to disregard."

"The motion is granted. The jury will please disregard the last answer. Proceed, Mr. Dandridge."

"Now doctor, did you examine the deceased to determine whether he had recently had intercourse and reached a sexual climax?"

"I did not."

"Did you make any such examination?"

"I did not."

"Could you have done so?"

"I could have."

"Would it have disclosed the answer?"

"It should have."

"But you were not asked to, and you did not?"

"Correct."

"And you did not hear the subject discussed?"

"I did not."

I stole a look at the jury. Some of the jurors were looking at each other in wonder. I turned toward the defense table and my client was staring straight at me with what appeared to be a half-smile on his face?

"Now, doctor one or two more questions and I think we'll be about done. Did you make any examination to determine the alcoholic content of the blood of the deceased?"

"I did not."

"Where you asked to?"

"No."

"Could you have made such a determination if requested?"

"Very easily."

"That's all, doctor. Thank you," I said, and I went back to my table.

"Nice going," the Lieutenant whispered.

"We've at least got our foot in the door," I whispered back.

"Any re-direct, Mr. Walker?" The Judge inquired.

I watched as Randall and his assistant Jean put their heads together, whispering to each other. "No further questions Your Honor," Randall said as he lifts up slightly from his chair.

The Judge turns to Doctor Kindleworth, "As there are no further questions, you are excused, Doctor Kindleworth. You can step down."

As the doctor gratefully hurried back to his seat, Judge Nicholson looked at the clock. "We will take a fifteen-minute recess," he said

One could almost hear each juror exhale audibly in a long deep breath before following the Commissioners of Jurors out the door. The rest of the court room empties as people head toward the exit their weariness and relief apparent in their haste to get outside.

Chapter 2

I couldn't see Pete anywhere around, but he didn't require a briefing on the coverage since he was there in the thick of it. Besides, right now it is important to meet with the Trapps in the conference room. As I hurry down the hallway, I see the Sheriff hovering importantly outside the entrance to the conference room and when I am in front of him I say pleasantly, "Good afternoon" and he moves aside. I know he is stationed here because the jury will have to pass this way. As I open the door, both the Lieutenant and Paige turn around to greet me. They had been gazing out the window and from their expressions, they are feeling happy with the case results thus far, except for one issue that they bring up.

"It looks like the prosecution doesn't want the rape mentioned at all."

"Yes, you're right. That is what they are trying to keep out of the court room. Doctor Kindleworth was very helpful for our side as well as theirs. But there will be other opportunities and definitely I will cover it in my closing argument. I pull out my notepad and jot down a reminder, just in case I haven't included it before.

"Listen, Lieutenant, and you too Paige. I believe we have nothing to worry about and I want to assure you of that. We have gone over every aspect of the case and you have given me honest answers to my questions so that we have a good, maybe a great case."

"Aren't you worried they could come up with something that throws you off your game?"

I look at the Lieutenant and then over at Paige. "No, not really. This is like the game of chess. The goal of the game is to checkmate the opponents king by maneuvering him into a positon to be captured. In order to win there are four simple rules. Protect your king, don't carelessly lose your pieces, try and control the center of the board with your pieces and pawns and use all of your pieces." I pause, looking deeply at each one of them. "Do you see what I am getting at?"

"Yes, I do, the Lieutenant says and Paige nods in agreement.

"So if I have all the pieces, which in this case would be all the details, then I can play, study and win.

Paige speaks up. "I don't care for that Jean Larson. She's so; so different from her appearance and that makes me not want to trust her."

"I can understand that very well. I am not fond of her either and would like to ignore her, but I can't. She is too shrewd to be ignored and I trust she has a lot more up those tailored sleeves of hers."

"Richard," the Lieutenant says from across the room where he has gone back to staring out the window. "When the Judge overruled Larson, when you were questioning the doctor, I happened to be looking at the jury and I saw one of them grin and almost laugh out loud."

"Let me guess. It was the young husky blond haired man, sitting in the first row, on the extreme left end?"

"That's the one." The Lieutenant walks over to stand just in front of me. "I think he is a fan of yours. He watches your every move and hangs on your every word."

"Well, Lieutenant, I followed the Shrek Rule in choosing the jury which is it is better out than in. It's related to the 'hair in the food' rule. If there's a hair in your food...and you should always assume that there is...better that you should find it. If the jurors have unpleasant or frightening ideas, and they always do, better that they should reveal them in jury selection than conceal them until deliberation."

I watch as the Lieutenant shakes his head, then my attention is drawn away when Paige says, "Excuse me, but I have a complaint to make."

"What's that Paige."

"These glasses are for reading. I can't see anything beyond my nose with these glasses on. I thought the purpose of them was to make me appear professional, not blind."

"It is. Maybe you need to just find some glasses that are just plain glass and wear them instead."

"Good idea. I just might do that."

I watched as the Lieutenant places his hand on the back of his wife's waist and guides her toward the window. They stand there the rest of our time in the conference room. With nothing more to say, my mind flashes pictures as I wonder if I am doing the right thing here. I recall Charles Crawford of Missouri who received a life term in 1965 for murder and was paroled 1990 and was convicted of murder again in 1994. Jack Ferrell of Florida committed Murdered 1981 and was given a sentence of 15 years to life in 1982. He was paroled 1987 and murdered again in 1992. Then Timothy Buss murdered a five-year-old girl and was sentenced to 25 years in 1981. He was paroled 1993 and murdered a 10-year-old boy. Why would someone who had paid the cost for murder, do it all again. Is it possible that committing one murder makes it easier to do it again? The Lieutenant had served his country by killing. Could that have played a role in him murdering Noah instead of letting the law handle the punishment?

Extenuating circumstances can cause lawyers to pull their hair out in frustration, but we do the best we can. Now as I look at my client that's what I have to believe if I am to defend him. It was a one-time thing. The door opens and the Sheriff peeks in. "Five more minutes, Lt. and Mrs. Trapp.

"Thank you," they say in unison.

The Sheriff then focuses his attention on me. "Richard, the Judge wants to see you in chambers."

I turn to my clients. "Come with me," I said and lead them back into the court room where I am happy to see Pete already seated behind the defense table. I then excuse myself.

The Judge, Randall and Jean Larson sit chatting in chambers. There is a photographer from the local paper there and I look quizzically at the Judge. "What is this?"

"Oh, Richard, this young man wants to get a picture of us outside of the courtroom," he says this looking at the prosecutors. "and I thought that it would be nice to have you be part of the picture as well."

"Thank you Judge," I said. "Thanks for thinking of me, but I'm sorry,"

I lie. "If you don't mind, I promised my clients I would talk with them before court is back in session."

"Very well," Judge Nicholson said. "You are excused."

I thank the judge, turn and walk to the door. I think I actually see an appreciative gleam in the old Judge's eyes and I wonder if he knows this is an excuse because I want to appear as individual as possible in the jurors' eyes and to have a photograph of all of us together would throw that out the window. As I head to the courtroom I am glad I had enough forethought to tell the Trapps that under no circumstances should they permit their picture to be taken. I know there will be many pictures taken during the court case, both inside and outside the court room, but I do not want them posing for any.

The rest of the afternoon session begins with the presentations of charts and photos introduced into evidence and projected for the jury. It is like a prelim of boring details before the session really gets underway.

Judge Nicholson turns and looks at the prosecutors table. "District Attorney Walker call your next witness."

"The People call Coroner Jennifer Pfeiffer," Randall replies.

Coroner Jennifer Pfeiffer stands and strides to the witness box. I wonder if the jurors, like me, cannot picture this young woman as a coroner and if that will work in her favor or against her.

As she reaches the front, Finn Landon walks purposely toward her. "Coroner Pfeiffer, please raise your right hand." She obliges.

""Do you swear to tell the truth, the whole truth, and nothing but the truth, so help you God?"

"I do," Jennifer Pfeiffer replies and takes the witness chair.

Under the guidance of the prosecutors questioning, Jennifer tells the jury after being let in by the bartender, she saw Noel Arietta's body lying face down behind the bar in a pool of blood. She felt for a pulse and found none. She stated that she had arrived around two in the morning along with the state police. After a quick examination of the body, the police took measurements and 'pics' and then she had been allowed to remove the body and place it in the medical examiner van for transport. She had transported the body to her lab in Lyons, New York where it was kept in cold storage until the autopsy on Sunday. The body was later transported to the Monroe County Crime Lab for the autopsy and she had been present at the autopsy. After that Coroner Pfeiffer said that she had taken the body back to Lyons where the body was embalmed.

It was dry details without much fill in to make the juror sit up and notice and I for one was glad when it came to an end.

"Your witness," Randall said.

I got up and slowly walked up to the witness. "Good afternoon Coroner Pfeiffer...I'm sorry, is that how you wish to be addressed?" I see the thankful look on her face as she smiles and says, "No, please call me Doctor Pfeiffer."

"Doctor Pfeiffer, can you explain the difference between your job as a coroner and that of a medical examiner?"

"Yes. Coroners and medical examiners both deal with death, and the two titles are often used interchangeably as a result, but this is technically incorrect. As a coroner it is my job to direct activities such as autopsies, pathological and toxicological analyses, and inquests relating to the investigation of death. It is my job to determine cause of death or to fix responsibility for accidental, violent, or unexplained deaths. Sometimes I am the person who makes the decision to initiate an investigation if they determine the cause of death to be questionable. I work closely with law enforcement officials and public health officials."

"For the record can you tell me the job of the medical examiner."

"A medical examiner is a licensed physician who specializes in forensic pathology. When a death merits an autopsy, this medical professional performs the autopsy and records the findings. Although they form an important part of a law enforcement team, they do not necessarily decide the course of an investigation or prosecution of a suspect. "

"Thank you Doctor. I am sure this is helpful to the jurors too." I sneak a glance at the jury and can see they appreciate my line of questioning.

"Now, can you tell me was the bartender who let you and the state police in, alone at the bar?"

"Yes, he was alone."

"Where specifically did this take place?"

"At the Founders Café in downtown Rochester, in the bar area."

I look down at my pad, "So, you received the body and was the one who removed the clothing."

"Yes, that's right."

"Was it over an hour from the reported time of the killing to when you turned the clothing of the deceased over to the state police who then sent it to the Monroe County Crime Laboratory at 85 W. Broad St. Rochester, NY."

"Yes, that is correct."

"Can you tell me for what purpose this was done."

"For evidence of sperm or seminal stain," the coroner answered.

I prepared myself for the thunderous voice of Ms. Larson and am surprised at no objection being made so I continued. "Do you know the results of those clothing tests, if any?"

"I do not." Doctor Pfeiffer replies, "But the State Police should."

"Were you present during the autopsy when the officers asked Doctor Kindleworth to determine the spermatic capacities of the deceased?"

"I was there at all times."

"And?"

"Yes, I was there then."

"And was that done for the purpose of refuting any possible later claim that the deceased might not have possessed those capacities?"

"That was my understanding, yes."

"Was there any discussion among the officers about asking the doctor to determine whether the deceased had recently ejaculated?"

I ask that and look at the jury to see how they are taking this. I notice that a juror I recalled was named Margaret Foster was sitting forward on the edge of her seat.

"There was some discussion, yes," Doctor Pfeiffer said.

"In the presence of the doctor?"

"No."

"And no such examination was made."

"I'm not sure."

"Oh? Were you here when Doctor Kindleworth testified earlier?"

"No, I just got here. I was in the lab until now."

I lifted by eyebrows in surprise. "More murdered people? I hadn't heard. Seems it never rains but it pours…"

"No, not murders, just two bodies."

"In your role as coroner or embalmer?"

"Waiting to be embalmed."

"My sympathies, Doctor Pfeiffer. So, as to my question, what is the answer?"

"What Question?"

"I asked you whether in fact Doctor Kindleworth made any examination to find out whether the deceased had recently reached a sexual climax."

"He did not."

"Or any test for the alcoholic content of the blood?"

"He did not"

"Was that discussed by the officers?"

"I don't know?"

"That's all the questions I have, Doctor Pfeiffer. Thank you.

"

Randall had no re-direct

"You can step down now Doctor. Pfeiffer," Judge Nicholson says.

Randall next called to the stand Manson Carpenter a commercial photographer who is sworn in and takes the witness stand and once he is seated; Randall addresses the jury. "It has been said, that which we drink in at our ears, doth not so piercingly enter, as that which the mind doth conceive by sight." He pauses for emphasis. "The using of photographs has long been accepted for the simple fact that it is not an easy matter for even a well-trained mind to get a clear conception of a place, or of a physical thing, from a description given in words. That is why we have shown and will continue to show personal photographs, maps, plans, and buildings, so that each of you will obtain a full and clear understanding of the evidence."

"Mr. Carpenter will you review the photographs that you have taken for this case."

Mr. Carpenter waste no time as he quickly identifies a flock of 8 x 10 glossy photographs he had taken for the prosecution, all of which had been entered into evidence. I pay close attention to each picture as it is projected on the screen, especially the various views of Noah lying inert and crumpled behind the bar; Noah lying exposed on the slap, full face, left and right profile, Noah on his back with the ventilation marks showing up splendidly. Mr. Carpenter carefully describes each photograph in detail.

"Your witness," Randall says.

I was about ready to waive cross-examination when Paige Trapp leaned over the railing to whisper in my ear excitedly, "That man! He took some pictures of me that night. I just remembered…"

"Good girl," I whispered, and slowly rose and left my table and walked thoughtfully up toward the witness. Well, here was the first switch in the expected dialog, I thought, with luck this time perhaps fortunately for our side.

"Mr. Carpenter," I said pleasantly, indicating the latest exhibits, "were these all the pictures you took for this case?"

He shot a look at Randall's table, obviously seeking some direction, but none came. "No, there were some others."

"Perhaps they didn't turn out?" I said.

"No, they all turned out." A note of professional pride crept into his voice.

"Of course, Mr. Carpenter," I replied. "And these you have produced here are great examples of your craftsmanship." I paused. "Perhaps you forgot to bring the others?" There was no answer and I did not press. "Perhaps the others were needless duplicates?"

"No, there were no duplicates of poses."

"Oh," I said surprised. "Perhaps the other pictures had nothing to do with the case at all."

The witness is not happy. "They were photographs of Lieutenant Trapp's wife."

I see expressions of shock and wonderment on the faces of jury members so I hurriedly say, "And these pictures of Mrs. Paige Trapp; they turned out well?"

"Excellent."

"When did you take them?"

"That very night."

"Then they would show just how Mrs. Trapp looked right after the shooting?"

327

Sternly Mr. Carpenter replies, "They certainly would."

"How many did you take?"

"Three."

As expected, I hear footsteps behind me and without turning I know it is Ms. Larson again stalking my rear.

"Would you mind showing them to me?"

"I don't have them, they're back at my studio."

"What a pity. And I believe you didn't answer me when I asked if you forgot them. How come you didn't bring them along?"

I am almost giddy now because if the answer is what I am hoping for, it will help my case.

"I was requested not to."

"Hm, certainly not by anyone connected with this case?"

"Yes, sir."

"Come, Mr. Carpenter, tell us by whom?"

"Objection!" The voice of Ms. Larson fills the room.

"Overruled," said the Judge as I flamboyantly immersed my little finger in my ear on the jury side. "The witness may answer."

"Mr. Carpenter," I said softly, "could you have been told not to bring them by anybody presently standing, say, within three city blocks of me?"

"She's standing right behind you. It was Mrs. Lambert there. She said it would not be necessary to bring the pictures of Mrs. Trapp to court."

"Larson!" Jean Larson's voice grated in my ear. "The name is Ms. Larson, not Lambert." One could almost hear the missing word, 'idiot' that she holds back.

"Ah, you mean Mrs. Larson." I start to stop there but can't help adding. "The Lamberts might not like any confusion either, you know, they might possibly know Mrs. Larson." I had to take my fun where I found it; because Larson's turn would inevitably come.

"I'm sorry," the witness said, adding. "Mrs. Larson told me not to."

"Well, if you don't have the pictures you can't very well show them," I said. "But perhaps you can describe for us the picture you saw of Mrs. Trapp that night with your own eyes? That might even be better."

"Objection," Ms. Larson said quickly, before the Judge could make his ruling. If Ms. Larson thought she was helping my case by keeping this testimony from the jury, which I guessed must be fairly consumed with curiosity about now, she could block away. Before the Judge gives his ruling I turn and say, "Your Honor, I would like to request to have Mr. Carpenter bring the three photographs to the court to be placed into evidence."

Judge Nicholson I withdraw the question, the witness is back to you." I bow and return to the defense table.

"No further questions," Ms. Larson said, glaring stonily at me.

"The witness is excused."

I looked around for Pete, to bask in his approval, but could not locate him. "Hell," I thought, "Just when I have a fairly good round.

***

"Call your next witness, Mr. Walker," Judge Nicholson says.

"I call Franklin Orwell to the stand."

Franklin Orwell is plain. He has a long, face, a pointy nose and a shock of black hair that is unruly. His thick brows give him a menacing appearance as he walks forward in a suit hanging loosely on his thin frame. As I watch his progress I can't help myself as I think about his namesake's statement, "If you want a picture of the future, imagine a boot stamping on a human face--forever." Again I have to squash an urge to laugh out loud.

Randall waits until the witness is sworn in and seated then he approaches the stand and says, "Mr. Orwell, can you tell us what you do for a living?"

Loudly, Mr. Orwell clears his throat. "I am a speech-language pathologist."

"Can you tell the jury about your education and place of work."

"Sure. I received my B.S. and M.S. in Speech-Language Pathology from Adelphi University in Garden City, New York and specialize in evaluation, diagnosis, treatment, and therapeutic support. I am the president and owner of Orwell Speech Language Pathologists."

Thank you Mr. Orwell. Now can you tell us what happened on July 31st when you were in the Founder's Café bar."

Mr. Orwell shifts his body on the witness stand as if trying to appear relaxed, but looking even more uncomfortable. He clears his throat again. "Well, I was having a beer at the bar, when I hear several shots and I turn toward the sound and see there is a man standing up on the rail in front of the bar and leaning far over the bar, clicking an empty gun at something behind the bar. I can't see what it is."

"What did you do?" Randall asks.

"What would anyone do. I got the hell..." Mr. Orwell turned to look at the Judge. "Sorry Judge. I mean I got out of there fast."

"Did you know the man who was doing the shooting?"

"Not by name, but I would recognize him."

"Do you see him in the courtroom?"

"Yes, he's sitting next to Mr. Dandridge there at the other table."

"You are referring to the defendant, Lt. Vincent Trapp?

"That is correct."

"Thank you Mr. Orwell. Your witness Mr. Dandridge."

It was my desire not to ask about any movements that Noah may have made before the shooting since I was pretty sure the witness would not remember or have seen anything and I didn't want to chance the jury hearing him say that so I steer clear and hope later I will find another way to broach the subject of Noah reaching for something behind the bar. So I begin saying, "Mr. Orwell, when you saw Lieutenant Trapp at the bar and he stood up on the bar rail and leaned down over the bar…," I paused. "Did the Lieutenant say, 'take that you s.o.b., or words to that effect?"

Mr. Orwell's tilts his head to one side and looks straight ahead, deep in thought. "Not that I heard. To the best of my recollection Lt. Trapp didn't utter a sound. He came in, went over to the bar and then left."

"Did you see any signs of anger on his face or in his movements."

This time Mr. Orwell doesn't hesitate. "None, that I saw. Of course I must admit I didn't get a good look because I did hurry out of there as fast as I could."

"Do you know what time it was? I mean the time of the shooting?"

"Not exactly, but it was close to one o'clock in the morning. because I don't live far from the bar and I was home by one in the morning.

"This is important Mr. Orwell. Did you pay for the beer at the bar?"

ɔ

"No, Noah wouldn't let me pay. He said it was on the house."

"I see. So you and Noah were close friends, I guess."

"No, hardly knew him. I did know the regular bartender though."

"Hmm," I say for emphasis, "And was the bar crowded?"

"Yes, practically the whole length, with just, like I said, the one open space that Lt. Trapp filled which was near some rails"

Rails, I ran the word over in my mind and finally understood. "By rails are you talking about the waitresses' service station?"

"Yes, I think so. It's where the patrons are told not to stand."

I can see Mr. Orwell is tiring as he continually reaches up and wipes at his eyes. "You're doing fine, Mr. Orwell." I give him a moment and then ask, "Did Noah buy the whole bar a round of drinks?"

"Yes, he did. I heard later that it wasn't the first round he bought that night either."

I try to control the building excitement at the answers he gives. "And was Noah drinking?"

"Well, let me see. He was drinking on the round he bought me. So, Yes."

My next question could ruin my line of questioning if the answer isn't what I hope it to be. I have to ask, "Do you know if buying house drinks was his usual practice?"

There is a slight pause before Mr. Orwell says, "It was the first time I'd seen him treat the bar. I can say that it was probably the first time this happened for me in three years."

"Three years?"

"Yes, three years."

"Would you say that you were a fairly regular customer at the Founder's Bar. I mean for an occasional nightly beer." I didn't want him to appear to be a heavy drinker.

Mr. Orwell nods and says, "Yes, a fairly regular customer. I am a snob when it comes to a bar. I look for safety, believe it or not," he says with a grin, "I don't want to have to look over my shoulder every time someone walks in. And it can't be too noisy because I like to talk to the people next to me without shouting and trying to read lips. Oh yes, and I don't like it when the jukebox is blaring or the sound system is so loud that I have to scream to hold a conversation. Until this happened, this was my idea of a great bar."

"I see. Do you remember who you were standing next to on the night in question?"

"I was seated by the end of the bar nearest the street and talking to two brothers Leo & Malcolm Parks,"

I am getting anxious and I want to lead the conversation down another path, but I know Ms. Larson would be all over me so I work around it.

"Tell me where was the bartender during this shooting?"

"Standing over near the door, I believe. At least I spoke to him there when I came in."

"Was it the usual practice for Noah to work alone behind the bar." I quickly add, "Answer if you know, if not, it's okay."

"No, it wasn't. In fact, I remarked about it to the brothers. He often stood at the end or behind the bar, but rarely waited on the patrons of the bar. His bartender or the barmaids usually did that."

"And was it equally unusual for the bartender to be out on the floor, standing by the door?"

Mr. Orwell places a fist under his chin. "Well, now that you mention it, it was unusual. Brook, that's the bartender, usually stayed behind the bar."

It is again going better than expected. "Tell me Mr. Orwell, just before the shooting, how did the deceased appear?"

"I don't know what you mean by that?"

"Did he seem nervous or fidgety. Was he acting like he expected something bad to happen or was he cheerful and calm?"

I waited for an objection but it didn't come.

"I would say he was perfectly calm and at ease." I could see the Cheshire smile on Ms. Larson's face thinking that was a leap in their direction. What man who had just raped another man's wife would be calm and at ease.

I continued. "Mr. Orwell, if you were not here testifying in the murder case of People versus Lt. Vincent Trapp, you could honestly say the same thing...that Noah Arietta was calm and at ease..., even if the case being tried here now were instead the trial of People versus Noah Arietta for rape?"

The witness' unmistakable "Yes" and Jean Larson's booming "Objection" exploded in the courtroom at the same time.

"Sustained", Judge Nicholson ruled sternly. "Mr. Dandridge you know better. Please rephrase the question or otherwise change your line of questioning."

The Judge says to the court stenographer, "the question and answer will be stricken from the record." He then turns toward the jury and says, "As for the previous question, the jury is asked to disregard the question and the answer."

"I'm sorry, Your Honor, I apologize. No further questions."

"We have no further questions for the witness." Ms. Larson curtly replies.

"Mr. Orwell, you are excused. Please step down."

As I return to the defense table I see Pete grinning from ear to ear. We had discussed that last strategy and Pete had said that we needed to bring it out early and as dramatically as possible. No doubt about it now. The rape had its foot in the door.

The witnesses that followed were all individuals who were standing at the bar that night. Each told their version and in general it was the same as that of Mr. Orwell. They agreed that the Lieutenant had walked up to the bar and though they had not seen the shooting they did see Noah standing up on the bar rail after Noah had fallen, and then had silently turned and left the place. All agreed that the shooting occurred around one a.m. Some said around 12:45 a.m. Many, including the Parks brothers, said that Noah had brought as many as five rounds of drinks that night and that this was as Mr. Orwell had implied, not his usual behavior or place to be.

It was all the same and on cross examination I received nothing new until the last two witnesses who were waitresses at the bar. When I asked them if Lt. Trapp had spoken at all, they said that they had spoken to the Lieutenant as he had approached the bar, just before the shooting, but that the defendant had not returned their greeting or looked at them. These same two witnesses also thought they heard Noah Arietta say "Good evening, Lieutenant." Or words to that effect as the defendant approached the bar.

Randall conducted the examination of all of these witnesses and I carefully cross-examined them.

By then it was nearing five o'clock. Randall Walker glanced at his watch, stood and looked in the direction of Judge Nicholson. "I'd like to call another witness to the stand."

"Fine, Mr. Walker. Go ahead."

"I'd like to call Kyle Redford to the stand."

I looked down at my pad and searched through the screens until I found the name, Redford. I quickly reviewed the information I had collected and then turned my attention to the court room. This would be interesting.

Kyle Redford is wearing a long sleeve plaid shirt and a pair of neat, clean blue jeans. With his shirt tucked in the girth of his waist was apparent and as he walked forward, the dent in the hair at the back of his neck showed where the strap of a hard hat would hit him. He was what one would call, his own man. As soon as the witness was seated in the witness stand, Randall said. Please tell the jury your full name.

"My name is Kyle Redford."

"Mr. Redford will you tell the court what you do for a living."

"I'm a plasterer. I apply coats of plaster, cement, and stucco to interior and exterior surfaces."

As if to give weight to this witness, Randall asked, "How do you do your job."

"I follow blueprints, architect's drawings or oral instructions."

"Interesting," Randall says. "So, can you tell me how you came to be at the Founder's Café?"

"Sure. My wife and I were out to dinner with another couple at the Founder's Café that night."

"So where were you seated in the café."

"At a table near the outside door."

"Did you go there often?"

"Often enough."

"Did you speak with anyone, besides the couple you came with?"

"Yes, we chatted for a long time with the bartender, a Mr. Brook Hamilton. He stood by our table."

"Can you tell the court what interrupted your conversation."

"Yes, we heard several shots. They sounded like giant firecrackers. And then we saw Lt. Trapp leaving the place and the bartender quickly followed out after him."

"Your witness," Randall said.

I wasn't sure if the prosecution thought they had gained anything from this line of questioning except that the bartender went out after Lt. Trapp. In any case, I began my cross-examination.

"Did the bartender, Brook Hamilton, return or remain outside?" I ask.

"He came right back in."

"Did he say anything to you?"

"Yes, he said he recognized it was Lieutenant Trapp."

"Anything else?"

"No, after that he hurried over to the bar."""

"Are you sure he said nothing else?"

"Not that I recall."

"How long had the bartender stood by your table?"

"Quite a while, I would say well over half an hour. We were in no hurry and it was a nice night and our table was right by the window."

"Did the bartender sit down and talk with you?"

"He talked but didn't sit down, though we asked him to several times."

"You asked him to sit down?" I said. That's interesting. Here was a tired bartender on break to rest a bit and he wouldn't even sit down when invited to.

"Yes, but he said he was expecting a friend from out of town and wanted to keep an eye out for him. He did keep looking out the window."

I glanced around to the rows of waiting People's witnesses and found the bartender, Brook Hamilton, sitting with folded arms and staring straight ahead. Tyra Pederson was not to be seen; in fact, neither Pete nor I had observed her around the courthouse since the case had opened. I turned back toward the witness stand.

"Mr. Redford, did you say the bartender talked to you and your party?"

"Occasionally. Just small talk, the weather, how busy the place was and, oh yes, how his boss Noah Arietta, had recently won another pistol shoot; casual stuff like that."

I could have gone up and kissed the man. "Casual stuff indeed. "So the bartender told you that Mr. Arietta had won another pistol shoot?" I said.

"Yes. We didn't pay much attention; it was an old story. Noah was always winning another pistol shoot. I guess he was one of the best in the business."

I paused thoughtfully. Trial lawyers who sought to polish perfection frequently only managed to cloud it instead. Perhaps I'd better leave well enough alone. I turned around toward Randall, ignoring Jean Larson, who was again lurking behind me. "No further questions."

"Do you wish to cross-examine the witness," Judge Nicholson says.

I watch as Randall glances at Jean Larson and see the slight shaking of her head.

"No further questions, Your Honor."

"All right. Then there being nothing else from either party, we're adjourned. Court will reconvene at nine a.m. on Thursday, September 16th."

I watch the court clerk walk gingerly to the front of the court room. He clears his throat and says, "All rise!"

Instantly I hear the usual sounds of fabric in motion as the full room stands. We continue standing until Judge Nicholson disappears behind the back door entrance and like trained seals the spectators move as one toward the court room exit.

***

I let out a breath of air and feel my body responding to the calm that now descends within me. I have made it through the first day of trial and I feel good. There is no doubt, I have earned my salary and I have made my client happy. I know it's too soon to bask in victory, but I'm going to enjoy it while I can. We had a great defense strategy for this case and it seems to be strong enough to keep my client from facing a long prison term or thousands of dollars in fines. All those hours of sifting through the evidence collected by the prosecution and listening carefully to the Lieutenant's version of what happened and reviewing over and over again the evidence collected from our own investigation of the case has paid off royally. I know the smile on my face has been earned.

Chapter 3

I am in the midst of packing up when Paige comes up to the front to join me and her husband. The Lieutenant is the first to speak.

"Richard, I am impressed. I had a hard time figuring out where you were going with your line of questioning, but when you got there...wow."

"Thank you Vincent. Thank you."

Paige reached across and touched my arm. "You are great. I am so glad we have you as our lawyer, Richard. Truly glad and grateful."

"I'm glad it is going so well and that you can see it is, but we still have a ways to go before I will feel comfortable. That Ms. Larson is clever and the perfect person to play off our capable prosecutor, Randall Walker. Together they are a force to be reckoned with so I must keep on my toes."

I am saying this as much to myself as to them. I then look at them and smile. "Well, you two, go home and get some rest and I will be in touch." We shake hands and then I watch them walk down the aisle toward the exit. I then finish gathering up my belongings, take one last look around and find myself whistling as I head toward the door.

The weather outside is perfect, hovering around sixty degrees with no humidity. The sky is clear which can be a rarity this time of year so it's greatly appreciated as I look around for Pete. I check the car, but he isn't there and his briefcase is gone. I lean closer and see something on the driver's seat so I dig out my keys and open the door.

It's a note from Pete.

"Richard, I got a new lead and waited as long as I dare but had to take off. I'll call you if I can, but definitely fill you in tomorrow. Don't worry. Get a good night's sleep. It was a long day."

I stand there reading the note over again as if there is a hidden message to be found. It's silly of me, but I start worrying, wondering if... No, I reprimand myself. Pete is fine. But, I remind myself, this is the second time he has disappeared today. What could be so important he had to leave quickly without giving me any details. I take out my cell and call Theresa.

"Theresa, has Pete checked in with you?"

"No, why?"

"I can't find him and earlier today he went missing."

"Well, I can't help you."

Something in her voice makes me think she is not being totally honest with me. She knows something. "Come on Theresa, you aren't a good liar. You know something so spill it."

She is silent on the other end. Finally, she says, "I can't tell you. I promised so stop asking."

"Theresa?" I practically yell into my cell and then the call is ended.

Chapter 4

On Thursday morning, I arrive at the court feeling a little side swiped by Theresa and Pete, but I need to put that aside. I have a job to do. I had hoped to hear from Pete before court reconvened but it was not looking like I would know what was up his sleeve anytime soon.

When I park the car, I am greeted by the Lt. and Mrs. Trapp in the parking lot and we all walk in together. I am glad that besides me, no one knows that my partner is missing, because no one knows I have a partner.

Inside the court room Lt. and Mrs. Trapp follow me and Mrs. Trapp takes her usual seat directly behind the defense table. I wait until she is seated then the Lieutenant and I walk ahead, opening the gate and proceeding to our seats at the table. I try to focus as I take out my files strategically placing them on the table before finally allowing myself to turn and look around to see if Pete is in the court room.

He's not sitting near the front, as I scan the area. I continue to let my eyes flow over the seating and still no Pete. Trying to remain calm I check out the witnesses, just because I can't think where else to look. As I allow my eyes to survey the full length of the first row behind the bar my gaze pauses as I see an unfamiliar face.

I turn my attention to a man with a rosy complexion, high cheekbones, and sparse hair, but enough to be respectable. He sports a short grey beard and mustache on his lean face. His eyes that are so deep set I can't make out the color seem to be looking right through me and I guess, this must be the prosecution's psychiatrist. This has to be Doctor Mason Anderson.

At that moment, Judge Nicholson is announced and I stand along with everyone else in the court room and watch as he walks to the bench and once we are all seated again, the Judge asks if we are ready to begin. Both Randall and I reply.

"The people are ready."

"The defense is ready.

"Call you first witness," Mr. Randall.

"I call Mrs. Kyle Redford to the stand." Mrs. Redford is sworn in. There is nothing noteworthy during the questioning by Randall or my cross examination of Mrs. Redford as she repeats basically what her husband has already stated. His next witness is the friends who were seated at the table with the Redford's and after being sworn in they agree to what we have previously heard, giving the same information as gleaned from the Redford's. They answer in their own words the conversation they had with the bartender and the fact that the bartender stood by their table during the shooting.

Next there were seven witnesses on the list that Randall addresses the court about. "Your honor, the remaining witnesses have left the state and cannot be produced at this time. The Sheriff has tried to issue subpoenas, but has been unsuccessful. These witnesses are beyond the confines of the state.

I look over the names on the list. "Have all of these witnesses been previously interviewed by the prosecutor?" I ask.

"Yes," Randall responds, "and I have their testimony for the court and the defense." I watch as Randall goes to his desk and produces papers that he distributes to me and to the Judge to review.

Actually, I do not foresee a need to interview these individuals since I had done so earlier but I know that the judge must determine whether the witness is material and necessary to the criminal proceeding and will in this case probably allow for their absence.

Some people take advantage of the moment, while others remain in their seats. I take the time to check again to see if Pete has arrived, but do not see him anywhere so I turn my attention to the Lieutenant and we talk quietly together. In less than 10 minutes, the Judge is back on the bench.

"The material witness statute permits the detainment of any person who may have information pertaining to a criminal investigation for the purpose of testifying before a grand jury or during a criminal proceeding. In the case of these witnesses, I can see no reason for pressing the issue of their attendance. The copies of their testimony will be entered into the record and supplied to the jurors."

"In that case, Your Honor, the defense waives the producing of these seven witnesses and further waives any cross-examination of them." I pause for effect. "Besides, the defense does not dispute the fact that my client, Lieutenant Vincent Trapp did cause the death of Noah Arietta by shooting him. We dispute only that it was murder."

As can be expected, Jean Larson is at the ready. "All counsel needs to say is he waives or he doesn't' waive." If looks could kill, I would be dead.

I can't help myself as a smirk plasters itself on my face. "Sorry, I waive the right to cross examine these seven witnesses."

"Fine!" the Judge replies with annoyance ringing in his voice, "Mr. Prosecutor, call you next witness.:"

"The People call Brook Hamilton,"

Finn Landon doesn't seem to tire as he moves to stand in front of the next witness. "Mr. Hamilton, please raise your right hand." Brook does as he is asked.

""Do you swear to tell the truth, the whole truth, and nothing but the truth, so help you God?"

"I do."

"Please be seated, Mr. Hamilton."

I watch Brook take the seat in the witness stand. I can hardly recognize the bartender from the Founder's Café He wears a sports jacket over a tan shirt and tie and unlike when I first met him, his colorful tattoos are no longer visible. Even his hair appears different with the tuff island at the crown neatly combed.

"State your name, please," Randall says.

"Brook Hamilton."

"Where do you live?"

"1093 East Main Street, Rochester.

"Where do you work?"

"I am the bartender at the Founder's Café on Marsh Road in Rochester."

"Were you on duty the night of Friday, July 31st, and during the early hours of Saturday, August 1, of last year?"

"Yes, I was."

"Did you know the deceased Noah Arietta?"

"I did."

"How long have you known Mr. Arietta?"

"Since taking the job as bartender, which would be almost two years. He was my boss."

"Do you know the defendant Lt. Vincent Trapp?"

"I do."

"How long have you known Lt. Trapp?"

Brooks eyebrows squeeze closer together as he gives the question some thought. "I would say I have known of Lt. Trapp for several years, but to have actually met and talked to him it has been more like a month. We would share words on his occasional visits to the bar."

"Can you identify in this courtroom the man you know as Lieutenant Trapp?"

"I can."

"Will you do so?"

"That gentleman sitting at the table over there." He points to the defense table. "The man sitting with the lawyer, Mr. Dandridge."

"Thank you, Mr. Hamilton. Now, can you tell us if you were in the bar when the shooting occurred?"

"I was."

"Where were you?"

"I was standing next to the table where Mr. and Mrs. Redford were seated with their friends."

"Did you see the actual shooting?"

"No."

I almost jump up off my seat. I don't believe that. I don't believe it at all.

"Did you hear the shots, Mr. Hamilton?" Randall asks.

"Yes, sir. I heard six shots fired. After about the second shot, I looked over and saw this man bending down and leaning over the bar."

"Then what happened?"

"Well, then this man stood up, turned and walked out the door near where I was standing."

"Did you recognize him?"

"I wasn't sure who it was at first." Brook answered.

"What did you do then?" Randall asked.

346

Okay, I think as I wait impatiently for Brook to reply. I am sure he will now tell the court that the Lieutenant said to him, "Do you want some, too, buster?"

"Well, I rushed out the door after him."

"Were you able to identify him outside?"

"I was. He turned and faced me and I recognized him."

"Tell the court, who was the man that faced you?"

"Lieutenant Trapp."

"Lieutenant Vincent Trapp?"

"Yes."

Randall turned casually around and glanced at Jean Larson and again I saw the little telltale nod. "Your witness, Mr. Dandridge," Randall said.

For a moment I sat there stunned. Here was one of the few People's witnesses who possessed vital prosecution information that would beat down our insanity defense. They had led this witness up to the threshold of that damaging information then quit cold turkey and turned him over to me. I smell a rat and I am not about to put my feet into boiling water.

"Reviewing my notes," I lie to the Judge. I need to figure out what Randall and Jean are up to before I say a word. The Judge nods at me granting more time and I stare sightlessly at the blank pad before me.

I arose and walked toward the witness. "did you speak to the lieutenant when you rushed out the door after him, as you have just so dramatically described it?"

"Yes, I said, Lieutenant Trapp?"

"I see, and this was the same man you have just testified you weren't sure you recognized?"

"Well, yes."

"The lights from the barroom weren't helping you when you correctly called him by name, were they?"

"Well, I guessed it was him."

"My question was, Mr. Hamilton, were the lights then helping you?"

"No."

"I see. Now a dozen odd causal patrons in the bar clearly recognized the Lieutenant but you, who had been standing by the door when he entered and when he left, you had to guess his identity?"

"That's right."

The lying bastard, I thought. The phrase was becoming a sort of a litany. "What if anything did the Lieutenant do when you spoke his name?"

"He whirled around."

And then you were able to confirm your shrewd guess as to who he was?"

"Yes, sir."

The stage was now set and I pressed on. "Did the Lieutenant say anything."

"Yes."

I glanced over at Jean Larson, who was staring up at the ceiling, doubtless with glee-crossed fingers. "will you please, Mr. Hamilton, tell us what it was he said?" I pressed.

"He said, 'Do you want some, too, Buster?'"

"Ah, and was he pointing his gun at you?"

"I believe he was.'"

"His empty gun?"

"I wouldn't know."

"You heard all the People's witnesses here who testified that the Lieutenant kept clicking his empty gun at Noah, didn't you?"

"Well, yes, but I didn't know then that it wasn't loaded."

I glanced around and found Randall and his assistant with their heads bent together in smiling and busy consultation. "Now, Mr. Hamilton," I said, "I assume of course you have told your story of the incidents of that night to the police, have you not?"

"Yes."

"And to Prosecutor Walker?"

"Yes."

"And to his part-time helper, Ms. Jean Larson?"

"Yes."

"And you of course told all of them, did you not, what you have just told me, namely that the Lieutenant wheeled around and said, 'Do you want some, too, Buster?'"

"Objection!" Larson yelled. "The defense is trying to infer that the prosecution is trying to conceal something. The reason we did not pursue this line of questioning was that it might create error or a mistrial, being possible evidence of the commission of still another criminal offense by the defendant."

I turned and stared across at Jean Larson. "The defendant is touched by your solicitude for his welfare, Ms. Larson," I said. "You would only have moved mountains to have brought this out if I hadn't."

"Tut, tut, gentlemen," the Judge reproved us. "I will take the answer."

"Yes, I told all of them about it." Mr. Hamilton finally had a chance to say.

"And when did you tell Ms. Larson?" I pressed on.

"Last night and again this morning."

"And did she or anyone ever warn you not to tell about this Buster business because it might be in error or hurt the Lieutenant's best interest?"

The witness tried to glance around me at the prosecutor's table. "Look at me and answer," I said.

"No, I don't believe that subject was mentioned."

Every lawyer has a juror that they focus on during the trial. I glance at my juror and noted that he was following this fairly intricate courtroom waltz. I paused and thought of what this devious character of a bartender had earlier told Paige and the Lieutenant about Noah, about his expression of sympathy and the 'wolf' business and all. Perhaps I had better get into that now, I thought, but I would have to do so obliquely, if I came at him cold and asked him straight out he would probably simply deny the whole thing.

"Mr. Hamilton," I said, "as a bartender what do you call your cheaper brands of whisky?"

Surprised by my line of questioning he takes a moment, "Oh, bottom shelf, red-eye or hooch. They're just slang names."

"Yes, of course. And your bonded bourbon?"

"Well, simply bonded or bourbon."

He apparently still did not see the drift. "I see," I said. "Now what do you call a man who has an insatiable penchant for women, any and all women?"

"What's 'penchant,' sir?"

"It means a desire, appetite, passion, taste, or hunger."

His eyes flickered and I now saw he'd got the drift. Cautiously he replies, "Why a lady's man, I guess." He glanced at the Judge. "Or maybe simply a damned fool." The courtroom tittered and the Judge glared the onlookers into silence.

"Anything else?"

Ms. Larson was on her feet. "We don't see the importance of all this. Your Honor. I…"

"You mean, Ms. Larson, you do see the importance," I broke in.

"Proceed, gentlemen, proceed," the Judge said sharply.

"Anything else, Mr. Hamilton?" I said

"Woman chaser," he ventured.

"Hm, pretty medieval. Please try again."

"Masher."

"Come, now, Mr. Hamilton, mashers went out with whalebone corsets and hair nets, but you're getting warmer. Anything else?"

Studiously, thoughtfully, "No sir, I guess I've run out of terms. You see, sir, I haven't had the educational advantages you've had."

The clever little bastard, I thought. "How about the expression 'wolf?'" I said. "Or perhaps you've led too sheltered a life ever to have heard of that?"

"Naturally, I've heard it. It slipped my mind."

"Naturally it would. Clanking around in there with all those rusty old mashers it naturally would. Do you ever use the expression yourself?"

"Nat.. he began but caught himself. "Of course I have. Everybody does."

"What does it mean?"

"Well, I guess just about what you said, an insatiable desire for women."

"Have you used the expression lately?"

"I couldn't remember that any more than you could."

"Maybe I can refresh your recollection," I said. "Do you remember driving Mrs. Trapp to Lyons the Sunday after the shooting?" The witness craned around to look at Jean Larson. "You needn't look at Ms. Larson," I said.

Ms. Larson leapt to her feet. "Let the witness answer," she shouted hotly. "Don't try to pretend he's being evasive."

"I wouldn't need to half try," I said.

The Judge spoke wearily; we were wearing him down. "I suggest both of you invoke a little silence and let the witness answer. In fact, I order you to respond, he said looking at Mr. Hamilton."

"Yes, I remember, the witness answered.

I decided suddenly to veer away from all this and let the witness sizzle a little, a slow broil was something good for the memory. "Now, Mr. Hamilton, "I said, "you knew the deceased quite personally, did you not?"

"Yes."

"And did you consider yourself to some extent his confidant?"

"Yes"

"Would it be fair to say that you were as friendly with him as any of his male acquaintances?"

Thoughtfully he replied, "Well, yes."

"And were you able to tell when he was drinking heavily or not?"

"I object," Jean Larson said. "Nothing in this case involves drinking. Had the deceased been dead drunk it still has no bearing. I see no connection. Your Honor," she concluded.

"You will, Ms. Larson, you will," I said.

"I think possibly the objection may be well taken," the Judge said, "but I will let the witness answer the question"

I nodded at the witness. "I do not believe he was drinking particularly heavily that night," Hamilton answered.

"I did not ask you if Noah was drinking heavily that night, Mr. Hamilton," I said," I asked you whether you were able to tell when he was drinking heavily."

"Yes"

"Thank you. Now, "Was he drinking heavily that night?""

"No," The man was lying so I pressed on.

"Or that day?"

"No."

"And how much did he drink when he was drinking heavily?"

"I object. The witness has said flatly that the deceased was not drinking heavily that day, which is the day that concerns us."

"Well, you're pushing this pretty far, Mr. Dandridge," the Judge said, "but since we're into it, I'll take the answer. But I warn you, the limit is near."

I decided to veer from this line of questioning before I got slapped down. "I'll withdraw the question, Your Honor," I turn back to the witness. "Now I ask you whether from your familiarity with the deceased you knew whether he was an expert pistol shot?"

"Objection. No self-defense in this case. All evidence points to the fact the defendant was unquestionably the aggressor. That makes this line of questioning immaterial and irrelevant."

"Mr. Dandridge?" the judge said questioningly.

I was in a dilemma. I certainly knew why I wanted to get in the drinking and expert pistol business and since the Judge had all our requests for instructions, he too certainly knew. And Ms. Larson was shrewd enough to sense that I was up to no good, so she was objecting and I had to admit to myself that as of now her objections were probably good.

"We believe this evidence may be material, Your Honor," I said, "and several of the People's witnesses have already indicated as such. For instance, the Redford's."

"I don't know what you are talking about," Ms. Larson said.

I ignored her. "I believe, that the deceased was considered to be an expert shot. We believe it has a connection with certain important issues in this case. However, we will of course abide by the court's ruling." It was a lame and reluctant retreat from a tense and touchy courtroom situation.

"I believe that I must withstand the objection," the Judge said slowly. "Until proper issues are raised making such questions relevant I don't think I can permit this line of questions. If and when whatever issues you may have in mind should properly be raised here, I will allow both sides to introduce their concerns. But not until then. That is the court's ruling."

I glanced at my juror and found him downcast; the only good thing about the Judge's ruling was that it now showed beyond any doubt that my juror cared. Jean Larson was beaming her satisfaction and approval over such an erudite judge. In the meantime, I needed to save face. "Your Honor," I said, "may it be understood, then, that the defense can reserve further cross-examination of this witness until these proper issues should be raised?"

"It may be so understood, and I so rule. This witness and indeed all witnesses are under subpoena here I will not permanently excuse them and they may not leave the jurisdiction of this court without my permission. If and when the proper issues are raised here to warrant these and similar questions, both sides may have at them to their hearts content and with the court's blessing."

"Very well, Your Honor," I said. "With that understanding we have no further questions of this witness at this time."

"Any redirect?" the Judge inquired, looking at Randall.

Jean Larson thought a moment, her chin resting on her hand. "No, Your Honor," she said. "No further questions."

"There has been a lot of friction and we will all do well to take a ten...no, a fifteen-minute recess. Court is adjourned for fifteen minutes." Counsel will meet me in my quarters.

***

That fifteen-minute briefing was to be expected. Judge Nicholson said he was "disappointed" about having to address the subject of lawyer behavior, calling it "at best, a distraction."

The rest of Thursday courtroom battle crept by slowly. The prosecution was bent on cleaning up the odds and ends of details from its remaining witnesses, saving the best for the last, which would translate to be the best for them, that is. Randall questioned the alert state police who were paraded to the stand, one by one to give their reports. Each one seems to want to outdo their predecessor on describing the details shown in the charts of the crime scene. There was no need to prompt them with questions as they repeated the accuracy of the measurements taken, described where the body was found and how far the body was from the door. From them the jury heard the location of the Trapp's residence and the distance from there to the Founder's Café and the distance to the park entrance. It was repeat after repeat and yet Randall kept them coming. I had all I could do to stay awake and I was not the only one.

I understood why Randall did this. He was hoping that something new might emerge, something that was not mentioned earlier because its significance wasn't realized but now with the competition of besting each other might lead to a new discovery. Only it was not happening. I glanced at the jury and could tell they were becoming disinterested too. I made a decision that I would not prolong the agony. So as Randall finished with each police officer and turned the questioning over to me, I no more than summarized what each had said, waited for their concurrence and went on to the next; skipping over several of the witnesses along the way.

There are some limits placed on the questions that can be asked during cross-examination by the defense. Typically, the questions are limited to matters testified to on direct examination by the prosecution. That's the rules, however, if a witness "opens the door" on cross-examination, by volunteering information not discussed on direct, then they can be questioned on that subject. Only to get that information out requires finesse and is best done with a witness known to the defense and one who I knew personally had more to share.

There was no need to bring up questions on Noah's personal life or his habits. I didn't mention his collection of guns and I definitely steered clear of any talk of rape or Paige Trapp. Oh yes, and one other area I left alone, the lie-detector test. My cross-examination was just perfunctory.

The prosecution was doing it right, only elongated. Randall was calling witnesses that favorably persuade the jury and though repeating themselves, his witnesses were the story-tellers. They're the ones who saw what happened, can explain the evidence and convince the jury. There was no doubt they were convinced, even if on overload.

Court mercifully adjourned a little early for the noon recess and needing to escape and clear my head I got in my car and drove over toward Main Street, parked in an outside parking lot and walked over to watch the Genesee River water cascading over the falls at the bridge. I didn't want to think about the trial or analyze how it was going. All I wanted was to watch the water and let the sound and beauty of its power fill my mind. I leaned back as I held the railing giving my body a good stretch and though I tried not to my eyes went to my watch and noted the time. I resignedly hurried back to my car and drove to the court house.

Outside the building I paused. The five-story structure spanned an entire city block and featured a limestone facade over modern materials such as concrete and steel columns and beams. It was majestic and deserved to be appreciated. I ascended the broad spans of stairs, recognizing several individuals I had seen in the courtroom. Inside the expansive main lobby that crossed the length of the building as the primary public space it was ornately finished with marble floors, baseboards, and walls of people everywhere. It is at this point all my relaxation ends.

With so many people, I am lucky to get on the elevator and take it to the second floor. When I begin to move from the back to the front I squeeze through the crowd in the elevator saying, "excuse me" until I can step out and proceed down the hallway pass the law library and several courtrooms before reaching my destination, only to join with several others pushing through the courtroom doors in front of me. Once inside I hurry up to the defense table where Lt. Trapp sits patiently staring at the front of the court room, not even turning to acknowledge my presence until I say, "Hope you got a bite to eat."

"What? Oh, yes, Paige and I went to a street vendor and grabbed a bite. Not the most nourishing, but it was good."

Knowing that I can look intense without even trying, I smile, hoping to soften that expression and take my seat, only to stand again with everyone in the courtroom when the Judge is announced. Then it is all business as I once more take my chair and get out my files.

"Call your next witness," the Judge said to the prosecution.

"We call Walker Appleton to the stand."

I watch as Mr. Appleton is sworn in and steps up to sit in the witness seat. I know this slight man with a receding hairline and I perk with interest.

357

"State your name and occupation, please," Ms. Larson said. As can be expected, she has saved the best witnesses for herself. I sneak a look at Randall, but he doesn't seem to mind the change.

"My name is Walker Appleton and I am the groundskeeper at the Trapp residence". He looks over at Lt. Trapp and smiles without showing any teeth, and then adds, "and the Caretaker at the Great Embankment Park in Pittsford".

"Mr. Appleton, aren't you also a deputy sheriff?"

"Yes, of course, yes, I am a deputy sheriff too."

"Can you tell the court what your duties are in the role of Deputy Sheriff."

"Well I enforce the law relating to public safety and welfare."

"And how do you do that."

"Well, I am assigned an area where I patrol for possible criminal activity or other conditions that could endanger public safety. I investigate complaints, report accidents, and other hazardous conditions."

"Tell me, Mr. Appleton, do you investigate crimes and interview witnesses?"

"Well, no." He pauses in concentration. "Actually the term used for my positon is Special duty officer. I was hired to maintain order. I provide security, and at times facilitate traffic flow. I can also take action against violations of the law."

"Oh, I see. Did Mr. Trapp know you were not a deputy sheriff?"

"Listen, Miss." Frustration is apparent in his voice. "I do not misrepresent myself and I have certainly told him and others my real title, but it makes no difference. I follow the rules and do not get involved in the enforcement of house rules or other administrative duties except to encourage compliance through police presence and take action to prevent illegal acts or disorderly conduct. That's what I do. Do you understand?"

"Yes, I understand," Ms. Larson says as she stares at the jury. "And, Mr. Appleton, is it not part of your duties to make sure that the gate is locked at the Great Embankment Park?"

"Yes, ma'am it is?"

After making sure that the jury heard mainly that Mr. Appleton was not actually a deputy sheriff she began her questioning covering the same ground as Randall had with the police, only heading it down a more personal aspect.

"Mr. Appleton, where do you live?"

"I stay at the cottage on Lt. Trapp's property."

"And how far is that from the Trapp residence.?

"Three hundred feet or so."

"So, you get up, put on your deputy badge and clothes and go to the park each day, or evening?"

"It depends, but most of the time it is in the evening."

"So, you are responsible for locking the gate each night."

"Yes, I lock the park gate every night at ten and that is well known to the guests using the park".

His body language is a telltale sign of irritability. When Ms. Larson talks, he now averts his gaze, looking beyond her, but she seems unaware.

"Now, Mr. Appleton, on the night in question, you are sure you locked the gate and went home to sleep?"

"Yes, I'm sure I locked it."

"Can you tell us what happened next?"

He paused and then added, "I went home and went to bed, but was awakened during the night."

I am impressed by his ability to remain calm as he continues to respond to her repeating questions. I listen and I have a feeling that Mr. Appleton might be the witness I have been looking for.

"And who woke you?" Ms. Larson elegantly continued.

"Lieutenant Trapp," the witness answered.

"For what purpose?"

"He wanted me to take him into custody, ma'am."

"What if anything did he say?" I sit up straighter in my chair and lean over the table.

"He said, you better take me in, Mr. Appleton. I've just shot Noah Arietta."

Just like me, I could see the jury leaning forward in their chairs hanging on Mr. Appleton's words. Jean Larson paused like a good actor to let these loaded words sink in. "And what time was that?" she continued.

"Just before one a.m."

"What did you do?"

"I walked him back to the house and told him that I would call the police."

"And did he go willingly?"

"Yes, ma'am, he did. And the police finally arrived and took over."

Ms. Larson looked pleased as she turned toward me and smiled, she actually smiled. "Your witness, Mr. Dandridge."

I nodded in her direction then walked nonchalantly to the front of the courtroom.

"Good afternoon, Mr. Appleton. May I ask how old you are?"

"Sure, "I'll be seventy-nine in February," he answered.

"And how long have you been custodian at the Trapp residence?"

"Going on nine years, sir."

"And who do you work for. I mean who pays your salary?"

"Well, Lt. Trapp does and I get a small stipend from the town for my duties as a Special Duty Officer." With a sneer on his face, Mr. Appleton looks across the room at Ms. Larson when he says this."

Not able to contain myself I say, "And how long have you been a deputy sheriff, ah, excuse me, a special duty officer?"

"Going on three years."

"And who pays your salary for that office?"

Mr. Appleton looks up at me with a surprise expression, "Why no one sir. I don't get paid to serve."

"I see," I reply trying not to smirk. "So your sole income from your work at least comes from being the custodian for Lt. Trapp?"

"Yes Sir."

I walk across the area to the defense table and pick up a sheet of paper that I take with me as I approach the witness. "It says here that a deputy sheriff can place a person under protective custody. They can transport prisoners and defendants to courtrooms, prisons or jails, attorneys' offices, or medical facilities. More importantly they can make arrests, even execute arrest warrants. This is what Deputy Sheriff Jeremy Sexton's job entails, but not yours?"

Again, the surprise is noted in his voice as Mr. Appleton says, "Oh, no sir, I only work at the park."

"As a matter of fact, Mr. Appleton, you've never done any of these things, have you; your deputyship is purely a convenience in connection with your responsibilities in the park, you've never made a dime as a deputy; you don't wear a uniform or carry a gun; and you've probably never arrested a man in your life?"

"All that is correct, sir, I don't even own a gun." He hesitates and smiles. "Perhaps I can explain. You see, Mr. Dandridge, about three years ago some of our town boys began coming around the park at night, singing, drinking and disturbing the residences. Nothing vicious, you know, just being noisy." He pauses. "Well, I thought if they saw me as a figure of authority I could scare them a little."

"And did they scare, Mr. Appleton?" I said smiling.

"Not readily," he said timidly. "It was Mrs. Appleton who finally solved the problem."

"How?" I inquire with interest.

"Cookies."

The jury and audience are forcibly trying to contain themselves. I look up and swear I see a smile on the judge's face.

"Cookies, Mr. Appleton?" I try to control the urge to laugh.

"Yes, Cookies, Mr. Dandridge, Isabelle..., Mrs. Appleton, I mean; silenced the boys at night by offering them homemade cookies." He shrugged his shoulders. "We haven't had any problem since."

There was no holding back as the courtroom erupted in laughter. It is inevitable in a case dealing with this sort of detail that members of the jury want to burst out laughing. I look at the jury and see they can no longer hold it back and I wait patiently.

"Order in the court," Judge Nicholson finally manages to say as he lowers the gavel on the sound block over and over again until order is restored.

"Mr. Dandridge, please continue."

I clear my throat and am back in control of my faculties. "Passing now to the locked gate," I said. "I believe you testified that you close and lock the gate at ten every night, and that this is well known to the patrons of your park?"

"Yes, sir."

"And I assume then that this would be even better known to the residents?"

"Oh, yes, sir—everybody knew that. It's been locked at that hour since the park opened—long before I became caretaker."

"So that if any local residents suggested driving into the park after that hour, he must surely have known that the gate would be closed and locked?"

"Objection," Ms. Larson said. "The gate is irrelevant and immaterial."

"Mr. Dandridge?" You're treading on dangerous ground, the Judge replies.

"I'll abide by your ruling, Your Honor."

The Judge pauses and then says, "The objection is overruled. The People have opened the gate, so to speak, and within reason, the defense "may close it. You may answer the question." The Judge says to the witness.

"Oh, yes, sir," Mr. Appleton says. "Everybody knew that."

After that I had myself a time getting out the details that mattered. I continued the questioning to bringing out that there was a foot stile at the side of the gate and that more than himself had a key to the main gate. Finally, I covered the fact that there was only the one entrance to the park. Just for fun I bought out the detail that coyotes had been seen in the park on several occasions and finally dropped the matter, changing again my line of questioning.

"Mr. Appleton?" I said. "How did Lieutenant Trapp appear when he told you what you say he told you?"

"Well, he was as white as a ghost and stood very straight, very erect and soldierly and he—he seemed to have trouble speaking. It's hard to describe except to say he acted like a man in a dream."

Bless Mr. Appleton, I thought. I stood quietly letting his description sink in. Yes, he was definitely the one to veer safely off the subject and allow me to get the information I needed for the jury. He managed to change the image of Lt. Trapp as a man in a cold rage to one in the grip of some grave emotional or mental disturbance. I decided to rest the subject there and tread off in another direction.

"When you walked Lt. Trapp back to the house, did you happen to see Mrs. Trapp," I asked?"

"Oh yes, I walked over to the house with the Lieutenant and she came out the door crying hysterically.

"Did she say anything?"

"Yes, she sputtered out the words, Noah did this to me," as if apologizing for the way she looked. She was a mess." He looked out in the court and found Mrs. Trapp. "Sorry," he said apologetically. The witness closed his eyes as though to banish a bad dream.

I waited, but there is no objection from the prosecution. I just assume that Ms. Larson is too smart to nail the point home by objecting. She's hoping that it had slipped out and maybe it would go away. Everybody in the courtroom and the county knew for sure now, that Paige Trapp had claimed that Noah had raped her. But this was the first sliver of actual evidence of the fact. The jury had to know we were skating on the very edge of the rape. And like the people sitting in the courtroom, they were also probably dying to hear about it. But I was damned if I was going to risk getting slapped down again. I thought a minute and decided I had to try to lay the jury's disappointment elsewhere.

"Your Honor," I said, "we seem to be veering rather close to a 'keep of the grass' subject. I have no desire to annoy the court or to try to circumvent its earlier ruling. I need your direction on this matter."

I attempted to appear nonchalant as I stood waiting for my orders. "Hm…" said the Judge, leaning back in his chair. I had passed him a little conundrum and we both knew it. But he was up to the challenge. He passed the ball off to the prosecution by addressing Jean Larson. "The People, Ms. Larson?" he said. "What do you say?"

"Absolutely not," Ms. Larson said as she stood up commandingly at the prosecution table. No longer did her appearance fit that of a pleasant grandmother with her brow pressed down and her lips tightly closed. "The court has ruled; counsel is aware of it'; and there is not a scintilla of evidence of any…" she paused and for once the lady was at a loss for words but I was certain she had nearly said, rape."

"Yes, Ms. Larson?" I leered at her helpfully.

"—of any issue to which this line of questioning would be relevant," she concluded, glaring at me.

"Perhaps, Mr. Dandridge." The Judge suggested, "perhaps in view of the People's attitude you had better push on with something else. You may recall this witness later, of course, as per our earlier understanding."

I swear I heard the entire courtroom sigh collectively as though someone had punctured a balloon. To stall, I studied the portraits of the deceased judges' portraits on the walls around the courtroom and then, I cleared my throat.

"Now, Mr. Appleton," I said, coming slowly to another delicate subject, "what time did you retire that night?"

"About ten-fifteen, my regular time, right after closing the gate and listening to the news."

"And was your rest disturbed between that time and when Lieutenant Trapp awoke you around one?"

"No" he said, then added, "though I am a light sleeper."

"And your hearing, Mr. Appleton?" I asked softly.

"I hear very good. Mrs. Appleton says I can hear a pin drop."

"And your cottage was about how far from the Trapp home?"

"About three hundred feet—just as the chart there says." He points to the chart that had been displayed during the questioning of the officers.

"And from your cottage down to the main gate?"

"About three hundred feet like it says."

"And nothing disturbed your slumber?"

"No, sir."

Treading carefully now, I said, "No boys messing around in the park?"

"No, sir."

"No woman screaming in the park?"

"The screams I heard were down by the gate…"

"Objection, objection!" Jean Larson was fairly breathing down my neck.

There was an edge in the Judge's voice. "Please let the witness complete his answer before you object, Ms. Larson," he said sharply He turned toward the witness. "Proceed," he said.

"Those were Mrs. Trapp's screams that the residents heard down by the gate."

"Objection, Hearsay," Jean Larson urged the Court.

"Your Honor," I said, acting on a sudden hunch. "I withdraw the question. The witness is back to you Ms. Larson."

"No questions," she snapped.

"Thank you, Mr. Appleton," I said enthusiastically.

"You may step down, Mr. Appleton," says Judge Nicholson.

***

The Judge excused the court a little early that afternoon. By four o'clock Randall had called several more routine witnesses to the stand giving testimony to back what had already been heard and my cross examination did not uncover much more. I was tired, thirsty and had the beginnings of a headache pounding just below the surface when the Judge said, "Court is adjourned." I shook hands with my client and touched the arm of his wife as I explained to them we all needed to get some rest. Thankfully they agreed and I found myself fairly racing out to my car and fleeing the courthouse. I headed not to the office but to my home in Irondequoit.

Chapter 5

It had begun to rain, gently at first and then with a kind of monotonous autumnal savagery. I drove home on back streets avoiding the expressway and splashing through colorful dripping tunnels and gently sloping hills of fading leaves. The day's courtroom hunting had resulted in a mixed bag, some good and some bad but I didn't want to think about it now. Instead I wondered where my partner, Pete was keeping himself. I could use some direction expertise from him, but I couldn't seem to reach him even on his cell phone.

On the outskirts of Irondequoit, I stopped at a little store and dashing through the rain, picked up a copy of the Democrat & Chronicle, which I flipped through avidly, sitting in the rain pelted car until finding what I was looking for.

'Lieutenant Trapp faces Second degree Murder Charges While Lawyers Clash", the headlines read. "Trial began for Lt. Vincent Trapp who shot and killed Noah Arietta on July 31, 2015, the owner of the Academy Building in Rochester, New York. He retained Richard Dandridge as his defense attorney a few days later. The trial that started on September 15, 2016 uncovered nothing new on its second day as the lawyers battled over what could and could not be presented. The prosecution is headed by the young, handsome District Attorney, Randall Walker and as his second chair, Jean Larson of the Attorney General's staff ...'

I read the coverage of the humdrum details coming out at the first days of the trial and the attention given to berating the lawyers as we fought for control. The young reporter, was doing a good job in his report on the murder trial but he was missing the nuances as is usually the case with newspaper reporters. I continue to follow the story and see the picture of the Judge and handsome crewcut Randall along with the gray haired Jean Larson leaping out at me. There was also a good shot of the Judge sitting imperturbable and alone at his desk, then another of Randall and his woman Friday. I carefully folded the paper back up and headed home, hoping there would be better coverage on the news this evening.

There was no relief from the rain as I finally made it home. I reached into the back seat and grabbed my umbrella and situated my briefcase securely on my shoulder before making a mad dash to the front door. On the steps, I reached into the mail box and tucked the contents under my arm as I turned the key in the lock. With the overhead coverage of the front steps and my umbrella I managed to stay dry.

Once inside, I dropped the umbrella in the rack and put my keys in the bowl before taking off my wet shoes and heading for my home office. It smelt musty in the room so I threw open the window on the side of the house where the rain wouldn't enter before pulling out the papers in my briefcase until I found the phone number of the psychiatrist. I picked up the receiver from its stand and stood punching in the number, then waited. I was all for the new technology, but for some reason I still had to have that landline. At first I kept it because the reception on the cell phone wasn't as good, but now I had no excuse except I just liked having it.

A recording played telling me to leave my name and number and the reason for the call. I follow the instructions and give my reason as being to inform him that he must arrive not later than

Saturday (this was Thursday evening), I hung up and then I read my mail.

There was a letter from my mother Laurel, who would be home in two weeks and hoped I wasn't working too hard and was getting plenty of sleep. Though efficient enough with the computer, mom tended to prefer writing her letters and I had to admit, I enjoyed receiving them.

She expressed her hopes that I also was regularly watering her flowers. I folded the letter and reprimanded myself because I hadn't gotten around to the flowers. Hopefully they were surviving and would not give me away. The rest of the mail included several bills and a bunch of advertisements. I set it all aside.

I made my way to the kitchen and found something eatable in the fridge. I threw it into the microwave and while it was heating I turned on the television. I flipped through several news stations but couldn't catch one talking about the trial. The microwave signaled and I took out my food, turned off the television and returned to the office. Soon I was engrossed in reviewing the case files. I turned on my Surface Pro and began a list.

Give jury true picture of tense setup in bar that night, I typed. Stress Noah knew gate was shut and Paige didn't. Give Larson hell. Show bartender is lying. I continued adding on snippets until I decided that if I wasn't going to get any rest I might as well go into my downtown office. The decision made, I went upstairs to change into clean clothes, brush my teeth and gather up my computer and papers.

When I opened the front door, I saw that the rain had stopped, but it had given everything a nice soak, making it unnecessary to go and water my mother's plants. I smiled as I climbed into the car and headed back downtown.

Passing the clock at the bank I saw that it was now nine o'clock. Though I was tired, my body just wasn't ready to call it a day that early so as I parked the car in the city garage, I knew this was the right thing to do. In a matter of minutes, I was in my office and seated at the desk with all my papers out and around me. I thought of a few more things to add to my list and then I was so overpowered by a numbness that stalled my train of thought. I must have fallen asleep.

"Richard," someone was saying softly. "Richard, Richard. Wake up, It's me."

Pete stood across from me his dirty blonde hair rowdily landing over one eye that his tinted lens shaded from site. As usual he was wearing a scarf tied to the side, an open collar shirt and a pair of tan khakis all of which I could tell had been worn in the rain without the help of an umbrella for protection.

He dropped his brief case and sagged into the chair across from me. "I had tire trouble...he murmured, wagging his head. "I'm not the driver I used to be."

I was only half listening as I thought, he's home, thank god the man is home. "Where have you been, Pete?" I said wearily, still only partly awake. I hadn't realized until then how much I loved this man, loved and depended on him.

Pete sighed and stretched out in his chair, his hands folded across his middle. "First fetch me one of those habit forming orange pops, Richard." He said. "You're asking where have I been?"

I handed him his pop and Pete rallied a little and leaned forward. "It happened this way," he began, and away he went.

Pete had been quietly working on the Noah Arietta will contest. He and Theresa had worked on it for days. He had briefed the whole subject, including the question of the Florida divorce, and had become convinced that legally the opposition didn't have a

Chinaman's chance to upset either Noah's will or the divorce. Then he had gone to Tyra Pederson's lawyer, Bryan Atwater, and put his cards on the table. He and old Bryan were contemporaries that had taken their last exams together years before. He knew Bryan could be trusted.

"But Pete," I interrupted, "why—why didn't you tell me? We were partners in this case...remember?"

"I didn't want you to worry. You had enough on your mind trying your case. If I failed, I—I didn't want..." He paused and held out his hands pleadingly.

"Not knowing where you were made me worry, Pete. I never worry about what you do. I trust you." I said. "Tell me what you found out."

Pete recited that he had gone over his brief with Bryan Atwater and he agreed my line of thinking was right. Bryan said they had receipts and canceled checks showing that Noah's ex-wife had collected alimony for years. Plus, he could vouch that Noah had indeed been sober when he made the will because before signing the will, Bryan had him get a physical with Doctor Henson. Pete added that Bryan had said that the will was signed that same day after the physical and that he himself drafted the will and had himself, his stenographer and the doctor immediately sign in witness right after Noah returned from the doctors. And for additional support to the case, another witness to the signing was the local Justice Of The Peace.

After the meeting Pete had given a copy of his brief to Bryan Atwater. He had then succeeded in getting Bryan to phone Tyra Pederson and try obliquely (keeping us out of it) to soften her up on the criminal case. Bryan had done so and in Pete's presence they met face to face, but the results had been inconclusive. Tyra Pederson had said she was reassured on the will authenticity, but she seemed plagued by the notion that Noah's former wife might still upset the divorce and take everything. She was equally stubborn on conceding to support anything that might blacken Noah's name or tend to show him guilty of the rape.

I felt as if I was in a soap opera with all the twist and turns that were coming out in this case.

Pete had then concluded that the only way to remove Tyra Pederson's fixation on the Divorce business was for him to go there.

I interrupted. "Where was the Will taken?"

"Tucson, Arizona"

I stared befuddled at Pete. "Don't tell me…you went to Tucson, Arizona?"

"Well, did I have a choice? If I wanted to get it all straight, I needed to check it out."

Pete told me how he had gotten copies of the alimony receipts and the signed checks from Bryan and then called the airlines to take their first flight out. He booked a flight on American leaving the next morning at 7:55 a.m. with a stop in Chicago and had arrived at 11:43 a.m. Once there, he rented a car and set out for the Tucson County Courthouse, only he had a flat and had to call Hertz to come and fix it; causing him an hours delay before finally reaching his destination. Once at the court house he showed his credentials, and the copies given to him by Bryan as proof he was legitimate and it all went smoothly, thanks to Bryan who had supplied me with the full legal name of Noah Arietta and Helena Buckus Arietta, his ex-wife.

"I had the year of the marriage and though not mandatory, the marriage license number. Thanks to Bryan's copies after showing my ID as a non member of the family, I had the necessary paperwork to allow me access to the records and soon I was hard at work in the files and records in the old divorce case of Noah Arietta vs Helena Buckus Arietta." Pete and made copies of papers on file that were missing from those given to him by Bryan.

"The original summons was missing from the courthouse file and this legal document tells the responding party that a divorce case has been filed naming the respondent as one of the parties. It also informs the respondent that a response must be filed within 20 days if he or she wants to have any input regarding the divorce case so it was important that he get a copy of this document as well."

So, Pete had climbed into his rental car and gone to the Pima County sheriff's office. He again showed his credentials and was able to find a record showing that a deputy sheriff named Griffin had handled the summons in the old divorce case and as luck would have it Mike Griffin, the deputy was retired and living in Phoenix, over 100 miles away. So after thanking the Sheriff Pete had driven to Phoenix, but during the hour and a half drive he had another flat tire and had to wait on Hertz, putting him into another hot long hour delay.

That delay proved worthwhile as Mike Griffin remembered personally serving a divorce summons on a Mrs. Noah Arietta and remembered Helena Arietta. Pete surprisingly had taped the whole conversation and on the tape Mike can be heard saying, "Damn right I remember that dame with the dyed red hair and discolored scar on her right cheek. She was no lady. She swore at me and called me names when I served her with the divorce summons."

At the end of the conversation, Pete convinced Mr. Griffin to ride with him back to Tucson and once there Pete and Mr. Griffin went to the Tucson sheriff's office where he solemnly swore to the legality of the documents and signed in the presence of the Tucson Sheriff.

"By then I was exhausted but there was one more thing I needed to get done and that was to meet with the Tucson lawyer of Helena Arietta," Pete added.

Pete had Mike Griffin join him for the meeting with Helena's lawyer and it went smoothly At the end, the lawyer had thanked Pete for his information and his brief and had prepared a document stating that he was dismissing the Tucson proceedings he had received to set aside the divorce and was promptly withdrawing from the New York case.

Not wasting any time, Pete had then phoned Bryan Atwater and given him the latest developments on the situation. He then asked him to pass this information on to Tyra Pederson, which her grateful lawyer agreed promptly to do. Then sure he had covered every base, Pete climbed into his rental car and headed toward the airport where he planned to find a motel and catch a few winks before his early morning departure to Rochester. But the rental had another surprise in store when it overheated and he had to again call in the troops.

It was too late to get a hotel room so Pete drove into the rental return at Hertz, then went into the Tucson airport where he found the gate his plane was scheduled to leave from, curled up on a couple seats and immediately fell asleep. The next morning Pete caught a flight at 5:40 am from Tucson to Chicago and arrived in Rochester at 2:20 p.m.

I sat staring at this gallant man. "Thanks, Pete," I said. "After all the trouble you went through, I hope it all works out as planned."

Pete shook his head soberly. "That's just the point, Richard. It surely won't work if we leave it rest there," he said. "This is only the foundation. Only you can really make it work."

I frown at him in confusion, "What do you mean, Pete?

"You must go see Tyra Pederson and personally plead your case." I start to protest. "You've got to. Don't you see? It's your case, it's your man who is in danger so you are the only one who can make her see it," he says determinedly

"Tyra Pederson? You want me to meet with Tyra. Where, when?"

"Now…tonight…We can't waste another moment. The trial maybe be over and done with in another day or so. Pick up the phone and call her."

I gave in. I glanced at the clock. It was one o'clock in the morning as I placed a call to the Frontier Café. The answering service picked up and I explained that I needed to talk with Ms. Pederson on an urgent matter. I gave my phone number and name, before ending the call. I didn't have to wait long before my phone rang.

"Hello," I said. "Is this Miss Pederson?"

"Yes, it is."

"Sorry to be calling you at this ungodly hour. This is Richard Dandridge, Lieutenant Trapp's lawyer. I'd like to see you tonight or, this morning, I mean."

"At this hour," she asked.

"Yes, I realize it's late, but tomorrow may be too late."

"Why can't you tell me over the phone…"

"I prefer not to. I can leave now and be there in a few minutes."

There is a nerve whacking pause as I wait for her answer.

"Okay," she says. My apartment is two o two in the Frontier Building.

"Thank you Ms. Pederson. Good bye."

"Ah great, she'll see you." Pete murmured, as he allowed his head to lower slowly on to my desk. In an instant he was asleep and snoring. I found an afghan to throw over him and then wrote a quick note to Theresa giving her directions to wake him up, find him something to wear and get him to the court on time. I then grabbed my brief case and gathered up the papers that Pete had accumulated during his trip and left the office.

The rain had finally stopped. Now in the darkness the moon peers through the clouds lightening up the dull, bleak atmosphere and water dripped off the leaves of the trees. The unprotected flowers along pathways have been drenched, and a damp, earthy smell now loiters. I am too hurried to enjoy it all. Pete had passed me the torch and it was my turn to get in and fight.

Chapter 6

It is a dark, serene evening as I make my way to Pittsford. I drive enjoying the quiet after the noise of this busy day that seemed to have no ending. I mechanically make the right turns until I arrive at my destination pulling into the first empty parking space and hurrying up the front door stairs. I press the buzzer at the side of the glass doors leading into the front lobby and there is the clicking sound announcing the release of the lock and I push through the doors.

I walk through the dimly lit entry, my shoes announcing my progress as I make my way to the elevator and press the button for Apartment 202. The lobby is bathed in silence so that I hear the traction steel ropes of the elevator car as it makes its descent. I know when to step forward as I can perceive the sound of the clutch mechanism unlocking the car doors and when the heavy doors open I step inside and press the '2'. Soon I am on my way to the second floor of the Academy Building that housed the Founder's Café and the apartment of Tyra.

I expected stylishness, but am instantly charmed as I step off the elevator and walk the runway carpeting of soft shades of color. There are oak paneled walls with built in bookshelves and seating running the full-length of the way across from the apartment doors, with huge one-over- one half round arch windows that would let in an abundance of sunlight. I stop in front of the oversized wood paneled door of apartment 202 and see it is slightly ajar. I knock softly and Tyra Pederson lets me in.

"Good evening, Mr. Dandridge," she said, smiling gravely and briefly shaking my hand as I look around in awe. The room, like its occupant makes elegance look easy as I glimpse the bright white living room with its clean, almost effortless look of sophistication. The room fits the architecture of the building with deeply coffered ceiling and gridwork of shelving that flanks the fireplace to define the space in bold, linear strokes. Symmetrical balance extends to both the architecture and the clean-lined furniture to impose formal structure on an informal, feel-good style. On the far wall inside the apartment is again two huge one-over- one half round arch windows that would welcome the sunlight in.

"How incredibly beautiful," I murmured.

"Why thank you, Mr. Dandridge." She offers to take my coat and as I shimmy out of it she says, "Can I get you something to drink?"

I start to say that a beer would be great, but somehow drinking a beer in this room seemed crude so instead I say, "Scotch with a little soda, if you have it?"

"Yes, I do." Tyra leaves the room and I take this time to concentrate on my mission. It is essential that I think about my strategy. I need to have the right approach if I want to get the information I require to win my case. I let out a sigh as I realize there is only one possible strategy really and that is true honesty. There is no time to waste in lawyer tricks or deceit.

I am ready when Tyra Pederson returns with two drinks and for the first time I take notice of the fact that her dark hair is piled up on top of her head and she is wearing what appears to be Chinese silk pajamas, in vintage turquoise silk brocade. I know this because it is the style that my mother has asked me to give her for Christmas.

The image of her now tends to off balance my initial sense of her being a gold digger with a personality flaw of being hard and demanding. That image would make it much easier for me to begin my task instead of facing off with this beauty.

"Thank you," I said, taking my drink. "this is very thoughtful of you."

Tyra glides across the room to the sofa near the window and motions me to follow. There are coasters on small tables and I sit my glass on one before taking a seat.

"Now Mr. Dandridge, tell me why you think I can help your case."

I take a sip of my drink. "Well, I will try by first telling you that I spoke with your bartender at the Founder's Café and found him to be very evasive. I could tell he was holding back then and still is. I want to give the jury a true picture of Noah, not some martyr who has met with danger, but instead an alcoholic who has an arsenal of guns at his disposal." I pause to see how she is taking all this and then rush on.

"Because of the Will contest, I think I understand why you have been so reluctant to let word of Noah's behavior and drinking get out. I think once I share what has been discovered concerning the Will, that it will no longer be a barrier." I proceeded to tell her everything that Pete had found out.

Tyra Pederson sat listening reflectively, occasionally sipping her drink. As I waited for her to express her thoughts, I begin to think that this may not have been the right way to approach this subject. Tyra may be obligated to the prosecution and to Jean Larson and this was not going to change her sense of loyalty to this man who didn't deserve it. Only it was too late now to pull back. Tyra doesn't say a word, and knowing that it is not the wisest thing to do, I rattle on.

"It is a fact Ms. Pederson that the proof of the rape is necessary to the case. It's just as important to let the jury know that Noah had a drinking problem and that he knew his way around guns."

Tyra got up quietly and looked questioningly in my direction. I nod and she takes my empty glass away. Once she is out of sight range, I pace up and down, nervously, reprimanding myself. I could have used tact in presenting the matter. Why did I go at it so directly? What an idiot I am proving to be. Finally, I manage to sit again hopefully succeeding in a façade of calm when she returns and finally speaks.

"How," she said quietly, "how can you be so sure that Noah raped this woman?"

I looked at her. Tyra sat very still and I could tell that she seriously wanted this to not be true. "At first I did have my doubts, because I thought maybe the Lieutenant had it out for Noah all along," I said soberly. "But I now believe it happened."

Tyra was looking directly at me. "Why?" she said in a low troubled voice. "Please explain, why."

Here was my chance. "There was a couple there that night that heard a woman's screams at the gate just before midnight and the time matched that of when Noah was gone from the bar. That changed my mind. Then, Paige Trapp was given a lie-detector test and I am certain that it showed she had told the truth about the rape."

I watched Tyra as she tried to keep her hands busy so that I wouldn't see them shaking. "Then," she said evenly, "If you have all this information why do you need anything from me?"

Good question, I thought, but more importantly it told me I had a chance of convincing her. "Well, the couple who heard the screams has gone back home and it will take more than just hearing the screams to force them back to town. I need to have a motive and to have the witness supply it and I don't think this couple can."

Now she knew how my hands were tied and in case she didn't, I added, "And as for the lie-detector test Paige Trapp was given, well it is not admissible in court. That's the reasons why I had to come to you."

I watch her reaction before saying. "All that I want; all that the Trapp's want is for the truth to be told."

She choked as she said. "I didn't know about the screams. I didn't know about the witnesses or the lie-detector test. I knew nothing about any of that."

She looked at me and I could see the tears glistening in her eyes. "Tyra... Miss Pederson," I said awkwardly as I started to get up.

"No, I am all right. Truly."

I had said my piece and there was nothing more to say. "I will go now. Maybe you want to be alone."

There was an awkward silence and then Tyra began, "You have been honest with me so I will be honest with you. Please sit," she said patting the cushion on the sofa. I obeyed.

"I came to Rochester on a vacation to visit friends and loved the place so decided to stay. I knew if I did stay I needed a job, but as a teacher that would mean getting my credentials to teach in the area first and so I began looking at alternatives. Out-of-state applicants from accepted states may be granted either a 2-year conditional initial or 5-year regular initial certificate, depending on qualifications and work experience. a full professional certificate may be issued once applicants have met all New York State requirements. All that would take time, just like bringing your witnesses back to testify."

"Lucky for me I met Noah at the bar in the Founder's café and he began a conversation with me and my friends. He told us how the building had needed attention and that he could see its potential only didn't have the eye to handle it all so he started small by setting up the café and bar. At the time we met, his dining-room hostess had quit and he was desperate for someone to replace her. I offered to help, temporarily, and took the job. It didn't pay much at first, but as he promised, Noah raised the salary far above what I could ever earn as a teacher."

Tyra stood and walked over to the window. She silently, stared off into the distance then finally, she turned towards me and said. "Whatever you may have heard, Richard, and whatever Noah may have been with others, he was a perfect gentleman to me, always. I regarded him almost as a father."

I nodded to let her know I understood.

Tyra quietly told me how hard she had worked building up the apartment section of the building and how fantastic things had gone, despite Noah's occasional erratic behavior, bouts of drinking, and even despite him having a witch of an ex-wife. Here she paused in reflection. "You know, I met Noah's daughter and was immediately drawn to her. She was a shy troubled child who desperately needed a savior and I wanted that to be me because I knew exactly what she was going through. I too came from a broken home so I know it's true what they say when you are an only child and your parents' divorce, you either use what you've learned from the abusive environment or you do the polar opposite. There is a wealth of data that shows children suffer badly from divorce or parental break-up, and that those brought up by a single parent are more likely to do badly at school, suffer poor health, and fall into crime, addiction and poverty. I saw a lot of myself in his daughter and I intended to help."

"I didn't know," I said. "I didn't know any of this."

"How could you," she said. Noah was not one to share his personal life with outsiders, but I could see he approved of my actions toward his daughter. Anyway, all was well until I met a man new in town. He was young, handsome and just so full of life that I was drawn to him and at that point Noah seemed to change."

Tyra took a sip of her drink and said, "Yes, he was always a womanizer, but in a different, more respectful way. He now was openly rude and obnoxious; especially when his drinking increased even more. To say it bluntly, his behavior was outright neurotic."

"Do you think it was because he cared for you in a different way," I asked cautiously.

"No, I don't think so because I know I was the only one he looked up to and saw as a loyal friend. I finally persuaded him to go see a doctor. I thought perhaps there was something physically wrong with him. Anyway, he went, but there was nothing wrong with his body." Tyra paused. "What was wrong with Noah had to do with his mind."

"Mentally, you mean?"

"Yes, in my opinion, not the doctors. In any case it was then that he took out two large insurance policies, one for his daughter and one for me. Maybe he had a premonition of things to come." Tyra paused and focused on me. "I knew nothing about the insurance or of his Will until...until after that horrible night. It was after he was deceased that I learned of my connection to anything belonging to Noah. That's the truth."

"I believe you," I said.

Tyra smiled sadly. "I suppose you must be wondering then, why I got involved in Noah's estate. It was a surprise for me as well. I didn't want anything to do with the mess; but when his ex-wife started going after the business I thought of how much Noah and myself had put into the building and I didn't want it to just be sold so I decided to fight like Noah would if he were here. I needed to fight for him and for his daughter too.

"His daughter?"

She glanced quickly at me. "It is my plan to share the estate with his daughter," she said quietly. "I have already made arrangements for a trust fund that the child's mother can never touch."

I could tell she wanted to say more so I remained silent. "I feel gratitude and loyalty to Noah for all he has done for me and maybe it had shut my eyes to the possible truth of what he has been accused of doing. How, I told myself, how could such a kind and generous human being possibly have done such a thing." Again she paused. "Then I guess there was a sense of guilt."

"What do you have to feel guilty about," I asked

"Guilt that I may have been to blame or partly at least."

"I don't understand," I said

"Well, Noah was upset about the man I was seeing. His name is Ian Solenhauser."

"Did he explain why?"

"No, but I think he was afraid I would get hurt. That and the fact that Ian was friends with Lt. Trapp didn't set well with him. Ian had a girlfriend back home and our relationship was a dance now and then, occasional picnic and swimming at the beach. He was always talking about his girlfriend back home and I am a good listener."

I looked at Tyra and wondered how a man who was out with her, could even think about another woman.

"Did Noah know the relationship between you and Ian was platonic?"

"No, and this is where the guilt comes in. Because knowing he saw me and treated me like his daughter, like any daughter, the more he tried to convince me I was making a mistake seeing Ian, the more I did the opposite. Here I am a grown woman and he is my employer, trying to control my personal life. I wasn't his daughter so I didn't have to stand for it."

"I can understand that," I said.

"There is something more. On the night in question, I wasn't here because I was with Ian and we were at the beach. Ian went into the water and I wanted to go for a swim too, so I changed on the beach into my swimsuit and someone turned a flashlight on me. Anyone could mistake the situation and gone and told Noah some cockamamie story. It might have even been Noah with the flashlight."

Wanting to assure her I said, "It wasn't Noah with the flash light. He was a devious and complicated man, but that I don't think was his style."

"I hope you're right."

Now I was the one on the hot seat, because I needed her help, "Tyra, I need you to do something for me. "

Without pause, Tyra surprises me. "Sure, Richard, I will if I can."

Taking care, I shared with her what I needed her to do. Afterwards she got my coat and walked me to the door. "Goodnight, Richard."

"Good night Tyra. It's been a pleasure."

Surprised, I felt Tyra grab my hands and hold them between us and then getting up on tiptoes she kissed me, very lightly, very non sexually. "You are a good man Richard."

With that, I walked down the hallway feeling happier than I had in days.

Chapter 7

After the long evening of confession with Tyra I was too tired to consider driving all the way to Irondequoit that evening so instead I slept at my office so that I would have a chance of making it to court in the morning. I took care to set an alarm.

By the time I turned in I was looking at two, maybe three hours of sleep and luckily I didn't waste a minute. When the alarm went off I was dazed but awake enough to shower, brush my teeth and shave, later in my office bedroom I found a suitable change of clothes, but wanted something more dynamic to awe the jury, but this would have to do. So, I wasted time I didn't have primping to make up for the uninspiring clothing and that threw me off my schedule. I find myself rushing as I take a final survey of myself in the mirror, then rush downstairs and quickly exit through the office door. On the steps outside I feel like an idiot as I reenter the office, gather up my briefcase and set the alarm.

I practically ran down the sidewalk to the garage and climbed into my car. My heart is pounding so fast I must do some deep breathing to calm myself before putting the key in the ignition. When the car comes to life I glance at the clock on the dashboard. "Damn, no way I can make it." I back out of my parking space and quickly turn the steering wheel. I was going to be late, but that wasn't a fact yet.

It is clear sailing and I make every light until I am minutes away from my destination. I find a parking space but the car on the left is over the parking lines. It would be a tight squeeze but I didn't have time to drive around and find another. Carefully I drive forward, using my side mirrors to keep me centered and I make it in okay.

Once I turn of the car, I go to open the driver side door, only to find it is impossible to get out. My mind is working overtime as I reach over to the passenger side and put my briefcase on the floor. I then raise the armrest, practically put my knees into my neck as I swing them over the console. I pause a moment trying to decide what to do next and find myself shifting my body over until I am sitting on the passenger side of the car. I open the door and slide out then reach in and get my briefcase. I try not to look at my watch as I lock the car and head toward the courthouse.

I see the coffee vendor on the sidewalk and know I don't have time to stop, but I am hungry and no matter what I do, I will still be late. I get a cup of coffee and a bagel that I choke down on my way up the courthouse stairs, through the hallway and into the court clerk's office. I am almost at the door leading into the court room when I hear the court clerk say, "Here he is now," and held out the phone in my direction. I stare at the clock behind her desk and see that it is now after nine o'clock, but I go over and take the phone from her outstretched hand.

"Hello," I said, this is Richard Dandridge."

"This is Tyra," she says in a low voice that is almost a whisper. She tells me that she has spoken to Brook and taken care of what I had asked her to do.

I am smiling as I say, "Thank you, Tyra."

"Your welcome. Please Richard, let me know what happens," she replies," and good luck."

"I'll call you. I promise I will."

I hand the phone back to the clerk and give her a big smile before hurrying through the side door of the court room just in time to hear, "All rise for the honorable Judge Silas Nicholson," I rush to the defense table and when the Sheriff says, "Please be seated," I take my seat and begin emptying my briefcase. The calamitous morning is no longer on my mind. All I can think about is that I finally have the ammunition I need.

"Call your first witness," the Judge said, nodding at Randall's table.

"I call Detective Sergeant Kenneth Parker," Jean Larson announces.

I look over at the prosecutors table and must admire their choice of clothing. Both Randall and Jean Larson are wearing charcoal color suits with bright white shirts. They look like a pair of bookends, except that Randall has a tie. Knowing Jean is not one to take chances, I have a feeling she made the call.

I turn my attention to Detective Sergeant Kenneth Parker and watch as he stands and walks with a confident gait toward the witness stand to be sworn in.

"Raise your right hand. Do you solemnly swear or affirm that the testimony you're about to give will be the truth, the whole truth and nothing but the truth, so help you God?"

"I do."

"Please be seated."

One could tell even from the side view as he takes the oath that he is indeed a handsome man. When he turns to take his seat, I swear I hear soft oohs and aahs from the woman in the court room. The Detective's hair is shiny like taffy with curls falling every which way. His brown eyes sparkle and the darkness of his lashes make it look as though he is wearing eyeliner. He even has a clef chin. There is nothing about his face that is not appealing. Even his closed mouth smile is acceptable because that smile goes all the way up to his brown eyes.

It is hard to see him as an officer of the state, but indeed he is and a good one at that. He had proven his honesty on numerous occasions and there was no reason to doubt anything he was about to share as nothing but the truth.

"Please state your name for the record."

"Detective Sergeant Kenneth Parker."

"How long have you been employed as an Investigative Detective at the Rochester Police Department.

"Just over fifteen years."

"Did you have occasion to investigate the fatal shooting of Noah Arietta?" Jean Larson asked crisply.

"I did. I headed the investigation," Detective Parker replied.

"Will you tell us what the investigation entailed?

"Well, as the officer first to arrive at the crime scene it is imperative to prevent any changes to the area. That means that I parked my patrol car a distance from the crime scene, both to prevent impacting evidence left by the suspect and to prevent any suspect still on the scene from observing my arrival. Even though in this case the call into the precinct stated that the shooter was not on the premises, a search for the perpetrator was done with officers limiting touching objects and places at the scene."

A glass of water sits on the witness table and Detective Parker pauses to take a sip. "When it is clear that the scene poses no danger, we barricaded the area with crime-scene tape and the posting of two officers at strategic spots. No unauthorized personnel, including police officers, were allowed to enter the scene. When done, the officers at the crime scene obtained names of possible witnesses. They documented in writing and pictures every action and movement that taken, keeping in mind that this is likely to be the subject of an examination and cross-examination during the trial."

"So, is this what you did?" Ms. Larson pauses. "Can I call you Detective?"

"Sure you can. No, it is not what I did. The 9-1-1 call into the precinct from the dispatcher at 1:15 a.m. informing us that there had been a shooting at the Founders Café, located at 13 Marsh Road informed me that shots had been fired in the bar area at the back of the café and that the person who had done the shooting; had asked a Mr. Walker Appleton, Caretaker at the Great Embankment Park to call the police. Mr. Appleton, told the police that he lived on the property of Lieutenant Trapp and that the Lieutenant had told him he had killed Noah Arietta, the owner of the Founders Café and wanted to turn himself in. Mr. Appleton gave the address of Lt. Trapp as 14 Epping Wood Trail in Pittsford. So the coroner's office was contacted and along with two other detectives they went to the crime scene to protect and investigate the area."

"So, Detective, what did you do."

"Well, since the caller had informed us that Lt. Trapp was the suspect and he was at his residence, that is where I, along with another detective headed. When we confronted him we read him his rights and placed him under arrest."

"Did you discuss the shooting with Lieutenant Trapp?" Jean Larson asked.

"I did. Both then and later."

"Will you tell us, Detective what he said?"

"I asked the Lieutenant where the gun was and he pointed at a table and said he would get it, but I said no, and instead got it myself," Detective Parker said.

Jean Larson nodded at the witness and then walked over to the table to pick up an object contained in plastic. She then walked up close to the witness and said, "And is this the gun?" She handed it to Detective Parker who turned it over in his hands, looking closely at it through the plastic.

"Yes, this is the gun."

Jean took the gun and placed it into evidence. She then turned toward the witness. "Were you present later at the bar when an effort was made to recover the bullets?"

"I was. I conducted the search."

"Were any recovered?"

"Yes. Four bullets were found along with five shell casings."

Jean again went to the table and came back to show the Detective the contents of another plastic bag. "Are these the bullets that killed Noah Arietta?"

"They are the bullets we found in the bar, yes."

Jean, paused a moment to stare at the bag holding the bullets and then slowly walked over to the defense table and said, "the People now put into evidence the bullets that killed Noah Arietta."

Jean was not done as she glided back before the witness. "Getting back to the defendant at his home, what else, if anything did he say?"

"He told us that his wife had been…."

"Stop right there, Detective. State the facts and not hearsay."

"Okay, Lieutenant Trapp said that his wife had some trouble with Noah Arietta and that he had left their residence and gone to the Founder's Cafe and shot him. He also asked if Mr. Arietta was dead and we told him that he was."

"What then?"

"Then we drove him and his wife to the county jail."

"Was there any further talk in the car on the drive down?"

"Yes, on the drive down the Lieutenant said he had thought the whole thing over before going to the bar and had decided that such a man should not be allowed to live."

Jean Larson paused to let this sink in. This was a massive blow to our insanity defense and she knew it. I made a few notations on my pad.

"Can you tell me how did the defendant appear?"

"He was upset and emotional and seemed very angry."

I could object to this being an unwarranted conclusion by the witness, but the witness had said it and the jury heard it so I remained silent.

"Anything else?" Ms. Larson asked.

"He said that he had no regrets over what he'd done and that he'd do it again. Then he asked us several more times if Mr. Arietta was really dead."

I now began to wonder if my client had signed a written confession that I didn't' know about. I again jotted notes on my pad.

"Then what Detective?"

"Then we arrived at the county jail and I asked the defendant if he cared to make a formal statement and he said, no. He was booked on a charge of murder in the second degree and locked up and we returned immediately to the Founders Café to continue the investigation."

Jean Larson looked over at me with a smug look and a nod, "Your witness," she said.

I nodded back and stood up, then walked slowly to confront the witness, a man I thought to be honest and forthright. Only now I must look at him in a different light.

"Good morning Detective Parker. I believe you testified that the Lieutenant told you that he had shot Noah Arietta after he had learned from his wife that she had 'some trouble' with the deceased, did you not?"

"I did."

"Now Detective Parker, were those words 'some trouble' the words Lieutenant Trapp used or rather are they the words that you have used here in order to briefly describe what it was he actually told you?"

"They were my words, sir. I don't recall that the Lieutenant used that expression."

"All right, Detective," I said, "will you now please tell the court and the jury what the words were that the defendant himself used when he described this trouble his wife had with the deceased?"

"Yes, sir, he said..."

"Objection! Objection, Your Honor," Ms. Larson practically yelled out. "The court ruled on that subject inadmissible for this case.

The Judge looked at Jean Larson and said, "You opened the door, with your line of questioning, Ms. Larson." He turned toward the witness, "I will allow it. Please answer the question."

"Yes, Your Honor," Detective Parker said. He turned to me and replied, "Lt Trapp told us that the deceased had beaten and raped his wife."

One could hear the intake of breath and see the wide eyed expressions on the jury as they absorbed this new information. I gave them a moment to let it all sink in before continuing.

"What else did the defendant say."

"He said that he had taken a nap earlier and that around nine o'clock his wife had gone to take the dog out for a walk and later stopped in at the Founder's café where he had planned to meet her that evening. Only he slept longer than anticipated and was awakened suddenly when he heard screams outside the gate to their home. He said it sounded like his wife so he had gone to press the button to open the gate and then hurried to the door where his wife fell into his arms."

"And when you arrived at the home, did you see his wife?"

"Yes, sir."

"What shape was she in?"

"She was hysterical and sobbing. Her face and arms were covered with dirt and bruises."

"And did she tell you what happened?"

"She did."

"And what did she say?"

"Objection, Your Honor." Ms. Larson gave a haphazard cry.

"Overruled. Proceed."

"She said that Noah Arietta had raped her and beat her up."

"And did she tell you anything else?"

"She said that he had taken her into the Great Embankment Park near their home in Pittsford and had beaten and assaulted her and that she had finally managed to escape, making it to the entrance gate to her home which was a short way down the road from the park and there he had caught up with her and further assaulted her and she screamed, scaring him off."

"And did she take you to where the first attack occurred?"

"Yes, sir."

"And did you find tire marks and dog tracks in that road?"

"Yes, sir."

"And looked for her panties but couldn't find them?"

"Correct, sir."

Now it was out and clearly the jurors were able to understand why Lt Trapp had murdered Noah. Now I needed to clear the Detective's name.

"So was it your decision to just say there was 'some trouble'."

"It was not, sir."

"Who's decision was it?"

"The prosecution attorney Ms. Jean Larson."

It was clear sailing now as I continued my line of questioning.

"There has been testimony here, Detective Parker, that you were given Paige Trapp's torn skirt for the purpose of having it tested for sperm or seminal stain. Was it tested?"

"It was, sir."

"And what were the results?"

"They were negative."

I should have known since there was no objection, but it didn't matter much to me now.

"And the clothing worn by the deceased, were they tested too?"

"They were."

"And the results?"

"Also negative, sir."

It was not going my way and I had to think quickly. I remembered an earlier conversation. "Was there evidence or reason to believe that the deceased had changed his clothes after raping Ms. Trapp and before entering his bar where he took over for the bartender."

"Yes, sir,"

"Now, Detective," I said, "I assume you conducted an independent investigation then and later to check on the story of the alleged rape, did you not?"

"I did, sir; an extensive one."

"And did that investigation tend to confirm or refute Mrs. Trapp's story of the rape?"

"Confirm it, sir."

"In every particular?"

"In every particular."

"And what were some of these things that confirmed your opinion on that score?"

"Well sir, the scene of the attack. It was obvious that a car had been parked there and the objects found as evidence at that scene, which I've described." He paused. "The biggest thing was the screams."

"Screams, Detective? What screams?"

"Mrs. Trapp had told us she had screamed several times at her front gate. We naturally checked on that, not only to find out if she had screamed but whether the screams might not have instead come from someone else."

"You mean, Detective, to find out whether it might not have been her husband who beat her up for staying out?"

"Yes, sir. Many times that has been the case so we try to rule that out first."

"And what did you learn?"

"We found four individuals who were visiting relatives who said they were awakened that night by screams around midnight and that looking out the window they saw a woman down the road in front of a gate, screaming. One said that she also heard moaning and a dull thud, like something hitting the ground."

"And you have the names and addresses of these witnesses?"

"I have."

"And you had long ago turned this information over to the prosecuting officials?"

"Yes, sir."

I paused and glanced at the juror. "Now, I ask you, Detective Parker, if you are an expert pistol shot?"

"Well, Mr. Dandridge, sir, I guess I am."

"And you are familiar with pistols and ammunition?"

"I believe I am, sir."

"And have you ever engaged in pistol shoots with persons not in police work?"

"Occasionally."

"In this county?"

"Yes, sir."

"Was one of them the deceased, Noah Arietta?

"Yes, sir."

"And was he also an expert?"

"Yes, sir. I would say he was among the best I have ever seen."

I walked over to pick up the pistol that had been put into evidence. Are you familiar with this type of weapon?"

"I am, sir. It is a German luger."

"What can you tell me about it."

"Well, the Luger is one of the first semi-automatic pistols designed to use a toggle-lock action, which uses a jointed arm to lock, as opposed to the slide actions of almost every other semi-automatic pistol. After a round is fired, the barrel and toggle assembly are both locked together at this point and will travel rearward due to recoil. After moving rearward, the toggle strikes a cam built into the frame, causing the knee joint to hinge and the toggle and breech assembly to unlock. At this point the barrel impacts the frame and stops its rearward movement, but the toggle assembly continues moving, extracting the spent casing from the chamber and ejecting it. The toggle and breech assembly subsequently travel forward under spring tension and the next round from the magazine is loaded into the chamber." During his talk, the Detective points out the areas of discussion to help the jury visualize what he is saying.

To be sure the jury can keep track, I go to the evidence table and find a chart drawing of the weapon with the points discussed labeled. I put this in front of the jury. Now that I have established that the Detective knows the weapon I ask, "What happens when it is empty?"

"Well, without getting technical, when it is empty, as it is now, the gun stays open, this gadget goes up, and the trigger clicks loose, like this." He points to the areas on the gun and I in turn point them out on the chart for the jury who may not see what he is doing.

"So a person familiar with that weapon could tell it was empty simply by looking at it, without opening it?"

"Correct."

I take the gun and return it to the pile of exhibits. This information will come in handy later. For now, I have another agenda.

"Returning now, Detective, to your confirmation of Mrs. Trapp's story of the rape, was there anything else that tended to convince you of the truth of her story?"

"There was."

"What was that?"

"Well, he said, "we questioned her again at length at the precinct."

"Who is we?"

"Lieutenant Gordon-Levitt, myself and..." The witness hesitates.

"And who else, Detective Parker?"

"Lieutenant Afflack, sir."

"What does Lieutenant Afflack do? I don't believe his name is mentioned on the information attached to this case?"

"He is our expert on the polygraph."

"And what is the polygraph?"

"It is generally known as the lie-detector, sir."

"You mean, Detective Parker that Mrs. Trapp was given a lie-detector test?"

"Objection. Results of polygraphs are not admissible in court as counsel well knows." Ms. Larson says irritably.

"Your Honor," I said, "no one is talking about the results of any lie-detector test, but whether one was given."

The judge thoughtfully pursed his lips. "The witness can answer the question. And, Mr. Dandridge, tread carefully." He added.

"She was given such a test, yes." Detective Parker replied.

"And was this test given before or after you had determined on your own whether she was telling the truth?"

"After?"

"At whose request?"

"Mrs. Trapp's."

"And after the test was given did you change your mind on that score?"

"Your Honor, Your Honor!" Ms. Larson was shouting behind me. "This is a sly maneuver to get around the ruling barring such tests. Besides the defense has never asked us for the results."

"I'm asking you now, Ms. Larson." I said to eliminate her objection.

"Gentleman, Ma'am., the Judge said, his voice rising. "There has been a question and an objection and I must make a ruling, which I cannot do if you keep arguing between yourselves. Now we are skating on thin ice, I realize that, but in all consciousness I cannot rule that the question is objectionable. Counsel is not asking for the results of any polygraph test but the opinion of the witness based upon certain knowledge possessed by him. The witness may therefore answer the question."

"My mind did not change." Detective Parker replied.

"So that before the polygraph test you believed she was telling the truth?"

"Yes, sir."

"And after?"

"Yes, sir."

"And do you still believe it up to this moment?"

"Yes, I do sir."

"Finally, Detective Parker, wasn't that the real reason you did not ask Doctor Pierson of the Medical Examiner's office during the autopsy to make any tests for possible recent intercourse or the alcoholic content of the blood?"

Nodding, Detective Parker replied, "Yes, sir."

"It was never with any idea, then or now, that you or your colleagues wanted to suppress anything here in court?"

"Certainly not."

"But rather because you and your colleagues were then satisfied beyond all doubt that the rape had in fact taken place and that no further confirmation was necessary?"

"Precisely, sir."

"And at that time, Detective Parker did you anticipate any question would ever be raised or issue made over the fact of that rape, least of all by the prosecution?"

Detective Park shot a look at Jean Larson's table. "I certainly did not, sir" he said.

"Thank you, Detective Parker," I said.

The Judge looked at the prosecution table and said, "Any further questions of this witness."

"Yes, Your Honor," Ms. Larson said.

"Detective Parker, couldn't the screams at the gate have been those of a man?"

"Possibly, Ms. Larson, except that all the witnesses said they were the screams of a woman."

"But did they know it was this woman's screams?" she said pointing at Paige Trapp.

"They did not, ma'am."

"No further questions," Ms. Larson said.

The Judge glanced in my direction and I got up.

"Detective Parker," I said, "during your investigation did you hear of any other woman or women who had screamed in that area that night? At the gate or anywhere else?"

Smiling briefly, "I did not, sir."

"You were unable to dig up any evidence of a general epidemic of screaming females that night?" I could hear the tittering sounds in the courtroom.

"Only the one occasion at the gate, sir."

"No further questions" I said.

The Judge looked at the prosecutions table.

"No further questions for this witness," Ms. Larson said the animosity apparent in her voice.

"The witness is excused," Judge Silas Nicholson said.

"The Judge added. "The court will take a fifteen-minute recess."

"All rise," the Sheriff said.

Chapter 8

I took advantage of the recess by having a parley with Pete in the conference room. There wasn't much time and I needed to bring him up to date on my moonlit session with Tyra Pederson. I told him everything in brevity but covered all the important points and when I finished I could see he too thought the meeting victorious. Because he had seen something in her that reminded him of his dead wife, Nora, I made sure to express the change I had seen in Tyra Pederson. How does that saying go, 'Sometimes it's not the people who change, it's the mask that falls off'.

"So, Pete," I said, "it appears now that all our work and worry over the Will contest was irrelevant. I guess it doesn't even matter much now whether the bartender comes our way or not.

Pete's head jerked up. "You've got your rape in now, yes, and thank goodness for that, but that still is not a legal defense for murder. We've still got that problem to face, and a motive for why the Lieutenant went to the bar that night carrying a concealed weapon. That's where the bartender can help us if he's willing. Do you think he's willing?"

"Lord knows, Pete," I said. "I told you what Tyra Pederson said to me on the phone. We'll have to wait and see what happens when I question the bartender again.

At that moment Sheriff Lincoln Harper popped his head in the door. "Second act curtain in two minutes, Richard," he said.

"Thanks, Lincoln," I replied, tightening my necktie.

"You know," Pete said thoughtfully as I snapped shut my swollen brief case and we began our walk back to the court room, "that Sheriff of ours might have possibilities if he'd only get out of politics. He, kind of grows on me."

***

Everyone is anxious to get started and the Judge doesn't waste a minute calling on the prosecution to present their next witness. To my amazement I am in for a surprise when instead of calling a witness, District Attorney Randall Walker stands and addresses the court. "Your Honor, before calling our next witness we would like to place into evidence, the missing three photographs taken by Mr. Carpenter."

You could hear a pin drop in the silence of the court room as Randall moves slowly to the front of the court and hands the photographs to the Judge, who looks then over and then hands them back to Randall, giving his approval to have them entered into evidence. All eyes are on Randall as he despondently takes them over to be logged in as evidence.

I wait with anticipation for it to be my turn to have a look at the photographs that I hope will have a huge factor on the defense side of this case. Randall keeps his head down as he finally walks over and drops the three missing photographs on my table and I gingerly picked them up, anxious and praying they capture the whole devastating results of the rape of Mrs. Trapp. I hold each photograph so that both the Lieutenant and I can scrutinize them together.

I remember how Paige had looked when I saw her after the rape, her eyes black and blue and her face puffy, but that was nothing compared to what I was seeing now. The woman in the pictures showed no resemblance to the beautiful woman sitting behind me. The photos show major contusions on both sides of her face — there is serious swelling and bruising. Her lip is split and her nose bloody. A closer look and I could confirm there are bite marks on one of her arms and on several fingers. There is no doubt she had been struck with his fists during this attack. No one in their right mind could believe she wasn't raped.

The Lieutenant is quiet as he observes what Noah did to his wife and once seeing all three pictures he just turns his head away. I then twist around to hand the photos over the railing for Paige to view and seconds later she taps me on the shoulder and I turn and take them back. I shuffle through the photos one more time.

I stood at the defense table and said, "Your Honor," the defense requests the court's permission to have the jury look at these latest exhibits at this time, that is, if the People raise no objection."

There is a slight pause and then, "No objection, Your Honor," Randall Walker says from the prosecutors table.

"Very well, Mr. Dandridge, the People's photographs of the defendant's wife may be shown to the jury at this time."

I leaned back in my seat and watched as Randall handed the pictures to the nearest juror who anxiously reached for them. The juror stared at the pictures intently while the others curiously leaned over and craned to see. Each juror in turn took some time registering the images of a woman who looked like she had gone through hell. When the last juror had finished, Randall reclaimed them for the evidence table.

I watch their faces closely as each in turn has a chance to see Paige as she was after the incident took place. Not one of the jury members shows anything less than disgust and several sneak a look at Paige with sympathy.

I remembered what the caretaker said to Pete. He had described Paige as a "mess," and these pictures richly bore him out; her long golden brown hair was tangled and streaming into her swollen eyes. There was streaks of dirt and tears on her face and a bruised discoloration of the flesh surrounding each of her eyes. There was no doubt when looking at the photographs that she was not a willing partner.

"Thank you, Mr. Walker," I said, handing him the three photographs and trying not to show the excitement emanating inside me because I knew he was aware how damaging these photographs were to his case.

Once Randall is seated again at the prosecutors table, the Judge Nicholson announces. "Call your next witness," nodding at Randall's table.

"I call Doctor Henrietta Pierson," Jean Larson announces.

Doctor Henrietta Pierson was a welcome witness even for our side. She was a young black woman with a mass of curly hair and a winning smile. Her unblemished caramel colored skin was tantalizingly smooth and her expression was one of someone who enjoyed what she was doing.

"Raise your right hand. Do you solemnly swear or affirm that the testimony you're about to give will be the truth, the whole truth and nothing but the truth, so help you God?"

"I do."

"Please state your name for the records.

"Doctor Henrietta Pierson."

Dr. Pierson, please state your educational background for the jury.

"I received my undergraduate degree from St. Lawrence University in Canton, NY. And graduated with the honor of Summa cum Laude. I received my medical degree from SUNY Upstate Medical University in Syracuse, NY and trained as a resident in the Department of Internal Medicine at the University of Rochester School of Medicine. I received the Dr. U.R. Plante Medical Award for excellence in medical school and as a resident, received the David A. Haller Intern of the year Award as well as the Pulsifer Award for dedication to patient care. I trained as a fellow in Gastroenterology at the Cleveland Clinic Foundation in Ohio with an interest in inflammatory bowel disease."

"Do you belong to any organizations?"

"Yes, I am a member of the American College of Gastroenterology, American Gastroenterology Association, Crohn's and Colitis Foundation of America, Medical Society of the State of New York, and St. Lawrence County Medical Society."

"Thank you Doctor." Randall quickly addressed the preliminaries for the record covering of course the fact that Doctor Pierson was a local physician and worked with the Police Department, providing medical assistance when needed. Once he had established her position and her credentials he began his interview of the witness.

"Doctor Pierson, did you examine the person known as Mrs. Paige Trapp."

"Yes, I did?"

"And for what purpose was the examination done?"

"When a patient claims to have been sexually assaulted arrives at the hospital, the hospital staff, usually an emergency room doctor, conducts a preliminary physical examination of the patient to determine if she requires immediate medical care, completes the necessary intake forms, and if the patient informs us that she has been raped, we ask permission to perform a rape test."

"What happens next."

"While the regular hospital staff treats the alleged victim as a patient of the hospital, the responsibilities of the physician working with the police is quite different. I perceive the alleged victim as my "patient," but as a possible crime scene. I am obligated to follow strict protocols as I collect possible evidence, document any injuries, and carefully memorialize the alleged victim's allegations."

"Did you personally complete a rape kit on Mrs. Trapp?"

"Yes, I did."

"When was the test performed?"

Doctor Pierson consulted her notebook and said. "I was called to my lab at five a.m. on August 16, 2015"

"Wow, five a.m. you say. Wasn't that an odd time to have you called in to perform this test."

"No, in order to collect evidence, a survivor must seek treatment at a hospital within 120 hours of an assault so it is always done as quickly as possible. The rape exam is the process used to collect the evidence for the rape kit."

"So what is this rape kit?"

"The Kit is a box that contains all the necessary materials to collect evidence. Each Kit has a unique number assigned to it and all evidence collected is placed in envelopes or bags and labeled with this number."

"How long would you say it takes to complete the test?"

I know what he is doing. He wants to establish a picture of a thorough test being done by this doctor so that the results will be a major shock, but with little doubt of its accuracy. Doctor Pierson pauses and then replies, "Well, The Kit has separate steps to collect evidence and it usually takes at least a couple of hours."

"So, Doctor Pierson, what was the results of your test?"

"They were negative."

There were surprise sounds and expressions on the face of the jurors who after seeing the photographs are shocked by the results expressed by the doctor. Randall is unable to hide his delight as he grins when looking at me. He says. "Your witness."

I stand and take my notes with me as I approach the doctor.

"Doctor Pierson. Can you tell us briefly what you are looking for and what the steps are for collecting this evidence?"

The Doctor is silent as she assembles her thoughts. "Let's see. We collect the clothing which frequently contains the most important evidence in a case of sexual assault. While foreign matter can be washed off or worn off the body of the patient, the same substances often may be found intact on clothing for a considerable length of time following the assault. Then there is what we call trace evidence which can provide evidence beyond DNA. This is materials or fibers that are found related to the assault. There are oral swabs and smears in cases where the patient was orally penetrated, the oral swabs and smears can be as important as the vaginal or anal samples. There are external genital swabs if the circumstances of the assault suggest there has been contact between the victim's genitalia and the offender's mouth or penis. We also collect pubic hair combings and pubic hair pulled samples, as well as pulled head hair samples. We perform anal swabs and smears as well as vaginal swabs. "

Again she pauses then continues. "We prepare cervical swabs and smears that are only collected in patients who are past onset of menses. The cervix provides an excellent source for sperm and DNA collection. Then there are fingernail clippings collected on patients which may have been in a physical altercation during an assault. They may contain skin cells of the suspect and are simple to collect. We do buccal swabs collection for DNA to determine the patient's DNA profile for comparison with such deposits. Plus additional evidence as needed, for example, it may be appropriate to swab a female's abdomen when she says the suspect ejaculated on her."

"My, that is intense," I reply. "Now regarding the vagina smear, how did you take it?"

"Well, I had Ms. Trapp lie down and I took four swaps and collected the sample and then wiped the four swabs across the middle surface of the labeled glass slide. "

"Hm, interesting. Did you dilate the vaginal orifice?"

"I didn't have to, there was no difficulty."

"Did you know when you came to the lab to take the smears that there was some question whether the woman had been raped?"

"Yes."

"Did you know her age? Did you know whether she was a mature woman or a virgin or adolescent?"

"No," Doctor Pierson said with discomfort.

"So you took a chance that you might not have to dilate with a speculum?"

"Well, yes." She spread her hands. "I didn't have a speculum."

"But isn't that standard practice, Doctor, to use a speculum or expander when taking a vaginal slide?" I asked.

"Not necessarily."

"But aren't there situations where a doctor might have to use a speculum to properly take a vaginal slide?"

"Of course."

"Wouldn't it be fair to say, Doctor, that the taking of vaginal slides is not and has never been one of your specialties?"

"No, yes…I can't say it is one of my specialties, but I am knowledgeable on taking one."

"Okay, let me ask this way. During the last ten years how many vaginal slides have you taken?"

"Well, I would have to say around four or five."

"And what did you do with these slides?"

"I sent them to the Monroe County Crime Laboratory."

"Do you know who worked them?"

This began to feel personal to Doctor Pierson and in an effort to gain respect she answered my question thoroughly. "When there is a murder, suspicious fire or hit-and-run accident, forensic scientists are called in. They will take samples collected at the scene and analyze them in a forensics laboratory. These are the individuals who apply scientific analysis to the justice system, to help prove the events of a crime. They analyze and interpret evidence found at the crime scene. When the report was completed, the District Attorney received a copy with the name of the scientists who performed the test."

"Thank you Dr. Pierson." I wait and then add, "Now, Doctor, the evening edition of the Democrat & Chronicle for August 2nd states that you reported you found no sign of rape. Is that a correct report of your findings?"

I walk over to the defense table and picked up a copy of the newspaper that had been folded around the article I was referring to. I hand this to the Doctor. Then I go over to the evidence table and take that copy and hand it to the jury to pass around while the Doctor looks over my copy.

Dr. Pierson reads the article and then says, "No, I didn't say anything like that."

"On any questions of rape, Doctor, are you willing to accept the word of those who may be in a better positon to explain the results of the tests performed from the rape kit you supplied?"

I registered the relief on Doctor Pierson's face. "Yes I am."

"Thank you Doctor Pierson. No further questions," I said.

"Any further questions, Mr. Prosecutor", the Judge asked.

"No further questions, Your Honor."

The Judge turned to the witness, "Doctor Pierson, you can step down."

Once the witness has returned to her seat, Judge Nicholson says to the prosecution, "Call your next witness."

"Your Honor," Randall said, "Lieutenant Gordon-Levitt, who accompanied and assisted Detective Sergeant Kent in the investigation of this case has been ill since the start of this trial. He is presently at Strong Hospital under a doctor's care. We could call in the doctor to collaborate if necessary."

I stood and said, "Your Honor, that is not necessary. I am aware of Lieutenant Gordon-Levitt's condition and waive the producing of this witness."

"Very well," Judge Nicholson said, "This witness is excused. Call your next witness."

Randall walked over to the prosecutor's table and whispered to Jean Larson. He then stood by the table and said, "Your Honor, the People rest."

I immediately jumped up out of my chair. "Your Honor," I said, "I believe the People inadvertently forgot some unfinished business. I had not completed my cross examination of the People's witness, Brook Hamilton, the bartender at the Founder's Café. Seeing as he is the prosecutor's witness I cannot call him to the stand.

"Your point is well taken, Mr. Dandridge," the Judge said, looking at Randall's table. "Your move."

Jean Larson half rose from her chair and irritably said, "The People recall Mr. Brook Hamilton and tender the witness for cross examination."

I watch as Brook makes his way to stand near the witness chair.

"You are already sworn in," the Judge says kindly. "Please be seated."

"Your witness, Mr. Dandridge," the Judge said.

This is my moment and I slowly walk to the front of the court room giving Randall and Jean a chance to gloat since they have no reason to assume I will get anything out of the bartender. Unless they have been tailing me, they have no idea of my visit to Tyra, let alone the outcome. This is going to be a bitter sweet moment and I am going to enjoy it immensely.

Chapter 9

"Are you comfortable Mr. Hamilton," I ask.

"Yes.

"Okay, good. I have a few more questions for you and I'll keep it as brief as I can." I take a few steps closer to the witness stand and give Brook what I hope is a pleasant smile. "So let's begin. Was Noah Arietta an expert pistol shot?"

"Objection, Your Honor," Ms. Larson barks, cutting off Mr. Hamilton before he can say a word. "The court has already ruled on that as being irrelevant and immaterial."

I avoid eye contact with Ms. Larson and instead look at Judge Nicholson. "But the People's own witness, Detective Sergeant Kent has now made the deceased an expert pistol shot," I said innocently. "We seek only to support his statement."

The Judge's navy blue eyes peer sternly over the top of his metal framed glasses. "Strictly speaking you may have a point, Ms. Larson," he says, "but as the defense has pointed out, the subject is now on record." The Judge pauses and turns to look at Mr. Hamilton. "The witness may answer."

Now it is my turn to feel hesitant as I hold my breath, hoping for the answer to be as expected. I can't trust that the prosecution hasn't schooled him on this matter. This is my punishment for feeling so superior before I had a right to be. Suddenly I have an overpowering sensation that Tyra might not have the pull when pitted against the prosecution; especially Jean Larson.

My mind is swimming when I hear, "I would say he was an expert, sir," Brook Hamilton answers.

"Objection, objection. Witness is not qualified to classify someone as an expert shooter."

It is going to be a battle to get anything out of this witness with all the protesting going on. I look at Ms. Larson and though her appearance still is one of a sweet grandmother, her constant outbursts and expressions has hardened that image to match that of the Wicked Witch of the West. "I'll get to that, Your Honor," I say with patience I am not feeling. I turn to Ms. Larson and plead sweetly, "Please permit me to go on."

"Proceed, proceed, I'll reserve my ruling," the Judge replied.

I begin again. "Upon what do you base your conclusion, Mr. Hamilton, that Noah was an expert pistol shot?" I ask.

It is easy to ascertain that Brook was not happy with Ms. Larson either, especially after this last objection that seemed to belittle his intelligence. Give them enough rope and they'll hang themselves, I think. Even if Tyra hadn't talked with Brook, I feel confident that he has had enough of Ms. Larson's insulting statements. I am feeling good and about to feel even better when Brook answers the question.

"Because I've seen him shoot against the best and beat them." He replied. "He's won dozens and dozens of first prizes at shoots all over the Country and I know a lot about guns. For instance, smaller caliber guns aren't necessarily just for newer shooters. Noah would always say that if you want to become an expert, practice with a light-kicking gun might be just the ticket."

"Interesting," I reply. What else did Noah share with you about guns?"

"Well he said that folks assume that since the .410 is small, light, and shoots a low recoil round, then it must be great for new shooters. With some exceptions, Noah believed the opposite true. He said that the .410 is really an expert's gun. If you see someone slinging a Beretta 687 Silver Pigeon on the skeet range, chances are they know what they're doing. It's hard to bust a moving clay target with a small shot charge. But if you can, then repeating the action with a 12 gauge will seem as easy as hitting water with a boat."

I glance over at Jean and can see her shrinking back in her chair as Brook more than proves his knowledge of guns. I am not about to stop him now.

"So, did Noah teach you how to shot?"

"Sure. Noah taught me that a .22 pistol is just as appropriate for an advanced shooter as a beginner. In his own words he said that if I wanted to be an expert shooter like himself I needed to master trigger press and so he had me practice daily dry fire practice, saying that the best professional shooters in the world practice dry fire drills every day. He regularly shoots guns of all types, in dozens of calibers and he rarely misses. He could shoot a target 100 yards away, and for those who are not up on it, to earn an 'expert' badge, soldiers must hit 36 out of 40 targets from distances of 50 to 300 meters. Noah could do that too. The man was deadly."

All of what he said was good, but that last statement was unexpected and superb. I glance at the jury and can see eyebrows raised and frowns on faces, but I want to push the point. "I'm concerned with this issue that you are speaking of" I say knowing that nothing shows concern like a couple of well-placed fingers on the chin, I take that pose and add, "Yes, the man was deadly."

I wait a few minutes to let it all sink in then add, "Well, that to me qualifies you on this subject." I turn toward Ms. Larson. "Wouldn't you agree?" She gives a slight nod.

"And was Noah's prowess with pistols generally known around town?"

"It was." Brook Hamilton began. "Mr. Arietta was never one to hide his light under a bush and he kept all his awards right on the wall behind and facing the bar."

I looked over at Jean Larson. "Do the people still want to object?"

"What is the ruling, Your Honor," Jean Larson said adamantly forcing the Judge to make the decision and pretty sure what he will say.

"The People's objection is overruled," The Judge said dryly. "Mr. Hamilton seems well versed on the subject.

I thought I detected a slight smile flit across the face of the witness. I continued. "Passing now to any pistols owned by Mr. Arietta," I said. "Did he own any?"

"Yes, he has owned many pistols. I would say as many as fifteen or twenty at one time. I suppose you could call him a collector. He kept buying and selling and trading them. At the time of the ah..., incident, he was down to six of his favorites."

Now it was time for the big question. "And where did he keep these pistols?"

Brook hesitated for a moment and then said. "He kept two in his quarters upstairs in the apartment."

"And the other four?"

The witness grew silent and looked around the room. About then I would have given anything to know what he was thinking about. The same could be said for those in the court room as the air was filled with silence and several jurors were actually sitting on the edge of their seats. Everyone was waiting to hear his reply.

"He kept them down in the Founder Café bar area,"

"Loaded?"

"Invariably."

I glanced quickly at Pete, who sat near the front of the gallery, to see his reaction and am pleased to see he is enjoying this line of questioning. I turn back to the witness. "And where in the bar area?" I asked.

"Behind the bar."

"And where behind the bar," I continued.

"He kept two on a little shelf he'd built in the middle of the bar-and one each at either end on other shelves he had built."

"Were they visible to persons standing in front of the bar?"

"No, they were not."

"And what was the purpose of keeping the pistols there?"

The eyes of Brook Hamilton flickered ever so slightly and I am afraid I may have pushed too hard, but Brook answers. "Protection," he says, "Protection against any trouble that may surface in the Founder Café."

I frown. "Trouble? What kind of trouble?"

"Holdups. That sort of trouble."

"And were these four pistols behind the bar the night of the shooting?" I asked, trying to relax as I wait for his reply.

"They were not," Brook said. My heart sank. Was all this a clever trap the witness and Larson had worked out? And why, oh why, had I asked that fatal question. But it was too late to back out now.

"Where were they?"

"I had locked them up."

"Why"

"Because of Mr. Arietta's drinking and general behavior."

"Did Mr. Arietta consent to this?"

"He did not."

I hated to ask the next question, but I had to because it might just be the right one. "Was it these four pistols in the bar that you locked up or all of the pistols?" I held my breath.

"Only the four. Mr. Arietta wouldn't give up the other two pistols no matter what we said or did. Besides he had told us before he wouldn't take them from his apartment. They would just stay there."

"We?" I ask.

"What do you mean."

"You said we. Who is we?" I asked.

"He promised Ms. Tyra Pederson and me. Tyra is the hostess at the Founder's Café and she lives in one of the apartment upstairs in the building.

"Was the fact that you'd locked up these four guns general knowledge?"

"It was known only to Mr. Arietta, Ms. Pederson and myself."

"And can you tell us more about why you felt obliged to lock up the four guns that were kept in the bar?"

Mr. Hamilton grew thoughtful. "Well, he said slowly, "about two weeks before the shooting, Mr. Arietta began drinking more than usual. He grew irritable and quarrelsome and difficult—and we decided it was best to remove the guns from the bar."

This was getting interesting now. "When did you lock them up?"

"Just about a week before the shooting."

I wanted to ask if Noah had asked for his guns back. I wanted to know where they were then and where were they now. but I held back. Instead I asked, "Could you venture to tell us the reason why Mr. Arietta seemed upset and drank more than usual?"

I asked, knowing it was what the jury expected me to ask but might not be allowed. It's one of those sticky wicky areas of the law. Like a hearing is held to determine a woman's mental competence. Out of court, when asked to identify herself, the woman said, "I am the pope." There is little question that the purpose of introducing that statement as evidence is not to convince the judge or jury that the woman actually is the pope; the truthfulness of the statement is irrelevant. Rather, the statement is introduced to show the woman's mental state; her belief that she is the pope may prove that she is not mentally competent. On the other hand, a defendant's out-of-court statement "I am the murderer," offered in a murder trial to prove that the defendant is the murderer, is hearsay. This answer may be objected to on the basis of hearsay. I wait for Brooks reply.

"No, sir," he said, and he must also have seen my look of relief.

"Could you tell us this, Mr. Hamilton, whatever the reasons, did they appear to have anything to do with the Trapps?"

"I would say definitely not, sir. None whatsoever."

I glanced at Jean Larson who sat staring stonily at the far wall, her arms folded. She was done objecting, at least during this part of the questioning.

After that I procured that Noah Arietta had been at the bar earlier that night; that he'd played Frogger with Paige, as she had claimed; that he'd left about the same time as she had, around eleven o'clock in the evening, that he'd returned to the bar shortly after midnight, that he'd relieved the bartender so he could 'rest,' and pretty much all that the bartender had told me on my earlier visit to the Founders Café I managed to bring out in questioning. There was an exception as I carefully avoided the subject of his possibly being a 'lookout' and I resolutely stayed away from the subject of Noah's

Will too. I decided that I could always argue the 'lookout' business to the jury later.

"When Mr. Arietta reappeared at the bar, "I continued, "did he come in the street door or from upstairs?"

"Upstairs, sir."

"Had he changed his clothing?"

Brook Hamilton blinked rapidly as if clearing something out of his eyes. "My best recollection is that he had," he finally replied. "I recall that he was wearing a loose sweat shirt after and he'd worn a white shirt before."

"Had it been a warm evening?"

"It was."

"Was it still warm in the bar after midnight?"

"It was, quite stuffy and warm."

Now it was my turn to be silent as I thought the answers through. It was a hot night and Noah had seen fit to change from a white shirt to a hot loose fitting sweat shirt. Could it be because there was dirt or lipstick or both on the shirt? Could he have worn loose clothing because he had one of the upstairs pistols on his person and he wanted to conceal that fact from the eyes of his 'pistol' caretakers?

"Mr. Hamilton," I said, "the other day when I was questioning you in court and we were so rudely interrupted, we were talking about Noah's drinking. Now was he drinking more than usual that day?"

I paused waiting for the objection, but it didn't come.

"I wouldn't say that day," he replied causing my spirits to sink. "I now recall he'd been drinking more than usual for about two weeks." My spirits rose as I asked. "And what was his daily intake during normal times?"

"Noah could easily drink eight or ten double shots a day."

"And how much was a double shot?"

"Two ounces."

I calculated that to be eighteen to twenty ounces of whisky a day. I would have been sick to my stomach if it had been me. "And was that whisky?"

"Yes, bonded Jim Beam' bourbon. Mr. Arietta drank only the best."

"Now how about during this two week period before the shooting; how much was he drinking then?"

The witness shook his head. "It must have been easily, a fifth. It got so I couldn't keep track."

"That was what you yourself saw him drink?"

"Yes."

"And that didn't take into account what he might take in his rooms or elsewhere?"

"It did not, sir."

I knew that Noah had at least four drinks with Paige and five more at the bar after the rape. That made nine. Eighteen ounces he'd had since nine o'clock that night besides whatever else he'd drank unobserved. It was faintly incredible. Lord, if I kept on at this rate I'd have the man blind drunk and I didn't want that either.

"Could Noah drink quite a bit without showing it?"

"Without showing it to strangers. We who knew him well could tell."

"He was not one to swagger and stagger and talk loud when he was drunk, then?"

"No, he tended to smile more; especially at the customers. It was a way he had."

"I'd like to change the question path for now. About the guns being kept behind the bar for protection against holdups, could you tell us how many holdups you had at the bar of the Founder's Café this past summer?"

Brook Hamilton frowned bringing his large forehead closer to his eyes, "None."

"Any attempts?"

"No."

"Had there been any such attempts during all the time you have worked there?"

"None."

"Have you ever heard of any holdups or attempts made before you came"

"No."

"But the loaded guns were kept there for; holdups?"

Brook, smiling slightly said, "Yes, for holdups, sir."

I abruptly abandoned Noah and his guns and drinking. The Jim Beam bourbon had reminded me of something else. I saw I'd have to lower the boom, still a little more.

"Did you drive Paige Trapp to the jail to see her husband the Sunday after the shooting?"

Brook Hamilton stirred uneasily, "I did."

"And did you tell Lieutenant Trapp in substance that the only thing you held against him was that he'd smashed your mirror and shot up a bottle of Jim Beam bourbon instead of some cheap whisky?"

Brook's eyes flickered and I saw that our brief honeymoon was about over. "I don't remember precisely what I said." His voice rose. "I was trying to cheer the man up. I may have said something like that for a joke."

"You wouldn't say you hadn't said it?"

"No."

"The fact was that your mirror was smashed and you did lose a bottle of bonded bourbon?"

"Yes."

"And were you trying to sympathize when you told Paige Trapp you could have warned her that Noah was a wolf?"

Brooks attitude was now dangerously changed and his dark features seemed stormy with anger.

"I didn't say I said that," he blurted angrily. "You're trying to trap me with sneaky lawyer questions."

"Answer the question, Mr. Hamilton. Did you say that to Mrs. Trapp? Did you refer to Noah as a wolf?"

"I don't recall saying any such thing," he snapped.

This was the end of the line with this witness in a sense. I had used him and finally betrayed him. But perhaps it was better to close on an angry note. I turned to Jean Larson. "The witness is back to you."

Jean Larson had grown grim and white. She evidently counted on this witness for big things. Now I watched as she walked toward the witness.

"How did Mrs. Trapp conduct herself at the bar in the Founders Café that night before the shooting?" she asked crisply.

I knew the question was objectionable on several grounds, including leading one's own witness, but I kept quiet.

"Well," the witness said, "at times I thought her behavior wasn't quite ladylike."

"Like when?" Jean Larson asked.

"Like once when she took off her shoes to play Frogger."

"All right. And did she do anything else while her shoes were off?"

"I don't recall, Ms."

"Didn't she also dance with a patron named Terry Kenion?"

This was objectionable but I still held back. I could feel the Judge's eyes on me wonderingly, but my gut said to be still. So I did.

"I don't know. I don't recall seeing her dancing with anyone," Brook Hamilton answered and as an afterthought continued. "You and I discussed quite a number of things and you may have misunderstood me," he paused. "Possibly you could ask Terry Kenion himself. He should remember an incident like that."

Terry Kenion had already been called. Evidence which goes to a matter that forms a fundamental part of the case which the prosecution is required to prove in relation to the charges brought in the indictment should be brought as part of the prosecution case-in-chief and not in rebuttal. The prosecutors can indeed apply to bring new witnesses to the stand under certain conditions and if the judges approves it as part of their evidence in "rebuttal." But not a previously called witness. Ms. Larson's hands are tied.

"Your witness," Ms. Larson shrugged.

I felt sorry for her and so I said, "I have but one further question for this witness. Was this man Terry Kenion that Ms. Larson just referred to the same big red-faced man who testified here as a People's eyewitness the other day and was examined by Ms. Larson?" I turned and pointed out in the galley. "The man sitting out there in the front row right now, grinning and with his hands on his knees?"

Brook Hamilton smiled, "Yes, that's Terry Kenion."

"No further questions," I said, happy to be done with this witness.

Jean Larson nodded her head grimly.

"Noon recess," the Judge said, and Sheriff Lincoln Harper has everyone rise as the Judge leaves the bench, then proceeds to clear the courtroom.

Chapter 10

I had one aim in mind and that was to have some alone time with the Lieutenant so as everyone cleared the court room I pulled him aside and lead him and Paige toward the conference room. Once settled, I began.

"I have been busy and unable to check out the psychiatrist that Ms. Larson retained. Have you noticed him watching you or did he say anything to you?"

The Lieutenant's focus was indeed elsewhere and I could see the fatigue on his face so I added, "I know your mind is elsewhere and I can't blame you, but I need to know."

"You need to know. You definitely need to know because you don't know anything about me." The Lieutenant said with sarcasm."

Where was this coming from. I couldn't think of anything that I did or said to cause this attitude in my client. Then it comes to me. It's not anything I did, it is about Paige. But, not being quite sure of it, I give him a minute before I respond. "I do know you. I know a lot about you. You are a longtime insomniac, and reportedly have been under psychiatric care in the past and have used medication for depression. I know you drink scotch and wine and enjoy eating peanuts and spicy food. You are intense and self-absorbed, prone to violent outbursts, and prefer a neat and orderly environment. I also know you are 6'1" and weigh around 180 lbs. You threaten without speaking a word because along with all of this you are a soldier and work as a United States Government Foreign Service Officer." I pause. "I think I do know you."

I see the look of amazement on his face as his anger begins to dissipate. He offers no apology but says, "I hadn't noticed the psychiatrist at all."

"Well I have," Paige said. "The man positively gives me the willies. Every time I glance over that way he's looking not at Vincent but at me. Once or twice I think he smiled."

"Well, don't worry, Paige, you are the prettiest person in that whole courtroom and I am sure many eyes have been turned toward you. Don't let it bother you."

"I have a suggestion," I said looking at the Lieutenant. "Can you put on all your ribbons and decorations tomorrow. I know we were going to save them for when you testify, but I think we need them displayed earlier."

"Sure, if you think it will help."

I turn towards Paige. "Paige, what about the insinuation that you were dancing barefoot with that man, Terry Kenyon? Is it true?"

"No," she replied vehemently. "I didn't dance with anybody," she said, "and if I had it wouldn't be that grotesque lurch, Terry. He's disgusting." She paused. "Why didn't they ask him that when he was on the stand?"

"Probably they were saving it for a surprise," I said. I knew differently. It was because during the early part of the trial this was all about the Lieutenant and a Mrs. Trapp was not even thought of until we mentioned the attack.

I sat there contemplating and then remembered something. "Paige, didn't you remove your shoes when you were playing Frogger?"

"Yes, now that you mention it, I did. I'd forgotten that. I took off my shoes near the end of the last game so I could stand on my toes and aim better. But the whole time my shoes were off my feet I didn't walk around or dance."

"Well, I want you to tell it that way when you are on the stand," I said. "Now, I have to leave. The sheriff will assist you back to the court room." I shook hands with both before leaving them alone. I hoped that the two would not get into it seeing as Paige has explained away the dancing barefoot issue.

***

The only sound in the back corridor was that of my footsteps echoing off the marble hallway. I found a good spot out of site and ear range and pulled out my cell phone to dial Tyra Pederson. She picked up on the first ring.

"I've been waiting for your call," she said. "How did it go, Richard?"

"Like a dream. At times Brook was reluctant and I could tell because his eyes were squinted and his lips set tight as he peered at me, but there were moments when he willingly spoke the truth. All in all, I think he definitely helped our case." I paused and then added, "Tyra I am most grateful to you for unlocking the truth. And I want to thank you in person as soon as this mess is over."

"Please do, Richard, I would like that. The whole thing has been worrying me terribly because I only now understand how much clamming up by myself and the staff had affected the case."

"The danger isn't over yet, Tyra, but I hope to see you soon."

"Me too. Good luck." She said and then disconnected the call.

I put my cell back in my breast pocket and walked gingerly down the hall and out the door of the court room. I had one more contact to make.

Pete was waiting for me in my car. I climbed in. "Richard, let's just go to Mickey D's and get takeout so we can talk in private." I shook my head in agreement.

We went through the drive-in placing identical orders and then drove to the High Falls walkway over the Genesee River. Here it would be quiet and though a bit cool, welcoming. At first we eat our burgers and fries and stare out at the falls, then I brake the silence. "What disturbs me most about this case is how I misunderstood Tyra Pederson and if I hadn't come around, how much further behind the case would be."

Pete doesn't say a word at first and then says, "The lack of communication and trust in the world today is why we have so many problems. It goes both ways and we are slow to realize it."

"What do you mean," I ask.

"Well take our situation in this case. All along we think that Tyra Pederson is a calculating and avaricious female. She in turn thinks we're nothing but a lot of controlling lawyers that can't be trusted. Well, we were both wrong and luckily we realized it before it was too late."

"You are right and I just hope I retain this lesson." I think before asking, "So Pete, what about judges. What makes a good judge?"

Pete thinks about this before replying. "There is a lot to consider, but to put it in a nutshell the most important characteristic is judicial temperament: A judge who has both the ability to apply the law to the facts and to understand how a judicial decision will affect the human beings appearing before the court is most important. In addition, his ability to communicate with counsel, jurors, witnesses and parties calmly and courteously, as well as the willingness to listen to and consider what is said on all sides of a debatable proposition is a close second." He pauses and looks at me. "I think I know why you are asking me this. You have nothing to worry about, Richard, Judge Nicholson is just and fair. I have no doubts about that."

I nodded, wordlessly and then we get into a discussion about the strategy to use and questions that still need asking. I hand Pete a copy of my opening statement and we discuss it; adding and removing points. When done, I feel comfortable and well equipped to present it to the court.

"Well, Richard, it's time we got back."

I stand up, stretch and then reach out and gather up our debris to deposit in the trash receptacle near the sidewalk. When I return, Pete has picked up our personal items and he carries them to the car. We climb in and I turn on the ignition. "Pete, wish we me luck."

"Luck, Richard."

***

Inside the courtroom every seat is taken. It seems that notoriety has grown and everyone wants to witness the case that now has more flavors. As I walk over to take my seat at the defense table, I nod at the prosecution then attend to getting my files out on the defense table. When Sheriff Lincoln Harper says, "All rise," and subsequently announcing Judge Silas Nicholson presiding, I am ready. We continue to stand until the Judge indicates everyone may be seated.

The Judge shuffles some papers on his bench and then peers over his glasses. "Is the defense ready to give their opening statement", he says.

"Yes, Your Honor."

"Please stand and present your opening statement."

I clear my throat and walk up to the bench and do a half turn toward the jury. I think about all the hours that Pete and I put into this opening statement and I am determined to present it with inflection that will award me the attention equal to the laborious hours.

"Insanity extinguishes criminal liability. Though a person committed a crime, the State does not impose any criminal sanction on that person because he was not in his proper mind when he committed the crime."

"Good Afternoon! My name is Richard Dandridge and though you have seen and heard me, we have not been properly introduced. I am the defense attorney of Lieutenant Vincent Trapp. This trial has been called in search for justice for my client, accused of violently killing Mr Noah Arietta on July 31, 2015. I stand here today however, to plead for justice for my client who has already been dictated guilty of the crime. I am here not to mislead the accusations that my client did not do the crime, but rather to explain to you all what happened. Allow me to begin my statement with a few pictures. I ask you however to brace yourselves, the things you will see are very gruesome.

These first are pictures of the body of Mr. Noah Arietta who was shot at his place of establishment while filling in for his bartender Brook Hamilton. He was shot over and over again until the gun was empty of bullets.

Next these are pictures of Mrs. Paige Trapp who was at the Founders Café earlier that evening, playing a game of Frogger with the deceased after which he offered her a ride home. She refused but then when pressured she allowed him to give her a ride home. The ride instead lead to Mr. Noah Arietta viciously beating and raping her. Looking closely at these pictures you can see that Mrs. Trapp was not a willing participant.

The question however my dear ladies and gentlemen of the jury, is how could a completely-sane person be able to do this much damage to Mr. Arietta and have the conscience to do it in a crowded bar in front of many witnesses and just walk away from it? Would you not agree that this is too unusual for a mentally stable person to do? Would you not agree with me when I say that Lieutenant Vincent Trapp could not have done this given he had a perfectly tranquil mind?"

"Fact and fiction have furnished many extraordinary examples of crime that have shocked the feelings and staggered the reason of men, but this is not the case here before you now. Mr. Noah Arietta, the owner of the Founder's Café and the Academy Building Apartments has been murdered. The murder has occurred at the hands of my client, Lieutenant Vincent Trapp, but it was not in cold blood. Look at my client, Lieutenant Trapp."

I walk over and stand beside him with a hand on his shoulder. "Many of you may know of him as he has resided in this town for some time now. Lt. Trapp is an avid outdoorsman, camper, and hiker. He has extensive camping experience. He also enjoys canoeing, swimming, jogging, tennis, and skiing. He drinks scotch and wine and enjoys eating peanuts and spicy food. He is like each and every one of us. He enjoys working out several times a week. He is also a licensed amateur pilot. He has an American Studies degree from Yale University and a Master's Degree in Italian from Middlebury College in Vermont. He is known to read extensively.

But what I am trying to show you is that like each of us, there are layers to his personality that you can identify in yourself."

"But then there is the fact that Lieutenant Trapp is a longtime insomniac, reportedly has been under psychiatric care in the past and has used medication for depression. He is described as intense and self-absorbed, prone to violent outbursts, and prefers a neat and orderly environment. One could say that these last characteristics are a direct result of his history as a decorated soldier, who now works as a United States Government Foreign Service Officer."

"The Prosecution claims that the crime was not done by an insane person. But still let me ask you this question. Where was the crime committed? The Founders Café! From that perspective alone it can already be said that the crime is not that of a sane person since the Founders Café is a highly frequented place owned and operated by Mr. Noah Arietta."

"We will present an expert witness to testify to the temporary insanity of Lt. Vincent Trapp. Dr. Milo Goodman will tell you how he examined the Lieutenant and how the results proved positive for a type of temporary insanity in Lieutenant Vincent Trapp."

"Do not hold it against me, Ladies and gentlemen of the jury, but this story never had a Happy Ending for Mr. Arietta. He drank heavily and as an expert shot could defend himself, but instead it was not to be. We will show that he was expecting the Lieutenant and had set the stage only he suffered and died. But we can still save someone who could not help what he was doing from dying in jail."

"There are two kinds of evidence, direct evidence and circumstantial evidence. Direct evidence is the testimony of persons who have seen, heard or felt the thing or things about which they are testifying. They are telling you something, which they have observed or perceived by their senses. Now in certain cases circumstantial evidence may be as sure and certain as direct evidence, in some cases more so because the eye and ear deceive as well as circumstances and events; but, members of the jury there is no class of evidence known that under certain circumstances is so dangerous and misleading as circumstantial evidence. Once you have heard the whole story, and have all the facts you will understand the Lieutenant's actions."

I pause and again walk over to stand beside my client and place a hand on his shoulder. "He became insane because of his overwhelming love for his wife Paige Trapp and this insanity made him unaware of what he was doing and therefore he should not be convicted for a crime which he did not mean to do. We will put the facts together so that you can see that Lt. Trapp is not guilty of murder or of any crime growing out of the fatal shooting of Noah Arietta, that he was actually and legally insane when he shot the deceased, and that he had a perfect legal right to go to the place of the deceased as he did and seek him out. I thank you."

I turned and went back to my table feeling good about my opening statement. I try not to smile too broadly as I take my seat. But it's hard.

"Call your first witness," Judge Nicholson says.

"The defense call Doctor William Henson," Doctor Henson was Noah Arietta's physician. All eyes were on him as he hurried up to the stand. He was a large sandy haired man, wearing a tweed suit that seemed warm for this time of year, but fit his nature.

The Sheriff came forward to stand beside him. "Raise your right hand. Do you swear to tell the truth, the whole truth, so help you God?"

"I most certainly do," he said sternly, but then remembering where he was and that this was not an offense against his character, there was a softening smile on his face as he made his way to the witness stand.

"Please state your name and occupation for the record."

"My name is Doctor William Henson and I am Mr. Arietta's medical doctor."

"Doctor, would you say that you knew Mr. Arietta well?"

"Yes, I would. I have been his doctor for some time."

"Doctor, did you have occasion during July of this year to give Mr. Noah Arietta a physical examination in connection with his application for some policies of life insurance?"

"I did," the doctor replied and I could feel the eyes of Ms. Larson on me. "It was on July twenty-eighth and in my office."

"Was the exam at the request of Mr. Arietta or the insurance company?"

"The insurance company."

"And in what kind of shape did your examination of Mr. Arietta disclose?

"Objection, irrelevant and immaterial. Anyway, results of an examination are privileged, even after death." It was the voice of Ms. Larson filling the courtroom.

"Mr. Dandridge?" the Judge asks.

"Yes, Your Honor," I search through the papers on my desk until I find what I am looking for. "Let me read this in response to Ms. Larson's objection. It will cover this objection and the possibility of further objections on this issue."

The main body of law that governs patient records is the Health Insurance Portability and Accountability Act's (HIPAA) Privacy Rule, which requires a covered entity (which includes a physician and/or medical practice) to protect the medical records, or "Protected Health Information" ("PHI"), of a patient. This obligation continues even post-mortem, and is quite similar to the obligation that exists when a patient is still alive. The primary, and obvious, distinction is that authority over records can no longer belong to a deceased patient. Upon death, this authority gets transferred to the patient's "personal representative." Under 45 CFR § 164.502(g)(4), a covered entity must treat a person as a personal representative, "If under applicable law an executor, administrator or other person has authority to act on behalf of a deceased individual or of the individual's estate."

A personal representative is generally appointed in a will, where an individual selects the person to carry out his wishes at death. This person is then granted either a letter testamentary or a letter of administration. If a personal representative has been appointed, it is important to note that authorization to release records then lies only with that person, who may be someone other than a former spouse or another family member. In fact, even if a decedent had provided a surviving party with a separate form granting authorization to obtain or grant disclosure of medical records, there is risk in relying on that as continuing authority. Even though the actual person whose records are at issue granted authority to another person to obtain or release the deceased's records, technically that person loses authority to the appointed representative immediately upon death. To avoid this conflict, a separate authorization should be included from the deceased's representative for any further disclosure of the patient's PHI. Any use or disclosure that has already been made in reliance on the now deceased patient's authorization is valid, however.

"Did Mr. Arietta have a personal representative," the Judge asks.

"Yes Mr. Arietta had designated a personal representative who in turn gave Dr. Henson permission to share the information with this court. The examination in question was done by Dr. Henson for the Insurance Company."

"The objection is overruled," the Judge said.

The Doctor has sat impatiently staring at each of us as we ascertained whether or not he could speak. Now, he is uncertain what to do so I say, "You may answer my question now. In what kind of shape did your examination of Mr. Arietta disclose?

"I found Mr. Noah Arietta to be in good health."

"Thank you Doctor. Your witness Ms. Larson."

"I don't have any questions for this witness."

"The witness is excused. Please step down," the Judge said.

Doctor Henson took his time getting down from the witness stand and walking slowly this time back across the room and finally taking his seat.

"Call your next witness." The Judge said when Doctor Henson was once again seated.

"The defense will call Doctor Augusta Ryan," I said and waited while she was sworn in and on the witness stand. This was the doctor who had examined Paige about a week after the shooting. This was the first time seeing her in person and I found her to be attractive with her white blonde hair in a pixy cut that made her look very young. She wore oversized silver framed glasses and a pleasant smile as she faced the court.

"Now, Doctor, do you have any specialties?" I asked.

"Yes, I am a doctor of obstetrics and gynecology."

"Can you tell the court what this means."

"Well as an obstetrician/gynecologist I am a physician specialist. I provide medical and surgical care to women and have particular expertise in pregnancy, childbirth, and disorders of the reproductive system. I serve as a primary physician and often serve as a consultant to other physicians." The doctor pauses and takes a dainty sip of water before continuing.

"I have more than two decades of experience, in the diagnosis and treatment of all types of gynecological and obstetrical issues. I provide medical and surgical care to women and have particular expertise in pregnancy, childbirth, and disorders of the reproductive system. I provide medical and surgical care to women and have particular expertise in pregnancy, childbirth, and disorders of the reproductive system, as well as routine gynecological exams aimed at identifying health risks and medical concerns in their early stages."

"Please share your educational background with the court."

"I received my Bachelor of Arts Degree in Biology and English from Canisius College in Buffalo and my MD from medical training at the University of Rochester School of Medicine and Dentistry. I am a recipient of the Charles Kochakian Award for outstanding research in endocrinology and nutrition. I completed my specialty training in Obstetrics and Gynecology at Strong Memorial Hospital in Rochester, New York and was awarded the Curtis J. Lund Award Research Prize. I am board certified in Obstetrics and Gynecology." Dr. Ryan pauses and takes another sip of water. "Is that enough?"

"Thank you doctor. That is definitely enough. It was indeed thorough and informative." I step back to allow the jury full few of the witness before I ask my next question. "Did you have occasion to examine Ms. Paige Trapp recently?"

"Yes I did."

"Can you tell the court when and where?"

"On August twentieth in my office."

"Will you please tell us the results of your examination?"

I survey the jury and see them leaning forward, anxiously awaiting her response.

"Yes, I found several areas of discoloration, from former bruises and contusions, around both eyes, the left shoulder, both buttocks and a large area over the left hip. This last measured six by four inches."

"Were these discolored areas what a layman might call black and blue?"

"Yes, but turning yellow when I examined her."

"And what might that indicate?"

"The duration of the injuries."

"And have you formed an opinion on that?"

"Yes, upwards of one week old."

"Now, Doctor, have you any opinion as to how the woman might have received the massive discoloration on her right hip?"

"Left hip, sir. Possibly a hard blow or kick."

"If you were called, say to the jail to take a vaginal smear to determine the possible presence of sperm in a woman, what would you bring?"

"I would bring a vaginal speculum or dilator so the tract could be exposed and inspected, and a light to illuminate the area. And some applicators, which are slender sticks of wood with cotton on the end, to swap up any secretions which are present, and glass microscopic slides on which to transfer these secretions."

"And I ask you how many glass slides you would probably take."

"At least two."

"In what areas?"

"Taken well up around the cervix, which is the mouth of the womb and well inside the vaginal tract."

"And having obtained these slides what would you do with them?"

"I would either send then to the New York State Department of Health or to a competent pathologist."

"Under any circumstances would you send them to a laboratory technician who was not a pathologist or a medical doctor?"

"By no means, sir."

"I ask you whether or not it would be possible to examine a dead body of an adult male and determine whether or not he had recently ejaculated?"

"Yes. An examination of the seminal vesicles would indicate whether they were full of seminal fluid or not."

"And if a doctor or pathologist were trying to determine that fact would you say in your opinion that that should have been done?"

"I would think so."

"Is that your opinion?"

"Yes."

"Now I ask you whether or not you made any further examination of Mrs. Trapp?"

"Yes, I examined her right knee and also did a pelvic examination."

"What, if anything, did you find about the right knee?"

"She complained of pain in the inner aspect of the knee. The knee was tender at that location."

"Any bruises?"

"There was no bruise apparent."

"Did she complain of tenderness or soreness in any other part of her body?"

"She complained of vaginal pains and disorders."

"And you made such an examination?"

"Yes."

I step back and look at the jury. They are on the edge of their seats, their ears perked waiting for the doctor's response.

"And I ask you, Doctor, whether or not such soreness could have been induced by a forcible act of sexual intercourse."

"I believe it could have."

"And what is the medical explanation of that?"

The Doctor leaned forward and spread her hands. "Well, ordinarily when a woman intends to have sexual relations there is a secretion of fluid, a natural lubrication. When the act is taken against her will there is no preliminary secretion, and consequently more friction and subsequent inflammation and pain."

"So now, Doctor, understanding that your examination was several days after the fact, to the best of your knowledge would you say that Mrs. Trapp had been raped."

"Yes, I would."

I look at Jean Larson not even trying to keep the smirk off my face. "Your witness," I said.

Jean Larson stood thoughtfully staring up at the skylight, rocking on her heels. "You did not specialize in pathology, Doctor?" she asks.

"No."

"And that is a specialty, as much as your own?"

"Yes, indeed."

"And the pathologist is usually more experienced and schooled in post-mortem procedures?"

"Yes."

"And would you concede that an experienced pathologist would be more qualified to determine the cause of death in a dead body and its physical condition?"

The doctor doesn't answer right away and when she does she speaks confidently. "Pathologists come in several types as they may specialize. For instance, a clinical pathologist oversees lab tests conducted on body fluids. A microbiology, pathologists identifies microorganisms that can cause infections, while an anatomic pathologist assists surgeons during operations by providing immediate diagnoses on biopsies. A forensic pathologist uses lab science to answer questions about evidence collected for criminal and civil cases and finally some pathologists devote their careers to research in pathology, developing new tests and new instruments to better diagnose diseases. It would depend on the type of pathologist of which you speak."

I have to control myself. That was indeed a blow to Ms. Larson, but I don't believe the doctor delivered it that way. An innocent but complete blow to the woman's effort to disqualify the doctor's opinion.

Jean Larson had stared up at the skylight during her brief examination. She now turned and gave me a dead sea scroll smile.

"Do you have anything further for this witness?" the Judge asks.

"I got up from my chair and walked to the front. Yes, I do. "Doctor," I said, "Would you equally concede that this experienced pathologist was more competent to test a dead male body for recent seminal ejaculation than yourself?"

Thoughtfully, "I should say that we were equally well qualified on that score and that if that were an issue, an examination of the seminal vesicles should properly have been made."

"Back to you Ms. Larson," I said.

Ms. Larson keeps her head down as she replies, "No further questions."

"Doctor, you are excused," Judge Nicholson states.

I wait until the doctor is back at her seat and then turn and look at Paige Trapp. I nod my head and say, "The defense will call Mrs. Paige Trapp to the stand."

The Judge looks out at the clock and batted his gray forelock out of his eye. "I think we'll take ten minutes before examining the next witness," he said.

The Sheriff stood and asked all to stand as the Judge left the bench.

Chapter 11

It was back to the conference room again for the Lieutenant, Paige and myself and once the three of us are alone, I said, "Lieutenant, I want you to go outside and get some fresh air, please. I need to talk with Paige alone."

I prepared myself for a rebuttal, but without a word the Lieutenant turns and left the room. In the hallway, I could hear Sheriff Simpson speaking with the Lieutenant and then I hear the sound of both their footsteps as they walk down the back hallway.

I turned to Paige. "Well," I said, "this is it. It's time for you to face the jury. How do you feel?"

Paige laughed nervously and laid a hand on her stomach. "I have butterflies in here," she said, "Do you have a cure for that?"

"Truth," I said. "All you have to do is tell the truth. Remember what I told you before? Don't be led into anything that can throw doubt on your account." Rape or sexual abuse can be very difficult topics to talk about, and many victims find it intimidating to speak in front of a courtroom. Just remember that these people are there to hear what you have to say as a witness for your husband and not to judge you." I pause. "Just because this case is not about rape, it still won't be easy."

"I know, I know." Paige replied. I feel a need to help her prepare so I add, "Some people find it helpful to focus on a person in the courtroom while they are speaking. Decide now who you want to focus on; I suggest not your husband so you can focus on me, a jury member, or someone in the gallery. Even though this is not a rape case you will be required to talk about the events in detail, and some questions may be uncomfortable. Take your time if you are struggling to talk about what happened. Remember to take deep breaths, and ask for a glass of water, a tissue or a short break if you need it. Whatever you are feeling is okay. It is incredibly difficult to share painful details, and you should do what you need to get through. Just keep in mind that the prosecution knows that rape is the most terrible thing for a woman and it harms them not only physically and socially, but also mentally."

I could see Paige tensing, but I had to go on. "When I question you I will try to be as kind as possible, but I need to ask a lot of insensitive questions." I smile at Paige. "The prosecution will not be as tactful so all I can say is think before you answer. You can be sure they have done their homework and will hit you with every negative detail they uncovered. Remember you are not on trial, the Lieutenant is and the case should be all about him."

"Why not, it....?"

"Because the Lieutenant's actions made him judge, jury and executioner and the law doesn't look kindly on that. Several points I want to stress and that is you must downplay the jealousy business if you can, but if they get into it don't lie about it. And don't answer more than you are asked, and if you don't understand the question or know the answer, simply say so. Truth must be the order of the day."

This wasn't the first time she has heard me say this but I felt a need to repeat myself. "Remember this case is not about the rape in the eyes of the law. It is about the murder so follow the instructions we discussed. If there are questions you do not understand, be sure to ask for the question to be rephrased and never guess at an answer; if you do not know or do not remember, just say so. Your job is to answer questions truthfully; the rest is up to the prosecution who will try to confuse you, so it is important to answer only the question you are asked, and to ask for clarification if you do not understand. This can also give you time to think about what you want to say, too." I wait for her reaction and then continue.

"One more thing," I added, "Don't feel you must dramatize any emotions you don't feel. Those women on the jury will crucify you if you dare pretend." I patted her shoulder. "You'll be fine. I know you will."

Paige nods and smiles tremulously. There is a knock on the door and Lincoln Harper sticks his head in. "So soon, Lincoln," I said.

"I'd like to see you for a minute, Richard," Lincoln looks at Paige. "Alone."

"Sure thing, Lincoln," I said wondering what this could be about. I nodded at Paige, who gave a nervous smile and left the room. I turned to Lincoln.

"First of all, Richard, I got an email here for you," he said, handing me the sealed envelope which I put in my breast pocket. "Then I want to thank you for that nice courtroom sendoff you gave me and our department when you were questioning Deputy Brown. I really appreciate that."

"That's all right, Lincoln." I said, smiling but puzzled as to his real mission. "You and your boys have been very nice to the Trapps and me

"Listen, Richard," Lincoln broke in, lowering his voice and speaking rapidly. "Recess is almost over and I got to talk fast. It's about the Lieutenant. I'm willing to testify for him."

"Testify for him?" I said incredulously.

Lincoln nodded. "Yes, testify. I feel sorry for the man and especially the way this lady Larson is piling on him, trying to block and keep out the truth. Like that lie-detector test. I've known all along that the test showed the Lieutenant's wife told the truth and the state police are fit to be tied the way this woman Larson has put them on the spot, making it look as though they were trying to hide the truth."

"Hm...what would you testify to Lincoln?" I said thoughtfully, my mind racing over the law. Other than a rebuttal witness, one usually cannot spring a witness on a party. However, if the reason the person is now to be a witness only arose very recently, which would be the case here, then there would be no way to have given advance notice of such a recent event. Your counsel would be given time to prepare to cross examine the witness.

"Insanity," Lincoln said. "Lieutenant Trapp was practically a basket case that first weekend, like a man in a dream. He didn't eat or sleep and just wanted to sit and mope in his cell. When the bartender came, and tried to cheer him up, he was like a zombie. I don't even think he recognized him.

"Lord, Lincoln," I said. "You really mean you're willing to testify for the defense on these things?"

Lincoln glanced at his watch and gave me his hand. "Any time, Richard, and now I must be going. And he was gone. I tore open the envelope containing the email. It was from our psychiatrist, Doctor Milo Goodman. "Arriving your airport at nine seventeen Sunday night. Please meet me," it said. I folded the email and put it in my breast pocket before entering the court room once again.

"Hear ye, hear ye," Lincoln intoned, and once more we were underway. The Judge nodded at me and I arose and addressed the court.

"Your Honor," I said, "with the court's permission I would like to change the order of my witnesses, if I may, and call another witness at this time in place of Mrs. Paige Trapp."

I turned and saw the relief on Paige's face and I smiled at her.

"Does the prosecution have a problem with this?"

"No Your Honor."

"Very well," the Judge said. "Call your witness."

"The defense calls Sheriff Lincoln Harper," There was a rustle and stir in the courtroom as Lincoln got up and marched determinedly to the witness stand and was sworn in and sat down. I stole a look at Jean Larson, who had her head bent in hurried conference with Randall. Glancing the other way, I found a perplexed Pete leaning forward with his brows understandably knitted. "Your name, please?": I said.

"Lincoln Harper," Lincoln answered.

"What is your occupation Mr. Harper."

"I am a Monroe County Sheriff."

"And as such do you have custody of the county jail and its inmates, Sheriff?"

"I do, sir."

"Did you at any time have the defendant in this case under your care?"

"Yes, sir."

"And how long was he under your care?"

"For almost a week until his arraignment."

"And did you see him almost daily when he was first arrested?"

"I did, sir."

"Now, Sheriff," I said, "how did his appearance, demeanor, and general behavior when he was first arrested compare with that of now?"

"Well…" Lincoln began.

"Objection, Objection. Your Honor. This is irrelevant and immaterial. If the defense plans to show mental state of the defendant, then this witness certainly is not competent to express an opinion."

I turned and looked at the witness and could see he was livid with rage. "Mr. Dandridge?" the Judge said questioningly.

I needed to calm the Sheriff down. "Your Honor," I said, "the defense would not for a moment try to pit our Sheriff against the psychiatrist for the People but the Sheriff has the advantage of having seen the defendant over a longer period and much closer to the time when we claim he was temporarily insane. However, we do not offer this evidence as the Sheriff's opinion on the sanity or insanity of Lieutenant Trapp, but as possible evidence by one of the few witnesses who was in a position to observe and tell, of certain symptoms from which persons who are competent to pass an opinion might do so." Not able to resist it, I add, "Ms. Larson, with her characteristic tactics, seems bent on keeping this out as well."

"You offer the evidence, Counsel," the Judge inquired of me, "not as an opinion, then, on either sanity or insanity, but rather as evidence on those disputed issues?"

"Correct, Your Honor," I said.

"The witness may answer," the Judge countered.

"Well," the Sheriff said, "Lieutenant Trapp was practically a basket case when he first came to the jail…"

"Objection, Your Honor, I am unacquainted with the idiom, the terminology…"

"One that is in a completely hopeless or useless condition," Lincoln broke in, his gray eyes flashing ominously. "Then he went into a short of gloomy depressed state, like a man in a dream. He didn't eat or sleep for two days and just wanted to sit and mope in his cell. We were so concerned we put him on suicide watch."

449

"And how did the Lieutenant appear, say, during the latter part of his stay?"

"Much better. He seemed to get a grip on himself, like a man coming out of a fog. He ate and slept well and did not give us any further concern."

"Thank you, Sheriff," I said, and turned to Jean Larson. "Your witness."

Ms. Larson stood glaring at the Sheriff, who glared steadily back at her, and Larson, sensing shrewdly that all she could do now was make matters worse by examining, murmured, "No questions," and abruptly sat down.

I stood for a moment silently reflecting that perhaps I had been lacks in not interviewing the Sheriff on all this beforehand. Supposing Lincoln had not come forward? All this testimony would have irretrievably been lost and it would have been my own fault.

"Since there are no more questions," Judge Nicholson turned and said, "the witness is excused. Please step down."

As soon as Lincoln was off the stand and seated in his chair, the Judge turned to me and said. "Call your next witness."

"I call Mrs. Paige Trapp to the stand."

I watched as Paige stood, walked to the stand and held up her hand for the oath. The jurors' eyes never left her person as she stood, her trim figure covered modestly and her russet color hair drawn back in a bun at the nape of her long neck. Before being seated she used one hand to smooth her dress under her, then sat very straight and poise in the witness chair. The glasses I had asked her to wear hid her green eyes and gave her a demurer appearance.

"Please state your name for the record."

In a shaky voice she responded, "Mrs. Paige Trapp."

"Are you Lieutenant Vincent Trapp's wife?" I asked.

"I am," Paige replied quietly, lifting her eyes to glance over at her husband.

"Now, Ms. Trapp, on the night in question can you tell me if you accepted an offer to ride with the deceased, Noah Arietta? That would be the night of July thirty-first."

"I did."

"In your own words, please tell us what happened on the evening of July thirty-first of last year, before Mr. Noah Arietta died."

There was silence from the witness and in the court room as everyone prepared to hear her story. It would be the first time that the events of that evening had been discussed by a witness.

"On that evening, my husband Vincent, er, Lieutenant Trapp took a brief nap before dinner. After dinner he was still tired so he excused himself and told me he was going to lay down and rest a bit more. When he woke he asked me to fix him a drink, but we didn't have any more of the whiskey he likes. I told him as much and he said he would settle for a beer, but when I checked, we didn't have any beer in the house so I asked if we could go out, and it being so nice I thought maybe going to the park would be fun. We could pick up some wine on the way."

"So what did he say?"

"He said he was still tired."

"What did you say."

"I said I wanted to get out for a while."

"What happened next"

"It being such a nice evening I decided to take Enzo, our dog, out for a walk, so at around nine o'clock or shortly before, I left the house with Enzo in tow. We walked through the woods next door to our property and then I took Enzo home and checked on Vincent. He was still sleeping so I woke him up and asked him if he wanted to go to the bar at the Founder's Café and he said, why didn't I go and he would meet me there later. So I left again with Enzo, who has learned to carry the flashlight in his mouth. We start walking in the same direction as before only continuing further through the woods for about a mile and a half, which eventually ends up at the Founder's café. So I tied Enzo up and went in."

"Was there anyone else there?"

"Sure. There were a few customers that I recognized as locals and some I didn't. There was Hamilton, the bartender and a dark haired waitress named Tyra something or other, not sure of her last name.

"Where was Noah Arietta? Wasn't he there when you arrived?"

"No, he wasn't. He came in later. I ordered a glass of wine and took it over to play the Frogger video game."

"Excuse me, what is the Frogger video game.?" I asked.

"If you grew up in the 80's you shouldn't need to ask." I could visibly see the tension leaving Paige as she talked about the game. "Frogger is regarded as a classic game from the golden age of video games and is noted for its novel gameplay and theme. You help froggy across the road avoiding the racing cars, trucks and hazards and use the arrow keys to move and cross the river by jumping on logs and turtles." She smiled. "Watch out for those turtles though, they have a habit of disappearing just when you don't want them to!" Again she smiled over at the jurors. "I just love that old game. It keeps the scores of all players so you can try and beat them."

Without realizing what she has done, she has managed to soften the jury members who now look at her as if she is a friend.

Her mood becomes soberer as she continues. "I had been playing for a while when Mr. Arietta walked in. I didn't see him

452

enter and only knew he was there when he came up to me and challenged me at a game of Frogger. The winner had to buy the other one a drink. Sounded innocent enough so I took the challenge and won the first game. Noah signaled Tyra and she served us drinks at the machine."

"What shape was Noah in?" I asked. "How did he act to you. Did he seem drunk or, did he make any kind of a play toward you?"

Paige thought for a moment before saying, "He seemed to be sober and he acted like a gentleman the whole time we were in the Founder's café. As for him making a play on me, I am sensitive to advances of that sort and I didn't sense anything in that way."

"Did the police ask you about his attitude toward you at the café?"

"Yes, and I told them the same thing." That is exactly what happened and I told them he was friendly and courteous the whole time we were there."

"What happened next."

"Well, Noah and I played several games and then I noticed it was almost eleven so I asked Brook, that's the bartender, Hamilton's first name, if he could sell me a six pack of beer. Brook said he could and when he gave it to me, I prepared to leave. It was then that Noah asked if he could give me a ride home, but I told him that I would be fine and would welcome being in the open air for a bit. I told him I had a flashlight and my dog with me so I would be able to see my way home. I thanked him and excused myself to go back to the restroom before leaving. This also gave me an opportunity to use the side door and leave without being noticed."

"So what happened next," I asked.

"I turned on the flashlight and put it in Enzo's mouth and that is when I saw a shadow at the side door. It was Noah. He was standing there with his car motor still running and expressed concern about me walking home that late at night. He asked again if he could give me a ride home. He was still courteous and seemed sincere in fearing for my safety so not wanting to appear rude, I finally agreed to let him take me and Enzo home. It was just a short distance anyway."

"Continue," I said.

"Well, at first we were heading in the right direction, but then he turned and sped up pass the house and turned into what I think was a driveway; a dirt road or driveway that I hadn't noticed before and that was when I began to be anxious. I asked him where were we going, but he didn't answer me. Instead he grabbed my arm and kept driving. I don't know how far we went when he suddenly stopped the car and turned off the headlights."

I could see the worry on her face as she paused to pull herself together before continuing.

"As soon as the car stopped I tried to get out, but he had a hold of my arm and pulled me back in. I tried not to show any fear. I thought I could possibly control the situation. I asked him what did he think he was doing and he grimaced at me and tightened the grip on my arm. He was too strong for me. He got his face up close to mine and said he was going to rape me." There was a catch in her voice as she said the word, rape. I gave her a minute to recover.

"He used those exact words?"

"Yes, those are his exact words. Then he said I'd better not give him a hard time or I'd never get out of the car alive. All the time he was talking he was groping at me, trying to pull me closer, but I kept trying to fight him off."

"Did you scream?"

"No. I think I knew we were not near any place where someone could hear me. We were in the middle of nowhere and I couldn't help thinking that he meant it, that he would kill me as he threatened to do."

"What happened next," I asked.

"He kept groping at me and beating me on my knees with his fists to force my legs open. I fought, I fought as long and as hard as I could, but I could feel myself getting weaker and finally said to him, hoping he would stop, that my husband would kill him if he didn't let me go."

"You told him that?"

"Yes, I was desperate and I thought by saying that I could scare him off and maybe he would come to his senses."

"Did it stop him?"

"No, it only made it worse. He laughed at me and said Vincent didn't have the guts to kill him and if he tried, that he, Noah would kill him first. He ranted on like a madman and I could barely understand his words as I kept trying to get away. He was swearing at me, yelling, take that you bitch amongst other things as he continued to force my knees open. I felt my panties being ripped off me and I struggled trying desperately to stop him. He was out of control acting like a crazy man, hitting me and squeezing my thighs, but by then I was too weak to give him much of a fight."

She managed to tell her story with only a catch in her throat and a few tears that escaped her eyes as she shared her unthinkable experience.

"I'm sorry, Ms. Trapp that you had to endure such treatment. I don't like asking you this but I must. Can you tell the court if Mr. Arietta climaxed?"

"He did."

"Are you sure of that?"

"I knew he had entered me and he came. I could feel it. I was just glad the nightmare was over. I felt the full weight of him on top of me, and heard him trying to catch his breathe. I must have fainted because the next thing I remember is the car moving again."

"Did either of you speak?"

"No, nothing was said. Noah was still breathing heavily. He was making funny sounds as he struggled to breathe. It was almost like he was about to cry. I don't know why it sounded that way, but that's the best way I can explain it."

"Go on," I said.

"Well, he drove back to the main road and when he slowed the car, I tried to open the door, but he grabbed my arm and pulled me back. He tried to rip off my sweater and I thought that he would kill me and that seemed to give me the strength I needed to wrench my arm away and get out of the car. I ran, but he caught up with me. He tripped me and then started kicking me after I fell down. He continued to hit me with his fists, hard, all over my face and body. I think he was trying to kill me with his bare hands and I felt as if I was going to faint. That is when I screamed. I think I screamed two or three times with all I could muster. I was so busy trying to scream it was a while before I realized I was alone. I managed to lift my head up so that I could look around. It took all my energy to just get into a sitting position before taking a deep breath and getting myself on my feet. I had to get away because he wasn't acting rationally and might just come back. I started to run, well not exactly run, but at the fastest pace I could muster. I didn't care what direction I was going, just so long as I was able to just keep going was all that mattered. Finally, I stopped to catch my breath and let out a sigh of relief when I saw the lights of my home just ahead. It was at that moment the fear I had felt was replaced with anger. Who did he think he was doing this to me?"

"You didn't see Noah at all after that?"

Paige closed her eyes and shook her head. "No, I didn't see him again. Not alive or after he was dead."

"Continue."

"I made it to the front door and just as I reached out for the door handle, Vincent opened it, scaring the bejesus out of me. He seemed only half awake but he told me later he'd dreamt he heard me screaming and it woke him up. All I could do was fall into his arms.

"Where was the dog, Enzo?"

"He must have at some point jumped out of the car and found his own way home."

I walked around the front of the court to give Paige time to recover. When I turned back to question her some more, she was back in control.

"Mrs. Trapp what else transpired that evening?"

"Well, my husband was arrested and I rode with him to the jail. A Doctor Henrietta Pierson, examined me and I had to repeat what happened to me over and over again with the last time being taken to the police department and telling the story with various gadgets attached to my body and arms."

I glanced casually out at Pete who stood up and quickly left the courtroom by way of the judge's chambers.

"That would have been a lie-detector test, I said. "And, Ms. Trapp, have you been officially informed of the results of that lie-detector test?"

"I have not," Paige said.

"Would you like to know the results?"

"I would."

"Would you for your part be willing that everyone in this room should know the results?" I asked.

Paige nodded. "I wo…"

"No, no! Objection!" Ms. Larson nearly shouted. "Counsel is plainly trying to circumvent the rule against admissibility of polygraph tests."

"I withdraw the question."

I address the court. "Your Honor," I said, "before I tender this witness I should like to bring in the little dog Enzo for a demonstration to the jury, if I may."

"Demonstration of what?" the Judge asked, startled.

"First, that the dog is both small and friendly and was unlikely either to dissuade the deceased or protect the witness and, second, that the animal and its flashlight could indeed have lit the witness through the park as she has testified." I paused.

Jean Larson glared at me and leapt righteously to her feet but the Judge held up a warning hand like a traffic cop signaling a motorist to stop. "The request is granted. Produce the animal."

I turned to Paige. "If you please, Mrs. Trapp."

Paige got down shakily off the stand and together we went to the lawyers' door by the side of the jury, which I held open for her as she stepped out of sight and was back in a thrice carrying Enzo, doubtless herself as surprised to have Pete thrust the animal at her in the corridor as was everyone in the court room to see her back so soon.

"Please release the dog, Mrs. Trapp," I said, and Paige put the dog down, with its flashlight lit in its mouth, and wagging its tail furiously, it ran gaily up and smelled the Judge, who frowned and turned quickly away and then, of all things, ran to the prosecution table, its tiny feet pattering, and tried to climb up on Jean Larson's lap. Ms. Larson flushed and lifted her legs to prevent it, and even the jury giggled. Then Enzo spotted Lieutenant Trapp and ran to him in an ecstasy of wriggling and whimpering joy, whereupon the Judge, who evidently had as dim a view of dogs in his court room as he did of cameras and cell phones, inquired, "Is the demonstration over?"

"Yes your Honor," I said, unless you think I should have him sworn in first." Everyone laughed, everyone but Ms. Larson. Even Randall had laughed. I watched as Paige fetched Enzo and went back to the door where Pete was waiting. She returned to the court room, reclaimed the witness seat and sat waiting.

I turned to the prosecution's table and said, "Your witness, Ms. Larson, or would you like Mr. Walker to question the witness.

Chapter 12

The Judge looked thoughtfully out at the courtroom clock and then down at the counsel tables. "Gentlemen, ladies, it's nearly four-thirty," he said, "which is too early to suspend for the day and yet perhaps too late to finish with this witness before five." He paused in reflection. "There is a chance that this case could end today if the jury and counsel would be willing to work a little overtime tonight."

Most of the jurors quickly nodded their heads and, swiftly getting our cues, Randall and I inevitably stood and nodded our approval. "Very well," the Judge said, "suppose we proceed with the cross-examination."

Jean Larson quickly stood and walked up to stand in front of Paige Trapp. She carried a sheet of paper and had an amiable grin, on her wrinkled face as if she was going to offer Paige a cookie. "Good luck, Paige," I murmured to myself.

"How long have you been married to the Lieutenant?" Jean Larson purred silkily.

"Three years," Paige answered.

"And have you worked during your lifetime?"

"I have, naturally."

"And what was your occupation?"

"Well, I was a housewife for twelve years before I married Vincent...I mean, Lieutenant Trapp."

"Oh," Ms. Larson queried, in false surprise. "You mean you were previously married?"

"Yes."

"Hm..And had you any other occupation beside that of housewife?"

"Yes, I once sold lingerie in a department store and another time demonstrated and sold cosmetics."

"Anything else?"

"Yes, I worked as a telemarketer and another time as a teaching assistant."

"Anything else?" Jean Larson pressed, appearing to consult a dossier she held in her hands, which indeed she might have held or, like a clever cross-examiner, it might have been nothing more than a blank sheet of paper. Neither the witness nor opposing counsel could be sure.

"No, I think that's all."

Still consulting her notes: "Weren't you once a Cosmetologist?"

"No."

"You mean you did not graduate from a beauty course you took in New York City?"

"You didn't ask that. I had the training but never actually practiced cosmetology." It was now plain that Ms. Larson indeed had some information on Paige's background and this was something I didn't know.

"But you did sell cosmetics on the road?"

"Yes."

"Now how long after the death of your first husband did you marry your present husband?" Ms. Larson asked with disarming innocence. I caught my breath for this was one of those trick questions that I had warned Paige about. Her question was so

461

framed that she might either deliberately lure her into a lie or she might innocently fall into one if she was not on her toes.

"Two weeks," Paige replied, and Jean Larson could not resist shooting a look of triumph at me as my heart sank. Good lord, she had fallen into the trap.

"So that two weeks after you became a free woman you got married to the Lieutenant?" Ms. Larson urged, luring her on and nailing down her lie.

"Yes, two weeks after my divorce was granted," Paige said, and once again I was able to breathe.

"Divorce?" Jean Larson said. "I though you just testified that your first husband died two weeks before your remarriage."

Paige shook her head wonderingly, and I was sure then that her flub had been innocent, she had misunderstood the earlier question. "He was and is very much alive, Ms. I have never told anyone he was dead. In fact, he has recently written my husband and me offering to help." This too I had not known.

"Objection," Jean Larson said. "The answer is irrelevant and unresponsive—at least the portion about the former husband offering to help, I move that portion be stricken from the record."

"Yes," the Judge ruled, "the reference to the offer to help by the former husband may be stricken and the jury is asked to disregard it."

I couldn't resist. "Your Honor," I said, "now that three people have already drilled into the jury the objection the defense agrees that the reference to the offer of help by the former husband may be stricken and disregarded. I am sure now that the jurors will resolutely banish it from their memories."

Jean Larson glared at me. "I further object to defense counsel commenting on an objection after the court has ruled," she said.

"Ms. Larson," I said, "I apologize for commenting on the fact that the former husband still wants to help."

The Judge stifled a smile and lightly tapped his bench with his gavel. "Gentlemen, Ladies," he said. "Time is flying. Let us get on with the examination. Proceed, Ms. Larson."

Jean Larson took her little setback and continued. "How long had you known the Lieutenant before your marriage to him?"

"Five months."

"And where was your first husband during all this time?"

"My first husband was in the army and stationed in Europe."

"So that all the while your husband was in the service in Europe you and the Lieutenant were conducting your little romance over here?"

Paige's green eyes flashed behind her glasses. "I did not say that. You asked me how long I had known Vincent, not how long he had courted me."

"Well, then, please tell me how long he courted you."

"One month."

"In other words, you and he were going steady, then, before you were actually divorced?"

"Well, yes."

Ms. Larson glanced at the jury and was rewarded with disapproving looks. "Now, coming to the night of the shooting," Ms. Larson said, "I believe you just told the jury you went to the Founder's Café bar that night to get a six-pack of beer?"

"Yes."

"And that was for your husband?"

"Yes, I rarely drink beer myself." She smiled a little and glanced nervously at the jury. "Too fattening."

"I see," Ms. Larson said and paused. "But if you went there for beer for your husband, why didn't you get it and take it home instead of staying there over two hours?"

She was giving Paige a bad time. I nervously waited hoping she would have the wits to wriggle her way out of this question.

She did, and with a vengeance she told the simple truth. "I did not go there primarily for beer, Ms. Larson. If you must know, going to the Founders Café to get the beer was only part of the reason I went. The other was to wait there for my husband who said he would join me later."

"To get out so that you could go drink whisky and play Frogger with Noah Arietta?"

"No, not at all," Paige shot back. "Just to get out."

"But you did drink whisky and play Frogger with Noah Arietta?"

"Yes, I've already told that here today and many times to the state police." Paige was getting her dander up and I wish I could calm her but it was out of my hands. So, just like Paige I had to endure this woman's trickery and hope for the best.

"And how many drinks did you have?"

"I didn't count, but maybe four."

"Double shots?"

"No."

"And over what space of time?"

"About two hours, with a large glass of water." Paige had an endearing expression as she added, "My dad taught me that."

"Did you feel the effects of those drinks?" Ms. Larson asked.

"Well, yes, I felt relaxed and was enjoying myself."

Jean Larson reflected for a moment. "Is it your practice to remove your shoes when you drink whisky?"

"It is not."

"Or when dancing?"

"No, I did not..."

"And were you served drinks with your shoes off?" Ms. Larson asked, interrupting Paige before she finished her response..

"Your Honor," I said rising, "I don't want to spoil the gallant Ms. Larson's fun, she's waited so long for it, but I wish she would let the witness complete her answers before she gets on to the next question. I object to her cutting her off."

"The objection is sustained. The witness will be allowed to complete her answer," the Judge ruled.

Paige glanced gratefully up at the Judge. "I was going to say that I did not dance with anyone and that I only removed my shoes once briefly during the last game of Frogger."

"Are you sure you did not dance with anyone?" Ms. Larson asked.

"I am sure."

"Didn't you dance with a tall red faced man?"

"No, not even a short pale one. I danced with no one, not a soul."

"Are you sure?"

"I am positive I did not dance. I am a poor dancer and I do not particularly like to dance."

"Do you recall any man having your shoes in his pockets while you danced with him? Answer yes or no and leave out the comments."

"No"

"Objection, Your Honor, the prosecution is badgering the witness. She has already answered the question by saying she hadn't danced with anyone."

"Objection sustained. Ms. Larson either excuse the witness or take your questioning in another direction."

"Sorry, Your Honor." Jean Larson had a cat and mouse smile on her face as she turned to the witness. "Now, after the shooting when your husband returned to the house did he then go to the cottage of the caretaker, Mr. Walker Appleton?"

"Yes."

"Did you hear the conversation between them?"

"No. I only saw Mr. Appleton when he came up to the house.

"Did your husband turn over his pistol to Mr. Appleton?"

"I don't know."

"Did you tell Mr. Appleton what happened?"

"Yes, I did." One could easily sense that she was trying desperately to hold back tears. Finally she replied, " I said, look what Noah did to me."

Jean Larson appealed to the court. "Objection. The answer is unresponsive and I move it be stricken."

"But you have asked the witness what she told the caretaker," the Judge said, "and she has answered. If you have something particular in mind, then ask it. Your objection to strike is denied."

"Did you tell Mr. Appleton your husband had shot Noah?"

"I did not."

"Now did you and your husband ever go out socially in Rochester?"

"Yes, of course."

"And did you and he once attend a cocktail party at the Academy Building apartments which is part of the Founders Café location?"

"Yes."

"And at one of those parties did your husband have an altercation with a young second lieutenant?"

"Altercation?" Paige said. "My husband knocked him down."

I had to admit she was being honest, but this was not going to sit well with the jury where the Lieutenant was concern.

"Why?"

"I don't know the answer to that. You had better ask him all the young man did was kissed my hand."

Rudely, Jean persisted. "Did you approve of your husband's behavior?"

"I did not. I would not approve of anyone attacking another person without a good reason," Paige replied.

Jean Larson turned and beamed at me. "Your witness," she said.

I pondered the skylight above me wonderingly. Was there anything I could say to help smooth the damage. No, there wasn't. "No questions." I said.

"In that case, we are adjourned," Judge Nicholson says. "As you were instructed before, during any of those recesses I direct you not to discuss the case among yourselves, and when we recess overnight, you must not discuss the case or the testimony with any members of your family or any other persons or provide an account of your juror service to others, including through any electronic means, such as shared Internet websites. Do not talk face to face or use any electronic device, such as the telephone, cell or smart phone, Blackberry, iPhone, PDA, computer, the Internet, e-mail, any text or instant message service, any Internet chat room, blog or website such as Facebook, MYSpace, YouTube, or Twitter, to communicate to anyone any information about this case." The Judge pauses and takes a sip of water before continuing. "The reason of course is that you should not begin any deliberations until the entire case has been concluded, which is until you have heard all of the witnesses, the final arguments of counsel, and my instructions as to the law. It would be improper for any outside influence to intrude upon your thinking. If anyone should attempt to discuss the case with you, you should report the fact to me or my staff immediately. Please be mindful of these instructions at all times. the jury is excused for the day and we will recommence at nine o'clock on Monday morning, the fifteenth. Court is adjourned."

"Bailiff," the Judge said.

"All rise." Everyone stands while the Judge leaves the bench and then the Bailiff goes over and leads the jury members out the door. We remain standing until we are dismissed by the Sheriff.

It has been a long, mind draining day to say the least and I am ready for a break.

Chapter 13

After the courtroom had thinned out I gravely nod my thanks at Lincoln, who stood over by the door, discreetly waiting.

"How did I do, Richard?" Paige asked as she leaned over the railing and tapped my shoulder.

"Beautifully," I said. "simply beautifully. I'm sorry I had to let Ms. Larson dig at you so, but there was no help for it." I did not tell her that I felt Jean Larson had scored heavily on us in her cross-examination, but I had told Paige to tell the truth and that she had, as Pete might say, the bad along with the good. I hoped that Pete and I could dream up some medicine to counteract it, for it was apparent now that Tyra Pederson or the bartender or someone from Downtown had furnished Jean Larson at least some of the material she had used. Probably before the change, else Ms. Larson could scarcely have asked some of the searching questions she had. Like the cocktail-party incident.

I patted Paige's shoulder. "Now you and the Lieutenant go on home and I'll be there later. I want to go over some head practice. Monday is the big day."

After the Trapps had left Pete shuffled over and stood silently watching me stash my papers back into my briefcase. I looked up. "Well, Monday's the day—the big pay-off, one way or the other. What do you think, Richard?"

"What do you think, Pete?" I countered.

Pete shrugged and held out his hands. "You've got most of the stuff in now, Richard. All we need is for the Lieutenant to tell his story and our doctor to say he's crazy and I guess then it's in the lap of the jury."

"Yes, Pete, and for me to make a decent argument to the jury, and for the Judge to give the jury our requested instructions, and then for the jury to understand and heed them and give us a brake...a hell of a lot of big ifs."

"You'll do it, Boss," the familiar voice of a woman said. "I, I'm also proud of you."

I wheeled around. "Theresa," I said. "What the hell are you doing here? I thought you were home minding the till?

Theresa snorted. "Till?" she said. "that's been repossessed. Stay home? Not on your life, Boss. Did you think for a minute I was going to sit around that empty old law office while the boss was on his way to rags or riches? And while the loveliest case that ever hit this county unfolds? I'll confess, Boss. I've been here every single day." She cocked her head defiantly. "Am I fired again?"

Pete stepped up. "Have you forgotten we're partners in this case, Richard?" he said. "It was my considered judgement that Theresa ought to be on hand. As a matter of fact we've still got important work to do."

I glanced at my watch. "I've got to go see the Trapps, maybe eat something, and then get some sleep." I closed my brief case together and stood up. "I plan on spending the next two days in seclusion; maybe do a little golf, but nothing legal.

"Come Theresa," Pete said, offering her his arm. He bowed and lead Theresa grandly out of the court room.

***

470

I arrived just in time at the airport and quickly looked for an arrival board to check were the passengers would disembark. With that information, I went to the waiting area for that gate. In a matter of minutes passengers began coming up the walkway and I stepped out of the waiting area so that I could be seen better. I had never met the doctor in person, only seen a photo of him. Who knew when that photo had been taken. He wouldn't have a clue as to who I am so we would each be looking for a stranger.

Several passengers passed me by without a glance until finally a light skinned black man with extremely handsome features, tall and walking with a confident gait came down the walkway. He simply had to be our psychiatrist; He wore an open collar blue shirt that highlighted his skin . His face was full of balanced features giving him a clean cut look. I had assumed he would be in first class and if so, this was near the end of the first-class passengers for this size plane so if he wasn't the doctor we were in one hell of a fix. As he walked towards me, I take a deep breath and say comically, "Doctor Milo Goodman, I presume?" and he replied with a smile "Richard Dandridge?" and I almost staggered with relief as I take his bag and lead him to my mud splattered car. We at last had our psychiatrist.

Doctor Goodman gestured at the three men walking into the lobby ahead of us. "Reporters," he said. "Your little murder trial seems at last destined for immortality. It seems that word of a little dog with a flashlight is what did it." We watched as the three reporters noisily commandeered a cab and whirled away.

"A little dog shall lead them," I murmured. "How was your trip, Doctor?"

"An amazing trip," the Doctor remarked as we left the airport. "Your towns are scattered amongst the lakes and woods. There's a lot of beautiful landscape here."

On the drive, I fill him in on the trial situation; how the People had not made any psychiatric examination of the Lieutenant or seriously attempted to make one. I also tell him the things, both good and bad, that had cropped up since he had talked with the Lieutenant. I was concerned over the testimony of Detective Sergeant Kent as it might modify or even completely change his previous diagnosis of insanity. And also over the evidence of jealousy that Ms. Larson had dug out of Paige. Doctor Goodman said very little, occasionally asking a question or two, and by the time we arrived at his hotel, checked in and proceeded up to his room I had exhausted my part of the conversation.

After Doctor Goodman tidied up I told him more about the case, including the whole tangled yarn of Noah Arietta and his guns and drinking.

"You say that this Doctor Mason Anderson proposes to testify as to the mental state of Lieutenant Trapp on the night of the shooting merely from observing him in court?" the Doctor said.

"Well, I can't be sure, Doctor" I replied, "but I think so. I can't see any earthly reason why they would have him here otherwise."

Doctor Goodman shook his head. "I am sorry to hear that. Very sorry."

"Why is that, Doc," I asked. "How can the People expect to rebut our proof of insanity based upon such counter-testimony? Yet they must do so under the law—and do so beyond a reasonable doubt."

"That's precisely it, Mr. Dandridge," the doctor said soberly. "You see; I wasn't thinking so much of your man as I was of my own profession. The profession or art of psychiatry has come a long way. Insane asylums, shock treatments, violent madmen: Clichéd images of mental illness abound. Yet much has changed in the last

20 years in the field of psychiatry. New treatments like TMS Therapy for depression have emerged; research has led to improved medications for schizophrenia. It is precisely practitioners like Doctor Anderson who tarnish the field of psychiatry by daring to pass a professional opinion on such a basis."

This young man, I saw was as dedicated to his profession as Pete was to his. I shrugged. "I see your point," I said. "I'm dismayed for your profession, Doctor, but very happy for my client." I paused. "And do I assume from what you've just said that you still are of the opinion that the Lieutenant was legally and medically insane when he fired the fatal shots?"

The Doctor glanced at me quickly. "Yes. There is not the slightest doubt about that. What you've told me tonight only serves to clinch it."

"Would you feel disposed to discuss it more now?" I said.

He shook his head. "I would rather do so in court, if you don't mind. It might lend my testimony a little more spontaneity, if nothing else, and at the same time spare you from being bored twice instead of once. But I assure you that in my opinion your man was clearly suffering from temporary insanity and that I will so testify. Is that enough for now?"

"As you say, Doctor." I stifled a yawn.

Doctor Goodman grew thoughtful. "I will say this, however, I believe that Lieutenant Trapp's case is routine compared with the dead man, Noah Arietta. There is a man whose mind I would really have liked to explore. There is a real challenge."

"Yes, Doctor," I said, "It seems to me he must have known that nothing but disaster would follow his rape and assault of Mrs. Trapp." I shook my head. "My biggest worry is that despite all our proof to the contrary the jury might still doubt that the man could be capable of such an act. The thing was so utterly savage and primitive."

Doctor Goodman responded. "We must remember that for millenniums in human race something very much like rape was probably the normal order of the relations between the sexes, anthropologically speaking, that is. and just as there are a surprising number of men today, so called civilized men, who somehow derive their greatest sexual satisfaction from colliding with the most depraved women they can pick up, so there are still many men who take their greatest pleasure from rape; especially after consuming excessive alcohol that liberates their thinking."

I watched Doctor Goodman as he mused over the matter. "I suspect," the doctor continued thoughtfully, "that Noah Arietta might have been one of them, a sort of frustrated throwback who suffered sudden atavistic regression to type especially when he drank. Maybe he needed to show the world what a dominant masculine fellow he was which corresponds to his hobby. I think his brain path would be most interesting."

The doctor moved about the room as if checking the place out. "Yes, to me the dead man is by far the most fascinating character to this whole drama and I would have loved to try to find out just what made him tick."

"Quite a character," I said, yawning and remembering that Pete had once made pretty much the same observation. "Your main diagnosis, then, Doctor is that the Lieutenant still was the victim of irresistible impulse that night, regardless of whether he remembered what he was doing or knew right from wrong?" I had at least to know that before I could possibly sleep that night.

The young doctor nodded his head emphatically. "Yes, irresistible impulse is a test applied in a criminal prosecution to determine whether a person suffered from temporary insanity. The

474

defendant may argue that because of mental disease or defect, he lacked the capacity to distinguish right from wrong. Or he may argue that because of mental disease or defect, he was unable to act in conformance with the law. This is volitional insanity, and it is known as the irresistible impulse defense. Under this defense, a defendant may be found not guilty by reason of insanity."

The doctor pauses. "It is quite possible that the Lieutenant remembers more about the shooting than he admits. He may in fact remember all about it, have clearly known right from wrong that night, and think he is pulling the wool over your eyes and mine by now saying he doesn't. Even so it wouldn't make any difference, because in my opinion he still couldn't help himself. He was nevertheless irresistibly impelled to do what he did and was therefore medically insane."

"But almost not legally insane, Doctor," I said, explaining to him what a cold sweat his diagnosis of irresistible impulse had induced in Pete and me until we had discovered that New York was one of the comparatively few states in the country that admitted the defense, and about the only one among the northern tier of states. "Had the Lieutenant shot Noah just over the border in Ohio or Wisconsin it would have been curtains for his insanity defense, at least on your diagnosis. Consciousness of right and wrong is the sole test in those and most of our states."

Doctor Goodman shook his head in dismay. "How primitive and medically unrealistic," he said. He walked over to me and held out his hand, smiling. "I don't want to appear to pass out diagnose but I suspect that the place you clearly belong Mr. Dandridge, is home in bed. Your head has been nodding and your eyelids drooping for the past hour. What time is court?"

"Sharply at nine," I said, "and our judge doesn't fool. I'd like you to be there to hear the defendant testify."

475

"Sharply at nine," he said. "And now home to bed for you."

I shook his hand and yawned prodigiously. "Good night Doctor."

"Good night Mr. Dandridge," he said softly and then shut his door.

Chapter 14

I arrived at the court house early on Monday morning, to see cars parked for blocks around the courthouse and I was glad that the Sheriff had reserved parking space between the courthouse and jail.

Just as bad was the line of people waiting to enter the courtroom. That line stretched from the marble stairs, along the entire main downstairs corridor and through the door and onto the cement stairs outside. It reminded me of the lines of people waiting to get into a mall during black Friday.

When I had fought my way upstairs and saw the crowd waiting to enter the courtroom, I was thankful I could enter from the back and hurried on my way. Inside the court room the jurors and the Trapps were already in their respective places. I nodded at Doctor Goodman, who sat in one of the chairs behind Paige; then swept over the vacant seats to locate Pete sitting gravely by the far side door, out of the way of the Sheriff's men who soon were trying to orderly allow the horde of spectators to enter.

There was a mass of city reporters huddled earnestly around the press table talking with Travis Walton, the local newspaper man. It was a circus and the star performer wouldn't be presented to repeat his feat. All of this for Enzo and his flashlight. I couldn't help smiling.

When I finally reached the defense table, Paige leaned over and whispered to me, nodding toward Pete. "That man sitting over there just left this envelope on the table for you. He's the same nice man who handed me Enzo when I testified yesterday. Who is he, anyway?"

"He's a very good friend," I said smiling and tearing the envelope open.

"Richard," Pete's note read," call the cafe desk clerk as your first witness. His name is Eric Rennert. Credit Theresa with a touchdown on this one. The rest of us clean forgot. Oh, yes, don't forget the money. Good luck. Pete."

I glanced anxiously over at Pete and he winked and looked away. I wasn't quite sure what it was all about, but I trusted Pete.

The door to the Judge's chambers open and the court was put on their feet by the Sheriff's announcement. Behind the Judge came Jean Larson and District Attorney Randall Walker. When the Judge was seated on the bench, Sheriff Lincoln gave the instruction to take our seats. Silence fell over the courtroom.

"Good morning everyone." The judge looks around the court room. On the other side of the aisle, packed into the courtroom and an overflowing gallery, were dozens of media and spectators. "I can see we have quite an influx of people, but the rule remains that there must be order in the court room at all times. He then looked at the defense table. "Please call your first witness."

That was my clue. "The defense calls Eric Rennert," I said, praying silently that Pete knew what he was about and that the proper channels for entering him as a witness had been followed. There were no objections, so I assumed they had been.

I couldn't recall seeing Mr. Rennert, Tyra Pederson's desk clerk, before. It was a curious feeling to question a witness one had never properly interviewed. I hadn't even heard his initial recitation of the facts in narration form or practiced direct-examination or cross-examination tactics. I just prayed that Pete had. I took a deep breath and plunged ahead.

"State your name for the record, please?" I said.

"Eric Rennert," the witness answered.

"Where do you live?"

"Fairport, New York."

"Your occupation?"

"Desk clerk at the Founder's Café."

"How long have you been employed there?"

"Nearly four years."

"And were you so employed on the night of July 31st and the early morning hours of August 1st?"

"I was."

"And where in the building section were you working?"

"At the desk in the main lobby."

"And I ask you whether or not your desk commanded a view of the main entrance?"

"Yes, sir."

"And also the stairway to the bar?"

"It did."

"In other words you could see anyone who entered or left the lobby by either route?"

"That is correct, sir."

"Now I ask you, Mr. Rennert," I said, "if you saw your late employer Noah Arietta in the lobby the night of the shooting?"

In a voice barely above a whisper. "I did."

"When?"

"He came in and passed through the lobby at approximately midnight, possibly five minutes before."

"Using what entrance?"

"The main entrance."

"Was there anyone else in the lobby?"

"There was not. I was alone."

I paused and took the plunge. "Will you now please describe the general appearance of Mr. Arietta when you saw him?"

Ms. Larson was on her feet. "Objection, Your Honor. The appearance of the deceased would have no bearing on the issues of this case. It's irrelevant and immaterial."

"Mr. Dandridge?" the Judge inquired. "Why do you offer this testimony?"

"Your Honor, both the defense and certain of the People's witnesses have now clearly injected the issue of possible rape into this case. If there is anything to this, Your Honor, the deceased must have come fresh from his attack." I paused. "It occurred to me that the jury might be interested in learning about the appearance of Mr. Arietta. I shall of course abide by the court's ruling."

I now felt that it did not make much difference which way the court ruled, if the Judge kept the clerk's story out, the jury would undoubtedly imagine it, if he let it in, well, then it was in. Perhaps it was even better to let it out or at least safer. The Judge resolved the dilemma. "I am going to permit the answer," he ruled.

"Mr. Arietta was disheveled and panting as though he had been running," the witness replied. "His hair was mused and his trousers and white shirt were soiled as though he had fallen."

I try desperately not to show my excitement as I continue.

"Did he pause or speak to you?"

"No, he hurried through the lobby and up the stairs without a word."

"Did you see him later that evening… in the lobby, I mean?"

"Yes, in about ten minutes or so he came downstairs and, after pausing at my desk a moment, proceeded down to the bar. I never saw the man alive after that."

"What was his appearance then?

"He appeared to have changed his clothes and washed and tidied himself up."

This was a gold mine. I could kiss Theresa for bringing this…this angel of mercy. I continue.

"How about his hair?"

"It was combed."

"How about his breathing? Was he still panting?"

"He seemed very calm and composed."

I took a moment and felt my way. "You have mentioned his pausing at your desk. Did any words pass between you?"

The clerk grew thoughtful. "No," he said. "Not any words."

The witness had stressed "words" and I still felt my way along. "Did anything pass between you?" It was beginning to dawn on me. Pete had cryptically mentioned money.

"Yes."

"What?"

"Money. He handed, rather slid me a hundred-dollar bill."

Ah so Pete had scored again. There was a rustle and stir in the courtroom and I paused to ponder the situation. The obvious thing was to press on and ask the witness why money had passed, but since no words had passed, I sensed he could not very well testify to that but could only guess, which would only give Ms. Larson an opportunity for another objection. Perhaps it was better to let it rest right there and let Ms. Larson dig it out herself if she dared. There was one final question.

"Mr. Rennert," I said, "had Mr. Arietta ever done anything like that before. Silently given you a hundred-dollar bill or for that matter, any amount?"

"No, sir," the witness answered.

"Thank you Mr. Rennert. You've been a big help." Mr. Rennert smiled from ear to ear and I smiled back at him then turned and said, "Your witness, Ms. Larson,"

Jean Larson and Randall were engaged in a whispered huddle while all of the jurors sat watching them with interest. I glanced at Pete who sat staring pensively at the jury.

Randall stood up. "No questions, for this witness, Your Honor" he said.

"The witness is excused," the Judge said. "Please step down."

Slowly Mr. Rennert vacated his seat in the witness stand and returned to his previous location.

"Call your next witness," the Judge said.

I rose to my feet. "Lieutenant Vincent Trapp," I said.

This was the moment that the court was waiting for. The faces of the jury were fixed on the Lieutenant and a low murmur could be heard from the galley. The Lieutenant made an imposing figure as he marched to the stand, erect and looking every inch the part of an Army officer in his fresh uniform with all the colorful campaign ribbons and battle stripes. There was a stir from the galley and the Judge scowled and tentatively fondled his gavel as the Lieutenant was sworn in and sat down to face me.

"Will you please state your name?" I said.

"Lieutenant Vincent Trapp," he replied.

"What is your business or profession?"

"Under Secretary of Defense for Intelligence."

"What is your rank?"

"First Lieutenant in the United States Army."

"What is your job as the Under Secretary of Defense for Intelligence?"

"It's a high-ranking civilian position in the Office of the Secretary of Defense within the U.S. Department of Defense. I am the principal civilian advisor and deputy to the Secretary and Deputy Secretary of Defense on matters relating to military intelligence."

"So, it is safe to say that you are no longer serving as a soldier in the Army."

"Yes, that is true."

"Now, Lieutenant, where were you when your wife left the house for the Founder's café the night of the shooting?"

The Lieutenant went on in a calm low voice and told of his taking a nap after supper and how Paige had awakened him to ask if he wanted to go to the Founders café bar. He had told her to go along and he would join her later, but he again fell asleep.

"When did you next wake up?" I said, plunging into the midst of it.

"When I thought I heard the sound of screaming." I could see that he did not plan on adding to this statement so I had to encourage him.

"Go on, tell us what happened," I said.

He hesitated and then said, "I was shocked awake by the sound of screaming and at first was temporarily unable to move, speak or react. When I was finally fully awake I jumped out of bed, thinking at first I must have been dreaming, but then I heard the scream again. I put all the safety steps to rest and didn't even look to see who was pounding on the door along with ringing the doorbell and screaming. I would have been upset if Paige had done that but when I pulled the door open there she was. Paige, my wife…fell into my arms."

"Please describe what you saw."

"Paige was hysterical as she fell into my arms and fought against me holding her at the same time. I tightened my grip on her so that she didn't fall down and then kicked the door shut. I stood holding her against me until I could feel her body relaxing and then I moved back a little so that I could look at her."

"What did you see?"

"I saw, I saw a harrowing image of my wife with deep bruises on either side of her forehead, blackened areas around her eyes and what appeared to be mud and blood at the corners of her mouth. Her hair was a rat's nest of tangles and her clothes were disheveled and torn as if someone had repeatedly pulled at them. She was crying so hard she couldn't speak."

"What did you do?"

"I had to pick her up and carry her across the foyer and lay her on the sofa in my office. I started to leave and she grabbed my hand so I calmly told her I needed to get a cold compress on her face to lessen the swelling. She then released me and I went into the kitchen and put ice in two plastic bags, wrap each bag in a towel and took them into the office and place them on each side of her face. I then sat down beside her and waited for her to quiet down so that I could find out what happened."

"Did you finally find out?"

"I did."

"Now, without going into details, will you tell us what your wife told you had happened to her?"

"Yes, she told me she had been beaten and raped by..." the Lieutenant paused and his face became unrecognizable. His dark eyes became mere slits on his face and his lips pressed tightly together as though trying to hold the name back, yet knowing he had to say it. The whole court room grew silent, waiting for the words that eventually were spoken. "by Noah Arietta."

I took my time and moved around the front area of the court room walking over to the jurors and back to the witness stand, allowing the Lieutenant a chance to recover, before asking him, "What happened then?"

"I continued to comfort her. I knew I should take her to be examined immediately and not change her clothes, but I had to, I just had to. And it was while helping her into clean under clothes that I…I saw the evidence on her legs."

"What did you do then?"

"I wanted to help her shower. Believe me when I say I know all the rules but it is hard not to clean up, and of course — it's a natural human instinct to wash away all traces of an assault especially when it is someone you care for. So I wiped it off."

"Then what did you do?"

"I was no longer able to keep myself under control so I made Paige as comfortable as I could and then waited until she began to fall asleep. I then left her side and went over to the side table next to the window where I kept my pistol, and took it out of the drawer to put in my pocket. I walked back by Paige and could see she was sleeping so I left."

"Did you tell your wife you were leaving or to your knowledge did she see you take the pistol?"

"No, I said nothing and I don't think she knew I was leaving." He paused. "She has already testified she did not."

"Then what did you do?"

"I stepped outside and stood in the dark for a few minutes to adjust my eyes. I also wanted to make sure that her attacker wasn't lurking around out there. Then I went to the Founder's Café."

"Did you walk or ride?"

"I rode in my car."

"Do you remember opening the gate?"

"I do not."

"Or remember driving to the Café?"

"I do not."

I paused. I was coming to one of the crucial parts of our case and I wanted to word it just right so that the jury had no doubts about the way the Lieutenant answered.. "Lieutenant," I said, "what was your purpose in going to the Founder's Café bar?"

The Lieutenant's handsome face changed again as his thick black eyebrows moved closer to his eyes and the way his mouth shifted from one side to the other, one could guess he was grinding his teeth before he spoke. "I was going to confront that individual and hold him, so help me."

"What were you going to do with him?"

The Lieutenant spoke rapidly. "I'm not quite sure. All I could think to do was seize him and hold him. A man like that could not be at large."

"I ask you whether or not you had any intention of killing or seriously harming him?"

The Lieutenant breathed deeply before he spoke. "I had no intention of killing or harming him but if that man had made one false move I would have killed him."

I paused. It was in now; for better or worse our man had declared that he had gone to the bar to seize Noah Arietta, not kill him, an assertion which I hoped gave us sufficient evidence to support our case.

"Well, when you got to the café with your car what did you do?"

"I remember I got out of the car and walked into the bar. I remember looking around to see if Arietta was anywhere in the room and was shock to see him behind the bar. He wasn't usually behind the bar. Plus, maybe I was paranoid, but it was like he was expecting me. I wasn't even in the bar when I felt his eyes on me; though his body was turned toward the café area. Then I began walking across the entrance way to the bar and saw Arietta whirl around to directly face me."

"What happened after that?"

"I can't remember from there on. It is a hodgepodge of disconnected visions. My next coherent recollection is when I was back at my home."

"Can you illustrate for us, Lieutenant, what position the deceased assumed when he turned around?"

The Lieutenant's words came in breathless spurts. "As I say, he turned…To the best of my recall he turned to his right…his left hand on the bar…I cannot recall seeing his right arm."

"You say his left hand on the bar or arm and hand?"

"I believe his left forearm. He kind of leaned."

"State whether or not you remember driving back to the house."

"I don't."

"What happened when you got back to the house?"

"I didn't realize until I was back home that I came to. I mean it was like I became conscious and was awake again." He paused and then said. "It was like someone threw cold water in my face."

What were you doing when you came to?" I pushed on.

"I was standing with the empty pistol in my hand."

"How do you know it was empty? Before you answer I would like to show you People's Exhibit Number Eleven, and I ask you if this is your pistol." I walked over to the exhibit table and picked up the pistol that was still in a plastic bag, and carried it back to the witness. "Tell me, Lieutenant, is this your pistol?"

"It is mine, sir."

"Now how did you know it was empty?"

It is like the Lieutenant has found a way to take his mind off of the initial discussion as he goes into extreme detail. "This is a semi-automatic pistol designed to use a toggle-lock action, which uses a jointed arm to lock, as opposed to the slide actions of almost every other semi-automatic pistol. After a round is fired, the barrel and toggle assembly both lock together at this point travel rearward due to recoil. The toggle strikes a cam built into the frame, causing the knee joint to hinge and the toggle and breech assembly to unlock. At this point the barrel impacts the frame and stops its rearward movement, but the toggle assembly continues moving due to momentum, extracting the spent casing from the chamber and ejecting it. The toggle and breech assembly subsequently travel forward under spring tension and the next round from the magazine is loaded into the chamber. The entire sequence occurs in a fraction of a second." The Lieutenant holds the pistol and points to the areas for the Jury. "This gadget sticks up on the top of the magazine when the last round goes off. And there is not another shell. The piece here holds it back…you can't aim it and you can't release this."

"In other words by looking at it you could tell it was empty?"

"Yes, sir."

"Is that substantially as Detective Sergeant Kent explained it the other day?"

"It was. I think he probably knows more about side arms than I do."

At this point I purposely did not get into how the Lieutenant had got the Luger, I had a little trap set out myself for this one, and if the clever Ms. Larson evaded it, I could still bring it out on re-direct.

"How many people did you see in the bar that night?"

"Only one. The deceased."

"There has been testimony here that a number of people were in the café and in the bar, and that some of them greeted you. Did you observe any of them or were you aware of their greetings?"

"I saw and heard nothing."

"Now you of course saw and heard these eyewitnesses testify here in court earlier this week?"

"Yes, sir."

"And did you know prior to that night some of those who claimed to have greeted you?"

"Yes, mostly by sight, but I had spoken to them on previous occasions. This is a neighborhood café and bar so people are very friendly."

"Did you speak to anyone at the bar that night?"

"No, sir."

"To your best recollection did any one speak to you?"

"No Sir."

"Including the deceased."

"That is correct."

"Do you remember leaving the café."

"I do not."

"Or talking to the bartender or anyone outside?"

"No, sir."

"Do you remember returning home."

"No, sir."

"What is the first thing you recollect?"

"I first recall sitting in the house with my wife and telling her I think I shot someone. And when she asked, who, I told her I thought it was the owner of the Founder's Café. I then said I was going to go see Mr. Appleton because I didn't know what else to do."

"That is the deputized caretaker who lives in a cottage on your property?"

"Yes, sir.""

"Why did you go to him?"

"Well, he was the only one I could think to contact right away. He was someone I knew."

"Did you go to him because he was in your mind a deputy sheriff?"

"I may have. At any rate I went to him."

Jean Larson was scribbling furiously and I knew she would pounce on all this deputy business. "Did you think of Mr. Appleton being a deputy before you went to the bar that night?"

"I did not. I did not think of Mr. Appleton or his being a deputy or about anything but seizing that man."

"Do you recollect what you told Mr. Appleton?"

"Not exactly. I assume I told him what he has testified to here."

After that I quickly took the Lieutenant over his knowledge of Noah's expertise with pistols; his medals; the fact that it was common knowledge that he possessed pistols and sometimes carried them, and finally that the Lieutenant possessed this knowledge the night when he went to the bar to 'seize' Noah. I then brought out, over Ms. Larson's strenuous objection, that the Lieutenant had been obliged to retain a psychiatrist. Then said, "Lieutenant Trapp, on the night of this shooting did you love your wife?"

"I did, sir."

"Do you still love her?"

He frowned and breathed deeply, clasping the arms of his chair until his knuckles showed white. "Very much, sir."

I turned to Jean Larson. "Your witness," I said and retired to my table.

Chapter 15

Jean Larson got her cross-examination under way with ominous calm. "You don't remember much about that night after you left the house, do you, Lieutenant?"

"Well, ma'am, it is just as I have already testified."

I happened to glance back at the People's psychiatrist and saw him taking notes. Until then I wasn't even sure he was awake.

"Have you ever had similar lapses?" Ms. Larson asked.

"Well, yes, when in combat its ordinary to have lapses in memory."

"What do you mean?"

"Well, quite often after a mission is completed and we go back to the barracks to talk it over, you can be sure if there were ten survivors there'd be ten different stories of what happened."

Can you give specific instances rather than generalities?"

I sit up straight in my chair. Jean Larson would surely have objected had I tried to bring out anything like this.

At first the Lieutenant looks thoughtful as he tries to recall an instant, but then his look goes faraway and he begins speaking. "It was when we were going on a mission in Afghanistan and our small unit was being flown in at night. Everyone on the choppers had already done this type of mission, so we weren't too nervous until there was a large bump and impact that was strong enough to send us flying uncontrollably around the interior. There was mayhem as we tried to grab hold of something to steady ourselves, but then there was an earthshattering noise and we again were thrown around the inside of the helicopter like rag dolls. I believe I was knocked out. After I came to, I realized we had crashed. I knew we were in a bad place for an ambush, so I started radio contact until finally we were rescued." The Lieutenant paused and looked over at the jury, apologetically. "My point of the story is that this is how I saw it happen but when we returned to our base, all of those on the mission told a different story. Some said that missiles were launched at us and brought down the choppers, while others, like myself did not register an explosion and thought the chopper hit something and just went down."

The jury was hanging on every word as the Lieutenant spoke. From the look on some faces I swear they were actually sensing they were there in the helicopter.

"How long did you serve in Afghanistan?" Ms. Larson asked.

"Most of the soldiers were working on their second, third, or fourth year of cumulative deployment duty and each deployment is around 12 months. I served two deployments."

Ms. Larson then had the Lieutenant talk about various missions during his deployment sharing the details that he could.

"Were you in constant combat?"

"No ma'am, no soldier is ever in constant combat. None that survive, anyway. We were under constant to intermittent battle; especially when in Helmand. Helmand has ranked as the deadliest, most violent province in Afghanistan."

"And you had clashes from time to time?"

"Oh, yes."

"Did you think we could win?"

"The issue has long ceased to be how we can decisively expunge the Taliban — we can't. Instead, the question is: How can we forestall its full-fledged resurgence upon our departure? Toward the end of this year's fighting season, just before the winter rains, I spent seven weeks with soldiers across much of Helmand."

Ms. Larson was presenting the Lieutenants familiarity with combat conditions. That was pretty clear as she continued on.

"Did you participate in these combats?"

"Yes, ma'am. As a platoon leader I had to."

"How many men in a squad platoon?"

I could see that Ms. Larson had done her homework or was just well versed on the terminology and the war in Afghanistan. I admittedly was not.

"It depends. Squad Sergeant - 9 to 10 soldiers, Platoon Lieutenant - 16 to 44 soldiers, Company Captain - 62 to 190 soldiers, Battalion Lt Col - 300 to 1,000 soldiers and Brigade Colonel anywhere from 4-6 men in a squad or as few as 2-3."

"About how long were you involved in combats?"

"Sometimes a day, maybe three or even four."

"Now, Lieutenant can you tell me if during this time you experienced any unusual mental state of any kind?"

Puzzled, he says, "Not sure what you mean by that, but most soldiers who have been in combat see someone so that would be normal. I once had a concussion from the firing of explosive shells but I was back in action the next day."

"Were you ever treated for mental disease?"

"No, ma'am."

"Were you ever hospitalized for mental neurosis or psychosis?"

"No, ma'am."

"You have testified here that after you found certain evidence on the person of your wife you immediately slipped your gun in your pocket and left the house. Is that right?"

"Well, not in those exact words, but that is what I did."

It was obvious Ms. Larson was trying to paint a picture of the Lieutenant as being in the grip of rage when he shot Mr. Arietta and that he was no way suffering from any insanity.

"Was your wife reluctant to tell you about the alleged rape?" she asked.

"Not reluctant, she was hysterical and she couldn't tell me anything in the state she was in."

"But you questioned her carefully?"

Again, there is a puzzled look on the Lieutenants face before he says, "I did."

"You wanted to be sure, Lieutenant that you did not kill the wrong man."

"Objection! No one has said, 'kill', I replied.

"Sustained. I would be careful Ms. Larson." The Judge ruled in my favor, but before I can stop him, the Lieutenant responded. "Not kill, ma'am, the word I used was 'seize' the wrong man." I say nothing because his explanation says it all and tThat was fine with me.

Ms. Larson ignores the reply and moves on. "Now you had a key to the gate, did you not?"

"Yes, of course I did and I had given one to Mr. Appleton."

"And you knew the gate was locked at ten every night?"

"Yes, I did."

"And you wife knew that, too?"

"Apparently not. I guess I didn't tell her. She had no occasion to use it alone and the few times we did together Mr. Appleton thoughtfully left it open."

"You thought he was a deputy, didn't you?"

"I don't think I did, but if I had it wouldn't have made any difference."

"Oh, so you preferred to take the law into your own hands rather than call on Mr. Appleton?"

I start to object, but stop. The Lieutenant seems capable of taking care of himself and I am not wrong.

"That's not my reasoning, it's your reasoning, ma'am."

"Lieutenant Trapp," one could hear the irritation in her voice as she spoke his name, "when you saw this stuff on your wife's leg you blew your stack and promptly went out to kill Noah Arietta and did kill him, didn't you?"

"Objection Your Honor. Relevance. The finding of something on her leg does not relate in any way to the issues being argued about during this trial. ."

"Objection sustain. Ms. Larson you know better. The jury will disregard the prosecution's statement."

"And you did carrying a concealed weapon?" Ms. Larson continued.

"The pistol was out of sight, yes."

"Concealed contrary to law?"

"An applicant for a license to carry outside the home must be required to show, in addition to the requirement for possession, that proper cause exists for the issuance of a carry license, including, for example, target shooting, hunting, or self-defense. A loaded handgun may be carried in a vehicle by a properly licensed individual. Possession of any loaded rifle or shotgun in a vehicle is illegal. It is unlawful for any person to carry, possess or transport a handgun in or through the state unless he has a valid New York license. Just so you know ma'am."

The Lieutenant was now in battle with Ms. Larson and was determined to hit her with everything he knew about anything she chose to bring up.

"Didn't you tell Detective Sergeant Kent that a man who did what Mr. Arietta had done did not deserve to live, and you'd do it again if the occasion arose?"

"I don't recall saying any of that." The Lieutenant paused and added. "I respect Mr. Kent's integrity, but I do not recall saying it."

"You don't deny saying it?"

"No."

Ms. Larson had drawn very near the witness wagging her finger at him. "I ask you now, would you do it again."

I got up. "Your Honor, if counsel gets any closer to my client with her wagging finger I'm afraid he might seize her. I object to counsel standing so close to the witness."

"Stand back, Ms. Larson," the Judge ordered. Ms. Larson quickly retreated. "Please answer my question, Lieutenant, would you do it again?"

"I rather doubt that I would dare, Ms. Larson, now that I have met you."

There were giggles in the courtroom, but it was quickly interrupted when there was a sudden thrashing in the back of the court. I wheeled around and saw a weird scene. It was a young man who stumbled to his feet, pounding on the chair in front of him while warding off the upstretched restraining hands of the officers, his mouth open, trying desperately to say something. "Let...let him go, go!" he shouted in a broken voice. "Let...him...go." Finally, he got it all out in one sentence. "For Heaven's sake, let the poor man go!"

The Judge's gavel sounded and a barricade of officers descended on the culprit and half carried and half dragged him outside the court room. "Ten-minute recess, the Judge stammered, then sent the jury to its room and called the Sheriff and counsel into chambers.

The Judge glared at all of us. "does anyone in this room know anything about this?" he demanded sternly. I could feel his eyes on me since the incident was plainly pro-defense. Though not guilty, I flushed and hung my head.

"Not I, Your Honor, I swear," I said "I like to win my cases but I wouldn't be a party to a thing like that for the world. I never saw the man before.

Jean Larson glared at me as though I was lying then the Sheriff came to the rescue. "Judge," Lincoln said, "If anyone is to blame for this incident it is me. This boy was in Afghanistan and was seriously injured. Knowing his mother, we try to take him off her hands for a few hours when we can. We'd kept him out of the trial until today and only let him in when he promised to behave. I guess we were wrong. It must have been all the war talk. In fact, that is more than I've ever heard him speak. None of the lawyers had anything to do with it. I'm terribly sorry, sir."

The Judge looked thoughtfully at Sheriff Lincoln. "I can understand why you did it, but I can't allow that kind of upset in my courtroom." The Judge added, "Sheriff Lincoln, that man is barred from the rest of the proceedings. Is that clear?"

"Yes, Your Honor."

"Okay, that will be all." The Judge said. Sheriff Lincoln pulled out his cell to call the jury room, then left the Judge's quarters ahead of us.

On my way back to court, I took a detour and met up with Pete in the restroom. While we were washing our hands, Pete was finally able to tell me the tale that had added the night desk clerk to the witness list. He told me that he and Theresa had driven to the Café the night before, following Theresa's inspired brain storm over the desk clerk, and had dined at the Café. After dinner Pete had had a long and friendly visit with Tyra Pederson in her room. When the night clerk had come on duty Tyra had summoned him so Pete could hear for the first time the full and significant details of Noah's appearance and actions the night of the shooting. From that they quickly had gotten a subpoena and the rest was history.

The prosecution and myself left next and hurried into the court room where the Jury was already filing in. We waited, standing until the Judge was back on the bench.

"Please be seated," the Judge said and then turning toward the prosecution he added, "Please continue."

Jean Larson continued her cross examination trying to poke holes in the Lieutenants account of what he had told Detective Sergeant Kent, and then going over and over the story of the actual shooting in an effort to get him to admit remembering some fragment of the events that he had earlier denied remembering. But the Lieutenant only repeated his earlier recollections.

"Is it true that you struck and knocked down a fellow officer who had paid some attention to your wife at a cocktail party?" Ms. Larson next asked.

"Yes, sir."

"Why?"

"Because he was intoxicated and was annoying her."

In a soft voice, Ms. Larson asked, "Where you jealous, Lieutenant?"

"I wouldn't say so. I didn't like it and I resented his actions."

"Were you angry?"

Frowning, he replied, "Well to some extent I was, yes."

"Do you have a quick temper Lieutenant?" Ms. Larson said and then added. "would you knock the prosecution down if he dared to kiss your wife's hand?"

Lieutenant Trapp stared at Randall Walker, admittedly a handsome man, with a half-smile flitting over his face as he answered. "No, Ms. Larson, but I think if Mr. Walker kissed your hand you might be nicer."

Unable to refrain, the courtroom broke out in laugher and Jean Larson flushed with anger. "Order in the court," the Judge said, bringing down his gavel until the room was again silent. Ms. Larson stood biting her lip as if fighting for self-control, then slowly she walked over to her table, drank a glass of water and then returned to the witness.

"Now, Lieutenant," she said, take this luger you used to shoot Noah Arietta with." Jean Larson turned and walked over to the evidence table, found the exhibit and spun it on her finger. "This luger pistol that you kept loaded in your home and carried concealed on your person that night, it was not regular Army issue, was it?" she purred.

"No, ma'am,"

"You hadn't reported it to your CO and as far as your superiors knew you did not even possess it?"

"That's correct, ma'am."

Pausing triumphantly Ms. Larson said, "Then please explain to the court and jury how and where you got it?"

"Yes, ma'am. I will be glad to. It was at the battle of Alasay on March 23, 2009. The French and Afghan troops defeated the Taliban insurgents in the Alasay Valley. It was dusk and I was leading about a dozen men out on night patrol. The area had been badly shelled and there was very little cover. Intelligence told us the Taliban were in full retreat, that the way was clear. They were wrong. Anyway, there was shots fired and one of the injured had a luger pistol clutched in his hand. I took the pistol as a souvenir."

Jean Larson shot me a grim nod of congratulation and swiftly changed the subject in an effort to cover up. "do you and your wife have any children?" she asked abruptly.

"No, ma'am."

"And is this your first marriage?"

"No, ma'am, my second."

"And did either you or your wife have children by your respective previous, ah, adventures in matrimony?"

Scowling. "No, ma'am."

"And both of your parents are dead, I believe?"

"Yes, ma'am."

"And you have no dependents other than your wife, Lieutenant?"

"None, ma'am."

Jean Larson was now cleverly showing the jury that there was no widowed mother or seven starving children standing in the way of the jury throwing the book at the Lieutenant by its verdict.

"And your wife has earned her living before and she is in good health and could do so again?"

"Yes, ma'am, if it came to that I believe she could, ma'am."

"The witness is back to you," Jean Larson said, turning to me.

"No re-direct," I said, tugging at the knot on my tie out of sheer relief to at last have the Lieutenant off the stand and out of the clutches of this diabolical woman.

"We'll take fifteen minutes," the Judge said to the Sheriff and the whole procedure played out again as the Judge left the bench. Because I felt I needed to, I assume that this break was so that the Judge could relieve himself which is what I planned on doing as I headed to the nearest bathroom. By now it was apparent that all of us hoped the case would be over and done by the end of the day.

***

Chapter 16

After the break things began moving quickly. Once the Judge was finally seated on the bench, he said, "Call your next witness."

"I call Doctor Milo Goodman," I said. All eyes were glued on Doctor Goodman who stood well over six feet with caramel colored skin, perfectly shaped eyebrows and full lips. He wore his hair short and close to his head and he walked with a purposeful stride to be sworn in and take the witness stand.

"Your name, please, Doctor?" I asked.

"Milo Goodman."

"What is your profession?"

"I am a psychiatrist."

The jurors glanced at each other surprised, and I was sure they were appraising his youth. Yes he was not only attractive, but young, acquiring proof of his credentials. "Are you duly licensed to practice medicine and surgery in the state of New York?" I went on.

"I am."

"For the record, please tell us about your background."

"I am an active clinician and expert witness. As a specialist in Forensic Psychiatry, my testimony has had a major impact in high profile cases. I am an Assistant Professor of Psychiatry and Human Behavior at The Thomas Jefferson University College of Medicine and a Special Guest Lecturer at Widener University School of Law. I completed a residency in psychiatry at the Albany Medical Center Hospital and Syracuse. I completed a fellowship in forensic psychiatry at Syracuse University College of Medicine. I have been an Expert Reviewer for the United States Department of Justice Special Investigation Unit and a Member of the Delaware Governor's Advisory Committee on Mental Health, Alcohol and Substance Abuse. I have been recognized by Delaware Today Magazine as a Top Doc three times in a row and as a Top Psychiatrist in America by the Consumer Research Council. I am Board Certified in General Psychiatry, Geriatric Psychiatry, and Forensic Psychiatry. I hold licenses in New York, Delaware, New Jersey, Pennsylvania, Massachusetts and Maryland, North Carolina and Virginia. I am active clinician in private practice in Wilmington, Delaware and have evaluated over 10,000 patients."

This put the jurors at ease knowing our Milo Goodman was indeed a recognized psychiatrist. "Are you a member of a board or organization devoted to your specialty?" I pressed on.

"Yes, I am certified by the American Board of Psychiatry and Neurology.

"What does that mean?"

"That means that the American Psychiatric Association has put its stamp of approval on me as a specialist to practice psychiatry."

"And are there practicing psychiatrists who do not possess this certification? I asked.

"There are."

"How many years have you spent actively in the field of psychiatry, Doctor?"

"Over eight years."

"How old are you?"

"Forty."

"Now, Doctor, I ask you were you recently asked to conduct a psychiatric examination of Lieutenant Vincent Trapp, the defendant in this case?"

"I was."

"Did you conduct such an examination?"

"I did."

"Where?"

"At Albany Medical Center Hospital."

"When?"

"From Thursday, September fourth through half of Sunday, the seventh."

"And will you tell us Doctor some of the things that were done in connection with this examination."

"The Lieutenant received a complete physical examination, which means that he went through each of the specialty clinics in the hospital. To begin we obtained a history giving the Lieutenant a chance to mention any complaints or concerns about his health and asking questions about lifestyle behaviors like smoking, excessive alcohol use, sexual health, diet, and exercise. He was then sent to the specialty clinics in the hospital for each phase of his examination. We discussed his vaccination status and updated his personal and family medical history. From there we checked blood pressure, heart rate, respiration rate, temperature, general appearance and gave him a heart exam, lung exam, head and neck exam, abdominal exam, neurological exam; to examine nerves, muscle strength, reflexes, balance, and mental state, dermatological exam, extremities exam; for physical and sensory changes, pulse check in arms and legs, testicular exam, hernia exam, penis exam, prostate exam and laboratory test."

"What did the lab test include?"

"There are no standard laboratory tests during an annual physical. However, we ordered certain tests routinely that include complete blood count, Chemistry panel Urinalysis (UA), and a screening lipid panel or cholesterol test. He was also given an electroencephalogram study."

"What is that?"

"Because there was in the history that the Lieutenant had been unconscious as a result of a concussion suffered in military service, efforts were made to determine whether or not there might be some residual effects. This would show in an electroencephalogram. However, it was perfectly normal."

"So, Doctor Goodman, that brings us to his mental state."

"Yes, Lieutenant Trapp also received a complete psychiatric review.

"Please explain the test for us."

"The most comprehensive and accurate information is obtained when the examination begins with open-ended questions and active listening followed by structured inquiry about specific symptoms and events. Open-ended questions give the patient the opportunity to tell things from his or her perspective, and active listening helps verify and enrich the patient's report. The clinician's listening attitude helps to establish trust and a collaborative, problem-solving partnership between patient and clinician."

"I ask you if some of the preliminary tests were conducted by persons working under you?"

"The tests were done by professionals in their field and the results presented to me for examination."

"Now, Doctor, are their modern psychiatric facilities and equipment in the Albany Medical Center Hospital?"

"Yes there are."

"And how do they compare with other equipment of that nature in other hospitals?"

"Our facilities compare favorably with that in any hospital I am acquainted with."

I paused. Doctor, I ask you whether you and I have heretofore reviewed together a hypothetical question based upon the issue of possible insanity in this case?"

"We have."

I walk over to the defense table and pick up a copy of this exhibit and carry it to the front. Your Honor, here is a copy of our hypothetical question. I wait until he has had a chance to peruse it. I then take it over to Randall's table and he reviews it and then I return to hand it to the witness so that he can verify it is one and the same as we had reviewed.

"With the court's permission I would like to read into the record our hypothetical question."

"You have the courts permission."

I read the report.

"Doctor, assume that a man of thirty-six is a Lieutenant in the United States Army, that he was a veteran of the war in Afghanistan and that he returned to the United States at the end of his final deportation. Consider he now serves as the Under Secretary of Defense for Intelligence and lives in Pittsford, New York with his lovely wife who is attractive and vivacious. As the establishment is close, they have gone many times to the Founder's Café in the Academy building. That he occasionally went to the café bar and that his relations with the proprietor were cordial though in no sense intimate. At approximately 9 o'clock at night on Friday, July 31st the wife of the lieutenant went to this bar and had some drinks and played the Frogger video game and that the Lieutenant went to bed and slept and that at approximately 11:45 that evening, he was suddenly awakened. That he hurriedly got up and thereupon heard a series of screams. That he then met his wife at the door of their house and that she was sobbing and breathless and hysterical. That she finally told him that the proprietor of the Academy building Apartments and Founder's café had threatened her life and assaulted and raped her; that he had again just assaulted her and beaten and kicked her just down the road from their home. That she was badly bruised and beaten. That her skirt was ripped and her underpants were missing. That the Lieutenant spent upwards of an hour attempting to calm and comfort her. That during this time she told him the details of these threats and assaults and beatings. That during this time he wiped a fluid from his wife's leg which he believed to be seminal fluid. Assume further, Doctor, that this lieutenant reasonably trusted that the man whom he believed had just assaulted, threatened and raped his wife was an expert pistol shot and that he kept pistols about his premises and possibly on his person. That he himself kept a loaded luger automatic pistol in his house for protection. That his mind was in a turmoil over what he believed had just happened to his wife and over her present condition. That he finally determined to seek out said proprietor, seize him and hold him for the police. That while he felt considerable anger and loathing and contempt for the proprietor he had at no time any intention of killing or harming him but felt that if the man made one bad move he would have killed him. That he went and got his pistol without his wife's knowledge and left his wife in the house and proceeded toward the Founder's café. That he does not remember what time it was or precisely how he got to the bar of the Founders café. That he finally got to the bar at the Founder's café and entered it. That he saw the proprietor standing alone behind the bar watching him. That he then advanced to the bar and the proprietor whirled around and the Lieutenant produced his pistol and pointed it at the proprietor and emptied its contents into his body, leaning over the bar to do so. That he had and has no conscious recollection of his act. That he then turned and left the bar and proceeded toward his home. That he does not remember anything after he entered the bar other than as indicated until he got home to his house. That he then first observed that his pistol was empty; that he then told his wife that he had shot the owner of the Founder's café. That he then notified a deputized caretaker of their property and the adjacent park. That he waited in his home for the police and was subsequently arrested and charged with murder. Assume further Doctor that this man had never before in his lifetime ever been arrested for or convicted of any criminal offense, including any civilian act of violence toward another human being." I paused and catch my breath, then walk over and take a sip of water before returning to stand near the witness. "Now, Doctor, assume all the facts herein stated to be true, have you an opinion based upon a reasonable psychiatric certainty as to whether or not it is probable that the hypothetical man was in a condition of emotional disorganization so as to be temporarily insane?"

"I have."

"What is that opinion?"

"That he was temporarily insane at the time of the shooting."

"Doctor, have you an opinion as to whether or not he was suffering from a temporary mental disorder at the time the deceased met his death so as to be unable to distinguish right from wrong?"

"I have."

"What is your opinion?"

The doctor hesitated here as he had the night before in his hotel room. "That the hypothetical Lieutenant was probably unable to distinguish right from wrong."

I pushed on. "Have you an opinion as to whether or not at that time he knew, understood, and comprehended the nature and consequences of his acts?"

"I have."

"What is that opinion?"

"That he was not."

"Was or did not, Doctor?"

"That he did not, I mean. Thank you."

"Do you have an opinion, Doctor, as to whether or not he was in such a state of mind that he did not have the benefit of his conscious reasoning mind, and rather was dominated by instinct and the unconscious mind?"

"I have an opinion."

"State your opinion."

"That he was completely dominated by instinct and the unconscious mind."

"Now, Doctor, I ask you whether or not you have a psychiatric basis or bases for these opinions you have just expressed?"

"I have."

"And is there in your opinion a condition presented here known to the profession of psychiatry?"

"There is."

"Would you please explain these bases and the condition, if any, which may be known to psychiatry?"

"The condition is known to psychiatry and it is not uncommon and after completing several sessions with the Lieutenant I have come to this conclusion. It is called, dissociative reaction. This is a common defense and or reaction to stressful or traumatic situations. Severe isolated traumas or repeated traumas may result in a person developing a dissociative disorder which impairs the normal state of awareness and limits or alters one's sense of identity, memory or consciousness. Once considered rare, recent research indicates that dissociative symptoms are as common as anxiety and depression. For those suffering such a reaction the shock would disturbed the mental and emotional equilibrium of the Lieutenant and be responsible for creating an almost overwhelming tension. In this state the one object the Lieutenant would seek would be anything that would reduce or alleviate the tension. His past history indicates he is a man of action and it was natural at this time that he should turn to action. It would also mean he would not be fully capable of understanding the significance of any course of action he followed. At such a time the only right that this individual may understand is the right that will reduce the unbearable tension."

"Does this mental state of dissociative reaction you have been talking about bear any other tag or label?"

"It does. It has also been known as irresistible impulse."

"Objection, Your Honor," Ms. Larson said. "The defense is leading the witness. Move that it be stricken."

"Mr. Dandridge?" the Judge said.

"Your Honor, the Doctor has called this condition one of dissociative reaction and I have asked him if it had any other name or label and he has just told us." I walked forward. "this is crucial to our case. Your Honor, and we will go to bat on that…"

"The Judge held up his hand "No need to make a speech, Mr. Dandridge," he said." The answer may stand."

"Now Doctor, I ask you whether in your opinion a man laboring under the mental state you have described would have been apt to have gone to a deputized caretaker and seek his help in seizing the deceased and holding him for the police?"

Jean Larson arose but the Judge silenced her with the upraised palm of his hand. I could tell that both Ms. Larson and I were wearing him down.

"Such behavior would have been incompatible with everything else you have enumerated in this hypothetical question, the witness replied. "the question indicates that this is certainly a hypothetical man of honor, a man who would sense that personal security depends upon self-respect self-esteem ideals and honor. To have such a man of this particular point turn to an unarmed caretaker would have been simply incompatible with the hypothetical man up to this point. I would not relish attempting to explain any circumstances under which such a hypothetical man could do such a thing."

"Doctor, I ask you whether or not he, the Lieutenant would have gone to the bar to seize the proprietor."

Doctor Milo Goodman smiled. "In the state in which this Lieutenant was at the time he would have gone to the café, in my opinion he would have done so with or without a gun, whether or not the proprietor had any guns available and whether or not he knew that they were there. In my opinion he would have walked into a cannon mounted on the bar, I think it is important to understand that the very essence of the Lieutenant's manhood was at stake here."

"Doctor, I ask you whether or not this mental state or condition of which you speak would necessarily interfere with the physical abilities or manual dexterity of the hypothetical lieutenant, as for example his ability to quickly produce a gun and aim it accurately."

"It would not, indeed it might well even facilitate whatever activity this man was following."

"Have you seen such phenomena in your experience as a psychiatrist?"

"I have seen and I have heard. I have heard of it from those in whom the phenomena took place."

"Doctor," I push on, "In your professional opinion is intensive and extensive psychiatric observation and examination of the individual important in reaching psychiatric conclusions about his mental state."

"I would say they were essential."

"Can you explain that?"

"To understand why the particular shock would result in a particular course of conduct or mental state in a given individual requires intense observation of the highest order. That, sir, is psychiatry."

"You may state, Doctor, whether or not you would venture or attempt to pass a psychiatric opinion on the past mental state of either the hypothetical lieutenant or the real Lieutenant Trapp on the basis of merely sitting here during the course of this trial."

Doctor Milo Goodman shot a quick look at the People's psychiatrist. "I would consider it impossible to pass any valid professional opinion on the state of this man's mind on the basis of mere observation."

I turned to Jean Larson "Your witness,"

Chapter 17

Well aware of the sexist connotation, I can't think in any terms than to say that Jean Larson, a visual picture of warmth and comfort was an irritating bitch; causing tension and annoyance. As effective as her stance she now had a new approach. "Doctor, during your examination of this defendant did you find any psychosis?" Jean Larson shot out as she lifted her body off her chair.

"I did not."

"Any neurosis?" she asked, advancing with her stealthy tread.

"That is a broad question." Doctor Goodman says. "I found no history of serious neuroses."

Ms. Larson now paused squarely in front of the witness. "Now, doctor, will you tell us what facts or factors in the hypothetical question you consider the most important?"

Now I am about to learn if my tactics of using a hypothetical case situation when questioning the medical expert would come around and bite me because it goes both ways. Ms. Larson was no dummy as she tries to make the doctor pull the facts apart and weaken the scenario. But my tactic has been successful in New York courts before and maybe, it would work for me. I anxiously await the Doctor's response.

"The whole hypothetical question is important," the Doctor replies thoughtfully. "It delineated a particular hypothetical man in its entirety so that I must say my answers were based on the whole question.

Ms. Larson tries again. "Weren't there any parts that were a little more significant than others?"

"No. No fact was so significant that I would say it was more important."

She would not give up, "You mean you don't recall the parts which were more significant?"

"I mean what I said, that the whole question as stated is significant and pulling out a part from the rest is like wearing one sock instead of the pair. Each part is as important and dependent upon the other."

Ms. Larson was getting no place so she wisely changed the subject. "How is dissociative reaction classified by psychiatrists?"

"Dissociative disorders are conditions that involve disruptions or breakdowns of memory, awareness, identity, or perception. It is classified as a temporary neurotic condition."

"It is not a psychosis?"

"It is not a psychosis nor is it ordinarily even a serious neurosis. This depends upon how you are referring to the reaction, it can of course be quite serious at the time that one is suffering it, both as to the consequences to himself and to others. But if duration is considered it is generally of a more temporary nature."

Doctor Milo Goodman, handsome, athletic and young knew without prompting that he needed to show the jury he was not just a pretty face and he was doing a bang up job of it.

"Now, doctor, just what test were made when you conducted your examination of the Lieutenant?"

"All the usual laboratory tests."

"Was he given a Wechsler Bellevue test?"

"He was not."

"Was there a Bender Gestalt test?"

"No."

"What type of tests are those?"

"They are psychological tests."

"And no psychological tests were given?"

"I didn't say that. The ones that I thought were indicated were administered and examined and appraised by me."

"What were they?"

"For one, the Thematic Apperception Test."

"Is it a psychological test or projection?"

"Both psychological and a projection test. The Thematic Apperception Test, must be administered by a highly trained psychologist or psychiatrist. The client is shown a series of several cards depicting people in various situations. The client is asked to tell a detailed story about each card and the story is then interpreted by the psychologist or psychiatrist. TAT for short, is often used to assess personality, depression, world outlook, etc."

"So tell me Doctor what is the purpose of the Wechsler Bellevue test?"

"The Wechsler Bellevue Intelligence Scale is a general test of intelligence, which Wechsler defined as, "... the global capacity of the individual to act purposefully, to think rationally, and to deal effectively with his environment." In keeping with this definition of intelligence as an aggregate of mental aptitudes or abilities, it consists of an information test, a general comprehension test, a memory span test, an arithmetical reasoning test, a similarities test, a vocabulary test, a block design test, an object assembly test and a digit symbol test."

That should have stopped Ms. Larson in her tracks but she bravely went on. "Did you have the facilities to administer this test?"

"Yes."

"And the Bender Gestalt test?"

"Yes."

"Did you administer either to Lieutenant Trapp?"

"I did not."

"Why?"

"Well to begin with because of its dated normative and psychometric data, today the Wechsler Bellevue Test is recommended for teaching purposes only. Now, the Bender-Gestalt II is an update of the Bender-Gestalt that you referred to. It is a brief test of visual-motor integration that may provide interpretive information about an individual's development and psychological functioning. It is clinician-administered. The second edition uses new recall procedures to assess visual-motor memory and provide a more comprehensive assessment of visual-motor skills and this test can also be used to assess neurological damage and emotional disorders."

Two strikes and yet she goes on. "Did you make a personality inventory study of the Lieutenant?"

"I requested no such study. I made my own individual psychiatric study of this man."

"What tests did you use, then?"

"I tested his perceptions rather carefully and then I used an electroencephalogram, also called a brain wave test, as a diagnostic test to measure the electrical activity of the brain which may help diagnose the causes of confusion, and to evaluate head injuries, tumors, infections, degenerative diseases, and other disturbances that affect the brain."

Ms. Larson paused and referred to her notes and glibly tossed out some more tests. "Did you give him the Szondi test?"

"I did not give him a Szondi experimental diagnostic examination. This…"

"No explanation is needed. You have answered the question, Ms. Larson interrupted him to say. "What about a Rorschach psychodiagnostic examination?"

"Objection, Your Honor," Ms. Larson has asked the question and is not allowing the witness to complete his answer.:

"The objection is sustained. The witness may continue.

"I will respond to both questions then," Doctor Goodman said and Ms. Larson cringed. "The aim of the Szondi Test was to explore the deepest repressed impulses of a person on the basis of sympathy or aversion caused by the specific photos of psychopaths. The test is based on the general notion that the characteristics that bother us in others are those that caused aversion to ourselves at an early stage of our life and that's why we repress them. The test was designed to make an assumption about the possible repressed impulses of each type of personality in accordance with the psychoanalysis theory and that is why I deemed it not necessary in evaluating Lieutenant Trapp."

Doctor Goodman pauses and takes a drink of water before continuing. "The Rorschach Inkblot Test for the 1940's and 1950's was the test of choice in clinical psychology. It fell into disfavor as many clinicians began criticizing it as "subjective" and "projective" in nature. With no clear leader to take the helm, at least four separate "systems" developed to administer, score, and interpret the test. Needless to say, questions and concerns regarding the test's reliability and validity was eventually brought into question. This explains my reasoning for not using either of the two test methods."

"So your answer is, No?"

"Yes, my answer is I did not." Doctor Milo Goodman glanced in the direction of the People's psychiatrist, Doctor Mason

Anderson who looked the part of the profession. "I may add, ma'am, I happen to belong to the school of psychiatry that tends to stress individual study and appraisal rather than to that group that has sometimes lightly been referred to as the slot-machine or gadget school of psychiatry."

Ms. Larson ignored the assault and pressed on. "From your examination of the Lieutenant did you find any history of delusions?"

"None."

"Or loss of memory?"

"None before this case."

"Or hallucinations?"

"No."

"Or conversion hysteria?"

"Well, the dissociative reaction itself embraces cases of what has been called such hysteria."

Ms. Larson paused triumphantly as though she had dug up a fresh bone. "In common language, doctor, isn't the conversion hysteria also known as a fit of temper?"

"It is not. I know of no reputable psychiatrist or psychiatric authority who would so describe conversion hysteria. A fit of temper is an outburst of anger which is not what conversion hysteria is."

"How would you describe conversion hysteria in common language?"

"I think I have done so already in the commonest language I could and still preserve accuracy," the Doctor replied coolly. "Dissociation is a common defense or reaction to stressful or traumatic situations. The hysterical reaction in modem psychopathology is explained as serving defensive function by which the individual escapes or avoids stressful situations and as a neurotic disorder, the symptoms of hysteria can take the form of widest variety."

Jean Larson eyed the witness and then referred to her notes. "Doctor, on direct examination you were asked if the hypothetical lieutenant was able to distinguish between right and wrong and you answered that he probably could not have. Do you still feel the same way?"

"I do," the witness answered.

"Then he might actually have known the difference between right and wrong?"

"He well might have."

"Then how can you possibly come in here and testify that the Lieutenant was legally insane?" She shouted at the witness. It was then that I knew Jean Larson with all her research did not know that irresistible impulse was a defense to crime in New Yok under a plea of insanity.

"I did not ever say here that anyone was legally insane, ma'am," the Doctor coolly replied. "I have said that I thought the hypothetical lieutenant was suffering from a medically recognized mental aberration known as dissociative reaction, sometimes known as irresistible impulse, and I say and repeat that a consciousness of doing right or wrong would not make much, if any difference to a victim of that mental disorder."

Jean Larson turned her back on the witness and shot a significant look at the jury and then over at me. Then, with her back still toward the witness, "And you are willing to rest your testimony in this case, Doctor, on that answer?" she fairly purred.

"I am, ma'am."

Jean Larson was going to have herself a little surprise, if the Judge gave the jury our requested instructions on irresistible impulse and if the jury understood and heeded them. Always there was the big uncertain if...

Ms. Larson deviated to another subject. "Might this man have felt anger toward Noah Arietta?" she pressed on, facing the witness again.

"Are you referring now to the real or hypothetical lieutenant, Ms. Larson?" the witness questioned calmly.

"Either one," she snapped. "As a matter of fact wasn't the Lieutenant angry at Noah Arietta and didn't he go over there in a homicidal rage to shoot him to death?"

The Doctor grew thoughtful. "He might well have felt some anger toward Mr. Arietta," he conceded. "It would have been rather abnormal if he hadn't. But we may be sure it wouldn't solely be anger. "He paused and smiled slightly. "Just as you have now displayed anger at me, Ms. Larson, yet your main desire is still the cool and calculated one, to trap me if you possibly can."

Jean Larson glared at the witness and decided not to pursue the subject of her own anger. "But wouldn't the defendant's main desire be to vent his wrath and anger upon Noah Arietta?" she persisted.

The Doctor shook his head. "Feelings and thoughts are different, but are also one and the same. We react to events with both thoughts and feelings. Feelings are emotions, and sensations, and they are different from thoughts, beliefs, interpretations, and convictions. Abstract words like anger and hate exist mostly as convenient labels for the complex emotion that men feel, Ms. Larson," the Doctor said. "To insist that the Lieutenant felt only anger is to isolate and stress but one of the many complex and conflicting emotions he was doubtlessly feeling at the time."

I glanced at the jury, fearful that they might themselves be sinking into a hopeless morass of semantics. Instead they were sitting alert in their chairs and appeared to be having the time of their lives.

Ms. Larson veered away from the topic of anger. "Are neuroses considered insanity?" she asked.

"Neurosis is a class of functional mental disorders involving distress but neither delusions nor hallucinations."

"That is all," Ms. Larson concluded, turning away.

"Redirect, Mr. Dandridge?"

"No re-direct examination, Your Honor," I swiftly replied. I was proud of the way Doctor Milo Goodman had handled himself and the prosecution.

"The defense rest."

"In that case, the court will take an hour recess for lunch. Everyone should be back by one o'clock.

Chapter 18

The hour went by swiftly as I concerned myself with what remained in court. With the conclusion of the defendant's case, the plaintiff would be ready to present rebuttal witnesses or evidence to refute evidence presented by the defense. Since that may include only evidence not presented in the case initially, or a new witness who contradicts the defendant's witnesses I needed to be prepared for anything.

I checked in with Pete and together we tried to cover all possibilities before the hour ended and we were back in court.

Sheriff Lincoln said, "All rise." And for the umpteenth time everyone in the courtroom stood. "The Honorable Judge Silas Nicholson presiding."

Judge Nicholson appeared and takes his seat on the bench. "This courtroom will now come to order." He bangs the gavel and says, "The court is now in session. Please be seated."

There is a rustle of fabric and activity then total silence. The Judge looks down at the People's table. "Does the People care to present rebuttal witnesses or evidence to refute evidence presented by the defense?"

"Yes your honor." Jean Larson said. "The people will call Doctor Mason Anderson to the stand."

Indeed, we live in a frustratingly perception-oriented society: A political candidate who is "baby-faced" is not only deemed less competent than his sterner-looking opponent, but he is also more likely to lose the election. So it is in the field of psychiatry as Doctor Anderson stood to stroll languidly to the witness stand with all eyes on him. As much as I hated to admit he looked the part with his thinning hair camouflaged by a slight comb over across the top of his high forehead. The addition of a short gray beard hid the contours of his face. He wore a black jacket over a baby blue sweater vest and tan trousers, giving him the appearance of being comfortable, yet intelligent.

Once seated, Ms. Larson began. Please state your name and occupation for the record."

"My name is Mason Anderson and I am a doctor of psychiatry.

"How long have you been a doctor of psychiatry?"

"Approximately twenty-five years."

"Doctor Anderson please state your credentials."

"I received my undergraduate biology degree from Southern California College in 1978 and my doctorate from Oral Roberts University School of Medicine in 1982. I did my general psychiatric training at the Walter Reed Army Medical Center in Washington, D.C., and my child and adolescent psychiatry training at Tripler Army Medical Center in Honolulu."

"And what if any is your present position Doctor?"

"I am the chief executive officer and medical director of six institutions for the medically insane."

"And what kind of patients are treated each year?"

"We specialize in the treatment of serious psychiatric diseases, such as clinical depression, schizophrenia, and bipolar disorder."

"And are you associated with any national psychiatric groups?"

"Yes, I am a Diplomate at The American Board of Psychiatry and Neurology, Inc." he replied, the pride apparent in his voice.

Jean Larson then read my precise hypothetical question to her psychiatrist word for word. When finished she asked, "Doctor, assuming all the facts here to be true, have you an opinion based upon reasonable psychiatric certainty as to whether or not it is probable that the hypothetical man was in a condition to be diagnosed as temporarily insane?"

"I have."

"What is that opinion?"

"That the information given regarding the hypothetical man is clearly not sufficient to warrant a diagnosis of insanity."

"Have you an opinion based upon a psychiatric certainty as to whether or not that hypothetical man was suffering from this dissociative reaction?"

"I have."

"What is your opinion?"

"I do not believe he was suffering from a dissociative reaction." he responded.

"What is your reason for that opinion?"

"A dissociative reaction is a severe type of psychoneurosis, a condition of long standing. I feel certain that the hypothetical lieutenant would have shown either one or repeated upsets of the dissociative nature during the time or times of his combat service."

As Ms. Larson continued her questioning it was presented that the hypothetical lieutenant could distinguish right from wrong, and he could understand and comprehend the nature and consequences of his acts. Further the lieutenant was in possession of his faculties.

"Now, Doctor, if the instances in question as set forth stating the hypothetical lieutenant had no memory of certain events were eliminated and it was swapped to say that he did have a memory of these events would that change your opinion?"

"No sir."

"Doctor, knowing all the facts as they have been stated to you putting them into one opinion, what would it be?"

"It would be that the hypothetical or the real Lieutenant was not legally or medically insane."

Jean Larson look back at me beaming "your witness," she said.

I rose and slowly advanced to destroy this man if I could. As I approached the witness, my mind churned over the facts until I felt comfortable with the way to approach Doctor Mason Anderson. I could do this.

"Doctor," I began softly, "so you're a diplomat of the American Board of Psychiatry and Neurology?"

"I am, sir," he said proudly.

"Since your colleague Doctor Milo Goodman belongs to the same group he would also be seen as a diplomat?"

Doctor Anderson showed his annoyance of admitting this by stiffly replying, "I assume so."

"How long have you been on the staff of various public mental institutions, Doctor?"

"Twenty-one years," he answered.

"And, is it correct to say that you head the staff of one now?"

"That is correct."

"Isn't it a fact, Doctor," I pushed on, "most of your professional career has been spent in public mental institutions where you deal largely with people who have already been adjudged insane by others?"

"Well, yes," he admits because he has to since he had already clearly testified to that fact.

"And a major portion of your work and experience has been in determining when and if those patients have recovered or been restored to sanity, rather than in determining if they were insane, the form of that insanity, or how they became so?"

"Yes, sir, that and in trying to cure them."

"And isn't it further true that all the public mental institutions you have been connected with, including the one where you presently work, suffer from long waiting lists of patients needing the facility?"

"Yes, sir, that is true."

"And as a consequence of that overcrowding is it also true that only those persons with the most advanced symptoms of insanity, are the ones most likely to be admitted to the asylums including yours?"

"Very true," he agreed."

"So that it would further be true then Doctor, would it not that those psychiatrists who work in such public mental institutions would rarely if ever get to study or observe subtle or subjective types of mental illness?"

"Yes, I suppose that is so."

"There is no supposing about it is their Doctor?"

"Well, no sir."

"And that would include persons allegedly suffering from this dissociative reaction would it not?"

Resignedly the good Doctor replied, "Yes. They would rarely be committed to a public mental institution."

It was time now to get down to particulars. "Now, Doctor," I asked, "when did you first lay eyes on the real and not the hypothetical Lieutenant Trapp?"

"On Thursday morning of this week."

I paused as if pondering this answer. "So you are saying that you have only seen the real Lieutenant Trapp in person for two and one half court days?"

"Yes, that's true sir."

"And did you see him at all outside of the courtroom during that time?"

"I did not."

"And may I assume Doctor That you did not conduct any personal examination of him?"

"Obviously not, sir."

"Nor did you conduct any of the various tests and whatever that have been mentioned here by Ms. Larson or by your colleague?"

"I did not."

"Now you were present, Doctor, were you not, when prosecutor Larson cross examined Doctor Goodman?"

"I was."

"And did you hear Ms. Larson question Doctor Goodman rather extensively on his failure to," I paused to view my notes. "On his failure to administer a Wechsler Bellevue test, a Szondi test, a Bender-Gestalt test, a Rorschach psychodiagnostic examination, etc. etc." I panted as if out of breath.

"Yes, of course, I was right here."

"Am I also correct in assuming Doctor Anderson that Ms. Larson got all this impressive sounding lingo from you?"

Doctor Anderson visibly drew back, offended. "Lingo?"

"Pardon me, Doctor, I meant to say psychiatric terminology."

"Yes, yes of course I told her. Many otherwise highly competent medical doctors wouldn't be apt to know those terms."

527

"Would it be fair to say that your criticism of Doctor Goodman's findings, would be on the methods he employed?"

"It would," the witness answered reprovingly.

"Doctor" I said, "do you assume and want this jury to believe that no personal screening or observation examination or test of the lieutenant whatever were better than the methods employed by Doctor Goodman?"

"I did not say that," he replied stiffly.

"I know you did not exactly say it Doctor but you have plainly inferred it and that is why I am asking you now. Were no test at all better than those given? Was it better to screen or not to screen?"

"What do you mean?" the witness parried uneasily.

"I meant exactly what I asked. Please answer the question."

Dr. Anderson frowned. "Are you trying sir to make a joke out of my profession?"

"Joke, Doctor?" I said softly. "I'm making a joke out of your profession?" it was time to lower the boom. "Look Doctor I ask you a simple question and I'd like a simple answer. Do you assume and want this jury to believe that no personal screening or observation examination or test of the lieutenant whatever were better than the methods employed by Doctor Goodman?"

"Objection your honor. He's badgering the witness," Jean Larson says with reserve.

"The objection is overruled."

The witness was fairly trapped, "No," Doctor Anderson replied.

"No what?" I dug away

"No, it would have been better to personally observe and test the subject."

"Now, tell us, did you make any request or was there any request made on your behalf to examine Lieutenant Trapp?"

"No request was made." The witness was literally squirming in his chair as he squeezed the words out.

My voice rose. "And yet you would dare come in here and pit your professional opinion against that of a reputable colleague who had actually examined him?"

"Objection your honor I…"

"Objection sustained."

My next question like the last was largely rhetorical, intended more for the jury than for the witness. "Perhaps Doctor," I said "since you were not inconvenienced by having ever seen him perhaps you would care to venture an off the cuff opinion on the psychiatric state of the dead man himself?"

"Objection! Clearly improper."

"Sustained." Mr. Dandridge, please get on with it.

"Now Doctor, let us forget about the hypothetical questions and the hypothetical lieutenants and look at the real man," I walked over and put a hand on Lieutenant Trapp's shoulder. "The real man who is under a real charge of second degree murder. I ask you if you now agree with Dr. Goodman that Lieutenant Trapp is presently sane?"

"I do. It is quite obvious."

"Thank you Doctor. Now I ask if you have an opinion as to whether the real Lieutenant was suffering from insanity at the time of the shooting?"

"I object. That would not be proper," Ms. Larson said.

"I asked your expert, Ms. Larson, if he had an opinion?"

The witness maintained silence. Finally, the Judge broke in, "Do you have an opinion or not?" He barely hid his annoyance. "Answer yes or no."

"I have an opinion, "Dr. Anderson replied.

"Good." I said. "Please state it?"

"Just a moment," the Judge interrupted. "Now if you have a real opinion I will permit you to state it. But I don't want any guesses. And you must be prepared to back your opinion up. Are you still prepared to offer an opinion?"

"I am," he said nervously.

"What is your opinion?" I asked.

"My opinion is that the real Lieutenant Trapp was not insane at the time of the shooting." he replied.

"And upon what psychiatric bases do you base that opinion Doctor?"

"From what I've seen and heard here."

"You mean to still venture an opinion on the sanity of this man without the benefit of any personal observation or tests or history whatever?" I shouted at him.

"Yes sir."

I pause for nearly a minute. "Doctor" I said slowly, "is that the normal and accepted method of psychiatric practice for a diplomat of the American Board of Psychiatry and Neurology?"

"I object to that," Ms. Larson quickly cut in. "Council is questioning now because he doesn't like the answer."

"The Objection is overruled," the judge said shortly. "Answer the question."

Doctor Anderson now looked as though he was sitting on a hot seat. "No, it is not normal practice to make a psychiatric diagnosis without the complete history and personal examination of the individual," he said.

"No further questions," I said, "your witness, Ms. Larson."

"I have no further questions," Ms. Larson quickly said.

"The witness can step down," the Judge replied.

Doctor Anderson didn't waste a minute getting off the stand and back to his seat.

"Call your next rebuttal witness," the Judge said to the prosecution.

"No further rebuttal witnesses, "Ms. Larson replied.

"Any further rebuttal witness, Mr. Dandridge?" the judge inquired."

"Nothing further, your honor," I said.

"Does the defense rest?"

"Yes, Your Honor."

"Let's take 10 minutes before I instruct the jury and we hear the closing arguments," the judge said. "Sheriff, clear the court."

I wheeled around and looked at the courtroom clock. It was now two seventeen on Monday, September the fifteenth. The battle was nearly over and hopefully the battle had been won.

I left the court room alone and entered the conference room, hoping to remain alone. I had done my best, I kept telling myself and anything said and done by others I could not control; could I? I got up and walked around the room going over what had transpired in the courtroom. The door opened and Pete entered. He didn't say a word, but instead stood near the door waiting for me to speak.

"This is it Pete." I said anxiously.

"Yes, it is. You did good, Richard."

I lean my head to the side, "And now we have to hope the jury does the same."

"They will, Richard, they will. You still have the closing argument, don't forget, that one more time to slam the door shut on the prosecution."

"Yes, Pete..." I started, but stopped when the door opened again. This time it was Dr. Goodman who entered.

"Sorry to interrupt gentlemen, but I was able to get an earlier plane back home and need a ride to the airport." He anxiously announced.

I walked over and offered my hand. "Doctor, you did great. We appreciate your help on this case."

"Thank you Richard. I was glad to be of service," he replied.

"I believe my friend Pete, here can take you to the airport." I turned to look at Pete, who nodded his head. "Again thanks for helping us out with this case."

"You are welcomed."

"Are you ready, Doctor?" Pete asked.

"Yes, I am." I watched as Pete and Doctor Goodman went to the door, opened it and with one more turn to say 'goodbye', left the room. I was alone again and I stood reviewing my closing argument.

The door opened again. "Two minutes," Lincoln said, popping his head in. I sighed and grabbed my brief case, straightened my tie and followed Lincoln back into the courtroom.

The tension could be cut with a knife as Judge Nicholson entered. I stood not making eye contact with the state prosecutors knowing that each person in that courtroom was aware this was the final act before the jury would make their determination.

"Please be seated." All that could be heard was the rustling of fabric as people take their seats and Judge Nicholson wastes no time in resuming the trial.

***

"Ladies and gentlemen, good afternoon." he says. "We are ready to proceed with the closing arguments of counsel in the case of Lt. Vincent Trapp vs the State of New York, Murder In the

Second degree. Because the State has the burden of proof in the case, you will hear first from counsel for the State. And counsel for the defense will have an opportunity to present their closing argument. Following the arguments, I will instruct you on the law. We want to give a full and fair opportunity to both sides to present their arguments in the case. So, if the prosecution is ready, lets proceed, Mr. Walker."

"The prosecution is ready, Your Honor." Randall Walker replied. He rose from his chair theatrically, his blonde hair smoothed back, a slight closed mouth smile on his handsome face and what from my side angle seemed to be a wink at the jury. Continuing his theatrics, he dramatically turned to face each person as he addressed them by name.

"Judge Nicholson, Mr. Dandridge, my colleague Ms. Larson, ladies and gentlemen of the jury, good afternoon." Randall remained facing the jury and the jury stared directly at him, taking in his every word and gesture, of which there would be many.

"The events that were set in motion a little over a year ago are ending. On July 31, 2015, a crime of ghastly proportions was committed..." Randall Walker proceeded to make a very capable review of the People's case. When done, he presented the elements of the charges. "Thank you for your attention in this matter," Randall begins. "Ladies and gentlemen of the jury, there is a difference between "self-defense" and vengeance. There is a difference between self-defense and unreasonable actions. Also, there is a difference between what constitutes reasonable doubt, and what amounts to just excuses by the defendant. Ladies and gentlemen of the jury, the defendant, Lt. Trapp saw himself as judge and jury when he murdered Noah Arietta at his place of business that night. His aggressive conduct has no defense since he admittedly entered the Founder's Café bar and unloaded his pistol into Noah Arietta who was standing behind the bar and offering no threat to his person."

"There is a saying that actions speak louder than words. That is a true statement. We ask you to judge the Lieutenant Trapp by his actions, by what he did that night, not by what he said today in the courtroom. His claims today do not match his actions on that day in question."

"We are a nation of laws, and every one of us must follow those laws. If you have a problem with someone, you do not have the right to kill them. We live in a civilized society and as such our law doesn't allow that. And we all must live by these laws. We can't take the law into our own hands and murder a fellow human being. Sure, we all have faced times when we want to lash out, but we resist that impulse…"

I sit up in my chair and look at Randall who has paused in his argument, knowing he has just used the wrong word in his argument. I can't help the smile that creeps over my expression as I look at the jury and sincerely hope they will remember that slip; 'impulse'.

Randall walks over to the prosecution table and deftly avoids Ms. Larson's eyes as he takes a drink of water, straightens up and returns to his post by the jury.

"Each one of us must be in control of our faculties. It is part of living in a civilized society. Our system is a system that holds people responsible for things we do and that is part of what makes this country great."

"This notion of culpability has a big place in our criminal justice system, that we are all responsible for our actions. Now we don't always like being held answerable, and we don't always own up to what we have done, but we all must face the consequences of our own actions. Every one of us, including Lieutenant Trapp."

"The defense has essentially tried to put the victim on trial, pointing out that Noah Arietta is a womanizer and an alcoholic. But that doesn't justify what happened to him. It cannot. We are all entitled to the protection of the laws. I would submit to you that Mr. Arietta has more in common with us than we might think. He aspired like we do, he felt pain like we do, and he deserved a future like each one of us does. No matter how Mr. Arietta erred, he didn't deserve what happened to him."

"I want to talk about what I need to prove in this case. I also want to talk about what I don't have to prove. The law says I must prove beyond a reasonable doubt that on Friday, July 31, 2015, that the defendant shot and killed Noah Arietta, and did so intentionally, and that there was an absence of self-defense. I don't have to prove why, what the motive was, or whether the injury was caused by any actions against the defendant. Just that an assault occurred. That is what I must prove. That is, it. I don't have to prove that the defendant is a bad person. And you know what, I maybe couldn't prove that. This case, no case, is a judgment of a person. Rather it is a judgment of their actions. Maybe the defendant had a bad day, maybe he had too much to drink. And defendant isn't the first guy who found himself a little trouble on a Friday night, and he won't be the last."

"Ladies and gentlemen, there has been a violent killing in this county and we believe that the People have shown beyond any doubt that the killing was done by the defendant Lieutenant Trapp. We further believe we have shown beyond any reasonable doubt that the killing was done deliberately, maliciously, and in a fit of homicidal anger, and that it was done without legal justification or excuse." Randall continued.

"If you tell this man he has done nothing wrong, aren't you thereby telling the one million, eighty-three thousand people of

Monroe County and indeed all of the State of New York that they may safely go and do the same thing. I would ask that you find him accountable for what he did. And that is murder in the second degree. Thank you, Thank you."

Dramatically, Randall turned and walked briskly back to the prosecution table where Ms. Larson rose and congratulated him, loudly, after which Randall reclaimed his seat. Once Randall was seated, Judge Nicholson began, "Mr. Dandridge, are you ready to proceed with your closing arguments for the defense."

"I am, Your Honor."

"We will now hear the closing arguments of the defense"

As usual I try to adjust my features into a more endearing expression. I can't change my deep set eyes, but I can surely soften my gaze. I have practiced it enough. I know that chiseled features and deep set eyes in some situations are assets, but not in court. As I rose from my chair and moved to station myself near the jury, I turned to face each person as I addressed them; just like my colleague did before me. I paused in front of the jury and standing by the rail I spoke directly to them. "In his poem *Gratitude To The Unknown Instructors*, William Butler Yeats wrote, 'What they undertook to do, They brought to pass; All things hang like a drop of dew, Upon a blade of grass.' You, members of the jury are the Instructors and it is in your hands what will become of Lieutenant Trapp."

"We have arrived at the time when we seek to sway your minds to our side. We do this even though the truth be told if we have done our job well, there should be nothing more to say. But that is not the way of the court room law. So, at this point in the trial all I can hope for is that I can reveal a point or two that you might otherwise have overlooked. For surely it is impossible in the brief time allotted us here to cover all the facts and angles of this tangled blade of grass."

"I appreciate the patience that you've shown to all of us throughout these proceedings; and I know I can trust that patience yet again, but it's important that we discuss and think about and reflect upon what we've heard in this courtroom. As I said, it's my opportunity to review some of the evidence. It's my chance and I will review the charges, what is at stake, what are the criminal charges against Lt. Trapp, what must the State prove to you beyond a reasonable doubt before we can prevail and you can convict. When I'm done, you will have concluded that the evidence does not in fact sustain the charges against Lt. Trapp."

"When Dist. Atty. Randall Walker first spoke to you in the opening and told you what the State intended to do, to fairly present the evidence against Lt. Trapp, he told you that the evidence would make your job easier, that it would amount to overwhelming evidence of guilt, that it would build brick by brick, witness by witness, a wall, a wall that added up to the guilt of Lt. Trapp. Well, Lt. Trapp has never denied that he pulled the trigger and the evidence presented for the defense has removed, brick by brick, that wall."

"I do not think it is necessary for me to tell you that knowledge of all the facts, not just part of them, not just the part that helps one side or hurts the other is necessary for a fair and just trial. But that is what our Ms. Larson would want, and speaking of Ms. Larson, there is no question that the young prosecutor, Mr. Walker, had a right to ask for assistance in trying this case. His right is clear and plain and I make no issue whatever about that. But I say that assistance should be that and not appropriation. You have sat here for days now and watched this case stolen away from our young prosecutor before his very eyes. You have watched a deliberate and at times brilliant effort made here by the People, but not the police officers, I hasten to add, to suppress or distort evidence that it was the clear duty of the People and not the defendant to produce. I am not talking about routine objections on procedural matters or the form of a question or about evidence which the court has ruled inadmissible. I am talking about the studied and deliberate suppression of truth, about fundamental and important matters of truth which it was the People's clear duty to bring out, not keep out."

I paused to catch my breath and to control my voice which had taken an upswing. I look at the clock and in so doing see Pete sitting white-faced and grave over near the door. He must have broken all kinds of records getting to and from the airport. I turn to face the jury once again.

"The unfair tactics of the prosecution have been double-edge; to keep out the truth where possible and to insinuate that certain things were so without bothering to prove them. As an example of this let us take the People's greatest fiction of all, the ludicrous assumption that Paige Trapp was not brutally beaten and raped by Noah Arietta that night. Yes, for days now you have watched, Ms. Larson fight the fact of that rape tooth and nail, with all the sidestepping and stonewalling she could muster."

"As a lovely example of the second tactic of perversion and sly insinuation let us take the incident of Terry Kenyon having supposedly danced with Paige Trapp with her shoes in his pocket. Yet I ask you now; who in this whole courtroom has ever once testified she did that? Who alone has inferred it but Ms. Larson herself? You will recall how she clawed away endlessly at Mrs. Trapp on that score. Yet if that had actually happened could not Terry Kenyon have testified to it when he was first called? Would the clever Ms. Larson have missed that chance to smear our lady?

And if he forgot to then could not Mr. Kenyon have been called in rebuttal after Mrs. Trapp had denied it?" If this thing actually happened Terry should have remembered it. Or if he forgot, surely there was someone in the bar that night who would have recalled it."

"But the most interesting thing about these tactics is the why of them. So what, you may be tempted to ask yourselves, so what if she did or didn't dance that way? Well, I'll tell you why. Because the clever Ms. Larson was trying slyly to plant in your minds the picture of a Paige Trapp as an abandoned and willful woman who would drink whisky neat and dance barefoot with strangers and thus presumably go out and lay up with the first man that came along. Because Ms. Larson, who dares not meet this rape issue head on, seeks subtly to confuse you and make you thing this brutal rape was a mutual affair. That is why."

"Consider if you will Ms. Larson's cross-examination of Mrs. Trapp's personal life while she was on the stand. Her gallant raking over of Ms. Trapp's background, bringing out the fact that she was divorced, the awful revelation that she once sold cosmetics and worked as a saleslady and even dared answer telephones. What does Ms. Larson mean by all this? What does it signify? Does she mean to stamp all divorcees as immoral? Does she infer that all beauty and telephone operators are abandoned women? If she didn't mean that, then why did she buzz away at her like a bee to bring all that out?

"Yes, ladies and gentlemen, she battered and tore away at this woman in every clever and insinuating way she could because in her heart of hearts she knew that what happened to Ms. Trapp would be important to you, the jury. But, let me remind you, never once did Ms. Larson refer to anything as coarse as the brutal assault and rape Mrs. Trapp suffered at the hands of the deceased man, Noah Arietta. Never once did Ms. Larson mention anything about a lie detector test which could have set her mind at ease. If Ms. Larson didn't and still doesn't believe Mrs. Trapp's rape story, then why in Heaven's name didn't she question her about the rape? Do you think for a moment Ms. Larson was gallantly trying to spare her feelings? Do you think she wouldn't have assaulted her with every offensive weapon in her arsenal if she had proof the rape had not happened?"

"Ask yourself, what does Ms. Larson need to become convinced of this rape? I wonder how much proof she would need if, she were instead defending this case? Ah then the proverbial shoe might be on the other foot or perhaps I should say, in Terry's other pocket."

"Have any of you so soon forgotten how, when the Judge was not looking, this morning, she several times got between me and the testifying Lieutenant? Why? I'll tell you why. In order to get me angry, in which she so richly succeeded, but mostly in order to plant in your minds the sinister notion that I was signaling to my client. I turned toward Ms. Larson as I spoke to emphasize my point, then turned back toward the jury. "But after all this case is not a gladiatorial contest between Ms. Larson and me. Your verdict is not a television giveaway price to be awarded the side that puts on the best show. No, ladies and gentlemen the stakes here are far bigger than Jean Larson, Randall Walker and Richard Dandridge. They have to do with some old fashioned things, big things like truth, and justice and fair play. They have to do with the fate and future of a man who sits here being judged by you."

The Sheriff appeared with a glass and pitcher of water that he put on the court reporter's table. I paused and nodded gratefully then turned, smiled at the jury before walking over and pouring a glass that I hurriedly gulped down. I sat the glass back on the tray then checked my facial expression before turning and walking back to the jury. "I wonder if any of you would ever have known that anyone had been raped in this case if I had not kept pounding away through the objections of Ms. Larson? And what purpose has all her objections served? Members of the jury, we could have been done with this case many hours if not days ago if the People had faced up to the reality of this rape, which they still do not admit. We didn't and we won't deny the shooting; as we have never denied it. That was obvious from the start of this case and the People knew it long before that, ever since we filed our written plea of insanity, way back in August. Yet they have spent hour after hour and witness after witness and incidentally dollar after public dollar blocking the obvious case of insanity issue. Ms. Larson has used up hour after dreary hour trying to hide and suppress this rape, the rape that surely no fair-minded person in this courtroom can any longer doubt took place. In a way, she is right to do so since it is not the rape itself or the man who raped Mrs. Paige who is on trial here. It is instead whether or not the Lieutenant believed, reasonably believed that it happened and how that reasonable belief affected him."

I then reviewed in detail the evidence pointing toward the rape as the reason why the Lieutenant ended up shooting Noah Arietta, reminding the jury that practically all of it had gone on record against the objection of Ms. Larson. I advanced closer to Randall's table and pointed at Ms. Larson. "You still do not admit this rape. You still want to picture Mrs. Trapp as a slut. You are still obsessed with your desire to go home in your state-owned car with the Lieutenant's life being a feather hanging from your rearview mirror. Well, Ms. Larson, I dare you to admit the rape! I turned toward Randall, "and I dare you to admit the rape took place, too!" I said this last as I leaned over the prosecution table with my face inches from Ms. Larson's.

I knew at that moment I could not face the jury because I could feel the tightening of my jaw and the lowering of my eyes into slits. Carefully I moved back and counted to five and when I turned and walked before the jury there was a hint of a smile on my face. As soon as I was ready, I began to review the harmful portion of Detective Sergeant Kenneth Parker's testimony. "As you will recall, the Detective told us that on the drive down to the precinct the Lieutenant said he had thought the whole thing over before going to the bar and had decided that such a man should not be allowed to live and that the Lieutenant appeared to him to be upset and emotional and seemed very angry."

As much as wanted to ignore this, it frankly had to be faced because it would not go away by ignoring it. "People," I continued, "maybe the Lieutenant did say these things. The fact that Sergeant Kent says so is pretty good proof that they were said. We cannot have our cake and eat it too. We cannot fairly pick out the parts of the Sergeant's testimony that please us and reject the rest. Only the hardy Ms. Larson seems able to undertake that miracle. But supposing the Lieutenant did say these things? Was he still not in the shock of his mental lapse, still gripped by the massive blast to his psyche, still groping his way back to reality, still trying to put a rational face on the dreadful thing he was slowly realizing he had done? In that case, I believe that the Judge will instruct you that you may acquit this man, even if he said these things and realized he was saying them, if at the actual time of the shooting you believe he was in the grip of what is known as irresistible impulse."

I checked my time and hurried on. I pointed out that if the Lieutenant had awakened and come upon Noah raping his wife and had killed him, there would doubtless have been no trial and the Lieutenant would instead have got a new medal to add to his combat decorations. "But here," I went on, "the difference is that the woman was not discovered in any act of adultery or while being raped, but had, however mistakenly trusted a wolf who had offered to drive her

542

home. Ah, yes, instead she was assaulted, pounded, choked, raped, mauled, tripped, kicked, repeatedly struck, the last time practically within a stone's throw of her sleeping husband, but now the killing becomes murder."

"Ladies and gentlemen, some of you may be asking yourselves why? Why have I been spending so much time here trying to show the obvious truth, namely that the dead man Noah Arietta was drinking heavily, that he was acting peculiarly, that he was an awesome physical specimen who kept in shape and that he was an expert shot who possessed pistols and knew well how to use them? Some of you may also have been wondering why our friend, Ms. Larson has so strenuously sought to keep these truths out."

I paused and drank some water before I continued. "Well, if Ms. Larson could suppress these truths she could then argue that Noah Arietta was unable physically to overpower and rape this woman and do to her the things he did, that in any case she should have put up more resistance and that therefore this sexual collision was not rape; that Lieutenant Trapp did not need to take a gun when he went to... in his words, grasp and hold this man for the police, that he therefore did so solely to slay him, and last but not least, that the unarmed caretaker, Mr. Appleton was the man he instead should have sent to grasp Noah Arietta." I again paused. "These I believe are the answers in a nutshell, this is why our Ms. Larson has spent days here trying relentlessly to baffle and block any attempt by me to show Noah Arietta as anything other than a nice, quiet, and harmless professional man."

I hurriedly gulped another glass of water. "Yes," I ran on, "the People, so zealously represented by Ms. Larson, will doubtless argue that the Lieutenant should have taken the unarmed caretaker out of his midnight bed to go over and arrest this man crouching in his lair behind the bar with his arsenal of weapons he so well knew how to use. Wouldn't that have been the fine, manly, legal thing to do?"

"People," I said, "to be competent jurors you need not check your hearts in the jury cloakroom. There is no mystery about your role here. It is to use your heads and also your hearts. If Noah Arietta did this thing to Paige Trapp, there were exactly three courses open to him. One, he could have given himself up. He didn't. Two, he could have run away or destroyed himself. He didn't. Three, he could have stayed and determined to brazen it out. He did. The great Noah Arietta, running true to form, returned to his bar and sent his bartender off, whether as lookout or whatnot we shall probably never know. He quickly replaced the bartender and with a buffer of patrons as his witnesses waited confidently for the showdown, primed by his whisky and his enormous ego, surrounded by his pals, his pistols and medals and his ever faithful lookout. Noah could not stand behind the bar staring at the door, he had desperately to play the part of the cool and calm one. That is why he had to give his tired bartender a 'rest' so he could serve drinks and chat with the clientele while his bartender stood nearly an hour over by the door and gave him the signal when Lt. Trapp arrived."

"But, you may ask yourselves, if Noah was waiting for the Lieutenant to come, with or without a lookout, why didn't he shot the Lieutenant the moment he entered the door? Ah, folks, that would not only have been murder, but murder added to a tacit confession of rape. That would have given the show away. Noah was on the spot. Noah knew what he had done but the others didn't. Had Noah mounted a Colt M-16 assault rifle on the bar and shot the Lieutenant down as he entered the door, he would by that very act have confessed his rape. Don't you see? Noah had to wait for the Lieutenant to advance into the room so that when the expected shoot-out came, the big scene, the accusation, the argument, even a hostile move for a gun, then the great marksman Noah could shoot the man down in front of witnesses and plausibly claim the whole thing was done in self-defense. He had to gamble that he was faster on the draw than Lieutenant Trapp. Can't you see, this tense bar drama was all carefully staged?" I lowered my voice. "The only thing that went wrong was that Noah forgot, or didn't know the Lieutenant was left-handed, that and the fact that at last he had met his match. He lost his grim gamble, he at last lost his first pistol shoot. This time the medal he lost happened to be his own life."

Time was fleeing as I rushed on. "No, the Lieutenant didn't send a sleepy unarmed man but went himself and did so legally, as I believe the Judge will so instruct you." This was the instruction that Pete had toiled over so long. "surely, people, this man Noah was not the savior of the world, but instead this handsome man with his tight curly black hair and blue eyes was a womanizer, a dangerous maniac and a sharp shooter. In either case he was a man who had just committed, in aggravated form, one of the gravest felonies on our books. I believe the Lieutenant had every right to go there and seize that man. I believe the Judge will tell you so. Because the taunting sight of his wife's tormentor may have unhinged the Lieutenant's reason, does it seem right that you are now asked to ruin his life."

I looked at the clock and stepped forward. "Our prosecutor has pointed out in his opening argument that if the deceased had intended any harm to Mrs. Trapp he would not have bothered to drive her to the park gate in the first place," I said, "The implication of that argument is, of course, that some mysterious thing happened between the bar and the gate that led Noah to believe his romantic advances would not be unwelcomed. Now, that argument has a certain glib plausibility, a surface persuasiveness, but I wonder if it will stand analysis? I wonder, people, whether this is not the true

545

reason why Noah Arietta drove her first to the gate. He knew the gate was locked. He had already formed his design to have at this woman. He already knew that she was reluctant and nervous about riding with him. By first driving her to the gate, which he well knew was locked, he could thus allay her suspicious and hide his real intentions. If on the contrary he had simply driven past the gate road without turning in, a point which the chart shows is still right in the town, she would immediately have become suspicious and could have caused a commotion, drawing the attention of a passing car or a pedestrian. His plan worked, when he made his final turn off on the 'rape' road, far down the main road, it was too late, any screams then would have been futile, she was finally in his power." I paused. "Is that not more obvious the real reason why he drove her to the gate at all?"

One of the jurors was all but nodding his head at me. Embarrassed, I looked at the woman next to him, an obese middle aged woman who had sat wide eyed during the entire trial watching rather beholding the proceedings, with a tense expression on her face. Now she stared at me openly, so I did a face check to be sure I was not returning her look with a stern expression.

I swiftly reviewed the testimony of the bartender concerning Noah's drinking and the guns and all the rest; the revealing wolf designation he had pinned on Noah, the unsought sympathy he had bestowed on the Trapps, and the expression of regret over the broken mirror and bottle of top shelf bourbon. My argument was verging on a sensitive area and for Tyra Pederson's sake I had to try to cover it obliquely. "And who was it that dragged whatever truth of these things we finally got out of this witness? Not our Ms. Larson, certainly. You will recall how hostile this bartender was when I first cross-examined him. At first he would have nothing unusual to share about his boss, Noah Arietta, either concerning his drinking or otherwise. He painted a picture of that night at the Founder's Café bar being the setting for a summer nirvana."

I glanced back at the frowning bartender and then returned to the jury. "I wonder why the witness changed? Could it have had something to do with Noah's estate or his insurance? Or was someone growing afraid of perjury?" I paused. "In any case, when I got him back again on the stand something certainly had changed, for whatever reason. I then dragged out of him over Ms. Larson's objections that things had been normal, indeed Noah normal. Because Noah was still gulping his double shots as greedily as ever, that his behavior was still normally queer, that things were so placidly normal and fine., in fact, that some of his arsenal of guns had to be locked up while at least two others were unaccounted for. Yes, that's how really normal things were around that seething apartment building, café and bar." I paused. "And isn't that what the bartender really meant when he told Mrs. Trapp it was too bad they had come to the Founder's Café when they did?"

I checked my time again. "We now come to our defense of irresistible impulse, to the battle of the psychiatrists. Doubtless, Ms. Larson will call our young doctor a charlatan and a faker for failing to use the impressive sounding tests that she, Ms. Larson, had so glibly learned by heart from the People's doctor. Let me review Milo S. Goodman M.D. Dr. Goodman is an active clinician and expert witness. As a specialist in Forensic Psychiatry, his testimony has had a major impact in high profile cases. He is Assistant Professor of Psychiatry and Human Behavior at The Thomas Jefferson University College of Medicine and a Special Guest Lecturer at Widener University School of Law. I could go on and on, but I won't. Does this sound like an incompetent charlatan to you?"

The jumbled mosaic of evidence pointing toward insanity had to be reviewed, and I swiftly reviewed it, along with the testimony of young Doctor Goodman. "Now, Dr. Goodman has told you of his intensive examination of the Lieutenant upon which he based his opinion." I went on. "this is flatly opposed by the testimony of Dr. Mason Anderson, the prosecutions psychiatrist. There is no way to reconcile their opinions, one of these men is dead wrong." I paused. "If the stakes here were not so high I might be tempted charitably to overlook Dr. Anderson's testimony and pass it by. This poor man in one breath tells us our doctor's tests were no good, that he would have given a whole flock of others, but then in the next breath he dares to pass a professional opinion on this man's sanity without any tests whatever. In his final breath, when he was cornered he reluctantly admits, over a final barrage of Ms. Larson's protective objections, that this is not normal or recognized psychiatric procedure."

I turned to look at Dr. Anderson. "This is the same diplomate who made no attempt to examine the Lieutenant although he had been here four days. I wonder what he meant by his testimony that no man could go mad when such a thing happened to his wife? He does not tell us. If he meant that none could, then I wonder when and under what circumstances any man could ever be expected to lose his mind over an emotional or psychic shock? If the Doctor instead meant that some men might go insane over such a shocking event, but not this man. Then I wonder what psychiatric basis of observation or examination he used to arrive at that conclusion? He does not tell us. "About this doctor we know very little. We know he has been in practice for around twenty-five years and is the chief executive officer and medical director of six institutions for the medically insane and specializes in the treatment of serious psychiatric diseases, such as clinical depression, schizophrenia, and bipolar disorder. Ms. Larson, couldn't hustle the poor man off the stand fast enough when I had finished examining him."

"If the doctor meant that he believed the Lieutenant was sane that night because he, the doctor, didn't believe his wife had been raped, then, along with our two die hard prosecutors, he is possibly the lone holdout in this room on that score. In any case I believe the Judge will tell you that it is not what actually happened that is the guiding test in these insanity cases, but what the insanity victim reasonably believed had happened. And this is true both psychiatrically and legally. People unfortunately go insane every day over something imaginary so does Dr. Anderson mean to say that men never go insane when faced with something real?"

I paused and shook my head. "There is something shameful about this performance we have seen here. If a medical doctor had done a thing like this he would be called a quack, a lawyer a shyster. When a man will casually make a mockery out of a whole profession, one to which he has presumably dedicated his life, then the lie takes on larger dimensions." I pounded the mahogany jury rail so hard with my fist that I wondered vaguely if I would ever again be able to use that hand. "And a lie of that kind is all the more vicious and reckless because we ordinary mortals lack the training to evaluate it." I shook my head. "It makes one think that a man must first be a good man before he can be a good psychiatrist."

"Ladies and gentlemen," I pressed on, "I take no pleasure in having to be so harsh on this doctor. His testimony would be laughable if the stakes weren't so high and the attempted use of his testimony so callous and mockingly bold. But when any man dares to come into court and tamper with the destiny of a man charged with second degree murder, then he is treating us as fools and he warrants our contempt."

I paused and mopped my brow. Both my temperature and voice were rising but it only helped to emphasize my point so I turned and again pointed at Jean Larson. "but however, we may criticize this poor doctor, it is the woman who instigated his coming here to testify on such a pitifully inadequate professional basis who deserves the full blast of our contempt. Was poor doctor Anderson sacrificed here on the altar by someone for whom law and justice and freedom is merely a cynical game?" I glanced back at the clock. "So much for Wechsler-Bellevue and the global capacity of a person to act purposefully, to think rationally, and to deal effectively with his environment."

"It is Lieutenant Trapp who is on trial here for murder and not his wife. It was the rape of his wife that he believed happened that made him snap. It is what Lt. Trapp believed happened that counts and how his mind reacted. And finally that it is his freedom and future that is at stake. We've had everything happen in this trial. We've even had a trained dog act with the little dog Enzo and his flashlight. Yes, Enzo was an important defense witness bearing on Mrs. Trapp's story of the rape. Having him appear here it was obvious that he was a friendly little animal who likely would not and obviously could not have prevented this rape, and, on a lighter note, he could indeed have shown his mistress through woods with his flashlight."

"There are things in this case we will never know," I raced on, "Things which seem to have nothing to do with the Trapps, and I have time but to suggest a few. Why was Noah drinking so hard? Why was it necessary to lock up his guns? Why did he apply for more life insurance a few weeks before that terrible evening? Consider soberly if you will the enormous sense of betrayal that must have afflicted Lieutenant Trapp that night. Why do I speak of betrayal? Not only had he the knowledge that his wife had been

raped and abused, but the almost as bitter knowledge that all this was done by a civilian, by one of those lucky ones for whom the Lieutenant had risked his life in two wars so that Noah might continue to drink double shots and blithely play wolf and shoot up empty whisky bottles. I do not try to turn this into an issue of the expectations of a man who has served his country against one who has not. These are the facts."

"Let me cite a case for your known as the M'Naghten's Case which may help you in deciding on the case before you. Defendant, M'Naghten was charged with the murder of Edward Drummond, secretary to the Prime Minister and used the insanity defense at trial. At the time of his arrest, he told police that he came to London to murder the Prime Minister because he was told to do so. The jury reached a verdict of not guilty and a meeting at the House of Lords ensued in order to determine what the standards for the insanity defense would be. What they decided was that in order to establish an insanity defense, it must be clearly proven that at the time of the act, the accused was under such a defect of reason from disease of the mind that he did not know the nature and quality of the act he was committing; or if he did know, he did not know what he was doing was wrong."

"I am seeking a verdict of irresistible impulse; an Insanity Defense of a special nature. The prevailing theory posits that two distinct and interconnected brain systems interact with one another and compete for behavioral outcomes. The impulsive system that involves the amygdala provides an immediate signal of pain or pleasure; the reflective system that involves the vmPFC, considers the long-term consequences of behavioral alternatives. Simply put, impulsivity results from an imbalance between these systems: the latter is unable to check the push for immediate action signaled by the former. This imbalance may derive from many different genetic and environmental causes and may be diagnosed or labeled in myriad ways. But for present purposes the end product is the same: the subject's ability to suppress impulsive behavior is substantially diminished compared to the average person."

"The behavioral manifestations of this imbalance have been studied in experimental settings. Remarkably, such persons usually know that their behavior is sub-optimal: they report an abstract understanding of the wrongfulness of their choices but cannot stop themselves from making them under the pull of emotion in the moment of decision."

"It is not surprising that people differ in their ability to control impulses. Nor is it surprising that impulsivity correlates with structural and functional differences in people's brains."

"That the brain and the nervous system are the organs by which all mental operations are conducted is now well established and generally admitted. When a man either feels, knows, believes, remembers, is conscious of motives, deliberates, wills, or carries out his determination, his brain and his nerves do something definite."

"It does not follow, however, that neuroscience can tell us whether defendants are morally or legally responsible for their actions. While informed by empirical knowledge, responsibility is a normative standard. But science does suggest that some people, in some situations, may find it next to impossible to control their behavior, even if they know it is wrong. Given the prevailing theories of legal responsibility, this raises the question of whether the punishment of such persons is either just or efficient."

"The legal answer to this question has varied both temporally and jurisdictionally. The history of control tests in the United States is illustrative. Before M'Naghten, most U.S. jurisdictions used a simple "right and wrong" test for insanity; by the 1950's, most had adopted common law or legislative versions of M'Naghten. But even before M'Naghten, a few courts had supplemented the "right and wrong" test with control tests.

"This fits Lieutenant Trapp. This too fits the position of Lieutenant Trapp. I say this to be true but to give you an example to help you see it too, suppose that a child has been brutally assaulted. If an otherwise conscientious and law-abiding mother shoots the perpetrator, the mother may argue that she was so enraged that she became mentally ill and incapable of exerting self-control."

I went on knowing that most jurors expect and thirst for a final statement that gives life to the person on trial. I paused and reflected a moment. "Can you possibly find it in your hearts not to add to the woes of my client. To subject him to the sentence of this court, will ruin his career and shut off his sole means of income. You will force his wife Paige Trapp to seek employment so that her husband will have a home to return to. How much ruin are you going to permit this Noah Arietta to leave in his wake? Whatever happens here has brought lasting degradation and shame on Lt. Trapp and his family. Mr. Arietta has beaten and raped and nearly killed another man's wife. He has set in motion the Lieutenant's arrest and this harrowing and expensive trial."

I paused. "Can you possibly want by your verdict to let the great Noah work one final bit of mischief from the grave?"

I lowered my voice and held up my cupped hand. "People, you are not dealing with a hypothetical lieutenant now, but a living, pulsing, suffering human being, a man whose destiny you hold in the palm of your hand." I turned and looked at the Lieutenant who sat white-faced staring at the opposite wall. "Look at this man, up here on trial for his freedom. Surely it would be an act of Christian charity as well as your legal duty to show by your verdict that up in our neck of the woods all decency is not dead, that justice is not a mere lawyers game played by a big voice like that of Ms. Larson that all our traditional friendliness is not a false prelude to betrayal."

So, ladies and gentlemen, this is where I finish. And I'll sit down, and I'm going to think of the five things that I should have talked to you about; and then tonight I'm going to think about the next five, and tomorrow the next five. I think I can speak for everyone about the attentiveness of you individually and collectively. I think we all sort of steal glances from each other from time-to-time. And we lawyers think, What are they thinking? And how are they going to do this important job in this case where it's so important to the defense, the prosecutors, the law enforcement, to the Trapp family and the other families and injured people

You have a terrible burden; and, frankly, I'm glad -- and I think I can speak for Ms. Larson, Mr. Walker as well as myself -- that we're thankful that we're not in your position. We can work hard and we can present away and we can try to do what we're supposed to do with a professional perspective. But our job is easy compared to yours. Good luck."

This has taken its toll. I wearily go back to the defense table and have barely sat down when there is a prolonged whistling expiring sigh from the courtroom behind me, like the sound of a truck tire going flat, and I looked around and see that people are standing around something or someone on the floor. "Move back," someone says and the crowd disperses and I see one of the homicide students has fainted dead away. She lays on the wooden floor, her arms bent at the elbows aligned on either side of her face. Her legs are straight out in front of her. I see the Sheriff coming forward with the left over water and he shoves his way through those standing in the aisle until he is able to hold her head up and pour water slowly into her mouth.

554

There is silence as all eyes are now on the woman and when she hiccups, there is a group sigh of relief. I watch as Lincoln helps her to her feet and then sits her down on a chair. It is at that point I wonder if she was overcome by my eloquent closing statement, but that is soon to be discounted.

I felt Paige Trapp taping my shoulder and I turned toward her. In a voice barely above a whisper she said, "You were wonderful. Thank you, Richard," she said, and there were tears in her green eyes.

The Lieutenant cleared his throat. "She's right, you did good," he said.

"Thank you, it means a lot to hear you say this. We still have to wait to see how 'good' I really did." I said, rising shaking their hands and making my way out of the courtroom. As I scrabbled to the conference room, Pete fell in by my side and grasped my hand in both of his. "Great," he whispered huskily, and then turned away, thoughtfully leaving me to sit alone in a chair by the window looking out over the manicured lawn, meditatively, until Lincoln Harper reminded me it was time.

"You were brilliant Mr. Dandridge," Lincoln said. "Good for you."

"Thank you, Lincoln," I said knocking knuckles with him and then grabbing my brief case."

Chapter 19

Judge Nicholson begins, "Ladies and gentlemen, we are ready to proceed with the closing arguments of counsel in this case. Because the State has the burden of proof in the case, you heard first from counsel for the State and counsel for the defense had their opportunity to argue. Now then counsel for the State have an opportunity for a rebuttal argument from the remaining prosecutor."

As I sit there at the defense table, I only hope I have covered everything; god knows I tried. That is my thoughts as I sit in a mental trance watching as the Judge nodded at the People's table and Jean Larson hoisted her amble body up then walked slowly to the front of the courtroom. She was already playing her last card by giving the jury a good chance to see this motherly, even grandmotherly grey haired woman with a chin length straight pageboy hair style that went well with her thin framed silver glasses. Even I was enchanted. Finally, she reached her destination and gave her broad and unpretentious smile a vision of softness and sweetness, the perfect ending to present the prosecutions summation.

During Randall's argument and the earlier phases of mine I had observed her busily taking notes, but now she carried nothing and stood thoughtful and empty handed before the jury, speaking in a low, almost conversational tone of voice.

"First of all, ladies and gentlemen, I want to compliment my young associate on the way he has conducted his case. It was a

556

pleasure to assist such a sterling young man." Having gracefully tried to give the case back to Randall she paused and turned, looking at me. "I also want to compliment Mr. Dandridge on his spirited and thorough defense of this case. If he thinks I am tough, then it has indeed been a good match. In any case, whatever happens, whatever you may decide, Lieutenant Trapp should never have any regrets over his choice of lawyer or over the capable and astute way that lawyer has fought for him."

She had drawn me into her act and having no other recourse, I nod gravely as Jean Larson turns back to the jury. "But I must remind you, ladies and gentlemen," she went on, "that it is not I who am on trial here as the astute defense has seemed to suggest. Nor, is it the deceased man, Noah Arietta who must answer to this crime. And finally, it is not the People's psychiatrist, Dr. Anderson who was attacked by defense for presenting an expert medical presentation. No, ladies and gentlemen it is Lieutenant Trapp who is on trial and if you will bear with me, I shall review the elements that lead to the proofs in this case and that in our view will show his guilt of murder beyond a reasonable doubt."

Jean Larson unfolded her hand. "Murder, my friends," she said leaning in toward the jury members. "Murder is a deliberate, malicious and premeditated killing of a person without legal justification or excuse."

"You have heard three detailed testimonies here that support our stance that this was murder by all definitions. First, there is the time lapse between Mrs. Trapp returning to her home, telling the Lieutenant she had been raped, and the time when the Lieutenant made his way to the bar at the Founders Cafe. It wasn't until he had helped his wife calm down and then help clean her up and saw the alleged telltale fluid on his wife's person did he make the decision to go to the Founders Café bar. This is when his true feelings began to surface. When it all boiled up to possess the Lieutenant in a grip of cold and merciless fury."

"But my friends, that wasn't the end of it. The Lieutenant's wife even predicted that her husband would kill Noah because she knew her husband's quick temper and jealous nature. She knew this because her husband, the defendant, had once struck a young fellow Army officer for kissing his wife's hand. You remember that testimony, my friends, the 'Buster' testimony of the bartender when the Lieutenant had asked him if he wanted some too."

Jean Larson persisted. "We have in addition the revealing remarks the Lieutenant made to Detective Sergeant Kent shortly after the shooting. I ask you are these," she demanded, "are these the actions and statements of an insane man or rather are they those of a man remorseful after a homicidal outburst of anger over the behavior of his wife with a strange man?"

She was good. In one breath she put a human swing on the actions of the Lieutenant so that it did not appear as though she was attacking him. Yet, that breath had me on the edge of my seat, for a brief moment when I thought she would slip and admit there had been a rape. I peered cautiously at the faces of the jurors and I could tell they were hanging on her every word. I lowered my eyes and said a little prayer for our side. That was all I had left to do, except listen to this expert do her job.

"Let me outline his movements. The Lieutenant deliberately and knowingly took a loaded gun; there is no question but he remembered doing that, and drove swiftly over to the Academy Building where the Founder's café and bar are located. Once there he did not look left nor right, but focused his eyes and his ears on Noah Arietta and not greeting those who spoke to him. He entered the bar and shot the man down like a dog and then returned to his home and told his wife what he had done. Next he gave himself up to the deputy sheriff who lived on his property. He would tell the sheriff that he had shot Noah Arietta." Jean finally paused to catch her breath. "Now if he was insane how could he have known he shot Noah? And if he remembered shooting Noah then he wasn't insane."

The jury's attention never wavered as Jean Larson quietly poured it on. "And if he was able to recount and remember what happened right before and again right after the shooting, why should he later and now conveniently forget the detrimental details he told Sergeant Kent upwards of an hour later?" she demanded. "Isn't this rather the picture of a calculating man who conveniently forgot whatever might harm him?"

I couldn't help taking another look at the jury. Several of the jurors involuntarily nodded and I turned and rolled my eyes as I looked over at Pete. I lifted my shoulders in a shrug as I turned my attention back to Ms. Larson. "And remember this, good people, this man took the law into his own hands. If the deceased had even done the things the defense claims, which we do not admit, there were legal ways to deal with Mr. Arietta rather than shooting him. There isn't any legal defense for what the Lieutenant did. I am sure the Judge will instruct you on this. And in taking the law into his own hands, the Lieutenant broke the law. And, do not forget that he also broke the law by carrying a concealed weapon on his person."

Jean Larson then moved on to the insanity issue and, in her adroit and plausible way, did a rather remarkable job of rehabilitating the People's psychiatrist.

"Even the defense's, own doctor found no psychosis, no neurosis, no delusions, no hallucinations, and no history of insanity or dissociative reaction." Ms. Larson insinuated that, Dr. Anderson was older and thus more experienced in the field of psychiatry, while our man, however sincere and dedicated, was still learning the trade. "The defense should not have used a boy to do a man's job," she said in her melodious voice.

"As for counsel's comment that we did not request a personal examination of the Lieutenant, I may add that no chance or opportunity to do so was offered." She paused and glanced back at me. "I have a suspicion, that had we tried to examine this man Mr. Dandridge would have thrown up stumbling blocks to prevented it."

I managed not to shake my head as I thought to myself, I should have known she would go there. I glance wryly over at Pete as Jean Larson continued soberly All I could hope was that the jury recalled that they did have an opportunity.

Ms. Larson skillfully drew the noose of argument ever more tightly around the neck of Lieutenant Trapp. There was something at once admirable and frightening as she sought only to convict. She was doing her job, I had to admit, so let her do her dance.

"Defense counsel and the psychiatrist make light of the fact of whether the defendant knew what he was doing and whether it was wrong. They tell you that it makes no difference but it does make a difference. If in fact he did know and remember what he was doing and lied to you about it, then he has not only lied to his lawyer and doctor but deliberately perjured himself on a material issue in this case. If so, then the court will instruct you, to disregard all of his testimony, including his defense of insanity, unless it is corroborated by other and credible witnesses whose testimony you do believe. So unlike you where lead to believe by the defense, it makes a whale of a big difference whether this man lied."

Ms. Larson walked over to the table and poured herself a glass of water. She turned to look at the jurors as she daintily drank, then checked her mouth before walking back to her station near the jury. "Now it is quite possible that Lieutenant Trapp has fooled his able lawyer, and that he has fooled his youthful psychiatrist. As Mr. Dandridge has so well pointed out, none of us is infallible."

Jean Larson paused and glanced at the clock. "Ladies and gentlemen, I am nearly done." Jean Larson went on. "Please keep in mind the difference between insanity and passion. There is an ocean of difference between insanity and passion. For one thing, insanity is a general condition of mental disorder. It is a state where one cannot discern what is logical or not and what is right from wrong. It is a general break of mind from the realities of life. Passion on the other hand is a very strong feeling about a person or thing. It is an intense emotion or a compelling enthusiasm or desire for something. Consider if you will how easy it is to simulate the one and twist the other into symptoms of mental abnormalities. Indeed, homicidal passion and murderous anger is in itself a form of mental lapse but, fortunately the law does not recognize it as a defense to cold and brutal murder."

Ms. Larson walked slowly down the length of the jury box. "This is a serious case. Certainly it is serious to the defendant. It is equally serious to the People because someone has been murdered at the hands of another. It is your job to conscientiously evaluate the evidence in this case and apply your logic and your common sense and your reasoning powers and the law given to you by Judge Nicholson to that evidence, and thereby reach a just and a fair verdict." She was pounding the nails in the coffin. "When you apply the law and your logic and your common sense and your reasoning powers to the evidence in this case, you won't have any difficulty whatsoever coming to the conclusion that the prosecution proved the guilt of this defendant beyond all reasonable doubt."

Jean Larson stared deeply into the eyes of each juror as she continued her march, "Ladies and gentlemen, the prosecution did its job in gathering and presenting the evidence. The witnesses did their job by taking that witness stand and testifying under oath. Now you are the last link in the chain of justice."

"Ladies and gentlemen of the jury, Noah Arietta is not here with us now in this courtroom, but from his grave he cries out for justice. Justice can only be served by coming back to this courtroom with a verdict of guilty. Under the laws of this state and nation this defendant was entitled to have his day in court." Jean swings her body around and points a finger at Lt. Trapp. "He got that. He was also entitled to have a fair trial by an impartial jury. He also got that. That is all that he is entitled to. Since he committed this savage, senseless murder, the people of the state of New York are entitled to a guilty verdict." She takes a visible deep breath before saying, "Thank you very much. "

Her presentation is over and all eyes watch as Jean Larson bows gravely and walks purposely back to her seat.

Chapter 20

It was now Judge Nicholson's turn as he looked down at the prosecutions table and asks, "Are there any additional requests for instructions from the prosecution for the jury?"

"No Your Honor," Randall replied, slightly rising from his chair.

The Judge looked next in my direction. "I have your request for instructions Mr. Dandridge. Is there anything you wish to add at this point?"

"No, Your Honor," I said. "At this time I also submit to the prosecuting attorney true copies of our requests."

"Very well, counsel," the Judge said, looking out at the courtroom clock and tilting his head back and peering through the bottoms of his bifocals as he opened a leather portfolio laying in front of him. He stared down at the papers before him then leaning slightly forward turned to the jury and cleared his throat. "Members of the jury, I will now instruct you on the law. I will first review the general principles of law that apply to this case and all criminal cases. You have heard me explain some of those principles at the beginning of the trial but I'm sure you appreciate the benefits of repeating those instructions at this stage of the proceedings. Next, I will define the crime charged in this case, explain the law that applies to those definitions, and spell out the elements of each charged crime. Finally, I will outline the process of jury deliberations. During these instructions, I will not summarize the evidence. If necessary, I may refer to portions of the evidence to explain the law that relates to it. My reference to evidence, or my failure to refer to evidence, expresses no opinion about the truthfulness, accuracy, or importance of any particular evidence. In fact, nothing I have said and no questions I have asked in the course of this trial were meant to suggest that I have an opinion about this case. If you have formed an impression that I do have an opinion, you must put it out of your mind and disregard it."

Judge Nicholson picked up his glass and drank before continuing. "The level of my voice or intonation may vary during these instructions. If I do that, it is done to help you understand these instructions. It is not done to communicate any opinion about the law or the facts of the case or of whether the defendant is guilty or not guilty. It is not my responsibility to judge the evidence here. It is yours. You and you alone are the judges of the facts, and you and you alone are responsible for deciding whether the defendant is guilty or not guilty. In your deliberations, you may not consider or speculate about matters relating to sentence or punishment. If there is a verdict of guilty, it will be my responsibility to impose an appropriate sentence. Ladies and gentlemen, under our law you are the sole triers of the facts, but I am the sole giver of the law. You will take your law not even from the attorneys in this case, but solely from me.

"When you judge the facts you are to consider only the evidence and the evidence in the case before you include the testimony of the witnesses, the exhibits that were received in evidence, and the stipulations by the parties. By stipulations I refer to information the parties agree to present to the jury as evidence, without calling a witness to testify. Testimony which was stricken from the record or to which an objection was sustained must be disregarded by you."

"Exhibits that were received in evidence are available, upon your request, for your inspection and consideration. Exhibits that were just seen during the trial, or marked for identification but not received in evidence, are not evidence, and are thus not available for your inspection and consideration. But, testimony based on exhibits that were not received in evidence may be considered by you. It is just that the exhibit itself is not available for your inspection and consideration."

"We now turn to the fundamental principles of our law that apply in all criminal trials which are the presumption of innocence, the burden of proof, and the requirement of proof beyond a reasonable doubt. Throughout these proceedings, the defendant is presumed to be innocent. As a result, you must find the defendant not guilty, unless, on the evidence presented at this trial, you conclude that the People have proven the defendant guilty beyond a reasonable doubt. In determining whether the People have satisfied their burden of proving the defendant's guilt beyond a reasonable doubt, you may consider all the evidence presented, whether by the People or by the defendant. In doing so, however, remember that, even though the defendant introduced evidence, the burden of proof remains on the People."

Judge Nicholson took another drink of water, wiped his eyes and then continued. "What does our law mean when it requires proof of guilt 'beyond a reasonable doubt'? The law uses the term, 'proof beyond a reasonable doubt', to tell you how convincing the evidence of guilt must be to permit a verdict of guilty. The law recognizes that, in dealing with human affairs, there are very few things in this world that we know with absolute certainty. Therefore, the law does not require the People to prove a defendant guilty beyond all possible doubt. On the other hand, it is not sufficient to prove that the defendant is probably guilty. Proof of guilt beyond a reasonable doubt is proof that leaves you so firmly convinced of the defendant's guilt that you have no reasonable doubt of the existence of any element of the crime or of the defendant's identity as the person who committed the crime. In determining whether or not the People have proven the defendant's guilt beyond a reasonable doubt, you should be guided solely by a full and fair evaluation of the evidence. After carefully evaluating the evidence, each of you must decide whether or not that evidence convinces you beyond a reasonable doubt of the defendant's guilt. Whatever your verdict may be, it must not rest upon baseless speculations. Nor may it be influenced in any way by bias, prejudice, sympathy, or by a desire to bring an end to your deliberations or to avoid an unpleasant duty."

"If you are not convinced beyond a reasonable doubt that the defendant is guilty of a charged crime, you must find the defendant not guilty of that crime. If you are convinced beyond a reasonable doubt that the defendant is guilty of a charged crime, you must find the defendant guilty of that crime."

"As judges of the facts, you alone determine the truthfulness and accuracy of the testimony of each witness. You must decide whether a witness told the truth and was accurate, or instead, testified falsely or was mistaken. You must also decide what importance to give to the testimony you accept as truthful and accurate. It is the quality of the testimony that is controlling, not the number of witnesses who testify."

"Now let's turn our attention to the witnesses you have heard from on this case. If you find that any witness has intentionally testified falsely as to any material fact, you may disregard that witness's entire testimony. Or, you may disregard so much of it as you find was untruthful, and accept so much of it as you find to have been truthful and accurate. There is no particular formula for evaluating the truthfulness and accuracy of another person's statements or testimony. You bring to this process all of your varied experiences. In life, you frequently decide the truthfulness and accuracy of statements made to you by other people. The same factors used to make those decisions, should be used in this case when evaluating the testimony."

"Some of the factors that you may wish to consider in evaluating the testimony of a witness are whether or not the witness has an opportunity to see or hear the events about which he or she testified and if the witness has the ability to recall those events accurately. Decide whether the testimony of the witness is plausible and likely to be true, or was it implausible and not likely to be true. Consider whether the testimony of the witness was consistent or inconsistent with other testimony or evidence in the case and did the manner in which the witness testified reflect upon the truthfulness of that witness's testimony. Consider to what extent, if any, did the witness's background, training, education, or experience affect the believability of that witness's testimony and did the witness have a bias, hostility or some other attitude that affected the truthfulness of the witness's testimony?"

I was growing tired and at this point was glad that all the Judge was saying would be supplied to the jurors for review because they couldn't remember all these basics and what will come later.

The Judge paused once again and I wondered if he was ready to present our points, or even if he would. I sat up straighter, my interest peaked.

"In this case you have heard the testimony of Detective Kenneth Park. The testimony of a witness should not be believed solely and simply because the witness is a police officer. At the same time, a witness's testimony should not be disbelieved solely and simply because the witness is a police officer. You must evaluate a police officer's testimony in the same way you would evaluate the testimony of any other witness."

"You have heard from expert witnesses that included Dr. William Henson, the private doctor of the victim Noah Arietta, Dr. Jennifer Pfeiffer, Coroner, Dr. Henrietta Pierson, the Medical Examiner, Dr. Milo Goodman, Psychiatrist for the defense, Dr. Richard Kindleworth, pathologist, and Dr. Mason Anderson, psychiatrist for the prosecutor. You should evaluate the testimony of any such witness just as you would the testimony of any other witness. You may accept or reject such testimony, in whole or in part, just as you may with respect to the testimony of any other witness. In deciding whether or not to accept such testimony, you should consider the qualifications and believability of the witness; the facts and other circumstances upon which the witness's opinion was based; the accuracy or inaccuracy of any assumed or hypothetical fact upon which the opinion was based; the reasons given for the witness's opinion; and whether the witness's opinion is consistent or inconsistent with other evidence in the case."

"Embraced in the information filed in this case are two separate offenses," he went on, "and the law makes it mandatory that you the jurors shall be instructed as to the different elements which constitute each offense so that you may determine the grade or degree of crime, if any, which was committed. "

"Murder is defined as the killing of another human being under conditions specifically covered in law. For the case in front of you today, the U.S., special statutory definitions include murder in the second degree as one ruling."

"Let me share with you now, New York Penal Section 125.25 - Murder In The Second Degree."

The Judge clears his throat and begins reading.

568

"A person is guilty of murder in the second degree when: 1. With intent to cause the death of another person, he causes the death of such person or of a third person; except that in any prosecution under this subdivision, it is an affirmative defense that: (a) The defendant acted under the influence of extreme emotional disturbance for which there was a reasonable explanation or excuse, the reasonableness of which is to be determined from the viewpoint of a person in the defendant's situation under the circumstances as the defendant believed them to be. Nothing contained in this paragraph shall constitute a defense to a prosecution for, or preclude a conviction of, manslaughter in the first degree or any other crime; or (b) The defendant's conduct consisted of causing or aiding, without the use of duress or deception, another person to commit suicide. Nothing contained in this paragraph shall constitute a defense to a prosecution for, or preclude a conviction of, manslaughter in the second degree or any other crime; or 2. Under circumstances evincing a depraved indifference to human life, he recklessly engages in conduct which creates a grave risk of death to another person, and thereby causes the death of another person; or 3. Acting either alone or with one or more other persons, he commits or attempts to commit robbery, burglary, kidnapping, arson, rape in the first degree, criminal sexual act in the first degree, sexual abuse in the first degree, aggravated sexual abuse, escape in the first degree, or escape in the second degree, and, in the course of and in furtherance of such crime or of immediate flight therefrom, he, or another participant, if there be any, causes the death of a person other than one of the participants; except that in any prosecution under this subdivision, in which the defendant was not the only participant in the underlying crime, it is an affirmative defense that the defendant: (a) Did not commit the homicidal act or in any way solicit, request, command, importune, cause or aid the commission thereof; and (b) Was not armed with a deadly weapon, or any instrument, article or substance readily capable of causing death or serious physical injury and of a sort not ordinarily carried in public places by law-abiding persons; and (c) Had no reasonable ground to believe that any other participant was armed with such a weapon, instrument, article or substance; and(d) Had no reasonable ground to believe that any other participant intended to engage in conduct likely to result in death or serious physical injury; or 4. Under circumstances evincing a depraved indifference to human life, and being eighteen years old or more the defendant recklessly engages in conduct which creates a grave risk of serious physical injury or death to another person less than eleven years old and thereby causes the death of such person; or 5. Being eighteen years old or more, while in the course of committing rape in the first, second or third degree, criminal sexual act in the first, second or third degree, sexual abuse in the first degree, aggravated sexual abuse in the first, second, third or fourth degree, or incest in the first, second or third degree, against a person less than fourteen years old, he or she intentionally causes the death of such person. Murder in the second degree is a class A-I felony."

"To simplify, "Murder Second Degree is an A-I Felony, an Intentional Homicide in PENAL LAW 125.25 The count is Murder in the Second Degree. Under our law, a person is guilty of Murder in the Second Degree when, with intent to cause the death of another person, he or she causes the death of such person or of a third person. The term "intent" used in this definition has its own special meaning in our law. I will now give you the meaning of that term."

Judge Nicholson looks up and focuses on first, the defense table and then at the prosecution before turning his attention to the jury.

"Intent means conscious objective or purpose. Thus, a person acts with intent to cause the death of another when that person's conscious objective or purpose is to cause the death of another. In order for you to find the defendant guilty of this crime, the People are required to prove, from all the evidence in the case, beyond a reasonable doubt, both of the following two elements: That on Friday, July 31, 2015, in the county of Monroe, the defendant, Lt. Vincent A. Trapp, caused the death of Mr. Noah Arietta and that the defendant did so with the intent to cause the death of Mr. Noah Arietta. Therefore, if you find that the People have proven beyond a reasonable doubt both of those elements, you must find the defendant guilty of the crime of Murder in the Second Degree as charged in the count. On the other hand, if you find that the People have not proven beyond a reasonable doubt either one or both of those elements, you must find the defendant not guilty of the crime of Murder in the Second Degree as charged in the count.

If after the review of all the evidence in this case you see the defendant as committing murder in the second-degree, you should enter second degree murder as your verdict.

I watch as Judge Nicholson again pauses and looks out over the courtroom before beginning again.

"Ladies and Gentlemen of the jury, as I said there were two verdicts for you to consider in this case. The second is voluntary manslaughter. A person accused of murder in New York State is typically charged with either first or second degree murder but other classifications also exist, such as manslaughter."

"Manslaughter is a very serious situation in the State of New York. Second Degree manslaughter in New York is the crime many people refer to as 'involuntary manslaughter' and there is basically not an element of intent behind this crime. First Degree manslaughter is often referred to as 'voluntary manslaughter and does in some cases require the intent to cause physical harm, but not the intent to kill. The New York statutes define the various forms of manslaughter in New York Penal Section125.20; Manslaughter in the first degree and, and New York Penal Section 125.15; Manslaughter in the second degree."

"Manslaughter First Degree is a B Felony an Intentional Homicide Under Influence of Extreme Emotional Disturbance and described in PENAL LAW 125.20. The count is Manslaughter in the First Degree. Under our law, a person is guilty of Manslaughter in the First Degree when, with intent to cause the death of another person, he or she causes the death of such person or of a third person. The term "intent" used in this definition is the same as covered earlier. Thus, a person acts with intent to cause the death of another when his or her conscious objective or purpose is to cause the death of another. In order for you to find the defendant guilty of this crime, the People are required to prove, from all the evidence in the case, beyond a reasonable doubt, both of the following two elements: That on Friday, July 31, 2015, in the county of Monroe, the defendant, Lt. Vincent A. Trapp, caused the death of Mr. Noah Arietta and that the defendant did so with the intent to cause the death of Mr. Noah Arietta. Therefore, if you find that the People have proven beyond a reasonable doubt both of those elements, you must find the defendant guilty of the crime of Manslaughter in the First Degree as charged in the count. On the other hand, if you find that the People have not proven beyond a reasonable doubt either one or both of those elements, you must find the defendant not guilty of the crime of Manslaughter in the First Degree as charged in the count."

"This charge should be used in those relatively rare cases where, having heard evidence of extreme emotional disturbance, you the jury find legally sufficient evidence of an intentional killing, but votes to indict the defendant only for Manslaughter in the First Degree, rather than for Murder. The details for this charge is presented in Penal Law Section 125.20. Accordingly, this charge is essentially identical to that for Murder in the Second Degree under Penal Law Section 125.25. "

"The maximum applicable penalty for second degree murder in the State of New York is life. Life imprisonment is the usual sentence, but a lighter one may be occasionally ordered. These lighter sentences would only be awarded if a strong case had been made by the defense, or in the case or special arrangements. The minimum sentence would be 15 years to life, and the maximum sentence would be 25 to Life."

"Most murders in New York will be second degree, unless further evidence warrants reducing the charge to manslaughter. In the case of manslaughter in the first degree, the minimum sentence would be 5 years and the maximum would be 25 years.

The Judge continued, providing additional explanation of some of the terms. During his rhetoric the Sheriff came forward with a fresh pitcher of water.

As Pete and I had anticipated the Judge went on explicitly to instruct the jury that they could not acquit the defendant simply because Noah had allegedly raped his wife, even if they firmly believed that he had.

Judge Nicholson looked at the papers on his desk and when he spoke my heart leapt. He began instructing the jury from our requests.

"The guidelines for evaluating the criminal responsibility for defendants claiming to be insane were codified in the British courts in the case of Daniel M'Naughten in 1843. This was summarized by the defense in our case as a defense asserted by an accused in a criminal prosecution to avoid liability for the commission of a crime because, at the time of the crime, the person did not appreciate the nature or quality or wrongfulness of the acts."

"The insanity defense is used by criminal defendants. The most common variation is cognitive insanity. Under the test for cognitive insanity, a defendant must have been so impaired by a mental disease or defect at the time of the act that he or she did not know the nature or quality of the act, or, if the defendant did know the nature or quality of the act, he or she did not know that the act was wrong. The vast majority of states allow criminal defendants to invoke the cognitive insanity defense."

The other form of the insanity defense is volitional insanity, or Irresistible Impulse. A defense of irresistible impulse asserts that the defendant, although able to distinguish right from wrong at the time of the act, suffered from a mental disease or defect that made him or her incapable of controlling her or his actions."

"A criminal defendant who is found legally insane or "not guilty by reason of insanity" cannot be held accountable for crimes resulting from the condition. After all, prosecutors are required to show a defendant's willful intent in order to prove guilt for most criminal charges. State courts use one of several established legal tests to determine whether someone was insane at the time of the incident or simply faking it."

"In this case they are leaning toward "Irresistible Impulse" defense. One of the major criticisms of the M'Naughten rule is that, in its focus on the cognitive ability to know right from wrong, it fails to take into consideration the issue of control. Psychiatrists agree that it is possible to understand that one's behavior is wrong, but still be unable to stop oneself. To address this, some states, including New York also has accepted the modified M'Naughten test with an irresistible impulse provision, which absolves a defendant who can distinguish right and wrong but is nonetheless unable to stop himself from committing an act he knows to be wrong. This test is also known as the 'policeman at the elbow' test: Would the defendant have committed the crime even if there were a policeman standing at his elbow?"

"At the outset there is a presumption in cases of this kind that the respondent is sane, but as soon as evidence is offered by the respondent to overthrow this presumption, the burden shifts and it then rests upon the People to convince the jurors beyond a reasonable doubt of the respondent's sanity as that is one of the necessary conditions upon which guilt in this case may be predicated. When any evidence is given on behalf of the defendant which tends to overthrow that presumption of his sanity the jurors should examine, weigh and pass upon it with the understanding that although the initiative in presenting the evidence is taken by the defense, the burden of proof in this part of the case is upon the prosecution to establish all the conditions of guilt, of which sanity is one. Where there is any evidence in the case by the respondent which tends to show that at the time of the commission of the offense he was laboring under either permanent or temporary insanity, it then becomes the duty of the prosecution to prove the sanity of the respondent beyond a reasonable doubt, as I have just defined that term and unless they have done so the defendant must be acquitted."

"It is claimed here on behalf of the defendant that he was insane at the time he fired the fatal shots. His defense, as I understand it, is one generally known as temporary insanity, and I charge you that such a defense, if proven to your satisfaction, is just as valid as though the defendant were shown to be totally and permanently insane. In other words, the duration of the defendant's insanity is not the controlling test, but the issue is whether his insanity, however brief, was of such a nature and character as to render the defendant incapable of either exercising his own free will and volition or of appreciating the difference between right and wrong. If you should find that at the time he fired the fatal shots he was suffering from either such insanity, then you should acquit him, despite the fact that prior and subsequent thereto he may have been as sane as you and I."

I glanced over at Pete, who's hair hung loosely around his handsome face and that expression on that face was of one in full concentration. It was now apparent that the Judge was going to give our requests on insanity, at least, and he had already injected irresistible impulse in the case.

The Judge continued his charge on insanity exactly as we had prepared our requests. "As I have said, the main matter of defense offered here on behalf of the defendant is that he was insane at the time of the alleged offense and was therefore not legally responsible for his acts. The defendant has introduced evidence on his behalf tending to show that one of the contributing factors to such alleged insanity may have been his belief that his wife had just been threatened and assaulted and raped by the deceased."

The Judge paused and I held my breath waiting to see if he would give the next part. "In this connection I charge you that if you believe the defendant was insane, as I have defined that term, it is not controlling on this issue of insanity that you should first find that the defendants wife was in fact actually threatened, assaulted and raped by the deceased or indeed that any of these things had happened to her. It is enough that you should find that the defendant actually believed that these things had occurred to his wife and that the deceased was guilty of them and that this belief of the defendant was based upon reasonable grounds."

I again glanced at a tense white faced Pete, who seemed to be moving his lips with the Judge as the Judge then delivered Pete's pet charge on irresistible impulse. "Expert medical testimony has been offered on behalf of the defendant that he was insane at the time the fatal shots were fired, and that it was a form of insanity generally known to the law as 'irresistible impulse.' I charge you that such a form of insanity is recognized as a defense to crime in New York and that it is the law of this State that even if the defendant had been able to comprehend the nature and consequences of his act, and to know that it was wrong, that nevertheless if he was forced to its execution by an irresistible impulse which he was powerless to control in consequence of a temporary or permanent disease of the mind, then he was insane and you should acquit him.

The Judge cleared his throat as he came to our crucially important request on the relative opportunities of the respective psychiatrists to obtain the knowledge upon which their opinions were based. "There has been expert medical testimony offered here on the question of the sanity or insanity of the defendant. In this connection I charge you to consider the testimony of the doctors and their opinions on the subject. Also consider what opportunity the doctors had to obtain knowledge upon which to base their opinions."

The Judge loosened his collar with his broad middle finger. "I have already told you that the fact that the deceased may or may not have raped the defendant's wife does not in itself, afford the defendant legal justification or excuse for taking the life of the deceased. But, as we have already seen, we must nevertheless consider the question of rape in this case as it might bear on the possible insanity of the defendant, but before I pass to that I must accordingly first define rape."

"New York criminalizes a wide range of conduct constituting "sexual abuse," which is generally defined as subjecting another person to sexual contact without the latter's consent. You will be given a copy of Section 120 and 130 of the New York Penal Code to help you in determining the degree of the offense as it pertains to this case. Bear in mind that there is also evidence that later the same evening the deceased may have again assaulted the wife of the defendant with intent to rape her."

"If you are satisfied from the circumstances detailed in evidence here that the deceased did later make a further attempt to have sexual intercourse with the defendant's wife and that he did this with the intent to accomplish it at all events by his strength and power against any resistance which might be offered to him then he would have been guilty of assault with intent to commit rape, no matter whether he actually committed the rape or not."

The Judge droned. "There has also been some medical and other testimony here on the subject of whether or not any seminal fluid or male sperm did or could pass from the deceased onto or into the body of the defendant's wife. In this regard I charge you that the presence of seminal fluid or sperm is not controlling on the question of whether or not the deceased raped the defendant's wife. Under the legal definition of rape that offense may be complete without the presence of seminal fluid or sperm because any male penetration, however slight or fleeting, is sufficient to constitute rape under our law provided that the intercourse was had against the will and without the consent of the woman."

The Judge signed heavily and took another drink of water. "It is claimed here on behalf of the defendant that he left his house that night and went to the Founders Café and bar in the Academy Building with the intention of apprehending and arresting the deceased. In this connection I charge you that it is the law of this state that a private person, that is, a person who is not a policeman or other officer, may make a legal arrest without a warrant when the person to be arrested has actually committed a felony even though such felony did not occur in the presence of the private person seeking to make the arrest."

"Therefore, if you believe here that the deceased did actually commit one or more felonies earlier that night then the defendant here had the legal right to go and seek to arrest the deceased without a warrant, and this right would apply to the defendant even if he were a perfect stranger to the proceedings here and had no relation whatever to the woman victim in the case."

"I further charge you that both an officer of the law or a private person may in such cases as outlined above use such force as reasonably seems to him to be necessary in forcibly arresting a felony offender or in preventing his escape after such an arrest, even to the extent of killing him. He must, however, first announce his purpose to arrest the person he seeks to arrest."

Jean Larson stirred and glanced uneasily over my way as the Judge continued. "On the other hand there is no claim here that the defendant actually did arrest the deceased, or announce his purpose to make such an arrest, or that he shot the deceased in order to make such an arrest or to prevent his escape. Rather it is claimed that the defendant here in became temporarily insane with the fatal results that followed. However, the aforementioned claims bear on the intent with which the defendant went to the bar. If he went there with the intent to kill the deceased rather than to arrest him, then if he were otherwise legally responsible, the offense is murder, but if he went there with the lawful intent to arrest him and not with the intent to kill him, and thereupon became insane as I have defined that term, then you should acquit him.

It was my turn to glance at Jean Larson as the Judge pressed on about the right of the Lieutenant to carry a gun the night he shot Noah. "There has been some testimony offered and argument made

579

here that the defendant might have been guilty of carrying an unregistered and concealed weapon on the night in question contrary to the law of New York. Now it is true that in this state it is required by law that the average citizen register any pistol possessed by him and it is also made a felony for the average citizen to carry a weapon concealed upon his person or elsewhere without first obtaining a license to do so. But in this regard I charge you, regardless of what you may have heard here to the contrary, that the New York pistol registration and concealed weapon laws do not apply to the defendant in this case. They do not apply here because in New York States the law reads in Penal Code Law Subsection 265.20 Exemptions to the concealed weapon gun law, and I quote 'Persons in the military service of the state of New York when duly authorized by regulations issued by the adjutant general to possess the same. Police officers as defined in subdivision thirty-four of section 1.20 of the criminal procedure law. Peace officers as defined by section 2.10 of the criminal procedure law. Persons in the military or other service of the United States, in pursuit of official duty or when duly authorized by federal law, regulation or order to possess the same. Persons employed in fulfilling defense contracts with the government of the United States or agencies thereof when possession of the same is necessary for manufacture, transport, installation and testing under the requirements of such contract."

The Judge paused, and looking over the top of his wire frame glasses as he continued. "In other words Lieutenant Trapp as a member of the United States army was exempt from the provisions of these laws and he had a lawful right to carry an unregistered and unlicensed concealed weapon on his person on the night in question, and under the law it made no difference whether he was on duty or off duty. So I repeat that regardless of what you may have heard here to the contrary, that is the law in this State."

The Judge closed his portfolio and removed some papers from another folder. I glanced at Pete and he grinned and looked quickly away. The Judge had not only given all of our requested instructions but he had measurably improved on one of the crucial ones, the one about the psychiatric examination.

The Judge sat erect and placed his big hands out flat in front of him. "I now draw near the end of my charge. I charge you that you cannot find this man guilty of anything if you find him insane as I have defined it. On the other hand, you must not infer that because a man acts frantically or in a frenzy that he is therefore laboring under irresistible impulse or any other form of insanity. Insanity must always be separated from passion or anger or our courts will simply become public arenas wherein to acquit murderers."

The Judge glanced at the clock and presses on. "Your verdict on each count you consider, whether guilty or not guilty, must be unanimous; that is, each and every juror must agree to it. To reach a unanimous verdict you must deliberate with the other jurors. That means you should discuss the evidence and consult with each other, listen to each other, give each other's views careful consideration, and reason together when considering the evidence. And when you deliberate, you should do so with a view towards reaching an agreement if that can be done without surrendering individual judgment. Each of you must decide the case for yourself, but only after a fair and impartial consideration of the evidence with the other jurors. You should not surrender an honest view of the evidence simply because you want the trial to end or you are outvoted. At the same time, you should not hesitate to reexamine your views and change your mind if you become convinced that your position was not correct."

"Any notes taken are only an aid to your memory and must not take precedence over your independent recollection. A juror's notes are not a substitute for the recorded transcript of the testimony or for any exhibit received in evidence. If there is a discrepancy between a juror's recollection and his or her notes regarding the evidence, you should ask to have the relevant testimony read back or the exhibit produced in the jury room. In addition, a juror's notes are not a substitute for the detailed explanation I have given you of the principles of law that govern this case. If there is a discrepancy between a juror's recollection and his or her notes regarding those principles, you should ask me to explain those principles again, and I will be happy to do so."

"You may see any or all of the exhibits which were received in evidence. Simply write me a note telling me which exhibit or exhibits you want to see. You may also have the testimony of any witness read back to you in whole or in part. Again, if you want a read back, write me a note telling me what testimony you wish to hear. If you have a question on the law, write me a note specifying what you want me to review with you."

"Under our law, the first juror selected is known as the foreperson. During deliberations, the foreperson's opinion and vote are not entitled to any more importance than that of any other juror. What we ask the foreperson to do during deliberations is to sign any written note that the jury sends to the court. The foreperson does not have to write the note or agree with its contents. The foreperson's signature only indicates that the writing comes from the jury. The foreperson may also chair the jury's discussions during deliberations. When the jury has reached a verdict, guilty or not guilty, the entire jury will be asked to come into court. The foreperson will be asked whether the jury has reached a verdict. If the foreperson says yes, he/she will then be asked what the verdict is for each charged crime. After that, the entire jury will be asked whether that is their verdict and will answer yes or no. Finally, upon the request of a party, each juror will be asked individually whether the announced verdict is the verdict of that juror, and then, upon being asked, each juror will answer yes or no."

"Finally, there are a few remaining rules which you must observe during your deliberations. While you are here in the courthouse, deliberating on the case, you will be kept together in the jury room. You may not leave the jury room during deliberations. If necessary, food will be provided and if you have a beeper or cell phone or other electronic device, please give it to a court officer to hold for you while you're engaged in deliberations. During your deliberations, you must discuss the case only among yourselves; you must not discuss the case with anyone else, including a court officer, or permit anyone other than a fellow juror to discuss the case in your presence. If you have a question or request, you must communicate with me by writing a note, which you will give to a court officer to give to me. The law requires that you communicate with me in writing in part to make sure there are no misunderstandings. You may reach one of five verdicts. If you find the defendant guilty of murder in the second degree, then bring in such a verdict; if not you should next consider manslaughter in the second degree. If your decision is guilty of this then bring in such a verdict; if not, you should next pass to manslaughter. If after due deliberation you cannot find guilt here, then having a verdict of not guilty by reason of insanity or plan not guilty."

"That concludes my instructions on the law."

The Judge looked down at Finn Landon. "Mr. Clerk," he said, "Please reduce the jury from fourteen to twelve."

Again Finn's hour had arrived and he stood, white faced and returned all fourteen of the jurors' name slips to his box. Carefully he shook the box elaborately and drew out the first name. I held my breath hoping my favorite juror would not be banished. "Mrs.

Natasha Krampsky," Finn called out, and a heavy set woman stood up and carefully edged her way out of the jury box.

"Thank you," the Judge said.

Finn again shook his box and pulled out another slip. "Daniel Brown," he called and every one watched to see who Mr. Brown was and then waited as he left the jury box.

"Thank you," the Judge said.

"Swear an officer," the Judge said, and Lincoln's chief deputy, Floyd Landes, marched forward and raised his hand and was sworn by Finn. "You do solemnly swear that you will, to the utmost of your ability, keep the persons sworn as jurors in this trial in some private and convenient place, without meat or drink, except water, unless ordered by the court; that you will suffer no communications orally or otherwise, to be made to them, that you will not communicate with them yourself, orally or otherwise, unless ordered by the court, and that you will not until they shall have rendered their verdict, communicate to anyone the state of their deliberations or the verdict they may have agreed upon, so help you God."

"I do," Mr. Floyd Landes replied, and he turned and beckoned the remaining jurors to arise and follow him to their room.

Judge Nicholson announced, "This Court is in recess until the verdict of the jury or the further order of the court."

Chapter 21

I watched as the jury file out, feeling the tension that wracked my body. My mind is blank. My senses, numb. There is silence and each second that passes seems like hours. After such a long arduous trial I was not only physically exhausted, but my over churned mind was buttery and numb and I had simply nothing more to give. Added to all this was my growing anxiety over the outcome of the case. I hadn't mastered a good night sleep since the start of the trial and now as it was ending, my body screamed for slumber. I didn't fight for control as I found myself leaning back in my chair with arms dangling over the arm rests and my head dropping back over the top of the chair. My eyelids drooped as I squinted up at the beamed ceiling so close to slumber when I heard my name being called.

"Richard!" Pete whispered in my ear which under normal conditions would have startled me, but I was too tired for that and too weary to even respond.

Pete didn't care. "Listen Richard, Paige and the Lieutenant have gone outside for some fresh air. I think you should go sit in the car for a while. You'll be more comfortable there.

"But…" I started finally able to form words again.

"But, nothing," Pete replied. "I'll keep the vigil here and call you." He pulled at my jacket sleeve, "Go on, while you can still move."

"Thanks Pete," I said as I struggled to find the strength to pull myself up out of my chair and once mastering that feat, I nodded my head gratefully and silently staggered out the doors and headed downstairs through the bustling and milling knots of people, until finally reaching my car. I slumped down and sat staring sightlessly out at the stone foundation of the courthouse both worried and desperately tired. I yawned. My eyelids grew heavy, my head nodded on my chest; and soon I was fast asleep.

Someone was shaking me and when I opened my eyes I am startled and can't remember where I am. "Come on Richard, it's not going to happen today. Let's go home and get some rest."

Chapter 22

I fill my time with arraignments as I await the jury return with a verdict. I try to call the Lieutenant to see how he is doing, but am unable to reach him. To keep my mind busy, I finally place a call to my golfing buddy, Travis and he agrees to meet me at the Genesee Valley golf course. I try to get Pete to join us, but he says he's not ready for embarrassment on the course.

The weather holds out and Travis and I have a good round of golf with us both doing quite well. I expected to be off my game since I hadn't been able to break away for some time. But I surprised myself.

I get a text from Pete who has been hanging out at the court house, informing me that the jury has requested additional information and finally, two days later he informs me that the jury has reached a decision.

The phone rings. "Hello?"

"Hey Richard, its time. The wait is over. The jury is on their way back into court. They've reached a decision."

"Thanks Pete, I'll call the Trapps and head your way."

I hang up the phone and place the call to the Trapps. "It's time. The jury is in. I'll meet you there.:

Pete's announcement brings me back to the mindset of whether we succeeded in convincing the jury. I reach over to the passenger seat and collect my brief case and then pull down the car visor and take a quick peek at my reflection, running a hand through

587

my hair. Satisfied, I exit the car and walk to the courtroom steps, take a deep breath and wait for my client.

In less than twenty minutes I see the Trapps pull into the parking area and go over to meet them, waiting patiently as they climb out of the car and then we walk quickly side by side until we reach the court room. I watch as Mrs. Trapp takes her seat behind the railing and I smile. I know that this was short notice so I am surprised and pleased to see Paige is dressed conservatively.

The Lieutenant and I take our seats at the defense table and shake hands.

The courtroom is deathly silent. A few of the spectators are whispering to each other, but most sit poised for the jury to enter.

"Is this a good sign?" the Lieutenant asks nervously.

I plant a smile on my face and reply, "Some people believe a short deliberation time means a guilty verdict and a longer deliberation means the jury -- or at least one juror -- thinks the defendant is not guilty. But no one knows for sure."

"What do you think?"

I take a moment and then reply. "I think we need to relax and not speculate."

"Really? I need you to give me more then that. I'm anxious here."

I know I need to give him more so I do. "Think about this. Jurors took nearly 15 hours to find Jodi Arias guilty of first-degree murder in the death of her ex-boyfriend Travis Alexander. Jerry Sandusky was found guilty of over 45 counts of child sex abuse after a jury deliberated for more than 20 hours over two days. After almost 14 hours, jurors found Drew Peterson guilty in the death of his fourth wife, Kathleen Savio. Jurors from the second Phil Spector trial deliberated for 30 hours and convicted him of second-degree murder in the death of Lana Clarkson. Scott Peterson was convicted of first-degree and second-degree murder for killing his wife and their unborn child. The jury deliberated for seven days. After four days of deliberations, the Menendez brothers were convicted of two counts of first-degree murder for killing their parents. Steven Hayes was convicted of capital murder in the deaths of three members of the Petit family. The jury deliberated four hours...At that moment, thankfully, the Judge entered the court room. I was about running out of examples.

On command, everyone is on their feet. Judge Nicholson takes his seat on the bench and says, "Please be seated. Bailiff, bring in the jury."

After two days of deliberations, the panel of five women and seven men would be back in their seats. I look over at the prosecution table only to find them looking at me. We knew something bad would happen, we just didn't know bad for who. The feeling in the courtroom grew until the atmosphere in the courtroom was exactly the same as it feels being on a deserted empty street during a blizzard. No place to go and no one to turn to. I turn my gaze to the spectator area and see everyone just waiting for what the jury will say. A look at the media standing off to the side sends out a feeling of an emotional radar waiting to pounce at the first opportunity.

Sullen and heavy, like a blanket of smog, tension had hung over the courtroom, but now it sprang suddenly alive, almost intolerably so. I moistened my dry lips. My stomach is in knots and I try to relax, but it is useless. It seems an eternity before the bailiff opens the heavy jury door and stands aside for the jurors to file in. My heart leapt and for some unexplained reason I am engulfed in the feeling that something's about to go terribly wrong. That which seemed under control, suddenly feels horribly wrong. There's no reason for this feeling that I can put my finger on because I know I did my job and the jury had to know that too. I squeeze my eyes shut and say a little prayer.

The Judge held up his hand and the already tense, silent room comes to attention. "I advise each of you present to not interrupt the taking and acceptance of the verdict," he declaimed sternly. "Proceed, Mr. Clerk."

Finn Landon stood and faced the jurors. This was his final role of the case. In a high tenor voice he began. "Will the jurors please answer as their names are called?" Each juror responds to their name by raising a hand.

"Members of the jury, I have your note indicating that you have reached a verdict."

The foreperson stands and says, "Yes, Your Honor, we have."

"Will the Clerk of the Court please take the verdict?"

Finn Landon walks over to the Foreperson who hands him the copy of the verdict. Keeping the page in sight, the Clerk carries it over to Judge Nicholson to proofread the verdict before the jury Foreperson reads it aloud to prevent any appellate issues with the judgment or sentence rendered by the jury. The Judge makes sure the verdict sheet is filled out as instructed and signed by the Foreperson. All this delays the knowing and puts more stress on me and a brief survey of the courtroom reveals that stress is shared.

All eyes watch as Judge Nicholson folds the sheet and summons the clerk who takes it and carries it back to place in the hands of the Foreperson.

"How say you?" the Clerk asks.

The jury Foreperson rises slowly. He holds the sheet of paper that's visibly shaking, but not shaking as violently as my hands. My breathing is quite labored. I'm so dizzy I feel faint. I turn and glance

590

at Paige and see she is remarkably calm. I sneak a look at the Lieutenant and he too seems poise and calm.

Now I am more determined to keep my face straight and display no emotion, regardless of the verdict so I scribble on a legal pad and a quick glance to my right reveals that the same strategy is being employed by the prosecution.

The jury Foreperson clears his throat, and reads. Everyone is on the edge of their seat waiting for the verdict. "We, the jury, We find," the Foreperson began, and his voice cracked, and he cleared his throat and began again. "In the case of Lieutenant Vincent Trapp vs the State of New York under Article 125.27 of the New York Penal Law, we, the jury, upon our oaths find the defendant not guilty of murder in the second degree by reason of temporary insanity known as irresistible impulse."

There is a slight uproar in the court, but it calms at the first hit of the gavel by Judge Nicholson.

"Members of the jury, your foreperson has announced the following verdict of not guilty by reason of insanity. Members of the jury I will poll you on the verdict by simply addressing you, by the chairs in which you are seated. The juror seated in Chair No. 1: Was this and is this your verdict?"

Juror No. 1 replies, "Yes"

"The juror seated in Chair No. 2: Was this and is this your verdict?"

Juror No. 2 replies, "Yes"

"The juror seated in Chair No. 3: Was this and is this your verdict?"

Juror No. 3 replies, "Yes, Your Honor"

"The juror seated in Chair No. 4: Was this and is this your verdict?"

Juror No. 4 replies "Yes."

"The juror seated in Chair No. 5: Was this and is this your verdict?"

Juror No. 5 replies, "Yes, Your Honor"

"The juror seated in Chair No. 6: Was this and is this your verdict?"

Juror No. 6 replies, "Yes, Your Honor".

"The juror seated in Chair No. 7: Was this and is this your verdict?"

Juror No. 7 replies, "Yes, Your Honor".

"The juror seated in Chair No. 8: Was this and is this your verdict?"

Juror No. 8 replies, "Yes, Your Honor".

"The juror seated in Chair No. 9: Was this and is this your verdict?"

Juror No. 9 replies, "Yes, Your Honor".

"The juror seated in Chair No. 10: Was this and is this your verdict?"

Juror No. 10 replies, "Yes, Your Honor".

"The juror seated in Chair No. 11: Was this and is this your verdict?"

Juror No. 11, "Yes".

"The juror seated in Chair No. 12: Was this and is this your verdict?"

Juror No. 12 replies, "Yes, Your Honor".

"Members of the jury, you have determined by your verdict that the evidence established the defendant, Lieutenant Vincent Trapp was suffering with the temporary insanity known as irresistible impulse at the time of the crime. The charge and your verdict is that the defendant was insane only at the time of the crime charged. So stating you believe that the defendant was unable to appreciate the nature and quality or the wrongfulness of his acts.

When an affirmative defense of insanity is submitted to the jury, unanimity is required on both questions of guilt and sanity. A jury united as to guilt but divided as to an affirmative defense, such as insanity is necessarily a hung jury. United States v. Southwell, 432 F.3d 1050, 1055 (9th Cir.2005). It is in this case the unanimous verdict of the jury."

Judge Nicholson pauses. "Members of the jury, you have determined by your verdict that the evidence established the defendant, Lieutenant Vincent Trapp as not guilty by reason of insanity beyond a reasonable doubt.

I am in shock. Did they say not guilty? I am positive that is what they have said. Not guilty by reason of insanity. We won, we won. I know my elation is written clearly on my face and I don't care. I did it. Pete and I really did it.

There are hushed whispers as people in the gallery talk amongst themselves.

Chapter 22

Turning towards me, Lieutenant Trapp asked, "That's good?" I replied, "Yes, that's very good. You're free." Lieutenant Trapp smiled briefly, then resumed his customarily serious, slightly sorrowful expression.

I sat back. The Lieutenant still faces one more hurdle -- a psychiatric examination that could last 45 days. The doctors are to decide on a course of treatment for the Lieutenant, which will determine how long he is held. He could be released early if we can get an order to seek private treatment. All these thoughts parade through my mind.

I learn that the jury agreed, that Lieutenant Trapp, flooded with nightmarish images of his wife being abused, snapped psychologically after learning that Noah Arietta had raped her. It was knowing this that yielded an "irresistible impulse" verdict. The verdict brought to an end the trial.

I am engrossed with the whole concept that we had won I have transported myself elsewhere until I hear a gasp from behind me then the bomb of realization explodes with a sharp hiss of indrawn breath, bringing the courtroom to life.

The incantations rise and the Judge raises his hand to silence the room, but when he lowers his hand chaos abounds. Everyone in the court room is on their feet. I turned around and watched as Paige threw her arms about her husband and wept against his chest. I reached out to take the Lieutenants outstretched hand behind his wife's back and shook it.

I try to maintain my composure, and simply whisper, "Congratulations," to my client. He says nothing. It's impossible at this point not to smile. I nod and silently say thanks.

I look at the prosecution table and my eyes veer toward Ms. Larson who is struggling to keep a straight face. She is not use to being on the losing team and I can imagine how hard it is for her to maintain composure. This should have been a slam dunk. It was the hardest defense a person can use in a murder case.

My attention is drawn to a spot just behind the row where Paige had been seated. People are gathering together, just before the exit, but no matter how I try, I can't see anything from my vantage point. Someone yells out, "He's in full cardiac arrest. Please help him."

From that announcement, a flurry of activity began. I hear someone say, "Hurry, we need to do something immediately. At that moment all eyes are on the collection of people and the trial is forgotten. Someone asks, "Is he breathing?" Another voice says, "His chest is barely rising, but I think he is breathing." Another voice says, "Check his pulse," and another person reacts. The Bailiff hurries over and pushes his way through the crowd to perform CPR.

"Does anyone have a phone?" Because the judge doesn't allow cell phones in the courtroom, all eyes survey the room to no avail. I hear someone whispering my name and look over at the court reporter who motions me to come over. "I have a cell phone and I called 911." I go back to my table. "Nine-one-one has been called. Someone should be here shortly," I announce loudly.

Within ten minutes the doors open and people are asked to step aside as the medical team takes over. People linger to watch as the team efficiently handle the situation and it is not until they wheel the man out of the courtroom on a gurney, does the crowd thin.

"He just got so excited on hearing the verdict." A woman who I assume is the patient's wife says. I wonder if it was because he was happy with the verdict or vis-a-versa. In either case I didn't want to know.

I stand with my client, his wife and others waiting to exit the courtroom. Eventually the bailiff comes over to us and says, "The man had a heart attack all right; what they called the 'widowmaker,'. He wouldn't have made it out of the courthouse doors if these individuals had not taken action and intervened when they did".

I looked across the room and saw Pete standing white faced and blinking by his chair, biting his tremulous lip. I turned and looked at the front of the courtroom and see the court reporter sitting with her head bowed over her desk working on a crossword puzzle and looking endlessly bored as if nothing was happening.

I look across the room and see Jean Larson coming over in my direction and when she is right in front of me she pumped my hand and in an effort to diminish the noise in the room, cupped her free hand to my ear. "Congratulations, Dandridge!" she shouted. "You're a worthy opponent, damn you."

"Thanks, Larson," I shout back, smiling. "That goes for you, too."

When Larson moves aside, Randall gave me his hand and smiled and said something and backed away. He grabbed the Lieutenant's hand and shook it before heading back to their table. I turned around to gather my belongings but then the newspaper men were upon us, their cameras reaching over heads to get the best shot, while others have out their cell phones trying to get pictures to post on Facebook or other media areas. It was a zoo. "Over this way, Lieutenant, please…"

"Hey, look this way, Dandridge..." their cheerful urgings ranted.

"Can't you smile, man? You won, damn it, you won..." "Will you please take off those glasses, Mrs. Trapp?" "Let's get a pic of the jury." Where in hell is the dog?. I need a picture of that dog with the Lieutenant."

Realizing there would not be a lull too soon and no one seemed to be responding to his pounding, Judge Nicholson, turned toward the jury and spoke.

"Thank you, ladies and gentlemen of the jury, for your loyal and attentive service in a long and difficult case", he said soberly. "You have handled yourselves well in one of the highest duties and privileges of citizens in a democracy." He looked at the clock. "I guess there is no more to say except you are excused,

The Judge nodded his head gravely and looked out at the milling newspaper men. "I order everyone to clear the court, Now! No more pictures are to be taken in my court room." When there is little reaction to his order, the Judge yells, "Perhaps I should add that any who disobey this order will spend at least the night as the guests of our sheriff."

I watch as the jurors stand in a line, filing out the door one by one and trying hard to ignore the pack of wolves trailing them. Even after the Judges warning they still try to snap their pictures, hoping to get that award winning shot. It is not until the last juror makes it through the door, that the cameramen turn and again head toward us, but then think better of it after seeing the look on the Judge's face.

It is finally quiet in the courtroom as the spectators, news people and photo snappers have left the room to the Judge, the Trapps and us; the counsel. I sit down realizing that I can soon get out of my suit and tie and when I wake up, not have to worry about being on time to court. I have been living under the processes of etiquette of the court and though I enjoy being a lawyer, the rules are a whole other thing. It's like being a child all over again and hearing your mother say be polite, stand when speaking to an adult, do not interrupt when others are speaking, and on and on and on.

***

I am pulled out of my reverie when the Judge clears his throat. "There is still one final thing that needs to be attended to in this trial," Judge Nicholson says. "I am prepared to rule on the jury's decision."

I sit up straight in my chair.

"Ladies and Gentlemen, as a result of the verdict, you, Lt. Trapp are now a free man in one sense, but there is more to contend with. Gentlemen, as all of you well know, the law now charges me, under this verdict, the unpleasant duty of sending this man away until he is pronounced sane. It is a dilemma all the more sharpened by the fact that two otherwise violently disagreeing psychiatrists agree on this one thing, that the man is now sane. It so happens that I too think he is sane, as I believe you do, and it strikes me as a travesty of justice that I should be compelled to send this man away."

The Judge paused. "As a matter of fact, I don't intend to do so. Certainly it would be unfounded to send this man away." The Judge again paused and drew a deep breath, "Gentlemen, Let me cite a basis for what I am about to say to you know. It deals with the case of a Mr. Steinberg."

"In the year 1981, Steinberg was charged with killing his wife Elena with a kitchen knife. Elena was stabbed 26 times. It should also be noted that Steinberg was the one who called the police reporting an attempted burglary gone awry, though the police found no signs of a break in. The case drew much publicity in Arizona not only for the heinous crime, but because it was a case of homicidal somnambulism, or simply known as sleepwalking murder. To quote legal argument, "The defendant was not in his normal state of mind when he committed the act. Sleep walking is a parasomnia manifested by automatism; as such, harmful actions committed while in this state cannot be blamed on the perpetrator." Steinberg claimed he did not remember the crime and was sleeping at the time, hence the murder while sleepwalking. Not only that, he did not deny the fact that he murdered his wife. In his criminal trial, the jury found him not guilty on the grounds that he was temporarily insane when he committed the crime. Although Steinberg fabricated the story about the intruders, he walked away as a free man. Members of the jury were also quoted later to saying they were aware that they were releasing a killer but he was not criminally responsible for his actions."

"In our situation here, we all know that we are not releasing a killer, no, not at all. Lt. Trapp is a true example of the meaning of irresistible impulse. So I ask if we can all agree to letting the Lieutenant walk out of here a free man and not subject him to any time incarcerated in a mental institution, it would be the picture of justice served."

I was speechless at first, but finally found my tongue. I look at the judge and then over at the prosecution table. "If the People will agree I am willing to proceed now."

Jean Larson whispered briefly with Randall and stood. "We agree, Your Honor."

"A generous and sensible suggestion, Ms. Larson," the Judge said, nodding.

"Lieutenant, please stand." Judge Nicholson waits while the Lieutenant stands and then proceeds.

"Lieutenant Vincent A. Trapp, after hearing the verdict of a panel of your peers as being found not guilty of the charge of murder in the second degree by virtue of being temporarily insane at the time the crime was committed, and with the consent of both legal parties, I waive the need for you to be sent to a mental institution for observation and declare you a sane and free man."

In seven minutes by the courtroom clock Lieutenant Trapp was really a free man. Detective Sergeant Kent came over and shook hands all around.

After thanking me, the Judge and the prosecution Paige and the Lieutenant prepared to leave. "Richard, we will see you later at the house."

I shook hands and said goodbye to Jean Larson and Randall Walker then I walked up to the bench and thanked the Judge for a fair and just trial. The courtroom was now deserted except for Pete, Theresa and myself. I stoically started stashing my papers away.

Pete came up to join me. "Well, you did it, you really did it." He said huskily, resting his hand gently on my shoulder. "You were magnificent."

I looked up at him. "We did it, Pete," I said quietly. "Never forget that my friend. We did it."

"Ahem," Pete said turning his head toward the front of the courtroom. I looked up to see Judge Nicholson, dressed now in his street clothes and wearing a gray fedora hat that seemed to suit him. In his hand he carried a swollen brief case and I could only imagine how much work he had to take home with him. I left Pete and went over to him.

"Congratulations," he said, squeezing my hand in his arthritic ones. "Congratulations on winning one of the strangest and most oddly brilliant criminal prosecutions I've ever witnessed. And I've seen a few."

I glanced at him quickly. "Prosecutions?" I said, puzzled, fearful that the poor man had grown daft and punchy from trial fatigue. Good God, he didn't take me for Jean Larson, did he?

"Prosecutions," the Judge repeated, smiling broadly I've known for years, of course, as you doubtless have, that murder juries invariably 'try' the victim as well as the killer. Did the rascal deserve to be slain? Should we exalt the killer ...? But this is the first time in my legal career that I've seen a dead man successfully prosecuted for rape. This is a new one. Quite more impressive, I may add, you seem also to have acquitted a man called Lt. Trapp with the Irresistible Impulse ruling. Very hard to win a case with that one!"

"Thank you, Judge," I said, smiling with pleasure. "I never thought of it that way." I paused. I must say it was a pleasure and privilege to have you as our trial judge. Winning a case takes a good jury and a good Judge."

"I was just doing my job by the letter of the law. I must say, your requested instructions were quite impressive. I plan on keeping a set as a model. As I hinted before they are among the best I have ever seen."

I had been told before that I did a good job, but never with such praise. As I stood bathing in this moment I knew I couldn't take credit for it all. I turned and motioned Pete to join us. "Judge Nicholson," I said. "I want you to meet the man who was mainly responsible for those instructions, and for that matter, a great extent for what happened at this trial. Meet my new law partner, Pete Adams.

Pete looked at me with a confused smile on his face before he turned and walked up to the Judge and grabbing his extended hand shook it warmly. "It always delights my heart to meet a real lawyer, Mr. Adams," the Judge said, still pumping away at Pete's hand. "I wish you much pleasure and success in your new partnership with Mr. Dandridge here. You two will make quite a team."

"Thank you for the compliment, Your Honor," Pete replied, still glancing at me questioningly.

"Well, gentlemen, good luck and good night," Judge Nicholson said. We watched as he turned suddenly away from us and soon disappeared.

Pete's glasses misted and for once that frown on his face was gone. "Did you mean it?" he said in a low voice.

"Did I mean what," I said huskily, knowing exactly what he meant.

"About, what you said about you and me being partners?"

I waited a moment watching as Pete shifted his weight from one side to the other. "Why sure, damn it, Pete of course I meant it. I'd consider it a privilege and honor, my friend if you'll be my law partner. From this moment on, the new firm name will be Dandridge and Adams Criminal Law Firm. I'm going to have Theresa order the new stationary and formal announcements on Monday. As for the rest, I've already drawn up the Legal Partnership Agreement and we can have Theresa notarize it. Everything fifty-fifty, the good and the bad starting now. Just say the word, partner."

"Are you sure, Richard? Are you absolutely sure?"

"Let me ask you something. Are you sure you are ready to practice law and put the bottle behind you?"

"What bottle," Pete said. I clapped him on the shoulder and then turned. "Come on Theresa," I called out in the hollow and echoing courtroom, "we're all going out and celebrate the big case and our bigger new partnership." I paused in mid step. "Hold on a second. Here come the Trapps."

The Lieutenant several times tried to draw me aside and bring up the subject of my unpaid fee until finally giving up and asking to meet with me the following day. I told him I'd call upon them in the morning at their home in Pittsford. After all, the winner of the big murder case, with a new partner in the new law firm of Dandridge and Adams, I had some upcoming expenses to handle. At the start of this trial I told Pete we split this paycheck fifty-fifty.

"Again thank you Richard. What time will you plan to be at our home?" the Lieutenant inquired. "There is something we want to share with you."

"Oh, does ten; ten-thirty work for you." I asked airily.

"That's perfect. We'll expect you then."

I stood and watched as again the Lieutenant and his wife left the court room and then I turned to my office family. "Okay, let's go celebrate."

"Where shall we go?" I ask

"I heard of a new place called Sinbad's Mediterranean Cuisine on Park Avenue. I've been wanting to go." Said Theresa.

"Well then, what do you say Pete? Want to go."

"Sure."

We all piled into my car and soon were on our way. The traffic was light as we drove the short distance to Park Avenue and in minutes I was parking the car. As if fate was on our side, we were seated almost immediately and soon introduced to our waitress for the evening. "What can I get you to drink," she asked.

I thought for a moment. "Tell you what. Can you tell us what you have that is champagne-like, but with no alcohol? Do you have anything along that line?"

"We sure do, sir. We have the best. It's called Ariel Brut Cuvee, a premium dealcoholized sparkling wine. I've had it and it taste exactly like a quality champagne."

"Richard, you don't have to…"

"Hey, Pete, we have a busy day tomorrow and she says it taste just like the real thing. I want us all to celebrate. Is it okay with you Theresa?"

"Yes, I'm fine with that. Besides, I'm hungry and the food here is supposed to be an experience in itself so I want to taste it.?

"That's settled, bring us a bottle on ice."

We placed our order for soup to begin our meal. Theresa ordered a lentil soup, while I decided to try the Cacik since it sounded light and refreshing. Pete ordered the same. We talked over the highlights of the trial and between the two of them I felt like some kind of hero.

When we finished our soup we ordered an appetizer that the waitress called Sambusek and it was very good. It turned out to be a medley of chicken, onions, tomatoes, mushrooms and parmesan cheese toasted in a pita.

The conversation flowed easily as we conversed about the hunt we underwent for information to support the trail and had a few laughs over that and then it was time for the salad. All three of us went for the Sinbad salad. Then it was time for the main course and we each chose something different so we could taste each other's. I went for the Funghi, sautéed fresh mushrooms, onions, tomatoes, feta cheese, and herbs. Pete ordered Ganbari Marinated sautéed shrimp, roasted peppers, artichoke hearts, parmesan cheese, and spices. And Theresa went for the Vaccina Grilled tender beef, onions, mushrooms, asparagus, feta cheese, and spices.

This was the first time there was complete silence at the table while we tried our exotic meals. When it came to tasting what the other had ordered, we laughed and made jokes about how much better our own choice was. But honestly, they were all good.

"Nothing like trying something new for a change," Pete said.

"You got that right. We have been trying something new and meeting with success." I looked at Pete. "After what we managed to pull off tonight, we are going to be bombarded with clients. Everyone is going to want to go with the miracle makers," I laughed and Pete and Theresa laughed with me.

When the waitress returned for our dessert orders, at first we looked at each other and said, "No way," but then she handed us the menus and we folded. How could you refuse choices like Baklava: Sheets of filo, richly endowed with pistachios or walnuts and sweetened with sugar syrup. Bird nest: Crispy layers of filo filled with pinenuts and baked to golden perfection. Ladyfingers: Flakey filo dough rolled around ground cashews. Mamoul: Cookie pastry made of farina, sweetened with rosewater, filled with walnuts, or dates, or pistachio nuts. Burma: Shredded filo dough wrapped around pistachios and baked to a golden brown. Ballourie: Lightly baked shredded filo and chopped pistachio with a hint of rose water. We couldn't pronounce half of what was on the menu, but boy did it sound delicious. We made our choices and then ordered coffee.

After the table was cleared and we were drinking our coffee, Pete said, "Richard, if you don't mind me asking, are you planning on seeing Tyra Pederson again?"

I had almost forgotten that I had promised to call her after the trial, but by now she had already heard and I didn't want to break up our evening with a call.

"I'm not sure, really."

"Why not?"

"I don't..." I paused as my mind began to race. Something was wrong. I recalled my conversation with the bartender Brook and what he did when I asked him if he knew of any other relatives of Noah's besides his daughter Bernadine who was listed as being sixteen. In my mind I could see how he first glanced toward the stairs that lead up to the apartments and then had nervously lowered his head and scratched the back of his neck. Then later in conversation he mentioned there may be a married sister and he had slightly raised his head and began biting his nail.

"Richard, are you all right?" Pete asked worriedly.

All I could do was shake my head as I continued to pore over the information. Tyra Pederson had filed the petition for probate of the Will, listing as required by law, a daughter, Bernadine Arietta, age sixteen, as the sole heir at law, living in Pensacola, Florida. Yet, the Will left everything to Tyra Pederson, and was dated as the bartender had said, about three weeks before the shooting. When I mentioned this to Tyra she had glanced quickly at me and said that it was her plan to share the estate with his daughter by setting up a trust fund.

It didn't add up. Then later to learn that Noah had also taken out two large insurance policies, one for his daughter and one for Tyra. And she had made it a point to tell me that she hadn't heard anything about any of this until after Noah was killed.

"Richard, are you okay? Please answer me." This time it was Theresa.

"Sure," was all I could say.

Finally, I thought, Tyra told me how hard she had worked building up the apartment section of the building and how fantastic things had gone, despite Noah's occasional erratic behavior and bouts of drinking. Then she had told me how she had met Noah's daughter and was immediately drawn to her. She described her as a shy troubled child who desperately needed a savior and she wanted that to be her because she knew exactly what she was going through.

She explained herself by saying that she too came from a broken home so she knew how it was."

"What is it Richard? What's going on?"

I couldn't stop thinking just yet. Tyra had said that it was true what they say when you are an only child and your parents' divorce, you either use what you've learned from the abusive environment or you do the polar opposite. Then she had said she felt guilty because he saw her and treated her like his daughter. Like any daughter.

I now knew what was bothering me. I looked up into two worried faces sitting at the table and finally put them at ease. "I was just thinking about something Tyra said when I spoke to her. That's all. Nothing to worry about. Really."

I hated lying to my new partner and even to Theresa but I had to be sure before I said anything. "Are we ready?"

"Yes, Richard, while you were wherever you were, she bought the bill and we took care of it. You can settle with us later."

Pete and Theresa kept up a steady chatter as we drove back to the court house to get their cars and then said our goodbyes.

I wasn't sure what to do now. I could go to Tyra's and ask her and hope she would be honest, or I could talk to Pete. I was sure he was as tired as myself and I didn't want to bother him with any of this. As I started toward home, it came to me. I found a spot to turn around and instead of going home, I went to my mother's.

***

My mother had returned home recently so she knew about the ending of the trial. I could use that as my reason for stopping if I decided not to discuss this with her.

Even though it was late, I could see lights in her living room. I took out my cell and placed a call.

"Hello."

"Hi, Mom, it's me. You busy?"

"Hi Richard, no, I'm not busy, come on over and have a cup of coffee, or wine; whatever you prefer to celebrate your winning."

"See you soon."

I disconnected the call and waited a minute before pulling the car into her drive. I got out and taking my brief case with me, I headed up the walk to her front door. I was just about to ring her doorbell when she opened the door. "When you say a minute, you mean a minute. Where were you? Sitting outside my door?"

"Matter of fact, yes, I was." Mom stepped aside and let me come in.

She had coffee and wine set out on a tray in the living room and I put my brief case on the floor next to the sofa and picked up the wine glass in front of me.

"Wait Richard," Mom said. "Let's have a toast."

"To your successful conclusion of a case well tried, my son."

"Thanks Mom."

"Richard, I can tell something is bothering you. What is it."

At that moment I decided to ask for her help. I shared what I had thought about at dinner and then went on to add what I had thought about later.

"So, after thinking about Tyra's connection in all this, I have two conclusions to draw. Was she the one who murdered Noah and the Lieutenant took the fall? And if so, why? Was it for the money?" I know it sounded wild, but the witnesses were those who had been in the café area and not one who had been at the bar. Why was that?

"I can see why you would think this. It doesn't add up. So what about the Lieutenant?"

608

"Okay. Here goes.

During the trial, Ms. Larson had asked the Lieutenant if he and his wife had any dependents and he had this funny look on his face and then he said, no. Later Ms. Larson; oh by the way, Ms. Larson was called in as a teammate for Randall for the prosecution, starts asking him about his service and he told her about his two years in Afghanistan and told her about Helmand which was ranked as the deadliest, most violent province in Afghanistan.". Now, that's all fine and dandy, but I knew he had been in another battle in Afghanistan much earlier and he mentioned nothing about that."

Mom slid back further on the sofa making herself comfortable, but I could tell she was really listening to what I was saying. After all she had experience doing this with my Dad who was also a lawyer.

"So, back in 1989 there was the Afghan Civil War which started after the Soviet Union withdrew from Afghanistan, leaving the Afghan communist government to fend for itself against the Mujahideen. After several years of fighting, the government fell in 1992. Our Lieutenant was there."

"So, Richard, were many other soldiers."

"It's not the fact that he was in the war, but he was there in 1989 and his wife was in Florida then and from our research earlier we learned that was where Noah and his wife lived."

My mother sat up straighter on the sofa and stared at me over her glass of wine. I had her interest now.

"So, let me show you something." I dug out some papers form my brief case and passed them over to my mother. It was my turn to lean back and get comfortable. I watched her familiar face as she read over the files and saw her expression change from paragraph to paragraph, page after page.

"Oh my, Richard."

"Yes, I think you see what I did. I think that Paige Trapp was lonely and met Noah Arietta back then while the Lieutenant was in Afghanistan. I think she got pregnant and, maybe refused to divorce Vincent and marry him. In any case, he left his wife; may or may not have divorced her, and came to Rochester where he was originally from. I think that when she realized that Noah lived here and it was where her husband was assigned, she went to see him and try to make sure he didn't' tell the Lieutenant, since he did not know who the father was. Of course that is my interpretation."

I continued with my speculation. "In any case, the situation became stickier when Noah realized from the adoption papers that Tyra was their daughter. I don't know if he shared that with her until I meet with them later tomorrow. But that would be the reason that the Lieutenant did what he did. And of course why Noah attacked her. I think he was trying to persuade her to leave the Lieutenant and be with him. Does that sound too outlandish to you?"

"It sounds pretty right on, Richard. But does it matter now that the trial is over.?"

"Not to me or my case, but it does for the battle on the Will. I don't know, but I don't want to share this with anyone but the Trapps and now you. I hate loose ends. Oh, yes, I also made Pete, my partner. Do you remember Pete?"

Mom shook her head. "Yes, I think that is great. Just great. I like Pete."

"I'm glad. I like him too and he is very smart. He will add a lot to the firm."

Now it was my turn to read her face. "Mom, what are you thinking?"

There was a pause while she just looked at me and finally said, "Well, if Pete is your partner and he's smart, you should share all of this with him and he should go with you to the Trapp's."

I thought for a bit and knew she was right. I got up and helped her take the tray to the kitchen then hugged her tightly. "Mom, thank you. Thank you for being my mom." I kissed her and said my goodbyes feeling much better.

I drove home and decided to wait until morning before calling Pete. That night I slept soundly

The next morning, I made coffee and hurried to Wegmans to pick up some bagels and cream cheese and then I called Pete and asked him to meet me at my house. While I waited, I gathered the papers that I had showed to my mom and had them ready when Pete arrived. I waited until after Pete had a chance to settle in with his coffee and bagel before handing him the papers.

I didn't have to go over the details as Pete was already aware of them, only now the facts were being shown together. I had no doubt he would see the connections. Pete was silent for a long time. Finally, he spoke. "In a way, Richard, don't you see? The Lieutenant used you and you used him. He got his freedom and you got whatever it is you've got." He paused. "Maybe," he said slowly. "Maybe in a certain sense you two got what Theresa would call, a kind of poetic justice."

I slowly nodded my head. "So you see the labyrinth?"

Pete is silent as he nods his head. "Well, I think that Tyra is Mrs. Trapp's child, with Noah and that she put her up for adoption. I think that Noah approached her about this and how he figured it out, I don't know, but he wanted something from her and she said no."

"Do you think the Lieutenants knows?"

"Well, that is the big question. If he does, it means nothing as far as our case is concerned, but I know it's eating you up. You want to know the whole story. Me, I only need to know if it did affect the trial outcome, for our client. It doesn't, really."

Pete cleared his throat and stirred restlessly. "Richard, don't get caught in the what ifs, please." He looked directly in my eyes and added, "Come on Richard, tell me what is the Lawyer's creed to our clients."

Begrudgedly I reply, " I offer faithfulness, competence, diligence, and good judgment. I will strive to represent you as I would want to be represented and to be worthy of your trust."

"Okay, what is the creed to the opposing parties and their counsel."

"I offer fairness, integrity, and civility. I will seek reconciliation and, if we fail, I will strive to make our dispute a dignified one."

"Now the courts"

"Come on Pete, this is ridiculous!"

"Now to the courts, Richard."

"To the courts, and other tribunals, and to those who assist them, I offer respect, candor, and courtesy. I will strive to do honor to the search for justice."

"To colleagues in the practice of law."

"I offer concern for your welfare. I will strive to make our association a professional friendship."

To the profession:

"I offer assistance. I will strive to keep our business a profession and our profession a calling in the spirit of public service."

"Finally, to the public and our systems of justice."

"I offer service. I will strive to improve the law and our legal system, to make the law and our legal system available to all, and to seek the common good through the representation of my clients."

Pete pauses and walks over to me, putting his hands on my shoulders as he says, "Now, did you meet the requirements of the Lawyers Creed? Answer truthfully."

I try not to smile, knowing why he is doing this. "Yes, I did."

"Well, then, its done, Richard, let's be on our way and not sit around here mopping all day."

That's not fair, but it is," I laugh and Pete joins me.

We left the house and climbed into Pete's car since it was parked behind mine. "Richard," Pete asks, "What about the District Attorney job? Are you still planning on running?"

"Now Pete, how can I do that and have my own firm. It's a big NO. I'm over it. I thought about it, because I saw it as the position of the white cowboy hat that show that you're the good guy, the one with the biggest horse, the one who knows the truth and will reveal it to your fellow citizens. But I know that isn't what it is about and it holds no interest for me."

Pete didn't say anything. I took a sidelong glance at him and could see from the lift of his cheek that he was smiling.

It had been quite hot most of the month, with the temperatures soaring early in the day, but now it was comfortable as we drove to Pittsford to the Trapp house. The leaves were just beginning to change colors in Irondequoit as we start our drive. The burnt orange, glorious gold and deep-red colors that would emerge in the coming weeks just put me in such an inspirational state of mind and with all the mature tree lined streets in the area, it was a thing of beauty. It was one of the main reasons I chose to live in Irondequoit; that and the nearness to the water.

"Let's change the subject," I said, "It's too nice out to be thinking about the ways of the law." I try to think of something and come up with, "Pete, Do you know what Irondequoit means."

"Ah…, no." Pete replies. I can hear the laughter in his voice.

"Irondequoit aptly means 'where the land and waters meet'. The Genesee River borders on the East, Lake Ontario, on the North and Irondequoit Bay on the West."

Pete continues to drive. "I do love this time of year. I can forsake the winter, but the autumn and even the spring I need to see," I add.

"Sure," Pete responds. Living in that house of yours I would enjoy it too. It's different when you live near downtown. Don't get me wrong, it's where I want to be. I don't know what I'd do with a house your size."

"A house my size? My house is not that big, Pete. Besides your apartment is not that small. That's a beautiful full-size one-bedroom apartment and you have that private front and back access. It's conveniently located to all the downtown sites of Rochester. In one of the most beautiful historic districts in the city."

"Yeah, yeah, but I don't own it. Actually, I don't own anything beyond my car and my clothes."

Pete is silent, thinking. "You've been in the Lieutenants house, right?"

"Yes."

"What's it like."

"Well, let me see,

We had just turned off Cranbrooke Dr and were now on Kings Highway. I remind Pete that they have put in a traffic circle off Titus Avenue and we would take the third exit. I guide him until we are finally onto the interstate and then try to describe the Trapp's house.

Pete would comment every now and then with a 'geez' or 'wow' and it makes me laugh.

"But Pete, it's the outside, the gardens that are the best. Colorful gardens bloom around the house from late spring through early autumn. A deck, linking the kitchen and backyard, affords shifting views: In June, lupines grow thick and wild in the fields surrounding the property. In cooler months, glimpses of harbor appear beyond the slope of those fields. In the true dark of the night sky, you might see the Milky Way – or a meteor shower – without ever leaving the yard."

"And you know this, how?"

"Right, I've never seen it all, just the gardens and the landscaping, but Paige told me the rest."

We were exiting the interstate and on the last leg of the trip which was all of maybe twelve miles from my door to theirs, only now we were dealing with the stop lights and lots of traffic. We pass an old church with its burial grounds along the side of the building. A quarter mile from the church is the Harbor, at Schoen place where there are excellent restaurants and cafés, both casual and formal; a food market selling fresh, local goods; a wine and cheese shop; galleries and gift shops featuring local artists and artisans. It was the real center of the suburb.

Then just as suddenly as we entered it, we are through the heart of the suburban area . Pass through the scenic Causeway -- an old, stone footbridge before entering the Great Embankment Park that runs for 12 acres along the Erie Canal.

"That's the Park," I say.

"Yes, it is."

"Do you know why it's called the great embankment.?"

"Hah, I do, yes I do. It's one of the largest filled in embankments holding in the Erie Canal, ah, and much more…"

I laugh and Pete joins in knowingly.

Soon we are coming up to 14 Epping Wood Trail in Pittsford, where the Trapp's live. As we drive up to the gate, I hear Pete whistle. "Wow," he manages.

"Yes, wow describes it all right."

I am surprised to find the gate is open and I look over at the groundskeeper's cottage as if expecting him to push a button and lock us out, but no one seems to be responding so I tell Pete. "It must be because they were expecting us. Let's go."

Pete drives cautiously up the long driveway until we are right in front of the house. There is still no movement inside or out so we sit there in the car wondering what to do.

"Oh, come on, Pete. I think we've seen too many Law and Orders." I open my side of the car and climb out. Pete does the same.

We proceed cautiously along the walk and are almost to the front door when a voice calls out.

"Hey, you, stop right there!"

Even though I know that voice, I am startled and Pete along with me, stops as if someone has shot at us. I am unsure what to do as we stand there whispering, "What now?" to each other. Finally I get a little nervy and begin to turn toward the voice.

It is a slight man with a receding hairline above a broad forehead who stares back at me and we recognize each other immediately. It is Walker Appleton, the caretaker. He smiles at me. "Oh, it's you. The Lieutenant said you would be stopping by, but nothing about there being two of you. Sorry."

"No problem." I replied letting air escape through my teeth as I realized I had been holding my breath. This is my partner, Pete. Pete say hello to Walker Appleton."

"Good morning Mr. Appleton."

"Good morning," he replies.

"So, Walker, where are the Trapps?"

He paused for a moment and then shuffling his feet around as if trying to kick leaves off the sidewalk, looked up and said. "They're gone!"

"Gone! I was to meet them here this morning. Where have they gone."

"Can't tell you that."

"Okay, when are they going to return?"

"Ah, never."

I was too shocked at first to be worried. This I hadn't seen coming. I didn't understand. "Well, since they obviously told you I would be stopping by, did they say anything about that?"

Walker looked up shaking his head. "Yes, Mr. Dandridge, yes, they did. I'm sorry. Wait here."

I watched as Walker went up to the front door and unlocked it. I started to move forward and he turned and said. "Wait out here, please." I stepped back. Pete and I exchanged looks and I could see he was as much in the dark as I was.

Shortly, Walker stepped back out of the house, locked the front door and came down the steps. When he was right in front of me, I noticed he had two envelopes in his hand.

"These are for you. Lieutenant Trapp said that they would explain everything."

I reached out and took the envelopes and looked at Walker. "Any message coming with these packages," I asked.

"No, just that they would explain everything."

I thanked Walker and he watched as Pete and I climbed back in the car. I was anxious and wanted to open the envelopes immediately and maybe I should have, but I decided it best to leave the property before I did. Pete turned the car around on the circular drive and soon we were heading out the gate. In a matter of seconds, Pete found a convenient place to pull over and park. He looked at me and I looked at him. "Well, what are you waiting for. The suspense is killing me."

We sat in the confines of Pete's car and I slowly opened up the top envelope. Inside was a typewritten letter with no signature or name on it. I read it out loud. The letter explained most of what we had finally figured out on our own and what we still didn't know, the letter didn't tell. The only new news was that they had decided to move away and start over as that was best for all concerned.

I looked at Pete. "So who signed it, or who wrote it?" I told him there was no signature nor a name so we could assume that Paige wrote it in explanation or the Lieutenant knew and he wrote it.

"Tyra?" Pete asked.

"Don't know if she knows or not."

"I can't believe we are to be left in the dark. They could have told us, just us. After all we were their lawyers."

"I agree Pete, but I think that they wanted to forget the past and go on from there. Sharing it all with anyone would just keep it fresh."

"You're right. Damn it, you are right." Pete was quiet. In all the excitement over the letter, the other envelope had slipped off my lap and onto the floor to be forgotten for a while. Finally, I remembered it and started looking under my legs, down the side of the car seat and finally leaned over and saw it lying inconspicuously near my shoe. I picked it up.

Pete turned to watch me, having forgotten about the other envelope too. I carefully opened it, hoping for a part 2 to the confession letter, but instead there was a check, drawn on a local bank. The Lieutenant had given me a $25,000 retainer that I was to bill against my $300 per hour rate. I had run over that amount and now as I reached behind me to get my briefcase, I opened it and found the billing I planned on giving to the Lieutenant. I looked at the bill. The Lieutenant owed me a balance of $4,500 only that was not what the check had been written out for.

"So, are you going to share that with me."

"Pete, this is unbelievable. The balance the Lieutenant owed us above the $25,000 retainer amount was $4,500."

"Yes, so what did he pay us."

"Hold on to your hat my friend, the check is for $200,000!"

Pete whistled a big WOW. I think we both knew at that moment that the money was not just for the legal fees, but also a payment to not expose their secret. They wanted us to forget and not try to figure it all out.

"Pete," I said. "I know, Richard. They want us to stop trying to figure all this out and to let it lie. You know I'm okay with that. It has no bearing on the case or the outcome."

"But Tyra!"

"Richard, Tyra has lived her whole life not knowing and came out fine. Or, maybe she did know. In any case, her life is her life and we shouldn't go throwing curb balls at it."

Pete carefully pulled the car back on the road and stepped on the gas. As the battered old car leapt forward, I began to feel free as a bird. A curious sense of relief and release came over me as we sped along finally shedding the last scars of the town of Pittsford and at length arriving in Irondequoit only to continue down Lake Shore Blvd until reaching the Ontario Shore. We pulled into the parking area and stood at the edge of the embankment overlooking the lake below and I felt as though I was breathlessly hanging in midair. Spread out far below us was the tremendous expanse of the lake. Beautiful, empty, glittering cold and brooding.

"Amen," Pete murmured huskily, spreading his hands and shaking his head in awe. "Sometimes Richard, sometimes when I behold a sight like this I, I just want to stretch out my arms and soar like a bird. Can you understand a grown man thinking such a thing, much less saying such a thing?"

"Yes, Pete I can and I know exactly how that feels." I know a poem that says it all."

"How do you know a poem?"

"Well, remember back when I was seeing Stacy...can't remember her last name, but she was a real nut about poetry and so I wanted to impress her so one day when she dragged me to the poetry corner, where people get up and read or recite poems, well, one time I got up and recited a poem that I had memorized."

"You must have really liked the girl."

"You know what, I did and because of her I have one more layer to my person. Anyway, here goes."

"It's called Spread Your Wings – by Gary Ferris." I paused to collect my thoughts.

"Take a deep breath, then let out a sigh. Spread your wings; soaring through the sky. Prior deep wounds, and all of their sorrow. Leave them behind; don't burden tomorrow. Forget the past, along with its pains. For a new future is all that remains. Gratefully exercise this brand new chance. Do not be fearful to learn a new dance. Approach each day with joy and a smile. Because this time, you're going in style. Discard the bad, and seek out love. Draw your strength from the lord above. Freedom's price is often very high, so spread your wings, and prepare to fly.,"

"Yes, that says it all."